Dedicated to Veronica Kirouac

I had seen a pair of eyeglasses in an on-line advertisement and said, "I see a story here." I described this new concept to my Arizona writing sister, Veronica Rose. She advised me to stop everything and run with it. I did. Thank you, Veronica!

A NEW VISION

A Recipe for Love

A NOVEL

In baking, as in life, timing is everything—

JANET JENSEN

This book is a work of fiction. Names, characters, places, and incidents either are products of the author's imagination or are used fictitiously. Any resemblance to actual persons, living or dead, events, or locales is entire coincidental.

A NEW VISION: A RECIPE FOR LOVE
Copyright © 2022 by Janet Jensen

All rights reserved. Printed in the United States of America. No part of this book may be reproduced in any form or by any means without prior written permission of the author, except in the case of brief quotations used in reviews.

Print ISBN: 979-8-35091-399-6
eBook ISBN: 979-8-35091-400-9

For Chelsi and Jake Reichenstein.

This story is for you. I hope you enjoy reading Chelsi and Jake's journey as much as I did in writing it.

To Bryn Donovan and Gill Donovan.

Though there have been several editors who have contributed to the completion of this novel, a huge shout out must go to Bryn and Gill Donovan from Lucky Author. Thank you for polishing my work to perfection and molding me into the best published author I can be.

To Tammy James.

A heartfelt thank you goes to my beta reader, friend, and Soléa Keller sister, Tammy James, who could not wait to get the next set of chapters.

And a special thank you to Mary Dana Hardin, friend, and Soléa Keller sister, for her expertise on the cover colorization.

What is Chelsi's recipe for love?

Mix one established female baker with a trustworthy knight in plaid flannel.

Add in his sweet, pint-sized daughter.

Combine a bunch of quirky British angels whipping up a pair of innovative eyeglasses.

Incorporate a heaping handful of family support.

Knead in an unlimited amount of love, respect, and forgiveness.

Bake in a 400-degree preheated oven, forever.

Serve daily, with a generous measure of laughter.

Credentials. The one essential element missing from Chelsi Burnett's career path. Or so she thought.

Table of Contents

1. THE BETRAYAL ... 1
2. THE PLAN ... 19
3. THE SNOWSTORM ... 31
4. A NEW VISION ... 37
5. THE BAKING DISASTER ... 59
6. NO BLACK JELLYBEANS ... 67
7. THE SNOWBERRY INN B&B ... 73
8. ANGEL COOKIES ... 87
9. A MOMENTOUS DISCOVERY ... 93
10. TRAVIS WAS SICK ... 103
11. A WALKABOUT TOWN ... 105
12. COCOA'S PRESENT ... 115
13. TWO IMPERFECT HALVES ... 121
14. A ROMANTIC RIDE ... 129
15. GLORIA'S MISHAP ... 137
16. COFFEE AND CHAT WITH DANIEL ... 143
17. JIM'S RETIRING ... 151
18. ROSIE'S SAD ... 157
19. WE'RE NOT IN HIGH SCHOOL ANYMORE ... 167
20. LITTLE BLACK DRESS ... 173
21. NEWS FROM PARIS ... 187
22. A SHADOW IN THE STREETLAMP ... 197
23. THE ATTIC ... 211
24. TWO CHOCOLATE EGG CREAM SODAS ... 221
25. AMTRAK ... 231
26. SAGE ADVICE ... 241
27. LETTER, FLOWERS, AND CHOCOLATE ... 253
28. KRINGLEFEST ... 265
29. CHELSI'S RECIPE FOR LOVE ... 287
30. A NEW VISION: A RECIPE FOR LOVE ... 313

AUTHOR BIO ... 315

Chapter One

THE BETRAYAL

BAKING IS LOVE MADE VISIBLE. It's more than mixing flour, sugar, butter, and eggs. It's priceless memories and indispensable life lessons instilling patience, passion, and pride. A baker must be organized, accurately measure ingredients, and follow directions…*in order*. But it's in the joy of giving, the happiness we bestow upon others, that replenishes our passion. When we bake, we give the recipient a piece of our soul… the gift of love.

Today, the enticing aroma of freshly baked bread drifted through the commercial kitchen at the Golf and Country Club in Redfield, Massachusetts. Chelsi's kitchen. The earthly scent of rising yeast, combined with roasted garlic and garden-fresh rosemary, never failed to evoke fond childhood memories of baking with her late aunt, Ann Marie, at her B&B in Racine, Wisconsin. Her aunt's kitchen had overflowed with valued teachings and much more. It had been jam-packed with the heady fragrance of proofing bread, warm morning sunshine, and unconditional love. For head pastry chef, Chelsi Burnett, baking was more than a means to the end…it was her way of life.

* * *

BEEEEEP... BEEEEEP... BEEEEEP!...

"Chels... *Chelsi?*"

The sound of Rosaria's voice startled Chelsi out of her reverie.

"What?"

"Where'd ya go?" Rosaria said, in her classic Brooklyn accent. "The oven's beepin.' Ya need me to check on the bread?"

Chelsi Burnett stood at a stainless-steel prep table, adding the finishing touches to the afternoon's dessert course, when her baking assistant, Rosaria Pingerelli, waived a hand in front of her.

"Nope, sorry Rosaria, I got it. You know how focused I get when wrapping up an event."

Chelsi turned off the blaring oven timer and guided a six-foot-tall cooling rack toward the commercial ovens, its wheels squealing across the room.

"Oh, my goodness!" Rosaria said, covering both ears. "When is he going to fix those wheels?"

"Who, Daniel?" Chelsi snickered. "I think the only wheel he's interested in these days is the steering wheel that's attached to his new midlife crisis vehicle."

Chelsi had met Daniel Wright on a blind date and was instantly pulled into his hauntingly blue eyes, scruff-lined, chiseled jaw, and raven-black hair. He'd blown the top off her hunk-o-meter, and since they had similar interests in the food industry, they'd formed an instant bond. Chelsi knew that being engaged to the food and beverage director wasn't the most ideal situation, but there was nothing written in the country club's handbook about dating.

Chelsi paused to inhale the bread's aroma as it escaped the confines of the hot oven. Unconsciously, she hummed to the holiday instrumental, "Ode to Joy," drifting from the overhead speakers. "Say, Ro, do you think he lived above a bakery when composing this piece?"

"When who… composed what?" Ro asked, lining a dozen wire breadbaskets with white cloth napkins.

"Sorry," Chelsi laughed. "Beethoven. He was totally deaf when he composed this symphony, so I figure he had to rely on his other senses to create his masterpiece."

"Another Aunt Ann Marie lesson?"

"Yup, she had classical music playing during afternoon tea. Aunt Ann Marie said eating in silence can be uncomfortable, and music can help customers slow down and enjoy their dining experience without hearing the clamor of pots and cooking utensils from the kitchen."

Chelsi slid the first hot pan of her freshly baked bread onto the metal rack. She leaned in a little closer and listened. She loved the sound of her hot crusty bread hitting the cooler air temperature; the crackling of their golden-brown crusts composed its own pleasant melody.

"*Ahhh*, singing bread… music to my ears."

"Perfection, Chels. Nobody bakes better than you. You truly are a bread artist."

"Thanks, Ro. I learned from the best. And the great part is, this art we can eat!"

"Yesterday we actually got a compliment. This customer called and said she loved the bread so much that on her way out, she took an untouched loaf home! Many are quick to criticize, but slow to praise."

"I'm glad she enjoyed it," Chelsi said. "It almost makes these crazy hours we work worth it."

The phone pealed as Chelsi removed the last hot tray of bread.

"I got it, Chels."

"Thanks!" she said, transferring loaves from parchment-paper-lined baking trays to the prepared wire baskets.

Rosaria placed the caller on hold and sang out, "Boss, it's for you."

Teresa, the lead catering server, appeared in the kitchen doorway and cleared her throat. "Say, Chelsi, some of the guests in the Par-3 room have been nibbling on bread fragments from the bottom of their baskets." Nodding at the cooling rack, she added, "Are those loaves about ready to go?"

"Sure thing, Teresa. Ro, will you…?"

"On it."

Chelsi wiped her hands on the blue-striped kitchen towel she had draped over her shoulder. She plopped down behind her grey metal desk tucked away in a corner of the kitchen's supply area, grabbed a pen and writing pad, then reached for the receiver.

"Pastry kitchen, this is Chelsi. How can I—"

"Hey, Chelsi. This is Brian from the pro shop. We just opened a box addressed to Daniel by accident. It was mixed in with the pro shop merchandise, and the new guy didn't catch it."

"Oh, I'm sure it's fine." She glanced up at the clock. *Daniel's late,* she thought. "Who's it from?"

"Hardscrabble Publishers in New York City. It looks like he ordered a book titled *The Only Cookbook You'll Ever Need.* Do you want me to bring it over?"

She wiggled her left fingers and watched the sparkle of her diamond engagement ring wink back at her. *Hmmm…* Could this be the surprise he told her about last night at dinner? He said he'd bought her an early birthday present. After all, it wasn't every day his incredibly wonderful fiancée turned the big 5-0.

"No thanks, Brian. I'll be right down," she said. She needed to head over to the supply closet for printer paper anyway, so it was a perfect time.

Chelsi undid the woven ties to her white apron, slipped it over her head, and lobbed it over the back of her chair. From her desk drawer, Chelsi removed a small mirror. She took off her glasses and checked her eye makeup, and then, with a quick adjustment of the bill of her ball cap, she was off. The other bakers donned white cotton head coverings but, being a former high school softball player, she preferred putting her auburn curly hair in a low bun and securing it with the embroidered Country Club of Redfield baseball cap.

"Ro, I'll be back in twenty. The holiday party in the Par-3 room is well underway. I'll be back in plenty of time to plate the dessert."

"Oh, fuhgeddaboudit!" said Ro. "There are only thirty-two guests in that room. I *certainly* can handle it."

Chelsi nodded. "I think there's a package for me in Daniel's office, and he should be arriving shortly. I baked an extra cheesecake for tonight's catering event, so we have a few extra portions. It's his favorite. I figured I'd bring him coffee and a slice. Hope the coffee's fresh in the main lobby."

"He doesn't deserve you…ya know that, don't cha?"

Plating a generous slice of dessert, she replied, "Oh, he's not that bad. Although, I do think he loves his new sports car more than me."

"Have you set a date yet?"

"For what? The wedding?"

"What do you think, Chels, for the Macy's Thanksgiving Day Parade? Yes, for your weddin'!"

Chelsi shook her head. "No, not yet. He said we'd discuss it after the holidays."

"*Mmm-hmmm.*"

Chelsi sighed. "At first, Ro, we were perfect for each other. He was so attentive. He wanted to know everything about me. What I liked to do in my off time. My hobbies. Then… shortly after we got engaged, he seemed disinterested. Closed off, distant. Secretive almost. Now I'm not sure if Mr. Wright is 'right' for me."

"Remember, I tried to tell you I thought he was up to something? On your days off, he would come into the kitchen and just look around. Said he'd been tipped off the health department was on their way. That he was looking for potential health hazards. But honestly, Chels, I don't trust him. And, the man's got commitment issues. *Big time.*"

"Ro, I'm beginning to agree with you," Chelsi admitted. "See ya in a few."

* * *

CHELSI SNAKED HER WAY AROUND the waitstaff in the main dining hall, setting up for tonight's Governor's Christmas Gala. They wore mid-calf Parisian waiter's aprons, black dress pants, long-sleeved white tuxedo shirts, and Christmas-themed ties. Juggling two cups of coffee, a handful of sugar packets wrapped in a cloth napkin, and a slice of her signature chocolate truffle cheesecake, she took in the detailed vision of tonight's themed celebration.

The glint from the crystal chandelier reflected off the mahogany ceiling like fireworks on Independence Day. The country club's engraved silverware, polished to its highest sheen, contrasted beautifully against the brilliance of the snow-white damask linens. Holiday centerpieces featured tall crystal candlestick holders, fragrant branches of white pine evergreens, homey Granny Smith apples, and silver glittered pinecones. *Hmmph. Looks like somebody spared no expense on* this *shindig.*

* * *

DANIEL'S OFFICE WASN'T VERY LARGE, but it did have an excellent view of the driving range and the practice putting green, both now covered in snow. Chelsi glanced at dozens of framed posters that lined his paneled office walls. Several portrayed famous golf legends as Arnold Palmer, Jack Nickolas, and the late Payne Stewart. Others acknowledged renowned golf holes, like number fourteen, The Floating Green, in Coeur d'Alene, Idaho, or the eighteenth hole at Augusta National Golf Club, where Daniel's golf idol, Tiger Woods, won his first Masters Tournament with a twelve-stroke lead.

Rounding Daniel's desk, Chelsi placed the two cups of coffee on the corner of his marred mahogany desk. She grimaced when a splash of coffee overflowed the rim of the disposable cups, sloshing into a freeform puddle. "I knew I should've taken a serving tray," she said, shaking her hands and exercising her stiff fingers. She wiped up the spill, then leaned over and peered at the addressee on the opened box. *Mr. Daniel J. Wright, Director of Food and Beverage, The Country Club of Redfield, Redfield, Massachusetts.* Beneath the return address— *Hardscrabble Publishing House, 200 West 42nd Street, New York, New York*—it read, *"The Only Cookbook You'll Ever Need."—Claire Wallingsford.*

Claire Wallingsford? The guru of B&B hotels endorsed this book? Chelsi remembered how excited she and Aunt Ann Marie were one summer when Claire Wallingsford had been traveling the country visiting B&B's. Though Ms. Wallingsford never made it to her aunt's B&B, due to an untimely knee injury, there was still hope she'd continue her tour at a later date.

She placed the packing material off to the side, a single sheet of paper rested on top of a hardbound book. It read, *Mr. Wright, enclosed is the final copy of your cookbook. The first 200 copies are in the print shop and will be ready for immediate shipment. Thank you for this delectable journey across the United States. —Robert Hardscrabble.*

She placed the letter off to the side, then ran her hand over the glossy cover. *The Bed & Breakfast Cookbook: Recipes from America's top fifty B&B's, by Daniel J. Wright.*

Wait. What? By Daniel J. Wright? What did *he* know about writing a cookbook?

Daniel hated B&B's. Last August, she thought she'd surprise him for his birthday and made reservations at an 1890s Victorian B&B. After spending hours scouring the internet, she had decided that the Windrose B&B in Northern Massachusetts was the perfect location. It was situated in a quaint town right on the Atlantic Ocean with great shops, food, boating, and fishing. But, to her dismay, he complained about everything. He hated that they only had a claw-foot tub in the bathroom with no shower. Why was there no elevator to their third-floor suite? And… there was no golf.

Her heart was pounding. Perched on the edge of Daniel's executive chair, Chelsi rifled through the pages of the cookbook. *Let's see what you've been up to, Mr. Daniel J. Wright.*

She took a sip of coffee while captivating photographs and mouth-watering recipes slipped past her thumb. *Huh? That recipe looked mighty familiar…*

She studied its ingredients. Suspicion grew at the recognizable names and photos. Adjusting her glasses higher on her nose, she turned to the previous page.

"The Elvis? Marion's Meatballs? Are you kidding me?" She couldn't believe this! These were *all* her aunt's recipes from her Willow Creek B&B! When did he do this? Why?

Fury consumed her like angry hurricane waves devouring coastal shores. With a quick swipe of her hand, she shoved the box and sent all its packing material flying off the desk.

Chelsi slammed the book closed—then opened it again and turned to the table of contents. *Okay, Wisconsin, page 224.*

Willow Creek Bed and Breakfast, Racine, Wisconsin. Mrs. Ann Marie Brummer, Proprietress. A burning sensation rose into her chest and Chelsi thought she might hurl. It consumed her… anger, hot flash, didn't matter. Why would Daniel do this without consulting her? Why the secrecy? Did he think creating the cookbook would make her happy? Did he even love her, or was he using her?

Chelsi stood up with such force that her chair rolled backward, hitting the back wall. "Oh Daniel, how could you?"

"How could I, what?" Daniel asked, strolling into his office, not a care in the world. He rounded the corner of his desk and leaned in to kiss his fiancée but she refused his advance.

"Ah!" he said, taking his seat. "You brought me coffee and my favorite dessert. Thanks, Babe." Peering into the brewed beverage, he added, "Coffee's cold, but I know how delicious this chocolate thing is." He cut a huge wedge. Mumbling, he said, "You would not *believe* the morning I've had."

Daniel reached for the catering organizer on the back edge of his desk. "By the way, why are you in my office? Don't you have an event in the Par-3 room?" He glanced from the schedule to his watch. "Like… now?"

Daniel finally made eye contact with Chelsi. "Something wrong, Babe?"

She picked up the cookbook and held it in the air like a school crossing guard holds up their stop sign. "Daniel. Exactly *what* have you done here?"

He stabbed another sizable amount. "Terrific! It arrived!"

Daniel froze at the sight of his well-guarded cookbook. The fork released from his grasp; ricocheted off the plate, and propelled the next bite of cheesecake onto his lap. He pushed back. A look of repulsion flashed across his face.

"Now look what you made me do!"

He reached for the napkin and concentrated hard on *not* smearing the confection near the crotch of his khakis. Nervously, he continued. "Oh, *um*, wait—now the surprise is ruined."

Chelsi stood there staring over the top of her glasses at him, seething.

"What?" The muscle along Daniel's jawline flexed. "Chelsi, baby. Why are you acting like this?"

"Don't 'Chelsi, baby' me!" She slammed the book down on top of his desk. "How am I supposed to act when I just caught my fiancé in a lying, deceitful act."

He lowered his eyes, then glanced around his office. "*Um*... deceitful? Me? Why did *you* open a box addressed to *me* in the first place?"

"Don't make this about me, Daniel," she said, her voice elevated another notch. "Besides, is that all you're concerned about? The fact that I opened your stupid box? Which, by the way, I didn't."

"Then who—"

"You knew I kept Aunt Ann Marie's recipe book locked in my locker, and what gave *you* the right to look up *my* combination?"

"It was—"

"Don't you *dare* tell me it was an emergency!" He knew she held her aunt's cookbook close to her heart and that those recipes meant the world to her. "How could you steal her recipes, copy them, and print them as your own?"

Daniel raised a stubborn jaw. "I-I didn't steal anything, I... I borrowed them one day when you were off. I thought you'd be happy that I branched out into a field that you enjoyed. I figured the cookbook would be released after we were married, and what's yours is mine, right?"

"Wrong!" Chelsi's voice wobbled with a mixture of tears and angst. "You got caught, buster! If the pro shop hadn't opened this box by mistake, they never would've called and told me about it. You would've strolled in, approved the final copy, hid it in your locked drawer, and I'd never would've known about it."

Chelsi held her left hand out in front of her, then repeatedly pointed to her engagement ring. "Do you see this ring?"

"Yeah. I outdid myself on *that* purchase. I know it's not exactly your style, but?"

"You don't get it, do you? This engagement ring is more than a sparkling accessory. It's a symbol of trust and commitment to each other. It takes two people, dedicated to the same values, to make a relationship work. Do you want to begin our marriage based on deception and lies?"

Daniel swiped his hand across the top of the desk seemingly to remove a miniscule speck of dust. He leaned forward, resting his elbows, then steepled his hands. "And your point is…?"

Tension built up between Chelsi's neck and shoulders. "You *can't* print these recipes as your own. They do *not* belong to you! You know I love B&B's, all you had to do is ask and maybe, just maybe, we could've collaborated on this book, *together*."

Chelsi's current suspicions were correct. She had planned to spend the rest of her life with Daniel, but he didn't love her. He was using her. Daniel was driven by money and prestige, no matter the consequences. "Do you even see me as an equal in this relationship? It appears all you're interested in is making a buck at my expense."

He closed his eyes, then lifted one shoulder in an I-couldn't-care-less shrug. "So now what?"

Chelsi's stomach churned. Her fiancé's blasé response infuriated her even more. Frustrated, she grasped her engagement ring and pulled it off her finger with such vengeance that her knuckle cracked. Staring at the ring poised between her thumb and index finger, her chest rose and fell with rapid breaths.

"Daniel, we're done!" Holding hot tears at bay, she continued, "Not only are you single again, but I want you out of my apartment…tonight!"

Daniel threw his arms up in the air. "Chelsi, I can't believe you're breaking up with me over this! If it's a menopause thing you *seriously* need to see a lady doctor and get meds to control these outbursts."

"This has *nothing* to do with my hormones, but *everything* to do with your betrayal."

"Betrayal?" Daniel sat back and rubbed the back of his neck. "Can we at least talk about it?"

"Not. A. Chance," Chelsi answered.

Daniel's cell phone vibrated. He turned away and leaned back to retrieve his phone from his pants pocket, then checked the screen for his incoming text.

Exasperation erupted deep within her. "Are you serious?" Chelsi slammed her open palm against the top of his desk. "I'm talking here!"

He set his cell phone off to the side of his desk, folded his arms across his chest, and gave her his full attention. "By all means. Continue," he drawled.

"Agh! Daniel, I *don't* know who you are anymore. But I *do* know you're not the man I fell in love with."

Chelsi looked Daniel squarely in his eyes. With a curt nod, she said, "I! Quit!"

Shock spread across his face. "Quit? You can't quit! You know we're booked solid this week with Christmas parties."

Chelsi squared her shoulders and struck her best-ever Lynda-Carter-Wonder-Woman pose. "Watch me!" She sidled up next to him, stuffed her diamond ring deep into his half-eaten dessert, then wiped her chocolatey fingers across his starched, white, Oxford shirt.

"Goodbye Daniel," she said, without a backward glance, and walked out.

"You're nothing but a wanna-be baker, Chelsi Burnett. A professional would *never* quit during the busiest catering season. Your catering days in Massachusetts… are over!"

* * *

BREATHING HARD, CHELSI RETRACED HER steps through the main dining hall. This time, she had blinders on to the festivities of the Christmas holiday. Instead of seeing bright colors of the season, her vision was shrouded in shades of grey. There would be no vision of sugar plums dancing in her head tonight. The only vision she would have was Daniel scrubbing the dessert from her engagement ring—and the ring sliding down the drain.

Muttering under her breath, she said, "I'll show him. 'Can we talk about it.' He didn't give a hoot about losing me. All he cared about was his precious catering."

Chelsi marched across the kitchen toward the staff lockers. "Rosaria, you might as well be the first to know." She jutted her thumb behind her. "Well, second, if you count Mr. Wheeler-Dealer out there. I broke off my engagement with Daniel *and* quit my job!"

"*What*? You were so happy when you headed to his office. What happened?"

"Let's just say, Daniel's not the man I thought he was. I can fill you in later. Right now, I just need to leave."

Rosaria walked over to Chelsi's desk and picked up her friend's glass apothecary jar half-filled with multicolored jellybeans. Removing the lid, she shook out a handful. "Don't worry, Chels, you'll be on your feet in no time." She replaced the cover, then offered the container to her friend. "Here, take this. Grab your recipe book and go. Rediscover your passion. Get that wide-eyed feeling you had as a teenager baking with your aunt. Hey, maybe you can find a B&B to work at."

Chelsi nodded, her gaze not reaching Rosaria's eyes. "Maybe you're right."

Scrunching her eyelids closed, she fought back hot tears. She shrugged on her jacket, grabbed her handbag, and accepted the jar of jellybeans from her best friend. Taking a deep breath, she removed her most prized possession from her locker—her aunt's recipe binder—and tucked it under her arm. The well-worn three-ring binder contained all the coveted recipes from her late aunt's B&B. The very same binder her now ex-fiancé, Daniel, intentionally copied in her absence, knowing it was wrong.

Chelsi pulled her friend into a warm embrace. "I'll miss you, Ro. We'll meet up for coffee soon."

"I'd like that. I'll text when I can."

She took a few steps toward the door, then stopped. "Oh, by the way, please go to the supply closet, we're almost out of printer paper."

"Sure thing, Chels. Now get out of here."

Chelsi exited the kitchen and trekked down the desolate back hallway. Void of holiday music, decorations, and framed art, its emptiness mirrored her spirit. Institutional flooring led the way to the employee restrooms and outside delivery doors. It would be a longer walk to her car, but she didn't want to risk running into Daniel via the main entrance.

She stepped outside. The bitter cold December air slapped her sill-burning face. The heavy steel door locked behind her with a final click, a sound that echoed endlessly through the snow-covered golf course. It closed the door on her three-year career and six-month relationship.

Her head throbbed.

Gazing into the distance, she forced herself to take a deep breath, but the severe temperature stung her lungs. Her breathing slowed, as did her pulse.

What have I done?

She retrieved her keys from her jacket pocket. Through tear-filled eyes, this time from the cold, she stared at the Eiffel Tower pendant dangling from her keychain. It was a high school graduation gift from her best friend, Jake Hollister. Crystal rhinestones, representing the twenty thousand lights covering the iconic wrought-iron structure, glistened in the mid-afternoon sun.

Daniel's hurtful words of her not being a real baker ricocheted throughout her mind. *Since I'm unemployed* and *unattached, maybe now* would be the perfect time to get certified. Tonight, I'll finally apply to Le Cordon Bleu, and if I get accepted, I'll go to Paris.

Willing her feet to move, Chelsi pushed away from the door. With each step toward her vehicle, the snow crunched below her shoes. She looked toward the snow-covered bridge leading to the eighteenth green. Fleeting memories of Daniel's proposal instantly came to mind. Even though he didn't get down on one knee to propose, blaming *that* on bad knees, it was still romantic.

In hindsight, he probably proposed because it gave him unlimited access to her cookbook. Daniel could've gotten all the recipes he wanted from the internet, but lately, he'd not been that motivated.

Leaning on the bumper of her secondhand burgundy Jeep Wrangler, Chelsi emptied the snow that had accumulated in her opened-back kitchen clogs. Backed in next to her vehicle was a brand-new, black, BMW sports car. Daniel's BMW. She snickered at his front vanity license plate boasting, *MRRIGHT*. It should have read, *MRWRONG*.

Chelsi was grateful the lock to her Jeep wasn't frozen and her ignition key slid easily into the vehicle's chrome lock. As she opened the car door, she happened to look down.

Her eyes widened. *Hmph*. A nail had penetrated the sidewall of Daniel's fancy tire.

"A flat. Now why didn't I think of that?" Nodding at the tire, she added, "Karma."

She put her stuff on the passenger seat, closed the door, and started the engine. Rubbing her ungloved hands together, she prayed for instant warmth, but knew better than to expect anything but cold air to circulate throughout the cab.

The early afternoon sun shone through the frozen layer of crystals that formed on her windshield. She watched the ever-changing kaleidoscope of shapes unfold until they melted away, trickling down the windshield like falling tears.

Chelsi pulled down the vehicle's sun visor, then flipped up the cover to expose the vanity mirror. Leaning forward, she removed her glasses. Bloodshot, hazel green eyes glistening with tears looked back at her.

"Well, that's not a good look." Chelsi wiped away the mascara-streaked tears. She pulled off her green, CCR ball cap, loosened her low bun, and attempted to finger-comb her unruly hair. Her hair had a mind of its own, especially after being restricted for work.

She remembered telling Daniel that lying to her was an instant deal-breaker. He'd assured her he loved her and would never hurt or disrespect their relationship. Yet, here she sat. Single. Next week she'd be turning fifty. Another failed relationship. Another broken engagement. She trusted Daniel like she'd trusted her first fiancé, Andrew. That also ended in a lie.

The pendant on her keychain swayed in time with the RPMs of the engine warming up. Chelsi closed her eyes and sent up a silent prayer. *Will I ever meet a guy I can trust?*

Another hot flash flared up from deep within her chest. She wiped away beads of sweat that had formed under her nose and along her hairline, hoping this menopause thing didn't last too long. *Hmmm*, men-o-pause… maybe she should take a pause-o'-men, for a while. She reached for the container of jellybeans on the seat next to her, removed the lid, and jiggled out a handful of her favorite chewy, sugary confections. Staring at the colors, she threw all the black ones into the cup holder, then popped the rest into her mouth. "No black ones for me."

Chelsi looked at her eyes through the reflection in the rearview mirror. Now what? She needed to formulate a plan. A plan that didn't include returning to her apartment… until she was sure Daniel had cleared out.

Kringle! Of course. Kringle, Vermont.

She could make it there in a few hours. Her father's house was there. Well, *her* house, now. She knew the utilities had been disconnected after her father passed, but she still owned the house. She had her car, a place to stay, and a few thousand in the bank. Now, all she needed was employment. Maybe Rosaria was right. Maybe she could work at a B&B in Kringle. Chelsi looked down at the Eiffel Tower pendant dangling from her keychain. Kringle… the town of her childhood. The town of her best friend… Jake Hollister.

Her emotions cooled, and the Jeep warmed. Chelsi backed out of her spot. She moved the gear control to drive, pulled out of the Country Club of Redfield's parking lot, and never looked back.

Chapter Two

THE PLAN

JAKE HOLLISTER AND HIS EIGHT-YEAR-OLD daughter, Penny, had returned to Kringle, Vermont three years ago after the death of his wife, Amelia. Penny had been struggling with the Christmas holiday since the death of her mother, but was beginning to show restored excitement about the upcoming events. She had signed up again to sing with the children's choir in the town's Christmas festival, Kringlefest. For the past fifty years, patrons came from miles around to enjoy the sights, sounds, and flavors of the upcoming season. Since Kringle was not a winter touristy town, the festival was a much-needed boost for some of the smaller businesses.

It was nearly 1:45 p.m. when Jake Hollister pulled into the Saint Michael's Community Center parking lot, put the truck into park, and left it idling for warmth. Yesterday, all the Saint Michael's participants had begun preparing for the pageant, and rehearsals were wrapping up for the afternoon.

Throughout the morning, the temperature had dropped considerably, now hovering just below freezing. Threatening clouds hung low in the darkened sky, and several dozen birds huddled close on the overhead powerlines. The town of Kringle, Vermont was bracing for a major snowstorm, this one predicted to be ten to twelve inches of snow beginning as freezing rain.

A friendly wave came from a female driver in the vehicle parked next to him. Acknowledging her, Jake rolled his window down.

"Shouldn't be too much longer," the woman said. "I try to arrive early so Reese doesn't have to wait outside in the cold." Jake returned the small talk but couldn't remember the woman's name. Luckily, she told him her daughter's name, and he remembered Penny going to her sleepover birthday party last month.

An alert chimed on Jake's phone. "Gotta go," he told her, waved, and rolled his window up.

Jake was an EMT with the Kringle Fire Department and had just completed this week's rotation. Hoping he didn't have to cover another shift, he removed his reading glasses from inside his puffer vest to read the incoming text. The sound of giggling girls exiting the rec center distracted him from his phone. Disappointment washed over him as he watched his precious daughter walk slowly toward the vehicle. Her head was down. A mane of dark brown hair framed the fur-lined hood of her red-quilted jacket. *This can't be good*, he thought as she got into the truck.

Trying to be as upbeat as possible, Jake said, "Hey, Pen. Have a good time at choir rehearsal?"

"No, it was terrible! I don't want to sing in the Christmas Pageant this year," she said, slamming the back door to the truck a little harder than she should have.

"But why, Sweet P? Yesterday you were so excited after choir practice you could hardly wait to show me your song booklet."

"That was yesterday. Before this." Without looking up, Penny tossed a crumpled-up piece of green paper over her father's shoulder.

"What's this?"

"Pageant information. Please read it, Daddy."

Jake removed his glasses from the dash, flattened the handout against his thigh, and began to read aloud.

"Kringle, Vermont's, Golden Jubilee, Christmas Pageant." He'd found it hard to comprehend the town of Kringle had been participating in the Christmas tradition since the year he was born.

Up until Jake graduated high school, he had always lived in Kringle. His family looked forward to Kringlefest every year. His mom organized the baked goods, while his dad built the outdoor Living Nativity scene. Jake had been excited the year his father told him if he could hammer fifty nails into a spare piece of lumber *without* hammering his thumb, he would be allowed to help. That had been the year his best friend, Chelsi Burnett, moved into town.

"Date, December 24th, yup. Time, uh-huh. Boy, I sure hope it won't be as cold as last year. Remember how windy it was, and how we had to bundle up, Pen?"

Penny sat in her seat, arms folded across her chest, unresponsive.

"Tree lighting ceremony, always a crowd favorite. I wonder who Mayor Schaefer will choose this year to have the honor of pushing the button."

Jake looked in his rearview mirror at his daughter. Nothing.

Um, a little help here, Amelia. You were so good at knowing exactly what to say to Penny.

"Okay, well this is a fun change. Instead of an electric light parade, a pet parade has been put in its place. Want to enter Cocoa? I'm sure she'd like to spend some time with other dogs."

She looked up. "Sure. Okay. I thought that sounded like fun."

"That's the spirit, kiddo."

"*Hmmm*…Children's art display inside the community center. Well, you've already completed your colored pencil drawing of a tea party in the gazebo. And it is quite lovely, I might add. I could never draw or paint as good as you. Even my stick figures were unrecognizable. You certainly inherited your mother's artistic flair."

Penny let out a quick laugh. A surge of tears streamed from her unsmiling eyes. "You have to say that. You're my dad."

"Gingerbread house competition at the firehouse." He sucked in a deep breath between his teeth.

"Yep. There's the first reason."

He turned around in his seat. "Well, Pen, we don't have to—"

"And we won't!" she blurted out.

He held up both hands in defense. "Hey, you can't blame me for that one. How was I supposed to know the paper pastry bag would explode?"

"You squeezed it too hard and the white icing squirted all over my lap. After I cleaned it up, I walked around all night looking like I wet my pants."

"And I did apologize for that. I guess I'm not as good of a gingerbread house assistant as your mom was. She *was* great at everything. Hey, to play it safe, I'll put an extra set of clothes for you in my truck. Okay?"

"I still don't want to decorate a gingerbread house," she mumbled.

"Oh, here! I know you'll love this one. Santa and his reindeer carousel ride. See, you'll miss out on a great experience if we don't go."

His daughter's eyes connected with his in the truck's rearview mirror. "Maybe I'll get to ride Rudolph."

"Good girl, Penny. There's the smile I've been waiting for. I hope you get your wish on that one. However, I won't be joining you on your carousel ride."

"But why not, Daddy? It sounds like so much fun."

"It's a long story, from when I was young."

"I don't mind," she said, sitting up a little taller. "I love hearing stories from when you were little."

"Well, I was a few years older than you when Grandma took me and Uncle Randy for a day trip to Coney Island in Brooklyn. The school year had just ended, and summer was right around the corner. We had had a lot of fun playing games, eating coney dogs and cotton candy, then laughing at each other in those distorted mirrors; you know, the ones that made you look tall and skinny or short and fat." His daughter nodded. "The line for the carousel ride was pretty short, and we had just enough time before the beginning of the Mermaid Parade."

Penny leaned closer and blinked her eyes several times. "You saw a mermaid parade?"

"Well, not exactly. You see, we missed it. There was this older kid in front of us in line who was bragging about how easy it was to get a brass ring from the carousel's dispenser. He must've been around twelve and said he already had a couple at home. He bet me I wouldn't be able to grab one."

"Ooooh, peer pressure! Not good, Daddy. Did you get the brass ring?"

"Nope. I couldn't quite reach it. So, when the bell rang indicating the last rotation, I took my safety belt off. When I reached for the brass ring, I slipped on the smooth surface of the saddle and fell off the horse. I landed hard on my shoulder. The pain was so bad, I thought it was broken. Haven't been on a carousel since."

Penny covered her mouth and let out a short gasp. "Did you break your shoulder?"

"Fortunately, no. But Grandma had to take me to the hospital for X-rays. The doctor said it was a bad sprain and I shouldn't use it for a few days. He put my arm in a bright blue sling to stabilize it."

"No wonder you don't want to ride the carousel with me."

Jake resumed his search for the offending item on the crumpled-up flyer. "Hot chocolate with marshmallows," he said, smiling.

"I was *so* embarrassed!" Penny said. "Every time I saw Jacob and Jordan at the festival, you know, the twins whose parents own Java Joes, they would puff up their cheeks, imitating you and Uncle Randy. Luckily, when school started, they had forgotten about it."

"Okay. You win." Her dad crossed his heart. "I promise this year not to compete with Uncle Randy to see who can stuff the most marshmallows in our mouths. Deal?"

"Deal."

"I love this one the best," he said, shifting in his seat. "A performance by the Saint Michael's Children's Choir. That's you! Homemade Christmas cookies. Yum!"

"What do you mean, Yum. Didn't you read the next line?"

"Let's see… four-dozen homemade cookies to be provided by the Saint Michael's children's choir." A heavy weight pushed against his chest.

Penny stood and reached over her father's shoulder, jabbing her finger at the flier. "Yeah, Daddy, that one!"

"I'm sure we could buy…"

Jake looked over at his daughter standing behind him. Silent tears slid down her somber face. "No," she said softly. "Mrs. Carmichael said it's for the Christmas Pageant, no store-bought cookies. No exceptions."

He rubbed his stubbled chin. "Maybe we can ask Miss Laura to bake cookies for us. Even though we never ask her, she seems to enjoy bringing dinners to us." Jake thought back to the first day he and Penny moved into town. Laura Schaefer had seen them in the grocery store, and knowing he was single again, quickly began showing interest; but he wasn't ready to bring another woman into his life. So, the interest was purely one-sided.

"Nuh-uh. Miss Laura doesn't like me and only brings us food to see you."

"I'm sure you're mistaken, Pen."

"Remember the night she brought spaghetti and meatballs to our cottage?" Penny asked.

"Yeah."

"Well, Cocoa barked at the front door to tell you she had to go potty. While you were outside, Miss Laura's phone rang. She told me she'd be right back and answered it in the kitchen." Lowering her gaze, Penny stared at her sparkly, red sneakers. "I don't know who she was talking to, but I heard her say I had a rat for a pet and that I complicate things."

Jake remained silent, mulling over what his young daughter had just said. How could Laura say something like that when Penny was in earshot? He knew she was trying to wiggle her way into his life, but that was all going to stop. *Now.*

Penny raised her voice a notch and started to cry. "I don't like Miss Laura anymore. How can she say such bad things about Whiskers? She doesn't even know her! Besides, she's a guinea pig, *not* a rat."

In tears, his daughter shook her head and covered her eyes with her little hands. Jake heard her muffled words. "I love Whiskers. She was the last present Mommy bought before…"

Jake's heart ached. He remembered how excited Penny was that morning nearly four years ago when she and his wife, Amelia, came home from the pet store. That was the last day Jake ever saw his wife.

"Why did she have to work late that night?" Penny cried. "Why did Mommy have to die?"

He clenched his jaw. Her gut-wrenching sobs tore right through his chest. "Pen, the doctors did everything they could to save her."

Jake remembered sitting helpless in the Bremerton Naval Hospital waiting room where Amelia worked. A nurse had taken little Penny to the cafeteria for a bowl of cereal and a glass of chocolate milk. Though he had a small Naval fleet surrounding him for support, he had never felt so alone. His entire life flashed before his eyes in the sixty-eight minutes from the time he had received the call about his wife's car accident until the team of doctors, with somber expressions, had entered the waiting room. Though Amelia put up a good fight, she had not survived her injuries.

Jake looked up to the heavens. *Amelia, I love you and miss you every day. But I think it's time. I'm ready to move on with our lives. I pray someday soon, I find a lady as caring and loving as you, who will love me and Penny with all her heart.*

Needing the warmth and security of her father's love, she climbed over the truck's console and snuggled into the comfort of his arms.

"Daddy, I wish you had your guitar here so you could play Mommy's favorite song."

Adjusting her better on his lap, he said, "You Are My Sunshine?"

"Yes. Please."

He kissed the top of her head, taking in the scent of her strawberry shampoo. "But if I had my guitar, I couldn't hold you in my arms."

"Then, will you sing it to me, please?"

"Of course. Will you accompany me?"

Penny nodded.

He rested his cheek on the top of her head, and together they sang the classic children's song.

She sat there. Eyes closed, listening. Sniffling. Her little body calming down.

Jake remembered Amelia baking. She'd pull her hair back, wash her hands, and put on her favorite apron; the one with pairs of tiny garden birds. She'd remove a cookbook from the shelf he'd built for her in their tiny kitchen, read the instructions, and put everything she needed on the counter. Using her mother's vintage harvest gold measuring cups and matching measuring spoons, she'd measure each ingredient into individual bowls, then line them up in order of incorporation. She was amazing.

"Okay. I know your mommy was a terrific baker. She would never bake those refrigerated slice and bake type cookies—said their first ingredient was chemicals. So, I guess there's no time like the present for me to learn how to bake. Hey, Pen? This cookie thing… we got this."

Penny wiped her runny nose along the sleeve of her jacket.

Craning her neck, she looked back at her father. He thought he saw a hint of sparkle in her eyes.

"Whatcha got in mind?"

"Atta girl. Since our cottage is still being repaired from the flood, we can bring all the ingredients to Grandpa's kitchen at the B&B and bake 'em. The first guests won't be arriving for a few days, so he won't mind if we use the kitchen. Let's see… we're gonna call it, 'Operation-Cookie-Bake.'"

"Whhaaat?" she asked.

"I used to watch your mommy bake the most delicious cookies, roll out the flakiest pie crusts, and knead dough into the best-tasting bread you've ever eaten." He shrugged. "How hard can it be?"

"Can we bake angel cookies?" Penny asked, nodding.

Jake tilted his head to the side. "I think I remember Grandma baking angel cookies at the B&B. So, sure."

"You can read, right?" he asked.

Penny rolled her eyes. "Of course, Daddy. I'm nine. Almost."

"And I can take hot stuff out of the oven. How 'bout, when we get home, I take out my phone and we'll look up Easy Christmas Cookie Recipes."

"Then, we can make a list—"

"And check it twice?" she asked, her eyes brightening.

"And, check it twice. Buy the ingredients—"

"Like flour, butter and eggs?"

"Yup, like flour, butter and eggs."

"Can we get red sprinkles?" she asked.

"Only red?"

"Daddy, you know red is my favorite color."

Wasn't it just last month she had to have everything purple? He looked down at her red sparkly sneakers and red jacket.

"Ah, yes. *Couleur du jour.*"

Her eyebrows knit together. "What does *that* mean?"

"It's French. Like in the country where the famous Eiffel Tower is. In the French language, *couleur du jour* means color of the day."

"Ooohh-kay," she said, after a minute.

French. I hadn't spoken any French since high school... Since Chelsi. Lost in thought about his childhood friend, Jake stared out the truck window, drumming his fingers against the steering wheel.

"When I was in high school, I gave my best friend, Chelsi Burnett, an Eiffel Tower keychain. She once had a dream of going to Paris to study baking."

"Did she ever go?"

"I don't know, Sprinkles, we lost touch."

"Daddy... Daddy!" She poked her elbow into her father's chest. "Sprinkles?" she giggled.

"Wha... What?"

"You called me, Sprinkles."

"Sorry, Pen. I meant to say, Sunshine."

He crooked his pinky and extended it. "Do you promise to put some sprinkles on top of the cookies?"

"I promise," she nodded, linking pinkies.

Smiling, Penny scrambled back over the truck's console to the backseat. "Oh dear," she said, buckling her seatbelt. "Better get going, Daddy. We have a lot to do."

Chapter Three

THE SNOWSTORM

CHELSI HAD DRIVEN ON I-91 a thousand times, but it wasn't until she spotted the familiar green and white sign welcoming oncoming travelers to Vermont, The Green Mountain State, that she realized she had been driving on autopilot since pulling out of the country club's parking lot. She lived and worked in Massachusetts, but loved Vermont. Kringle, Vermont, to be exact. It was a quaint New England town on the Connecticut River where everyone participated in seasonal festivals. Baconfest began with all things… you guessed it, bacon. Townsfolk would walk around wearing outlandish bacon costumes while eating bacon-wrapped hot dogs on a stick, bacon-roasted nuts, and finally, the ever-popular bacon butter on a toasted egg bagel. Then there was Flowerfest, a festival for the senses, followed by Applefest, with crisp apples, delicious fresh juice, and those outrageous apple cider donuts. Lastly, on December twenty-fourth, came Kringlefest. Chelsi loved them all. With that much local flair, why were teenagers, herself included, in such a hurry to leave their hometown after graduation?

A rumbling sound emerged from deep within her stomach, and Chelsi realized she hadn't eaten since breakfast. A glance at her gas gauge, hovering at the quarter tank mark, told her to exit the freeway at the Vermont Welcome Center or she'd soon run out of gas. Besides gasoline,

The Welcome Center had a huge assortment of vending machines, a fabulous food court, and clean restrooms. A win-win-win in her book. A full tank of gas for her Jeep, "Ruby," a hamburger, sweet potato fries with a side of warm, ooey-gooey marshmallow fluff, a large Sprite, no ice, and a clean place to wash up. Now, if she could meet a single man inside who didn't lie, cheat or deceive her, she'd put on her best apron and together they'd bake up some delicious memories, for as long as they both should live.

Chelsi had watched the outside temperature gauge drop over ten degrees in the time she had been traveling. Luckily, she scored a parking spot close to the food court entrance. A bone-chilling gust pelted her face like a snowball thrown at full force, tempting Chelsi to return to the warmth of her vehicle. She gathered the front of her jacket, lowered her head, and covering her nose and mouth, hunkered down into its warmth. Her hair whipped around with the same angry emotion as the wind, creating an untamed mass of curls.

Chelsi held the door open, allowing a young mother and a preschool child to exit.

"Mama, did you see the picture of Santa Claus in that parade?"

"I sure did, sweetie. That's a poster for this year's Kringlefest. Santa's always at the end of the parade. I remember when I was…"

Chelsi stopped. *Did she just say this year's Kringlefest?* She closed the door and read the poster tapped to it.

Kringle, Vermont's Golden Jubilee, Kringlefest, and Christmas Pageant. December 24th.

Fifty years. Wow, she thought. She was thankful to see that some traditions had continued. It was a way of bringing the community of Kringle, Vermont, together. When she got up today, she had no idea she'd be driving back to Kringle, but she still doubted she'd be in town long enough to see this year's pageant.

Fully fueled and ready to return to the road, she looked at the late afternoon sky. Its color resembled the concrete parking lot, stone-cold and grey. The television at The Welcome Center was tuned to a local channel. The meteorologist had said a nor'easter was blowing up the coast with blizzard-like conditions dumping close to thirty inches of new snow in some parts. Vermont was in for a doozy of a storm, and the promise of snow was undeniably in the air.

Chelsi sat in her Jeep, heater going full blast. "Okay, Ruby, we have two choices." She ticked the options off her fingers. "One, we turn around and head back to my apartment. But I certainly do *not* want to run into Daniel, so that's out. Two, we continue heading north and hope we make it to Kringle before we get stranded in the storm."

She sat for a minute, half expecting her car to tell her to put the pedal to the metal and pull out of the parking lot.

What was the overwhelming force drawing her north? There was nobody left in town she cared about—not that she knew of, anyway. Her mother had passed shortly after they moved to Kringle, and Dad four years ago. Being an only child, she'd always wished she had a brother or sister. She had her softball teammates. They were all close once, but that was thirty years ago. Most of them had left town on scholarships and had probably never returned.

Chelsi turned on the radio. Adjusting the volume, the ending chorus from "Angels We Have Heard on High" drifted from the Jeep's speakers. After she broke up with Daniel, the Christmas music descending from the country club's overhead speakers had annoyed her, but this one had the opposite effect. Chelsi smiled. That was the first song she had sung after joining the Saint Michael's Children's Choir. Goodness, that was over forty years ago. Christmas hadn't meant as much to Chelsi after her mom passed. Sure, Dad did his best, but Mom had always made all the holidays special.

Her mind was lost in childhood memories. She remembered moving from Leesburg, Virginia, to Kringle, Vermont, the winter she turned nine.

Standing on risers behind the live nativity, the Saint Michael's children's choir had opened the festivities. Over their winter jackets, the choir wore long, navy blue choir robes with a golden yoke. The 4-H club members brought their well-cared-for animals as participants in the live nativity. Every night for two weeks, Mom went to the church hall to help sew choir robes and nativity costumes. That's when Chelsi met Jake.

Warmth spread up her body and filled her heart. *Oh, Jake Hollister. My best friend. The fun we had. The trouble we got into. We were always together.*

Absent-mindedly, she rubbed the scar on her chin, thinking, *Stitch and Einstein.* The jock and the valedictorian. She never would've made it through the spring Mom passed without him. She wished they hadn't lost touch after only a year, but their lives had branched out in very different directions. She wondered how Jake was and where he was living.

As predicted, the snow began. Flake after flake danced with the wind to the silent song of nature.

"Well, that's my cue. Two it is, Ruby. Kringle's less than an hour's drive from here, without traffic. Hopefully, I don't get snowbound before we arrive."

Fiddling with the keychain dangling from the ignition, she looked at the old house key. *Home.* She hadn't been home since her dad's funeral. Despite the utilities being disconnected, she figured she could light the fireplace and crash on the couch for the night.

The horn blast from an anxious customer waiting to use the gasoline pump jolted her from her reverie. "Oh, sorry." Chelsi turned off the radio and buckled her seatbelt. *Better concentrate on the road, Ruby. According to the forecast, this storm's going to be ruthless!* She pulled out of the gas station onto the frontage road. Returning to the I-91 intersection, she looked south, but headed north. South was turmoil. South was Daniel. North was solace. North was home.

Vermont's interstate looked like a winter wonderland. Despite the snow, traffic remained at a constant speed, preventing the thick flakes from sticking to the pavement. Tall barren trees, weighed down with heavy snow, seemingly whizzed by. An unexpected gust of wind blew across the treetops, scattering clumps of snow in every direction. It looked like the trees were having a snowball fight.

Exiting the freeway at Maple Highway, Chelsi glanced down at her clock. Four forty-seven. Not bad timing, considering the weather. *Only six miles from here. Piece o' cake.*

As if waiting for her Jeep to exit the freeway, the foreboding sky opened. Howling wind and blinding snow exploded from the clouds. She put her windshield wipers on high and slowed her speed down to a mere crawl.

Where had this blizzard come from? True, the weather station had predicted a heavy storm, but this was crazy. She'd assumed it would arrive gradually—not like this!

Over an hour later, she approached the barely visible town sign. *Welcome to Kringle, Vermont. Home of the state's best Danish Pastry. Population 6,759.* She shook her head. That sign hadn't changed in thirty years.

The giant maple trees along both sides of the roadway had been planted over a hundred years ago. Their barren branches knit together like gnarled fingers above the narrow country road. Returning for her father's funeral, she hadn't perceived the trees as threatening. Now they were ominous. A brittle, snow-covered tunnel, certain to collapse in the blink of an eye. She crept along, watching. Waiting.

It was dark.

The snow, relentless.

The wind, unceasing.

Branches, moaning.

Crack!

A huge tree limb momentarily suspended… then plummeted toward the icy pavement.

Thud!

Chelsi was helpless.

Too late to stop. Nowhere to go. No way to avoid the deadly obstacle.

"Noooooo!"

Chapter Four

A NEW VISION

"WHA... WHAT HAPPENED?" CHELSI ASKED, blinking.

"You have been involved in an automobile accident," said a man in a thick British accent. "The roadways are extremely icy."

Startled at the sound of someone responding to her question, she turned her head in the direction of the voice.

"Who… who are you? Where did you come from?"

"My name is Dr. Jasper Aldridge. I heard you scream. I pray you are not seriously injured."

As if shivering from the cold, the Jeep's engine shook, sputtered, then stalled. Chelsi looked down at the dashboard and turned off the ignition.

She squinted at the man standing outside her window. "I'm fine. I think," she said, unbuckling her seatbelt. "The airbag didn't deploy, but my seatbelt prevented me from hitting the steering wheel."

"I am very glad to hear that, my dear. My fiancée and I own the establishment across the street." Jasper pointed in the direction of a weathered, wooden structure set back in the woods. "I am here to offer assistance."

"But… everything's so blurry."

Dr. Aldridge nodded toward the passenger seat. "Your vision is impaired because you have broken your spectacles. They're on the seat beside you, next to your handbag."

She picked up what was left of her eyeglasses. Peering at the cracked lenses and mangled black frame, her eyes widened in panic. "How am I supposed to drive with these?"

"I'm an optometrist. I will craft you a new pair of eyeglasses straight away."

The doctor pointed toward the maple tree which abruptly halted her vehicles' forward motion. "At present, this tree has rendered your vehicle… immobile."

She turned around to look behind her. Across the desolate road barely visible, a ten-foot tree limb blocked the icy roadway. "I couldn't stop in time."

Jasper opened the drivers-side car door. In a voice barely above a whisper, he said, "You were very lucky, my dear. Your vehicle can be repaired." Leaning inside her vehicle, he extended his hand. His benevolent eyes encouraged her to accept it. The stranger's straightforwardness was both persuasive and comforting.

Why did she trust this man? She hit a tree. He came out of nowhere, yet she felt as if she'd known him her whole life. He was an odd fellow. Compassionate, but strange.

Chelsi removed her keys from the ignition and dropped them into the front pouch of her handbag. She grabbed her cell phone and clutched it close to her chest. Accepting his hand, she slid out of her seat; her feet sank into a foot of fresh snow.

Jasper offered Chelsi his arm while they trudged through the snow to assess her vehicle's damage. The storm had diminished to mere flurries. The moon, but a sliver of its completeness, shed solitary gloominess upon the snow-covered country road.

Her shivering body, a combination of cold and shock from the accident, was instantly calmed by his warm touch.

A sudden gust of wind slapped her face. Chelsi pulled the zipper of her jacket up to her chin, then blew warm air onto her hands. She glanced over at her Good Samaritan; he appeared to be unaffected by the sudden squall of wind and blowing snow.

"Sir, how can you not be cold?"

"I am not usually affected by the outside elements."

Hmmm… bizarre.

She tapped the flashlight icon on her cell phone. Using her phone as a spotlight, they had a clear vision of the accident scene.

The Jeep's front end, wrapped around a century-old maple tree.

Hood crumpled.

Radiator, destroyed. Steam rising.

Right headlight, shattered. Shards of glass embedded somewhere into the snow.

"I'm afraid your vehicle will require extensive repair," Jasper said.

Chelsi stood motionless; eyes fixed on the front end of her Jeep. Unconsciously, she raised her cell phone, pried her frozen fingers away from the case, and unlocked the screen.

Through chattering teeth, she said, "Of course. No service."

"Once inside, I will call a tow service to assist you with your vehicle. If you wish, I will also call an ambulance to take you to the local infirmary."

"That would be very kind of you." Chelsi dropped her head to her chest. "No fiancé, no job, no glasses, and now, no car!"

He looked down at her feet, buried deep beneath the snow.

"You are badly shaken from the accident and must be thoroughly frozen from the elements. Come, let me get you inside to warm by the fire. Mrs. Winters, my fiancée, has prepared you a piping hot pot of tea."

"But—"

"She had just put the kettle on when we heard the crash."

Chelsi smiled. "Thank you. Tea sounds lovely." Trusting the kind-hearted stranger, she followed Jasper toward the store.

"I must warn you though, Miss, we have two endearing, four-legged rascals who adore callers. Their names are Maximillian and Gwendolyn. They are quite harmless, I assure you."

"It's Burnett," Chelsi said. "And I love dogs."

"I beg your pardon?"

"My last name is Burnett. Chelsi Burnett. And you are, again, Dr.…?"

"Aldridge. Dr. Jasper Aldridge." With a tip of his dark fedora, Dr. Aldridge added, "Good evening, Miss Burnett. It is a pleasure to make your acquaintance."

"Same here. But I wish it were under different circumstances!"

Chelsi accepted Jasper's arm and they trekked through the snow-covered street. A split rail fence, loaded with heavy snow, marked the boundaries between two large parcels of land. A For Sale sign dangled from one hinge, lashed about in the wind.

Turning one last time, she looked over her shoulder at her mangled car. From the corner of her eye, she studied how oddly Jasper was dressed, starting with his snow boots. What kind of outfit was he wearing? He looked like someone straight from a 1940s movie.

"I can't believe how shaken I am," she said. White puffs of steamy breath were visible in the icy air. "This was my first car accident in almost twenty… no, twenty-five years."

"Adversities are never easy to overcome, my dear. We must learn and grow from whatever life hands us. Sometimes, we live with a memory in our minds and our hearts forever."

"Like the loss of my mother when I was ten. It's as vivid today as the day she passed," she said.

"Preciously."

Just past the bend in the road, an old two-story colonial house came into view. Years of harsh Vermont winters and humid summer days faded the façade to a weathered shade of silvery-brown. Coach lights flanked the lacquered wooden front door, peeling from years of neglect. A swag of fresh-cut pine boughs, intertwined with sprigs of white berries tied together with a red bow, brightened the shabby front door.

Chelsi stopped at the end of the walkway and examined the dormant bushes which bordered the wooden front porch steps. She bent down and snapped off a six-inch twig laden with white berries. "I thought these were wild snowberry bushes peeking out from beneath all that snow. How I miss them."

"My fiancée had taken a fancy to them as well and incorporated them into the store's Christmas wreath. She's quite good with a pair of pruning shears," Jasper said, with a dose of pride in his voice.

"The birds and the squirrels will enjoy the fruit from this twig," said Chelsi, tossing the stick off to the side. "Nature's way of feeding the animals and spreading the enclosed seeds."

"Now, please come inside Miss Burnett. You must be quite frozen." The walkway and front porch steps were cleared of snow, but she was grateful Jasper took her elbow to help her up the timeworn wooden steps.

He escorted Chelsi inside. The tinkling sound of brass sleigh bells, tied to the old-fashioned doorknob, jingle-jangled when Jasper opened and closed the door. Two corgis, Maximillian and Gwendolyn, stood patiently at Mrs. Winters' feet, anxious to greet their visitor.

"Olivia Winters, may I present Miss Chelsi Burnett. Miss Burnett, my fiancée, Mrs. Olivia Winters."

Olivia offered her hand. "Good evening, Miss Burnett." With her charming British accent, she continued. "I am saddened by your untimely automobile accident, but it is lovely to meet you." Chelsi shook her outstretched hand which was then joined by Olivia's left hand. Chelsi looked down at their connected hands and again was immersed in warmness. The moment their hands had touched, a peacefulness encompassed Chelsi's body, like the feeling she got when she immersed her tired body into a hot bubble bath after a long day on her feet.

Chelsi stood there, not sure what to make of the feeling which engulfed her. It was, yet again, an uncanny feeling of complete calm.

Jasper hung his beige herringbone tweed wool coat and fedora hat on the hook near the door. "Miss Burnett's feet are quite frozen from the elements. Olivia, please see if you can find a hot-water bottle and a blanket."

"Yes, of course. Please, come warm yourself by to the fire."

Jasper sat on a chair near the front door and removed his black galoshes. Chelsi noted how the fuller cut of Jasper's outdated sport coat hung comfortably on his medium frame. The brown trousers were equally old-fashioned, buttoned just below the knee with brown cable knit knee-length socks tucked snugly underneath.

Nodding to Maximillian and Gwendolyn, he said, "Go ahead, mates, I know you're excited to greet Miss Burnett."

Chelsi bent down at the waist to greet the two spirited dogs. Accepting an abundance of doggie kisses, she patted their heads and ruffled the fur behind their ears. She looked from one set of expressive eyes to the other, each pooch vying for more attention. "Now, which one are you?"

"The impatient one here is Maximillian. He knows it's ladies first, but sometimes forgets his manners."

He offered his paw for a proper introduction. Chelsi accepted it, saying, "Very nice to meet you, Maximillian."

"And this is his sister, Gwendolyn," Jasper said.

Her face lit up. "Brother and sister?" Talking to the dogs, she continued, "How fortunate you were to have had each other growing up. I was an only child. I was kind of jealous of my friends who had siblings. I always wished I had a brother or a sister or both!"

Separately, each pooch let out a low bark.

Amazed, she said, "Oh! You're happy, too? I think they understood me!"

"In truth, they comprehend more than you conceive," Jasper said, directing her to sit by the fire.

Chelsi studied the enthusiastic pooches and her new surroundings. "They're Pembroke Welsh Corgis, aren't they?"

"They are indeed," he said. "Are you fond of animals?"

"Yes, very much so. A few years ago, I remember seeing this breed on the cover of a magazine posing with Queen Elizabeth II on her ninetieth birthday."

"Queen Elizabeth II's, ninetieth birthday, you say?"

"Yes, I don't remember much of the particulars from the article, but the magazine had photos of the queen and some of her corgis. It stated she'd had more than thirty dogs during her rein."

Olivia arrived and wrapped a dark gray woolen blanket around Chelsi's shoulders.

"There you go, dear. If you would please remove your wet shoes and stockings, the hot water bottle will soon warm you quite nicely."

Almost as if she were providing extra warmth, Gwendolyn rested her head on top of Chelsi's feet.

"It seems our dogs have taken quite a liking to you," Olivia said.

The familiar shrill from a boiling tea kettle directed their attention toward the sound.

"That's my cue, Miss Burnett. Tea will be ready in a jiffy."

"Please. Mrs. Winters. It's Chelsi."

"Then you must also call us by our given names as well. Jasper and Olivia."

Chelsi nodded and watched Olivia set off, presumably to the kitchen. Her gaze was drawn to Olivia's apparel. Shiny, black patent-leather shoes with a sensible heel, seamed hosiery with a one-inch hole just below her knee, and a slightly tattered green suit. Jasper had been dressed similarly to Olivia. Though both Jasper and Olivia had quirky taste in clothing, it suited them.

Chelsi looked around the room. From the various amount of mismatched kitchenware and linens to several lamps without lampshades, her first impression was an antique store, but she had the intense feeling the store was more than that.

Jasper excused himself for a moment and withdrew toward the back of the store.

"How are you feeling, Chelsi? May I check your eyes?" he asked.

"*Um*, sure."

He shined a handheld light into Chelsi's eyes and moved it back and forth. "Now if you will, please, without moving your head, follow my finger."

"Your pupils are responding nicely, but you should have a medical doctor examine you to ensure you do not have more serious injuries."

The enticing aroma of flour, butter, sugar, and possibly pecans drifted in from the direction Olivia had retreated to. "What is Olivia baking? It has one of the most heavenly aromas I've smelled in a long time. Whatever it is, I'd love to get her recipe."

Jasper's bushy gray eyebrows raised in uncertainty. "I believe she has scones in the oven. To my knowledge, Olivia does not follow a specific recipe. She knows exactly how much of each ingredient to add, how thick the dough should be, what gas mark and how long they should bake."

Chelsi picked up a delicate embroidery project from the side table and admired the tiny, precise stitches.

"Jasper, this is lovely. How long has Olivia been working on it?"

"On and off, whenever she has the time." He lowered his voice, barely above a whisper. "I'm not supposed to know she's working on it. Livy usually has her stitchery hidden away in a sewing basket. I suspect it's my wedding gift."

"Your wedding gift?" she beamed. "The two of you make such a cute couple. When will you be married?"

Jasper tapped his sport coat's breast pocket. "Christmas Day."

"Christmas Day? But that's only—"

"Tea's ready," Olivia said, in her chipper British accent.

Smiling, Jasper rose and removed the cumbersome tray from her petite hands, placing it in the center of the tea table.

Chelsi leaned forward. She closed her eyes and inhaled the delectable aroma of freshly baked scones.

"*Mm*. Delicious. I thought I smelled scones."

Chelsi took in her surroundings. "I lived in Kringle for ten years before moving away. I can't recall a store like this one ever being here. When I returned four years ago for my father's funeral, I believe this place was boarded up."

Jasper lifted a saucer, rattling the delicate teacup slightly. He placed a silver tea strainer onto the cup and extended it to Olivia.

With a gleam in his eye, he replied, "We haven't been here very long. Seems like we've only just arrived." Olivia poured the steaming amber liquid, filling the teacup only halfway.

Look at those two. The love they share is like none other. Now, here's a match made in heaven.

"Lemon, or milk and sugar?" Olivia asked.

"Just sugar, please." Chelsi smiled at the elegant tea service.

"Have you seen this pattern before?" Olivia asked.

"Similar. Mom passed when I was ten. Every summer, I'd stay with my aunt and uncle in Racine, Wisconsin. They owned the Willow Creek Bed & Breakfast. It was a beautiful, white Victorian built in the early 1900s. Every morning, it was my job to sweep the wraparound porch and set the outside tables. Aunt Ann Marie used a similar pattern for afternoon tea. While baking side by side with her, I learned the importance of using delicate hands while preparing scones. *That's* when my love for baking and afternoon tea began."

Olivia poured just a splash of milk into her cup. Holding the saucer in one hand, she raised the cup and took a quick sip of her tea. Replacing the cup onto its saucer, she asked, "Chelsi, what brought you to Kringle, especially on a snowy evening such as today?"

"I needed to clear my head, so I decided to come back to Kringle. I got in my car and just drove. When I left for work this morning, the Massachusetts weather had predicted snow, but nothing like what's on the ground here in Kringle. The sky didn't look bad when I left Redfield."

"Redfield?"

"Redfield, Massachusetts. That's where I work. Well... used to work."

Prompting her to continue, Jasper said, "If I might be so bold, what had you so upset?"

Chelsi picked up her teacup, rubbed the pad of her thumb over the silkiness of the scalloped cup's rim, and took a contemplative sip of the calming liquid. As if confessing to the ladybug accent inside the cup, she said, "When my aunt passed away, she left me the recipe binder from her B&B. I kept the book locked in my staff locker. On my day off my fiancé, Daniel, took that binder and copied all the recipes. Today, I found an advance copy of a cookbook, written by Daniel J. Wright in his office. A portion of those recipes he claimed as his own were my late aunt's."

Chelsi broke off a piece of her scone, slathered some orange marmalade on it, and continued. "Daniel was not only my fiancé… he was also my supervisor. Today I broke up with him *and* quit my job. I had hoped things would be different with Daniel."

Olivia reached over and patted Chelsi's hand. "Go on, dear."

"I was engaged about ten years ago. Andrew, he was my first fiancé, and I had a big wedding planned. Proud as a peacock, my father walked me down the aisle; a hundred happy guests watching every step. But Andrew wasn't gazing at me with happiness and love, like most grooms when they catch the first glimpse of their brides. His eyes darted nervously from me to a woman seated in the front row of the congregation."

Chelsi reached for her teacup, took a sip, and cleared her throat. "The minister had just begun the ceremony when my fiancé shook his head and told him to stop." Tears welled up in Chelsi's eyes, and Olivia handed her a lace hankie with the letter "C" embroidered on one corner.

"If this is too difficult for you, my dear, you don't have to continue."

"No, Olivia, it's okay."

Chelsi took a deep breath. "Andrew looked at this woman and nodded. With no remorse, he said, 'Chelsi, we need to talk.' Nothing good ever comes after someone says that to you. A woman from the front row on the groom's side stood up and left the church. He took my hand and led me out through the side entrance. He confessed he had reconnected with this woman on social media, and they were in love."

Olivia refilled Chelsi's teacup. "Oh my, how deceitful," she said.

"That's when I left Kringle and moved to Massachusetts to heal and begin my new life."

Chelsi glanced up and squinted at the old-style kitchen clock hanging on the wall. "I really must be going. Thank you for your hospitality. The tea was delightful, and Olivia, your scones were heavenly."

She stood up to leave. "Wait, I can't go anywhere until I get my glasses. Jasper, you mentioned you're an optometrist, but I don't see any eye equipment in here."

"Yes, yes, of course, my dear." He pointed toward the back of the store. "My office is this way. Come, let's examine your eyes so you can continue on your journey. Join us, Livy, won't you?"

Jasper nodded to the dogs. "Stay with your sister, Maximillian. You both will get t-r-e-a-t-s if you behave." He gave the dogs a wink.

Max turned and led Gwendolyn to the braided rug in front of the fireplace, where they both settled down with a loud huff.

Chelsi followed Olivia through the store. They walked past display tables of mismatched dishes and glassware, many of which had small chips or a slight crack. A toy train set circled the track, puffing smoke from its chimney. She commented to Jasper that when her dad was a boy, his parents had given him a Lionel train set for Christmas. Then she added that she thought it was still packed away in the attic. Chelsi couldn't resist running her fingers over a cast iron foot-pedal-driven Singer sewing machine. She could still smell the oil used to service the moving gears. Her eyes were drawn to the suit and blouse pattern for sale on the machine's cabinet table. She held it up and compared the pattern to Olivia's outfit.

Olivia smiled. "Yes, it *was* a very popular style."

Along the back wall, next to a roll-top desk, stood a mahogany telephone chair table. On the table, sat an antique, gold embossed, rotary dial telephone. The grouping resembled one Queen Elizabeth II might have sat upon in a Buckingham Palace foyer.

"Chelsi, what is it?" Olivia asked. "You appear to be puzzled."

"I am. I've never been inside an antique store before. I guess I never knew what kinds of things were for sale. Your merchandise is amazing!"

"Thank you. I like to offer a little bit of what a family might need and afford."

Chelsi picked up an antique brown bear. "Look at this adorable old bear." Staring into his eyes, she said, "Mr. Bear, I love your expressive button eyes; they tell me how much you were loved."

Jasper stood in the doorway of his examination room waiting for Chelsi to join him. "Mind the step," he said, pointing to the uneven flooring. "It appears this room was an addition to the existing structure."

Chelsi narrowed her eyes to read the sign above the doorway to the exam room. "'All you need is a new perspective.' Boy, if that isn't the truth!"

"Am I safe to assume you are not speaking of your damaged spectacles?"

"You've got that right." She looked up at the ceiling deep in thought. "In my late aunt's recipe book, the table of contents was separated by chapters, like *Julia Child's Mastering the Art of French Cooking*. One chapter was breakfast offerings, then breads, another evening snacks. I'm ready to turn the page and delve into the next chapter in my life. Something that will challenge me."

Olivia walked over and stood next to Jasper. Standing side by side, Chelsi looked at the outfits her hosts were wearing. "I like that you're playing the role with your clothing from the '40s. It must be great for business."

Olivia nodded. "It's what we're most comfortable in."

Jasper switched on a light. Once inside, he closed the office door and motioned for Chelsi to stand behind the blue line.

She took her position. His office was sparse and clinical. There were no carpets; only an oval braided rug, similar to the one in front of the fireplace, beneath an unadorned window. Chelsi visualized the dogs lying there, enjoying the warmth of the sun.

"Miss Burnett, would you please direct your vision to the eyeglasses on the chart straight ahead. Now, cover your right eye and read lines two through nine."

"VISION 2

IS THE 3

ART OF 4

SEEING 5

WHAT IS 6

INVISIBLE 7

TO 8

OTHERS." 9

JoÚathan Swift (1667-1745)

"Vision… is the… art of… seeing… what is… invisible… to… others."

Chelsi shrugged. *What a bizarre eye chart.*

"Excellent. Now if you would please cover your left eye and do the same."

"'Vision is the art of seeing what is invisible to others.' *Umm…* Jasper, where is the challenge in reading this eye chart? The chart is comprised entirely of words."

"My dear, it is the message from the chart you are reading. As we go through life's journey, each person's existence touches many lives. The effect ripples throughout time."

She knit her eyebrows together. "Time. Just to think, a few short hours ago, I thought I was happy with Daniel. And now look at me."

"Ah, but if the events of the day had not happened, you would not have returned to Kringle, and our paths would never have crossed. That would have been most unfortunate."

Jasper stood behind a metal straight-backed chair. "Now if you will, please sit on the examination chair for one last examination, we'll be finished in a jiffy."

Chelsi took a seat, perching on the edge of the white institutional chair. "Will you be able to make my new glasses, here? Now?"

"Yes, my dear."

"But I don't see a selection of frames to choose from."

"I have superior equipment. It's the only one of its kind." Jasper pointed to the metal chin rest. "Please place your chin here, and look straight ahead, my dear." Jasper flashed a light back and forth from one eye to the other. "Here, at A New Vision, the patient doesn't choose the frames. The frames choose you."

"You mean you don't have a selection?"

"No, my dear. Your eyes are the windows to your soul. The shape and color of the frame are similar to a butterfly. The style is 07-147-3301. The lenses are, well… innovative. They will help you see what your life is lacking."

"You mean, like a job, a boyfriend, and a car?"

"Precisely, my dear."

"No, wait! Scratch the boyfriend," she said, shaking her head.

Jasper clicked his tongue. "But a life without love is an empty life."

She snickered. This place was getting more bizarre by the minute. How could a pair of glasses, no matter how innovative, help her see what her life was lacking?

"I have completed your eye examination. Please visit with Olivia in the resale store. Your spectacles will take no time at all to complete."

* * *

ON HER WAY THROUGH THE antique store, Chelsi stopped again to pick up the bear. Max and Gwen snored quietly on the braided rug in front of the fire, Max with his head on top of Gwen's back. Or was it Gwen's head on Max? Anyway, the scene was endearing. Something straight from a Norman Rockwell painting.

"Olivia, how did you and Jasper meet?"

"Some time ago, Jasper moved from Liverpool to Manchester. Next to my thrift store, A Second Chance, was a tobacco store. I would see him from time to time exiting that store, but he never stopped into mine. One afternoon he paused to read the sign in the window advertising a room for let and walked in to inquire. I had unused space in the back, and he needed a place for his optometry practice. We've been together ever since."

"You're engaged to Jasper, yet I was introduced to you as Mrs. Winters."

Olivia looked down and rubbed her ring finger. "Yes. I married Robert Winters when I was seventeen. We were only married a short time. He died in the war."

Chelsi saw the pain on her new friend's face. "I'm so sorry for your loss, Olivia. Did you have any children?"

"Yes. Well, no. I had conceived shortly before he left for the front lines, but after he was killed, I suffered a miscarriage."

Chelsi reached over and clasped Olivia's hand. "I can't imagine losing your husband and your child at such a young age. But you're still young enough. I'll bet you and Jasper have a dozen kids."

"I'm afraid I'm well past child-bearing years. But Jasper and I will enjoy a lifetime together."

"I'm almost fifty," Chelsi said. "I would've loved to have had children. A little boy or girl to teach the fundamentals of baseball. Or A little girl to French-braid her hair and enjoy tea parties with."

Chelsi leaned over and glanced at her embroidery. "Speaking of French, your French knots are incredible. Every Saturday morning, the ladies from the Saint Michael's community center taught an embroidery class. Being left-handed, I had difficulty learning the French knots."

Olivia picked up her embroidery project. "I can show you a trick when making a basic French—"

"Ah, there you are, Chelsi. Your spectacles have been completed, and I have taken the liberty of calling you a towing service."

"So soon?"

"Aren't you anxious to be on your way?"

"*Umm…* yes. It's just that… well, I can't explain the feeling of complete calmness ever since we met."

Jasper looked at Olivia and smiled. A smile so warm that it would melt a dish of ice cream before you scraped the bottom of the bowl.

"Jasper, earlier, you told me not to worry, everything would work out. I had no doubt then. I have no doubt now."

"The source of change is inside each of us. You simply have to look for it."

The two pooches sat up, panting. Chelsi bent down and accepted doggie kisses from them. "Yes, even my new four-legged fur buddies have comforted me."

"Would you like to try on your glasses?" Jasper asked. "I think you will be quite satisfied.

Jasper handed Chelsi her new glasses. They looked like nothing she'd ever seen before. The mottled blue, purple, and brown colored frames looked like plastic but didn't feel like it. They looked like a combination of retro mixed with futuristic.

Chelsi took her new glasses from Dr. Aldridge. "Jasper, thank you. They look… *perfect.*"

"I assure you, my dear, they are the latest style. Perhaps, even a little ahead of their time," Olivia said.

"Enough dilly-dallying, you two. Time to see how this prescription measures up to your previous pair."

Though no gold or silver-tone was present in the frames, her glasses seemed to shimmer. She held them by the rim in her fingertips moving the frames back and forth. "Are they glowing?" Chelsi knew there was something special about them, but she couldn't figure it out.

"May I assist you?" Jasper unfolded the arms of the frames and slid them behind her ears, resting the frames on the bridge of her nose.

Her whole body quivered.

"My dear, are you cold?" he asked.

Blinking, she shook her head. It was quite the opposite. She felt warm… contented… loved. *I haven't experienced those feelings since… before Mom passed.*

"And how is your vision?"

She looked around the room, then back to Jasper. "Better than it's ever been. I don't think I've been able to see this clearly with any other pair."

Jasper nodded. "Olivia, do you have the looking glass?"

"Of course, Jasper. How silly of me." Olivia went to the table and retrieved an antique, jeweled, handheld mirror. Smiling, she handed it to Chelsi.

Olivia stood close to Jasper's side. They observed Chelsi watching for her reaction. She peeked over at them and smiled.

Her eyes widened. *Wait! What's going on?* She leaned forward and studied the figure before her.

"It can't be!" In the mirror image, a handsome man with brown eyes, as warm as hot fudge, looked back at her. His chestnut brown wavy hair, with streaks of grey, was cut short. Though not quite a beard, his square jaw was scruff-lined with mostly grey facial hair. She cocked her head to the side. "Is that Jake?"

Chelsi placed the mirror on her lap and removed the glasses. Holding them in her hand she examined them, turning them over, then back again.

"My dear, is everything all right?" Jasper asked.

She remained silent.

"This can't be," she whispered.

The dogs walked over to her and sat down at her feet. They too were staring.

She tucked her hair behind her ears, closed her eyes, then repositioned the glasses. Raising the mirror, she took in a deep breath, and opened her eyes.

This time she saw her own reflection. "Phew. For a minute, I thought my eyes were playing tricks on me."

"Tell us exactly what you saw, my dear."

"The first time I held up the mirror, I expected to see my reflection, but instead I saw, or *thought* I saw, the vision of an old friend."

"Jake?" asked Olivia.

"Yes. Jake Hollister. The last time I saw him, we were eighteen years old and had just graduated from Kringle High School. It was the night before he was to leave for the US Naval Academy in Annapolis, Maryland. He had brown wavy hair and was clean-shaven. In this, 'vision' he looked like, well… older."

Chelsi shifted her eyes back to the mirror. "It appeared to be an age progression of his senior picture." *What am I saying? He looked handsome. No, wait! Make that drop-dead gorgeous!*

The beeping of a vehicle horn outside startled them.

Jasper opened the door and peered out. "I believe that would be your tow service, my dear. The snow is falling again. And quite heavily, too, I might add. I'll escort you to your vehicle and see that you are well taken care of."

She stood and handed Olivia the mirror. "I'll be fine, Jasper. Really. You and Olivia have done so much for me already."

"Well, if you insist, my dear. The pleasure has been ours."

She gave Mr. Bear one more hug. "Goodbye, Mr. Bear. I hope you find the arms of a loving child to care for and love you."

"Oh, please take him with you, Chelsi. Perhaps during your stay in Kringle, you might find a child in need of a special friend."

"Thank you, Olivia. I promise to find him a good home."

Sitting on the floor, Chelsi talked to Max and Gwen, eye to eye. "It was a pleasure meeting you both. Now you two, behave yourselves. I hope our paths will cross again, soon."

Saddened to see her go, they plastered one last doggie kiss on the sides of her cheeks.

Olivia handed Chelsi an engraved white notecard. "If during your stay in Kringle, you have the need to speak with us, here is the telephone number that rings the store. We do not own cellular devices, but we do spend most of our time here."

"Thank you, Olivia," Chelsi said, embracing her. "Jasper, what do I owe you for the examination and the glasses?"

"Nothing, my dear. It was our pleasure."

"But you have done so much for me. How can I ever repay you?"

Jasper helped Chelsi on with her jacket. "Just follow your heart, my dear."

"I will," she said, stuffing the card deep into her pocket. "You both have been so kind."

Surprised to see a butterfly flit over and perch on Olivia's shoulder, she asked, "Olivia, a butterfly… in winter? Where did she come from?"

"Oh. This is Lady Vanessa. She comes and goes."

Chelsi looked closer. "Oh… poor thing has a damaged wing."

The horn outside blared again, only this time, a lot longer.

"I'm coming, Mr. Impatient!"

Olivia stood by Jasper's side. "Let go of the past. Embrace the present. Trust in the future."

Chelsi nodded at them, eyes glistening. "Goodbye," and walked toward the waiting vehicle.

Jasper turned to the glowing butterfly.

"As Vision Ambassador angels, our assignment has just begun. Set off now, Lady Vanessa. Help heal their wounded hearts."

Chapter Five

THE BAKING DISASTER

JAKE'S PARENTS, JIM AND JANE Hollister, had bought the Snowberry Inn B&B in Kringle, Vermont, about ten years ago. Jake's mom had a natural flair in the kitchen, and Jim enjoyed tinkering around with the B&B's upkeep. The inn had one two-bedroom suite, and six rooms. Two cottages and a gazebo were added that following summer. Jake and Penny moved into the two-bedroom cottage after moving back to Kringle, while Jim and Jane, before her passing, occupied the other.

The B&B was the perfect place for Jake and Penny to try baking cookies together. But unfortunately, it wasn't going well.

"They look *nothing* like angel cookies!" Penny cried.

Huddled together in the B&B's kitchen, they glared at the unrecognizable, red-sprinkled, globby-looking mess cooling on the counter.

Jake pinched his mouth closed as tight as he could, trying *hard* not to laugh. Operation Cookie Bake was a disaster! He felt terrible. Where did he go wrong? Cookies shouldn't be this difficult. Amelia had made them look so easy. Once a month she'd bake cookies for the doctor's lounge at the hospital, and they were always incredible. He'd mixed the ingredients just like she did, or so he thought.

"Oh Daddy, what are we going to do?" Panic rose in her voice.

He ruffled his daughter's hair, sending a cloud of flour everywhere.

Umm… Amelia, if you have any heavenly connections, I could really use a little interference here. I'm doing the best I can in raising our daughter. But this baking thing has me stumped.

"I promise you, Sprinkles, we *will* get it right."

Penny laughed. "There you go again, Daddy, calling me Sprinkles."

"I kinda like it. It's growing on me," he said, with a wink. "But we *do* need a better plan."

"Dad, what we *need* is a real Christmas angel!"

Her father nodded. *Yeah, like your mother.*

While loading the dishwasher, Jake's cell phone rang. He looked over at the screen. "Hey, Pen, Uncle Randy's on the phone. Please put him on speaker and tell him to hang on."

"Sure thing," she said, reaching for his phone. "Hi, Uncle Randy."

"Hey, precious. How are you?" Randy asked.

"I'm good. Dad said he'll be with you in a few. So, how's your new puppy?"

"She's good. Finally stopped crying during the night. She was used to being with her other litter-mates at the shelter. We were tempted to adopt two, but Aunt Jess said only one."

"What did you name her?"

"Maggie Mae."

"Aw, how sweet. I can't wait to meet her."

Jake dried his hands and reached for his phone.

"Okay, here's my dad. Bye, Uncle Randy."

Jake took him off speakerphone and pressed the cell phone against his ear. "Hey bro, what's up?"

"Daddy. Wait, wait!" Penny said, jumping up and down. "Maybe Aunt Jessica can help us bake cookies."

Jake had a hard time listening to both conversations. He held up one finger, momentarily, to quiet his excited daughter.

"There was an accident on Old Post Road, South of Wilton Woods Bridge. Where are you?" his brother asked.

"We're at the inn. Penny and I just finished baking cookies." He looked over at the baked blob. "Well, if you can call them cookies."

"Cookies, huh? Save me some. Listen, I hate to ask you, but could you do this tow for me? Jessica's got a bad stomach bug, and I don't want to leave her."

Jake glanced to the key rack near the back door. "Keys in the usual spot?"

"Yeah."

"What happened?"

"Jeep hit a tree."

Jake cringed. "Ouch! What's the name?"

"I couldn't make it out, the phone line kept cutting out. But the man, with a thick British accent, said it was a damsel in distress."

"A damsel, huh?" Jake looked down at his flannel shirt. "Well, in that case, consider me her knight in… plaid flannel."

"Ha, ha. I owe ya one," Randy said.

"My best to Jessica," Jake said, before disconnecting the call. He untied his apron and slipped it over his head.

Jake looked down at his daughter poking at their cookie catastrophe. He hated to leave her this way, but it was almost her bedtime anyway. "Sorry, Pen, I have to leave for a little while."

"Now, Daddy?" The little actress put on the best pouty face she could. "But we have to make another batch of cookies."

Jake bent down and pulled his disappointed daughter into his arms. "Afraid so, little one. Uncle Randy just got a call. Some lady hit a tree and needs a tow to the repair shop. Aunt Jessica is very sick. Uncle Randy can't leave her."

Jake surveyed the kitchen disaster.

"Go upstairs and take a good shower. Wash your hair, *with shampoo*, and get ready for bed. I'll be home shortly to tuck you in."

Penny looked around at the mess. "But—"

"It's okay, Pen. I'll clean up after I get home. Grandpa turned in early tonight, probably has the same stomach bug as Aunt Jess. Just *please* keep him upstairs so he doesn't see the kitchen!"

He looked at the gloopy-looking-mess, leaned forward and kissed the top of his daughter's head. "You know, this *was* our first test batch, we still have a week to get it right." Reaching for the tow truck's keys, Jake closed his eyes and sent up another silent prayer. "We will get this cookie thing right, I promise. You will have four-dozen amazing cookies for the pageant!"

* * *

EVER SINCE JAKE WAS A teenager, he never liked wearing bulky jackets. His typical winter outerwear consisted of either a hoodie or a plaid flannel shirt under a puffer vest. Tonight, he was grateful for the hood on his sweatshirt but wished he had gone back inside to snag his navy-blue beanie.

Jake made quick work with the snow shovel and cleared the back steps, then pulled out his cell phone and tapped the flashlight on. His brother's tow service was in its early stages, and Randy was grateful his dad agreed to parking the truck on the side of the garages. But access to the vehicle needed better lighting. Jake had made a mental note to install spotlights back there.

Southern Vermont wasn't even partway through the year's snowfall, and he was glad to see Randy had the snowplow blade hitched to the front of the truck. He pulled out onto Belmont Avenue, then made several passes back over the inn's three-car driveway, clearing away most of the fresh snow. He noticed the town had been behind on their snow removal—again. He figured on his way to pick up the tow, he'd help by clearing a bit of the newly fallen snow.

What had Randy called the stranded motorist? Oh yeah, 'a damsel in distress.' *Crazy lady. Nobody should be out on the roads tonight.*

Jake turned on the radio. He smiled at the selection of music his brother had been listening to. "Ticket to Ride," from the 1965 Beatles' CD album, *Help!,* blasted through the speakers. Teenage memories floated through Jake's mind. Funny how songs from the past could trigger emotions, both pleasurable and heartbreaking. He and Randy had played nightly duets in his parents' garage before Jake left for the Navy. Randy had played bass guitar, and Jake, rhythm. Jake's senior year, they won the Kringle High School's talent show with their version of the 1968 Beatles' song, "Ob-La-Di, Ob-La-Da." But how could they not? They were the last entrants to perform for the evening, and the school's auditorium had erupted in an earthquake of thunderous applause.

In addition to his brother being a shift captain of the Kringle Fire Department, Randy Hollister owned R & J Towing Service. Unlike his older brother, Randy had not followed in his father's footsteps by serving in the US Navy. After college, Randy married his high school sweetheart, Jessica Sanders, and they quickly set up home in their childhood hometown of Kringle, Vermont. Although they'd been married for over twenty years, Randy and Jessica never had children. Several years ago, they were both tested, but never revealed the results.

How grateful he was to have Penny in his life. From the minute Amelia had put their daughter into his arms, he was in love with her. This innocent little person they created. She truly was the sunshine of his life. If only—

The *rat-a-tat-tat* of sleet pounded on the tow truck's windshield.

Great! Just what I need now. Sleet!

The roadways were treacherous. He knew the town had to tighten their proverbial belts, but if the salt trucks and plows didn't arrive soon, he'd be out half the night towing in accident victims.

Approaching Wilton Woods Covered Bridge, he removed his foot from the accelerator. As he coasted through it, the image of fishing in Skunk Creek with Chelsi came to mind. Jake's mom would pack them bologna sandwiches on squishy white bread. One with mustard, the other mayonnaise, a dozen homemade peanut butter cookies, and a thermos of pink lemonade. They couldn't have been more than twelve.

A half-smile emerged from a corner of Jake's mouth. Chelsi Burnett… number eleven… four-year Varsity Kringle High School Stallions softball catcher and first baseman. His best friend. He hadn't seen her since graduation. He hoped she was doing well.

Jake had been so deep in thought about their childhood shenanigans, he nearly ran into the obstruction covering the roadway.

After removing the accident-causing tree limb, Jake approached the disabled vehicle twenty feet away. He cringed at the sight of the Jeep's front end wrapped firmly around the tree. *Good thing she wasn't driving anything smaller, or that tree would've been sitting in her lap.*

Not seeing the driver, he pulled forward to the two-story house with the porch light on. He beeped the horn and waited.

No response.

Jake leaned forward in his seat, drumming his fingers in time with the song, as he waited for his fare to appear on the porch steps. He beeped the horn again, this time, with two short blasts and one long. He was a patient man, but he wanted to get back to his daughter *sometime* that night.

The front door opened, and a woman emerged backlit from the porch light. *Wow! Randy was right. Definitely… a damsel.*

Motioning to Jake that she'd be with him in one minute, she said her final goodbyes to the couple in the doorway and carefully made her way to the tow truck.

Jake glared at her feet in disbelief. "Where are your boots?" he yelled from the drivers' seat window.

Clutching her jacket tightly under her chin, she said, "Um… I sorta left them at work." She waved him on. "Go ahead. I'll meet you next to my Jeep."

"Yes, ma'am," he said, and moved the truck into place, readying it for the tow.

He turned off the radio and set the gear control to park. After removing his gloves, he reached for the metal clipboard from the dash to log in his arrival time and location. Tapping his shirt pocket, Jake clicked his tongue. *Great move, Hollister! How could you have forgotten your reading glasses?* He stepped out of the truck and walked to the front of the vehicle. Shining his cell phone light onto the driver's side windshield, he snapped a picture of the VIN. He enlarged the picture and squinted at the phone's screen as he copied the seventeen-character code onto the invoice.

"Thank you for coming out on such an awful night," she said. "A fallen tree limb blocked the road. I saw it too late to avoid it."

Without looking up, he replied, "Ah-huh. I've already removed it, and several others from the roadway. Keys and name, please."

She reached into her pocket and removed her keys. Holding them out to him, she said, "Chelsi… Chelsi Burnett."

"Chels—" Jake stopped writing, his pen firmly set in place. He looked up and stared at the woman before him, then down to the Eiffel Tower pendant dangling from the offered keys.

"Chelsi?" Ten years of childhood memories sailed around him like bubbles on a breezy summer day. "Wow! Burnett. Look at you!" *Why is this grown woman clutching an old stuffed bear?*

Chelsi knit her eyebrows together, lowered her arm to her side, then leaned in for a closer look at the man standing a few feet in front of her. Snowflakes whirled around, frosting the tops of their heads like two figures standing inside a snow globe.

Chelsi had a strange look on her face. "*Jake?*"

She leaped forward to hug him but lost her footing in the snow. Falling forward, he reached out and caught her in his arms. Holding her tight, they stared into each other's eyes, unable to speak.

"*Um...* up ya go, Chels," he said, righting her to a standing position. Jake retrieved the stuffed bear half-buried in the snow, shook it, then handed it back to her.

"Thank you, Jake," she said, unable to take her eyes off him. "*Um...* How are you?"

"Frozen, at the moment. How 'bout we drop your vehicle off at the repair shop, then continue this conversation someplace warm, maybe over coffee."

Chelsi looked over her shoulder. From the porch, Jasper and Olivia waved goodbye. Closing the door, a stream of incandescent sparkles meandered through the snowy moonlit night, then faded away into nothingness.

"Yes," she said, handing Jake her keys. "Coffee sounds good."

Chapter Six

NO BLACK JELLYBEANS

CHELSI BURNETT COULD NOT BELIEVE she was sitting in a tow truck next to Jake Hollister. Jake Hollister! Her best friend since third grade. Growing up, Chelsi hadn't been a girly girl, playing with dolls, trying on makeup, or dressing up. She'd climbed trees, played neighborhood stickball, and helped her dad build a treehouse in their backyard.

She remembered the afternoon Jake had received his acceptance letter into the US Naval Academy at Annapolis, Maryland. He ran across the street, waving the letter high above his head, and without ringing the bell, ran straight into the Burnett house.

In appearance, how he'd changed. But then again, so had she. They both were grownups.

Chelsi blabbed on about nothing in the short drive to the repair shop. At times, even she couldn't make sense of what she was saying. *What's going on with you, Chelsi? This is Jake!* She should be able to string two words together without getting tongue-tied. Could she still be harboring romantic feelings for him?

He backed the tow truck up close to the oversized garage door, then radioed the repair shop owner for the garage code.

"Stay in the truck, Chels, where it's warm. It'll only take me a few minutes to settle your Jeep inside the bay."

"It's a deal," she said.

A frustrated sound came from deep behind her throat. *It's a deal? Did I seriously just say that? Do I think I'm on a game show or something?*

Jake opened her door. "On second thought, get your stuff out of the Jeep before we leave."

"Stuff?"

He looked at her lap and smiled. "Yeah. Stuff. Like your bear, a suitcase… or whatever."

"Of course. No, I don't have any luggage, but I will grab my handbag, Aunt Ann Marie's recipe binder, and my jar of jellybeans."

"Traveling light these days?" he asked, with a half-grin.

"*Um…* I sorta left straight from work. Then I got stuck in the snowstorm."

"And slammed into a tree," Jake added.

"Yeah. And that, too."

Chelsi held up Mr. Bear. "He is adorable, isn't he? A quirky British couple from the antique store, A Second Chance, gave him to me. I promised to find him a loving home."

"Antique store? A Second Chance?"

"You know," she pointed back to where he picked her up. "The old Colonial house is an antique store with an eyeglass store in the back. How long has it been there?"

He scratched the grey stubble on his chin. "Never noticed it before. It must be new."

She popped a few colored jellybeans into her mouth, then offered the jar to Jake.

"Do you still throw away all the black jellybeans?"

I can't believe he remembered that. "Yup. But when we were kids, I threw them *at you*."

Jake winced and rubbed his shoulder. "After thirty years, I think I still have welts."

I was flirting with you, Jake! Why were guys so clueless?

"I thought you'd outgrown not eating black foods by now. What about eating black beans, black olives, or black poppy seeds on an everything bagel?"

"Nope. Nope. And… unfortunately, nope."

"The black jellybean thing started when you mom passed, right?"

She nodded. "After Mom's funeral, everyone came over to the house. It was Easter week and Aunt Ann Marie had brought me a bag of jellybeans. She opened it, poured them into Mom's crystal candy dish, and placed it on the dining room table. I spooned a dozen or so jellybeans onto a napkin and watched the grownups around me. Some were helping themselves to coffee and cake, others were in the living room talking quietly in groups, and a few ladies were in the kitchen doing the dishes. They all had one thing in common…they all wore black. When I looked down at the napkin, I'd eaten all the jellybeans except the black ones. The color of suffering. The color of death."

"I remember now," Jake said. "After that, we sat on your porch and didn't come in till after dark."

"Speaking of outgrowing… do you still segregate all the food on your plate?"

He lowered his head, then kicked a clod of snow off the rear tire. "When I was a plebe at the Naval Academy, the upperclassmen quickly broke me of that habit."

My, Jake Hollister, you certainly have grown into a handsome man. He looked like life had treated him well. But wait, what was she thinking? She'd sworn off men. *All* men.

* * *

INSIDE THE GARAGE OFFICE, JAKE opened the middle drawer of Carlos's desk and removed a numbered tag. He wrote Chelsi's telephone information on the back, then attached it to the ignition key. Satisfied that her Jeep was safely tucked inside the repair shop's middle bay, he placed her key in the overnight slot and punched in the code to lower the overhead garage door.

"Let's get going, Stitch," he said, handing her the remainder of her keys. "So… no toothbrush. No luggage. Did you at least make a hotel reservation?"

And what are you planning to sleep in tonight?

Why was he thinking about what she might, or might not, be wearing to bed?

Um… 'cause I'm a guy.

"I think I left a tee shirt and some softball sweats in my old room at my dad's house. Thought I'd stay there for a few days, then figure out what to do with my life."

Huh… So, she was at a crossroads in her life and it led her back to Kringle? *Interesting.*

"Chels, you can't stay at your father's house. The utilities have been shut off for years. You'll freeze. Come back with me. My dad owns a B&B in town. He has plenty of room. In the morning, you'll get to meet Penny."

She looked down at his ring finger. "Your wife?"

"No. Sadly, my wife, Amelia, passed a few years ago. Car accident. Penny's my eight-year-old daughter."

"Oh! Jake! I'm so sorry. It must be hard raising your daughter alone."

"Thanks. I'm doing okay." He put the truck into gear, but his right foot remained on the brake. Jake stole a sidewise glance at Chelsi.

It had been a long time since he'd had a woman sitting next to him. It felt comfortable. It felt… right. Even if it was only Chelsi. But man, look at her now! Stitch was all grown up. She was quite a woman! If only…

"Are we going?" she asked. "I'm getting a headache from the accident, and I'd like to take something for it."

"Where is my brain? That should've been the first thing I checked at the accident scene. Your welfare!"

He put the truck into park and pulled out his cell phone. Shining the light into her eyes, he said, "Follow my finger. Have you experienced any vomiting or dizziness? Short-term memory loss? Are you intoxicated? Over sixty?"

Chelsi slapped his hand away. "Sixty?" she yelled. "Jake James Hollister, you know darn well how old I am. What are you, a doctor or something?"

He smiled. "No, I was a corpsman in the Navy, and now I work with Randy at the fire station. We are all EMT-trained. Now more than ever, you need to not be alone tonight. When we get to the inn, I'll give you something for your headache."

He put the truck into drive, eased down on the accelerator, and pulled out onto Bloomfield Road.

"You mentioned it was your dad's B&B," Chelsi said. "When did your mom pass?"

"Two years ago. She was sick for about a year. Cancer. It hit Penny pretty hard. First her mother, then her grandmother."

"I can't imagine the heartache you and your family endured in such a short time."

"Yeah. When we moved back, Mom was terrific. She adored Penny. She was her little shadow. Penny loved doing everything Grandma did."

"I'll bet. Your mom *was* amazing."

"Thanks. Even on her bad days, Mom still insisted on doing all the baking. Nothing store-bought for the inn."

"I remember coming home from school, she always had a fresh-baked pie or cookies hot from the oven. Where does your dad get his baked goods now?"

"Gloria Alvarez. She owns the Kringle Bakery on Main. Every morning she'd bring an assortment of breads and pastries for breakfast, but Mom's were better. *Way better.*"

Chelsi sat up a bit straighter in her seat.

"Even when the inn has no guests, she comes over. Gloria and my dad sit at the kitchen table, drink coffee, eat pastries, and enjoy spending time together. They 'shoot the breeze,' as Pop puts it. I think they have a thing for each other, though he's not said anything about it one way or the other."

"Cute," she said. "Puppy love."

Chelsi opened the jar of jellybeans. Grabbing a handful, she plucked out the black ones and handed them off to Jake.

Jake snuck a glimpse at Chelsi and smiled. "I'm glad you're okay, Stitch."

She smiled back. Her smile warmed his heart.

I can get used to this.

Chapter Seven

THE SNOWBERRY INN B&B

"THE BACK DOOR TO THE inn is unlocked," Jake said. "Follow my footpath and let yourself in. Be careful going up the back stairs, they might be slick. On the dryer, you'll find dry socks and sweatpants. Help yourself. Oh, my dog Cocoa's probably going to greet you once she hears the truck pull down the drive. She's harmless."

"You know I love dogs, so she won't be any problem. Thanks for the offer of socks, my feet are freezing."

Jake cocked his head. "Chelsi, I have one word for you."

"What's that?"

"Boots."

Chelsi looked over the rim of her glasses. Trying hard not to smile, she pursed her lips together and closed the door to the truck.

Cocoa, a chocolate lab, came rushing to the back door and greeted Chelsi as Jake had expected. Hanging up her jacket on the wooden coat rack, she said, "Well hello, Cocoa, I'm Chelsi, nice to meet you." She ruffled the dog behind her ears and bent down and accepted an abundance of doggie kisses. "I can see by the color of your fur why they named you Cocoa." The dog thoroughly sniffed one pant leg, then the other. "Ah, yes,

I'm sure you smell Max and Gwen on me. They're corgis. I met them earlier today." Cocoa stood at the back door and waited for Jake. Chelsi grabbed a balled-up pair of white athletic socks, sat on the floor, and switched them out for her wet ones. "Jake will be in in a minute. He's parking the truck."

Chelsi scrunched her face at the condition of the inn's kitchen. "Goodness, Jake! What exploded in this kitchen?"

Jake spoke in a hushed tone. "Well, you see, Penny needs to bring four-dozen homemade cookies to Kringlefest next weekend. We were practicing."

Chelsi put her stuff down on a work surface that was relatively free from scattered flour. She picked up the red bag of self-rising flour and the can of baking powder. "No wonder your cookies turned into a blobby mess; you used two rising agents in the dough."

"Penny said the red bag was pretty."

She shook an accusatory finger at him. "Don't you dare blame your daughter for this."

After eyeing the baked blob on the cookie sheet, she dumped the disaster into the trash. "I'll help you clean up."

"No need, Chels. I can handle it. I'm sure you're exhausted from your ordeal today."

The cuckoo clock on the wall began its hourly countdown. "It's only nine o'clock. Besides, I'm *never* too tired to bake. It's my release from negative emotions. Baking sets my blood pumping. Baking is my happy place."

Jake tapped her playfully under her chin. "Thanks, Stitch. If there's anyone who can pull it off, it's you."

"It won't take me long to work some cookie magic. Anything for your daughter."

"You're the best. I'm gonna go upstairs and look in on her, then I'll get you something for your headache."

Jake stopped and looked over his shoulder. "By the way, Chels, love the glasses."

"I know your tricks, Hollister, don't try to butter me up."

Chelsi turned back and smiled. Terrible baker. Good friend. Great dad.

A quick search of the kitchen yielded all the ingredients and tools necessary for *edible* Christmas cookies, and what a kitchen it was. For a minute, Chelsi stopped and looked past the goopy mess and examined the prep and baking area. Top of the line stainless appliances, oversized six-burner stove, and dual ovens. What she wouldn't give…

Jake strode back into the kitchen, and she asked, "How's your daughter?"

"She fell asleep reading a book to Rosie."

Her lips curled into a smile. "Who's Rosie?"

Jake opened the fridge and took out two bottles of water. "One of her mother's childhood dolls."

"If that isn't adorable. The second generation loves her doll as much as the first."

"Yeah, she's never without Rosie."

Chelsi held out a plain green apron. "Here. Wash your hands and put this on. Lord knows what else you've done in those clothes today."

"At least you didn't give me the frilly one like my daughter did," he said, slipping the neck strap over his head.

"Don't think I didn't think of that. I also planned on texting pictures of you wearing it to the fire chief, but I'll hold that card for another time."

"Thanks for the heads up," he said, handing her a bottle of water.

"Let's start over." She held up the angel-shaped cookie cutter. "Fancy cut-out angel cookies?"

Jake raked his fingers through his wavy hair. "*Um,* if you say so."

The two of them baking together tonight should be interesting. Fortunately, time hadn't changed his fun-loving, playful personality. She pulled out her aunt's recipe book and opened it to the cookie section. Scanning through dozens of well-loved, butter-stained recipes, scattered with handwritten notes in the margins, she decided on the sugar cookie her aunt had so lovingly named The Best-Ever Sugar Cookie.

"Okay, here we go. Get me three sticks of butter out of the fridge. Just… three. Not a little extra for the mashed potatoes, like your mom always did. Three. And crack four eggs into this bowl. No shells! Got it?"

"Ma'am, yes, ma'am. Got it."

Chelsi set to filling a large mixing bowl with five cups of all-purpose flour. "So…when did you start working at the fire station?"

"Shortly after Amelia passed away, we moved from Bremerton, Washington back to Kringle. My brother Randy told me there was an opening at the fire station. With my medical background, they hired me immediately. Mom and Dad were a terrific help with Penny. There are two cottages built on the back end of the property. When we're full up, Pop usually stays in the one-bedroom; Penny and I moved into the two-bedroom. This last cold snap came on suddenly before we had a chance to winterize the cottages, and the pipes burst. We're staying here at the inn until the repairs are completed."

Sneaking a glance at Jake, she put his three sticks of butter, along with two cups of granulated sugar, into the bowl of a stand mixer and set it to medium speed. So… he was a single dad, and a fine-looking one at that.

She shook her head. Why was she thinking like that? She'd *just* broken up with Daniel. She'd been stung twice before by untrusting liars. Zero for two. One more strike, and she was out. But then again, she could get a walk… A walk right back into Jake's life.

Chelsi scraped down the sides of the stainless-steel bowl, added the rest of the ingredients, and turned the mixer back on. When the finished batter was the perfect consistency, she dumped it out onto the counter, flattened it into a large disk, and cut it into four pieces. She wrapped them individually with sheets of plastic wrap and placed them into the freezer.

"Why are you freezing it?" Jake asked.

Searching through the pantry, she said, "It rolls out better when it's chilled."

"A rolling pin? You have to roll out the dough?"

She shook her head as she pulled out a rolling pin. "You're hopeless, Jake. Simply hopeless. Did your wife bake?"

Handing her the angel cookie cutter, he said, "Yeah, she was the best. I'd watch her bake all the time."

"You obviously didn't learn anything."

"I said, 'I watched *her* bake,' not *what* she was baking."

Good answer.

A little while later, Chelsi sprinkled some flour onto the granite countertop and rolled out a portion of the chilled dough into a quarter-inch thick circle. Picking up the bottle of red sprinkles, she said, "There are only enough sprinkles left for this batch. I'll ice the rest. Hope that's okay with your daughter."

"I'm sure that'll be fine. Kringlefest's not 'til next weekend, so these will be a test run."

"Great. The dough's just about right. Come stand over here, and I'll show you how to cut them out."

Jake stood next to Chelsi at the kitchen counter. At this close proximity, she could feel the heat radiating off his body.

She closed her eyes. *Shake it off, Chels.*

Clearing her throat, she said, "Place the cutter on top of the dough and gently press straight down. Don't twist the cutter." She leaned in closer to him. Reaching around his arm, she placed her hand on top of his. "Like this."

Jake looked at her hand on top of his. Aware of their intimate contact, sensations stirred up deep within him. Feelings he hadn't had since before Amelia's death.

She picked up his hand and repositioned it to cut out the next cookie.

Jake tried concentrating on the cookie cutter, not the feeling of Chelsi's hand touching his. Like that was really going to happen. He took in a slow, deep breath.

"After the cookies have all been cut out, slide a spatula underneath, lift them carefully, and place them onto the cookie sheet. Wanna go get one for me?"

"Get what?"

"A cookie sheet, please?"

"Since you put it that way." Jake walked across the room, took the cookie sheet from the dish drain, and grabbed a clean kitchen towel.

"Thought you might need this as well," he said, tossing the towel at her.

"Thanks," she said, and flipped the clean towel onto her shoulder. She tore off a sheet of parchment paper, placed it on top of the cookie sheet, then spaced the cookies two inches apart.

Jake picked up the binder. "How long do they have to bake for?"

"Take a look. Should be 400 degrees. Six to eight minutes in a preheated oven."

"Dad's oven is gas. Isn't it automatically 400 degrees when you turn it on? That's what they do at the station. Turn it on and put the food in."

She closed her eyes and shook her head. " 'Fraid not. Stick with me, Jake. I'll turn you into a bona-fide pastry chef in no time."

No complaints here. He kind of liked this baking stuff. Playful. Intimate. *Oh man, stop thinking like that, you fool! This is Chelsi!*

He snuck a quick peek at her. *But then again… she's not twelve anymore.*

Chelsi put the first tray into the oven and set the oven timer. "Wanna try rolling this next batch on your own?"

He moistened his lips. "Sure. Why not."

"Don't forget to sprinkle some flour on the counter before rolling out the dough."

Jake shot a grin at her. "Like this?" He grabbed a handful of flour and flung it over her head. The powdery substance flew all over the top of Chelsi's head, down her nose, and onto her shoulders.

She slid her towel off her shoulder and slammed it on top of the counter, scattering flour everywhere.

"Jake Hollister, I can't believe you just did that!"

Laughing, Jake tapped her nose and wiped some flour away.

"Twenty-some odd years in the Navy, and you're still that little boy I first met all those years ago. You know what this means, don't you?"

"*War*!" they both yelled out in unison.

Chelsi flung her towel at him.

He caught it, balled it up, and threw it back at her.

Running around the kitchen island, she picked up a handful of dough and threw it at him like a snowball.

"No fair!" he yelled.

"All's fair in love and war!"

Flour and cookie dough flew everywhere. The next thing they knew, they were rolling around on the floor, covered with flour, laughing.

Jim Hollister stood in the doorway between the living room and kitchen. "What's going on here?" he boomed.

Jake helped Chelsi off the floor. She untied her apron, pulled it over her head, and attempted to smooth her flour-tangled hair. "Hello, Mr. Hollister."

"Umm... Pop, do you remember Chelsi Burnett? She used to live here in town."

"I remember," he nodded. "That still doesn't explain why you two supposed-grownups are creating havoc in my kitchen."

"Sorry, sir. Chelsi's car hit a tree on Old Post Road and Randy asked me to tow her Jeep to the repair shop. She was helping me bake cookies for Penny."

"I'm sorry we woke you, Mr. Hollister. We promise to clean up the mess."

Jim gave Chelsi a questioning gaze. "You're all grown up now, young lady. You can call me Jim." He lifted his nose and sniffed the aroma drifting from the oven. "Besides," he continued, removing the container of milk from the refrigerator, "you didn't wake me. Whatever you've got bakin' in my oven, did."

Buzzzzzz.

"They're ready, Pop. Would you like some of Chelsi's homemade Christmas cookies to go with your evening glass of milk?"

Grumbling, he answered, "Might as well. Can't let any of them go to waste now, can I?"

Jim Hollister's broad hand shook while he poured a glass of milk. Dark veins were easily traceable through his aged skin. He studied Chelsi. "Where are you staying tonight? Your dad's house has been closed up for years."

She looked back and forth between Jake and his dad. "*Umm...* Jake said you had a few open rooms, and that I could stay here tonight. In the morning, he'll take me over to my dad's, or should I say my house now."

A slight smile creased the lines of his weathered face.

"If it's okay with you, I'll make an early breakfast," Chelsi added. "What would you think of ham and egg pie, or say, stuffed French toast?"

His voice softened a bit. "No need to fuss over me. Gloria delivers pastries here every morning."

"Jake told me Gloria does all the baking for the inn. This would be my way of thanking you for allowing me to stay the night."

Jim put the milk away and rubbed his chin. "Ham and egg pie, you say?"

"Yes, sir. It's supposed to be made with puff pastry as the base. I see you've got crescent roll dough in the fridge." With a nod, she added, "That works almost as well."

Chelsi grabbed three Christmas napkins from the holder on the kitchen table. As she was transferring the cookies from the cooling rack to a plate, one broke in half.

"Can't serve that one now, can I?" She placed that one on her napkin before handing Jim and Jake their two, perfectly baked, angel-shaped cookies. "Enjoy!"

Jake removed two glasses from the cupboard. What was it with Chelsi? He'd known her all his life, but seeing her today was like seeing her for the first time.

Jake stood at the table and poured himself a full glass of milk.

"Where are your manners, son? I thought your mother taught you better than that."

"Mom taught me just fine, Pop. Chelsi's lactose intolerant. Milk doesn't agree with her." He handed her a glass of water. "Water, no ice."

"You remembered that too, Jake?" she asked.

"Yup," he said, slowly releasing a breath. *I remember everything about you.*

Jim Hollister took a bite of cookie and chewed thoughtfully. Then he said, "My goodness, girl, these cookies are as good as my late wife's. You can bake in my kitchen anytime!" Then, popped the rest into his mouth.

A broad smile crossed her face. "Thanks, Jim. I was hoping you'd say that."

The Hollister men dunked and munched. They reached for seconds.

Jake reached for a third and Chelsi smacked his hand. "Save some for your daughter."

"Yes, ma'am."

"Don't stay up too late, you two. You workin' tomorrow, son?"

"No sir. Just completed my rotation. I'll take Chelsi to her dad's first thing to check on the place, then swing by the car rental office. I think it opens at eight. Her Jeep will be laid up for at least a week, maybe more."

Jim Hollister brought his empty glass to the sink, rinsed it, and loaded it into the dishwasher.

"Set her up in the Rudolph Room."

He nodded to Chelsi. "It's a small room, but comfortable. Used to be the Mrs.'s sewing room."

"Thank you again, Jim, for your kindness."

"You're welcome. Stay as long as you need."

Chelsi smiled.

"When I get back tomorrow morning, Pop, I'll help out with the snow removal. Penny has a Christmas party at the library at two."

"If it's okay, I'd like to make supper tomorrow night," Chelsi said. "Baked chicken or bacon-topped meatloaf?"

The Hollister men looked at each other. "Meatloaf!" they said in unison.

"Meatloaf, it is."

"Night kids," Jake's father said, heading upstairs.

"Good night, Jim."

"The Rudolph Room?" she asked Jake.

Jake turned off the kitchen lights but left the light above the sink on. "Something Mom started years ago for the holidays. Each room is holiday-themed. I'll get your key from dad's office."

Unlike the hardwood flooring downstairs, the second-floor hallway was covered in plush beige carpeting. Its walls displayed a creamy wallpaper with clusters of pastel pink, bell-shaped snowberry blossoms surrounded by thin, light green oval-shaped leaves. The inn was called the Snowberry Inn, so of course the wallpaper would feature Vermont's familiar springtime blossom.

Chelsi pointed to the framed, hand-colored artwork depicting the theme of the approaching rooms. Santa Claus, Mrs. Claus, Christmas Tree Lane, and Alabaster Snowball, Chief Elf.

"Your daughter's artwork?"

Jake nodded. "After we moved in, Mom bought Penny a Christmas coloring book. They cut the pages apart and she 'commissioned' her to color these framed pages. It helped Penny make the transition."

"How sweet."

When they reached the Snowflake room, Jake closed the door. "Penny's room," he whispered. He opened a door with a likeness to Rudolph portrayed on the outside. "This is you," he said, switching on the light and handing her the Rudolph key. "Make yourself at home. I'll be right back." He opened the room next door named Silver Bells and went inside.

Chelsi went inside and ran her hand over the soft red, white, and grey checkered flannel comforter. The decorative pillow shams depicted whimsical pictures of reindeer playing "Reindeer Games."

"Here ya go," Jake said. He held out a US Navy tee shirt. "It was in my dresser. I think it's clean." Giving it a sniff, he replied, "Yeah, mostly. But I think we're out of fabric softener."

Chelsi stared at the shirt.

Avoiding eye contact, he pushed the shirt forward. "For you to sleep in tonight?"

"Oh yes, of course. Thank you."

"Coffee will be ready at six-thirty. Sleep well. You've had a tough day."

"Thank you for everything, Jake." She reached up and gave him a warm embrace. An embrace that lingered a tad longer than a friendly hug.

Jake rested the side of his face against the top of her head, inhaling the essence of her. After all she'd been through today; she still had a sweet fragrance about her. Sweet like… like cherry pie. He took in a deeper breath. Cherry pie… a la mode. He was certain that for the rest of his life when he smelled cherry pie, he would always think of Chelsi.

Tearing himself away from her embrace, his emotions were filled with her sweetness. Her tenderness. The only words he could say, were, "No problem. Good night."

"Night," she returned.

* * *

CHELSI CLOSED BUT DIDN'T LOCK her door. She clutched his tee shirt to her chest and plopped onto the bed. A few seconds later, she heard another click. She looked in the direction of the noise and noticed an interior door. Did they have adjoining rooms?

She crossed the room and tried the knob. Locked. She put her ear against the door. Nothing. Chelsi looked at the tee shirt lying on her bed, then back to the door. Could that be what Jake was going to sleep in tonight? She shook her head when her mind wandered where it shouldn't have. What was she thinking? Less than ten hours ago, she'd broken up with her fiancé. No way, no how, did she want to get into a relationship now. Even if she did just have the best evening of her life. Even if it was with Jake Hollister, the guy she knew best in this world. The guy who sat up all night with her before the calculus final, cramming. The guy who bought all the fundraiser candy she sold for softball. Twice. The guy who's so smoking hot he should be illegal. The guy she'd been secretly in love with her entire life.

Chapter Eight

ANGEL COOKIES

PENNY WALKED INTO THE KITCHEN rubbing the sleep out of her eyes. "Daddy, did we miss breakfast?"

Jake scooted his chair back, and Penny climbed onto her father's lap. She snuggled her doll, Rosie, tight to her chest. "Nope. You're both right on time," her father said, kissing the top of her head. "Penny, I'd like to introduce you to a very—"

A glimmer of excitement rose in Penny's eyes when she eyed a small plate of cookies next to the coffee maker. "Cookies! Dad, I told you a Christmas angel would come and bake us cookies." Penny placed her doll on the table and leaped from her father's lap. At the counter, she helped herself to the cookies, one in each hand, then returned to the table, nibbling on her first.

Jake cleared his throat. "Penny, as I was saying, I'd like to introduce you to a very special friend."

Chelsi came into the kitchen, a smile lit up her face.

"Penny, this is Miss Chelsi. When we were kids, she lived across the street from us on Cottage Lane. Remember, I talked to you about her?"

"Very nice to meet you, Miss Chelsi," Penny mumbled, through a cookie-filled mouth. "I dreamt an angel came last night and baked us cookies, and here they are!"

"I hope you like them, sweetie." Chelsi walked over to the stove and dished up a child's size portion of her still-warm ham and egg pie.

"Miss Chelsi went to Paris, France, and learned how to bake these amazing cookies, among other delicious treats."

"Jake," she said, placing Penny's breakfast plate in front of her, "I never made it to Paris…" Her voice trailed off.

His eyes locked on hers, questions escalating. "But Miss Chelsi and I did bake these cookies last night while you were sleeping. Do you like them?"

Penny nodded and she licked all the crumbs from her lips. "I sure do. Are there more? Can you bake these for me to take to Kringlefest?"

"Slow down, little one." Jake went to the counter, turned off the coffee pot, and poured the remaining brew into his and Chelsi's mugs. "Pen, how 'bout if the roads are clear enough, we leave a little early for the library. I'm sure you want to check out some books—"

"Can we pick up Travis, too?" Penny asked.

"Yes, if it's okay with his foster mom, Mrs. JoÚson. First, we'll need to drop off Miss Chelsi at her house so she can pick up some clothes and see if she has any boots."

Penny raced to the kitchen window. Her overstuffed white unicorn slippers flashed on and off in a rainbow of hues with every step. "You don't have any boots, Miss Chelsi? But there's like… a ton of snow out there."

Chelsi joined her at the window, then, put her arm around Penny's shoulder. "Yesterday, I left straight from work and forgot to take my boots from my locker."

"Come back to the table, Pen, and finish up."

She picked up her plate and fork. "Daddy, can we be done now?"

Jake gave his young daughter that doubtful look. "Is your tummy full?"

Penny nodded. "And Rosie's full, too. May we please be excused?"

"All right. You know what to do."

Penny took her plate and scraped what was left into the trash, then loaded it into the dishwasher. Skipping her way back to the table, she stopped next to Chelsi and gave her a light kiss on her cheek.

"Oh, my goodness, thank you, sweetie. What was that for?"

Matter-of-factly, Penny answered, "Breakfast. We always kiss the cook." She picked up Rosie from the table and skipped away.

Chelsi touched the side of her face where Penny had just kissed her. How complete her life would be to have a loving husband, like Jake, and a caring daughter, like Penny. "Oh Jake, she's adorable. You've done such a wonderful job in raising her."

"'Twasn't me. She's got her mother's spirit."

What a happy family they must've been, until… Chelsi stood and began to clear their plates.

Jake put his hand on top of hers. "The cook doesn't do dishes." Then he, too, leaned in and kissed Chelsi on her cheek.

She'd forgotten what a caring guy Jake had been in high school. She'd known he wanted the Navy to be his career, but why had they lost touch after such a short amount of time?

* * *

"LET'S GET GOING GIRLS," JAKE yelled, standing at the back door. "We've got a lot to do before the library."

The thunderous sound of Cocoa sprinting down the stairs told Jake his chocolate Labrador retriever was on a mission. She raced straight to the back door, nearly colliding into Jake, sat down, and looked back at him with her pleading eyes.

"Sorry, girl, not this trip. Maybe next time, okay?"

Jake took the tow truck's key from its place on the wall of keys for the inn. He'd plow Chelsi's driveway and whatever else she might need clearing.

He took out his phone. "What's keeping them?"

"Coming Dad," Penny said, "I have a surprise for you."

"*Mmm-hmmm*," he replied, typing a text message.

Penny stood in front of Jake and cleared her throat.

Without looking up, he said, "Glad to see you're finally ready, Squirt. Get your stuff on and let's get going."

Penny shook her head, then sat on the floor to put her boots on, but she could not stop smiling.

"I just contacted the repair shop," he told Chelsi. "Carlos is inspecting the damage to your Jeep and will call later with an estimate."

"Thanks, Jake."

He looked up. "Penny, it's cold outside, *please* put your hat on."

Chelsi came and stood behind Penny. "*Um*, Jake?"

"Yeah?"

She motioned with a tilt of her head for Jake to look at Penny.

"Sorry. So, what's the surprise?"

Chelsi stroked one of Penny's French braids. "Doesn't Penny's hair look beautiful?"

Jake tucked his reading glasses into his vest pocket. "Oh, yeah, Pen, your hair looks pretty today. I like the ribbons."

Penny looked over her shoulder and smiled at Chelsi. "Miss Chelsi French braided my hair. She even braided a ribbon through it like her mommy used to do."

Jake reached out and ran his fingers over both the braids. Penny was missing out on so much by not having a mother in her life. Look at what Chelsi had done for her already. Baking cookies last night and now, doing her hair. He hadn't seen a smile like that on Penny's face in a long time. "I see that. You know, I do remember Miss Chelsi wearing her hair like that when we were kids."

"Really?"

"Really," he replied.

"Miss Chelsi said she found some ribbon in Grandma's white sewing basket on the floor of her closet. She also said that when I take the braids out tonight my hair will be curly like… like Mommy's was."

"Sorry, I went into Penny's room to get her hairbrush and I saw a photo of Penny and her mom on her dresser."

"You still need to put your hat on, young lady."

"But—"

"But nothing. Do you want to be sick for Christmas?"

"No, Dad."

Chelsi bent down and helped Penny on with her hat. "Your hair will be fine, Sweetheart. If it gets a little messy from your hat, I can fix it, I promise."

Penny threw her arms around Chelsi and gave her a big hug. "Thank you, Miss Chelsi."

"Are we going to my house first? If any of my old stuff still fits, I'd like to run it through your washing machine later if that's okay."

The corner of Jake's mouth lifted a notch. She sure had filled out nicely since high school, but she didn't look like she'd gained an ounce. "Sure, Chelsi. I'll drop you off after we get Travis. Are you sure you'll be okay?"

"I'm as ready as I'm going to be. Don't forget, I haven't been home since Dad's funeral."

"You'll be fine, Chels. I'm here for you."

Chapter Nine

A MOMENTOUS DISCOVERY

THE MOOSE ANTLERS BOBBED UP and down on Penny's winter hat as she ran up to Travis's front door. The moment he opened the door, she grabbed the front of his jacket, nearly dragging him out of the house. "Hurry up, Slowpoke. I have someone for you to meet."

"Slow down, Munch. My arms are full of books to return, and I don't feel so good today."

"You're just a faker 'cause you don't want to race me to the car. And don't call me Munch, Pokey."

He grabbed her hat, trying hard not to drop the books in his arms. "As long as you wear this silly hat, I'll call you Munch. Race ya!"

They took off running down the sidewalk, both touching the car at the same time. "I won!"

"No, I won!"

"Remind you of another childhood friendship?" Jake asked.

Chelsi smiled. She reached over and gave him a quick backhanded slap on his arm. "The apple doesn't fall far from the tree, Hollister."

Travis and Penny settled in the back seat, still vying for the winner's title. "Buckle up, you two wiggle worms."

"Dad... you're hilarious."

"Thanks for the ride, Mr. Hollister." Travis put his pile of books on the seat between him and Penny. "My books are a little overdue."

"Overdue, huh?" Chelsi asked. "Did you bring a can of food in exchange for the late fines?"

"Hey, how'd you know that?" He reached into his jacket pocket and produced a pouch of tuna fish. "I took this from the pantry. Mrs. JoÚson said it was okay."

"Trav, this is Miss Chelsi. She and my dad grew up together."

"Cool." Travis crossed his arms over his stomach and took in a deep breath.

Penny grabbed her hat from Travis's hand and smoothed some of her wayward hairs. "You'd better not have messed my hair up, Buster."

Jake looked in his rearview mirror, concern for Travis crossed his face. "You okay, buddy? You look a little pale."

"Yeah, I'm okay, Mr. H."

"Travis, we're going to drop off Miss Chelsi at her old house before heading to the library. Do you guys know she and her father built a treehouse in the backyard?"

"Is it still there?" Penny asked.

"It was a few years ago when I was last in Kringle," she answered.

"I can't wait to see it. Can Travis come too?"

"Sure, but first, I'll have to make sure it's safe for you kids."

They sat in silence for the remainder of the drive, Jake checking on Travis every few minutes.

Jake stopped in front of Chelsi's house, put the truck into park, and pointed across the street. "See that house over there, that's where I used to live."

Penny unbuckled her seat belt and climbed over Travis to get a better look. "Wow, Daddy, I really like your old house. Did Grampa, Grandma, and Uncle Randy live there too?"

"They sure did. It was a wonderful place to grow up."

"Well, this is me," Chelsi said nervously. "I'll let you guys get to the library. Call me later?"

Jake reached across the truck's console and touched Chelsi's shoulder. "Sure. You got this, Chels."

* * *

JAKE'S TRUCK STOOD IDLING AT the curb in front of 28 Cottage Lane. Chelsi got out of the truck and stared at the front of her father's house. How the years of neglect had aged its façade. Memories of her childhood popped in and out of her mind like hot kernels of corn popping in a microwave. She glanced over her shoulder to Jake's house. Her stoop had five cement steps leading to the front door, and Jake's only four. So, every day she and Jake had played stoop ball at her house. They'd stand behind the third crack in the front walk and toss a bright yellow tennis ball ten feet toward the steps. If it bounced off the step and was caught, it was a five-pointer. Catching the ball on a fly was worth ten.

Chelsi looked at the spot where three days after varsity softball tryouts she found a sign announcing that a "KHS Varsity Softball Player lives here," and then across to Jake's to the baren mimosa tree where their graduation photo was taken, two weeks before he left for Annapolis, Maryland.

He rolled down the passenger side window. "You okay, Chels?"

She turned around, visible tears welling up in her eyes. "Yep. Gotta do this some time. Thanks for dropping me off."

"It'll be pretty cold in there. Any wood stockpiled?"

"I think I remembered there being a stack in the fireside basket on the hearth when I was last here. Hopefully, the lighter hasn't dried up after all these years."

Jake opened the console of his truck and tossed her a lighter.

"I don't remember you being a Boy Scout growing up," she said.

Giving her a sly grin, he said, "You're right, I wasn't. But I *am* prepared for almost any situation. I'll text you later, say around three," said Jake. "Then we can figure out what to pick up from the grocery store for supper."

"Chicken fingers, and sweetie potato fries," Penny piped up.

"Or, I can make Uncle Randy's Tuna Noodle Surprise, what about that?"

Penny wrinkled her nose. "Daddy, I don't think Miss Chelsi will like it. Mostly, I don't even like it. I pretend to like it so I won't hurt your feelings."

"What would you think of Bow Tie Taco Casserole, or Wagon Wheel Pasta Mac and Cheese?" Chelsi asked.

"I looove Mac and Cheese. My daddy makes it a lot."

"Penny, you're gonna turn into a Mac and Cheese ball," Jake said.

Chelsi rubbed her cold hands together, then blew some warm air onto them.

"She's freezing out there, Pen, why don't we try her Bow Tie Taco Casserole."

"Okay, Daddy."

Oh, drat, Chelsi thought, pulling out her cell phone. *I'm only at twenty percent.* Her phone charger was back at her apartment.

Chelsi tucked her phone away, waved goodbye to Jake and the kids, then watched him pull away.

She walked up the cement steps and ran her hand over the black painted wrought iron railing. Every night after supper her dad had sat on the top step and "watched the grass grow." He'd smoke a few cigarettes and drink a bottle or two of his favorite beer before retiring for the night. Chelsi smiled when she saw an old bottle top peeking out from underneath a dormant azalea bush. Her dad had said he was hoping, someday, the bottle tops would take root and he'd be the first to grow a beer bottle bush.

She opened the metal screen door with her left hand, then held it open with her elbow. Staring at the front door key still attached to her Eiffel Tower pendant, she inserted it into the lock. Chelsi had to jiggle the key just so for the inside tumblers to catch. Her first attempt at pushing the painted front door open failed. Putting her hip into it, the slumbering door released a loud yawn, then irritably swung open.

Closing the front door to her family's 1950s tri-level home, vivid childhood memories surrounded Chelsi like a warm towel. Sing-song echoes of *Mom I'm home, can I have a snack*, or *Dad, can we finish my treehouse this weekend?* came to mind. Where had the time gone? Automatically, she hung up her jacket on the same hook of the wooden coat rack as all those years ago. Walking through the foyer, she looked up. Still pressed deep into the arched sheetrock was the thumbtack she used as a teenager to hang fresh mistletoe in hopes of stealing a kiss from Jake at Christmas. But that kiss never happened. She remembered Jake dating in high school, but she guessed he never thought of the girl across the street as girlfriend material.

In the living room, mounds of white cloth resembled the bunny hill at the Mount Snow Ski Resort, where she first learned how to ski. In reality, it was furniture she'd covered in bed linens after Dad's funeral.

Spying the stack of wood and long matches on the hearth, Chelsi rubbed her hands together. *Enough traveling down memory lane. It's freezing in here. Time to build a fire. Now, make sure the flue is open.* She remembered how angry her dad was the time she'd forgotten to check it. That day, she had two options for removing the black soot off the living room walls. Either get a bucket of soapy water and wash walls or grab paint and a roller. She chose the latter.

Satisfied with the fire, she rubbed her cold hands in front of it, then pulled the protective wire-mesh curtain closed. A short stack of grocery store boxes, a black marker, and several rolls of packing tape sat off to the side in the dining room. "Well, let's get to it," she said, tossing the marker into the empty box. With a box in one hand and a roll of tape worn around her wrist like a bracelet, Chelsi took a running start up the stairs to her bedroom. Not even halfway through, she decided one step at a time would suffice.

Her bedroom was at the end of the hall. It was just as she had left it all those years ago. Her bed with a maroon and gold print bedspread, her no-name pink floppy-eared bunny, and several throw pillows filled out her twin bed. She picked up the bunny and hugged her tight to her chest. On her dresser was a framed photo of Chelsi standing in front of her mom and dad the New Year's Eve before she passed. She dusted off the silver frame and touched the faces of her parents. "I miss you guys," she whispered.

Taped to the mirror above her dresser were the photos of her softball sisters and the graduation picture of her and Jake. She in a gold-colored cap and gown, Jake in forest green.

One drawer at a time, Chelsi glanced at her old belongings. What had she been thinking? Nothing here would fit her. All this stuff would go to Goodwill. Later she'd ask Jake to drop her off at the store so she could pick up a few pairs of jeans, tops, and some underwear. She scooped everything up and tossed it into an empty box.

Chelsi walked over to the window, opened the blinds, and moved her white Priscilla curtains off to the side to look at Jake's house. She was glad the new owners were taking such good care of the Hollister family home. Jake had played a big part in her life. Until now, she'd never realized just how much.

Chelsi taped the box closed, stifled a yawn, and went back downstairs to grab a few more boxes. She wished she had brought a bottle of water or some coffee in a to-go container.

Next, she headed to her parents' room. She could never get used to calling it her father's room, because to her, it would always be her mother's, too.

The door was closed. She raised her hand, ready to knock, then realized what she was about to do and turned the knob. She peeked inside and eyed her mother's dresser. The only items displayed were a blue Chinese vase, a dried-up bottle of Chanel No. 5, and a two-inch, hand-carved wooden fish. She picked up the bottle of cologne and removed the top, exposing the spray nozzle. Inhaling what fragrance was left, she said, "Miss you, Mom."

Her dad had donated all her mother's things shortly after she passed, so she knew those drawers were all empty. Chelsi put two boxes on the bed and marked the sides, Homeless Shelter. She'd ask Jake if the shelter for displaced veterans was still in town.

She stood there staring at her father's five-foot-tall armoire. "Let's start from the bottom up this time." She opened the bottom drawer and removed a stack of sweaters and some plaid flannel shirts. They were all in decent shape, and as she placed everything into the box, she knew someone would be pleased to get them.

She opened two large louvered doors and removed Dad's Bible and the notepad and pen he always took to church. She opened the Bible and ran her fingers over the underlined and highlighted areas that were important to him from that day's scripture reading. Then she held his Bible close to her heart. Dad's Bible would come home with her. She had been away from the church for a while; now would be a good time to return.

All that was left to pack away was his jewelry box organizer that sat on top of the dresser. Her dad would come home from work and put his watch, loose change, and his billfold on top of the organizer. When Chelsi came home for her dad's funeral, she wasn't ready to get rid of those personal items, but she'd removed the cash from his billfold and canceled his credit cards.

She needed to see what was inside the drawer housed below the organizer. A strange feeling overtook Chelsi when she placed her fingers on the silver-toned drawer pulls. *Well, that was odd.* She looked around the room as if someone was standing behind her. *Sorry, Dad, but I've got to do this.* She hated disrespecting her father's privacy, but he had been gone for several years.

Pulling on the knobs a little harder than she thought, the entire drawer pulled out. Surprisingly, it was fairly empty. A Kennedy half-dollar, some silver dimes, and a few tie tacks. Chelsi removed the coins and held them in the palm of her hand, supposing she could find a coin dealer to see if they were worth more than face value.

Chelsi had a difficult time returning the drawer to its original position. She removed it and tried again. Same outcome. The drawer was stuck. Peeking inside the empty slot, she couldn't find any reason why it wouldn't close. She turned the drawer over.

Taped to the underneath part of the drawer was a 5"x7" manila envelope with a bent corner. *Ah-ha.* Chelsi removed the envelope and sat down on the bed. "Okay, Dad, let's see what you've been hiding."

Downstairs, her cell phone rang. Taking the envelope with her, she jumped off her dad's bed and ran down the flight of stairs to answer the call.

"Hi, Jake."

"Hey, Chels, how's the packing going?" he asked.

"Okay, but there's nothing here I'll be able to use. Looks like I'll need a quick shopping spree when you have the time."

"Oh, you women are all alike. You'll do anything to buy new clothes."

Chelsi rolled her eyes. "Sure. I'll see you later. I found a sealed envelope my dad had hidden, and I'm intrigued."

"Can't wait to hear about it. Gotta go, too. Penny's running towards me; looks important."

Jake disconnected the call without saying goodbye. "Well, alrighty then."

Chelsi sat on the floor in the living room and crisscrossed her legs. She picked at the corner of the envelope, then slid her finger underneath. Pulling out the contents, Chelsi placed one color photograph on the floor followed by a folded a sheet of goldenrod paper, then checked inside to make sure nothing was left behind. The first was a picture of two women; one was pregnant. *That's Mom and Aunt Ann Marie!* Turning it over, Chelsi recognized her mother's handwriting. In blue ink, she had written, "Three months to go."

"Wait, what? Aunt Ann Marie never had any children." Chelsi looked off into the distance. "At least I *think* she didn't have any."

She looked closer at the photo, but couldn't recognize where it had been taken. Why would her father have it hidden away? What could the significance be? Her mom had known about the picture, since she was posing with her younger sister. Placing it back into the envelope, she leaned back against the couch, straightened her legs out in front of her, and picked up the folded piece of paper.

Hmmm... this looks like some sort of official document.

"State of Wisconsin Certificate of Live Birth." Chelsi's eyes grew larger, and she stood up so fast she made herself dizzy. She wasn't sure if it was from the speed in which she stood, or what she had read on the document, or a combination of both.

She read: "CHILD-NAME: Chelsi Ann Singleton. DATE OF BIRTH: December 16, 1970. MOTHER-MAIDEN NAME: Ann Marie Singleton. AGE: 19. FATHER-NAME: Unknown. "What? Aunt Ann Marie is my biological mother?" That was the last thing Chelsi remembered before she blacked out.

Chapter Ten

TRAVIS WAS SICK

JAKE UNZIPPED HIS PUFFER VEST. "Hey kids, hang up your stuff and make sure your boots are dry before walking inside the library. You don't want the librarian, Miss Maureen, to put you on the naughty list this close to Christmas now, do you?"

Penny's eyes widened. She looked over at Travis. Animated, they both shook their heads.

"Boots all dry, Dad," said Penny, wiping her feet for a second time. "While Travis returns his books, I'll go inside and save our spots for the puppet show, 'kay?"

"Sure thing, Pen. I'll be upstairs for a while if you need me. Enjoy. But behave yourselves."

Penny gave him a big hug. "We will, Daddy."

Travis put his stack of overdue books on the counter, immediately followed by the package of tuna fish.

Maureen Doyle reached for the stack of books. "Late again, Travis?"

Travis looked down at the counter while his books were being processed. "Yes, ma'am. Sometimes after school, I have to go to work with

Mr. Johnson. With the cold weather and all, his broken foot's been bothering him."

"Helping your foster father with trash and recycle collection is mighty hard work for someone your age," said Maureen.

He lowered his voice. "Don't mind it, really."

Travis spotted Penny waving at him, trying to catch his attention. "Need anything else?"

"No, ma'am."

Maureen handed Travis back the pouch of tuna fish. "You're all set. Go on and catch up with Penny."

He smiled up at her. "Thank you, Miss Maureen."

Jake was on his phone when he saw Travis wince again in pain. He sat at the children's computer table, folded his arms, then dropped his head onto the table.

"Travis, don'tcha wanna see the puppet show? I saved ya a spot."

"I think I'll pass, Penny. My stomach hurts. Bad."

"Stay here. I see my dad. I'll go get him." Penny ran up to him yelling, "Dad, Dad! Come quick! Travis said he's real sick."

Jake disconnected his call.

"Thanks, Penny, I'll check on him."

He knelt on one knee and put his hand on the boys' shoulder. "Hey, buddy, what's goin' on?"

Travis lifted his head. With the back of his hand, Jake stroked his cheek, then across his forehead. "You're burning up." Jake pulled out his cell phone and called the boy's foster mother. He put her on speaker and set the phone on the table next to Travis. "Fern. Jake here. We're at the library. Travis is running a high fever and is complaining of a bad stomachache. He needs immediate medical attention."

"Thank you, Jake," Fern said. "I'll be right there."

Chapter Eleven

A WALKABOUT TOWN

"GOOD MORNING, LIVY. ISN'T TODAY the most glorious day?"

"Oh, Jasper, you startled me!" Olivia wiped her hands on the hem of her apron, removed it, and hung it on a nail in the kitchen.

"Worry not about my seeing you wearing an apron, my dear. The bouquet of ingredients you have baking this morning has created havoc with my senses." He looked at the oven, then leaned in and kissed her cheek.

Her glare spoke volumes. "Don't you dare open my oven door, Jasper Aldridge, or Max and Gwen will be enjoying your breakfast."

Respectful of her wish and yearning for a warm, tasty breakfast, Jasper slowly backed away. "Is that the kettle I hear?"

Olivia turned away and smiled. She measured the appropriate amount of loose tea into the warmed teapot, then half-filled it with boiling water.

"Orange zest."

"What, my dear?"

"The added ingredient to our morning scones. Before slicing the oranges for Lady Vanessa's breakfast, I grated a tad bit of orange peel and incorporated it into this morning's scone dough."

"Livy, you never fail to astonish me."

The early morning sun drew Jasper to the front window. Her warm rays shined through the trees like fingers reaching, drawing him outside.

The clinking of teacups against their saucers removed Jasper from his reverie. "Livy, it is such a lovely morning. Might I interest you in a walk-about town? Perhaps browse a yarn store?"

"You're always thinking of me, Jasper. That would be delightful, but I do have plenty of needlework to keep myself busy during our assignment in Kringle." After filling Jasper's cup, she repositioned the silver strainer onto the rim of her cup. The familiar aroma of strong English Breakfast tea filled the room. Adding just a dash of milk to each cup, she carried their morning breakfast to the tea table.

"In fact, we would both benefit by an early morning browse through the local library."

Placing the cloth napkin across his lap, Jasper contemplated the beauty of her face. The twinkling green eyes which gazed back at him were brighter than his emerald green ring. He reached across the small table and covered her hand with his. "Olivia, how do I deserve such a beautiful, loving soul as yourself. I count the days 'til we wed. Dr. and Mrs. Jasper Gregory Aldridge. It has a jolly good ring to it now, doesn't it?"

Olivia's smile softened. Welling tears shadowed the surface of her eyes. "Like the sound of angels' bells ringing on Christmas Eve."

Vying for a share of some of Olivia's attention, Maximillian tilted his foxy-looking face up towards Jasper and let out a series of low woofs. Gwendolyn soon followed suit.

"Come here, you rascals," said Jasper, tapping his thighs. "Fancy a romp in the snow now, do you?" Running in circles, their four-legged companions conveyed their excitement.

"After breakfast, I'll go to the powder room to fix my hair and get my hat and handbag. It shouldn't take me but a few minutes."

Jasper clicked opened his timepiece. "You're never lackadaisical with your appearance, Livy. This morning, you were up much earlier than usual. Might I ask the importance of your early waking?"

She smoothed the Peter Pan collar on her white blouse. "You are always so perceptive. I had a bit of mending to tend to, and my shoes were looking a tad bit worse for wear."

After breakfast, Olivia accompanied Jasper outside. It was quite amusing to watch the dogs keenly dig in the snow, attempting to retrieve the snowball they were certain had landed in that exact spot, only to return to their master's feet wanting more. After several unsuccessful attempts, Maximillian had picked up a fallen stick, then proudly returned it to Jasper, the victor.

* * *

WITH HIS OLD WAR WOUND acting up, Jasper was glad he brought along his cane, as he and Olivia wandered through the crowded town of Kringle, Vermont. Fragrant evergreen garlands, twinkling Christmas lights, and plate-sized bows of red and gold dressed every Main Street store, vintage streetlamp, and even the attached trash cans. The windows of the coffee shop, Java Joes, advertised the twelve coffees of Christmas, and on its door was a life-sized, hand-painted Santa holding a steaming cup of coffee.

A Santa Claus volunteer stood in front of the Bank of Kringle, ringing a silver bell. He was collecting change and nonperishable food items for the less fortunate. Happy shoppers, their arms loaded down with must-have treasures, bustled through town, stopping only briefly to greet a neighbor. Weary shop owners accepted new deliveries, then began to restock their dwindling merchandise. Excited children pressed their noses against the toy store's front window, pointing to the very items on their wish lists.

"Oh look, Jasper, tomorrow night at the Kringle Hotel, the Vermont Theatre Company will be performing a play titled, 'Angels on Assignment, A Journey of Love.' I do hope we will have the time to attend."

Jasper walked quietly, not replying to Olivia's request.

"Jasper?"

"Livy. I wish, just once, I would be able to surprise you. I also viewed the advertisement, and we will indeed make the time to attend the most captivating performance."

"I'm terribly sorry for ruining your surprise, Jasper, but I am most excited to experience some more of the local flair."

Jasper and Olivia entered the library through the front entrance. Children's winter jackets, scarves, and woolen hats hung from hooks along the library's highly polished mahogany walls. Snow boots lined the wall beneath the jackets like multi-colored soldiers standing at attention.

"Good morning, folks," said the front desk clerk. Her broad smile was as bright and cheery as her red lipstick which contrasted beautifully against her alabaster complexion and long black hair. On the wall behind her desk hung an artificial Santa Claus landing his sleigh atop a black pitched roof. Rudolph, complete with his blinking red nose, helped guide Santa and his overflowing sleigh across the cloudy, midnight sky.

"My, you have a splendid library here," Jasper said. "Two stories, is it?"

"Yes. This is a county library," the young woman said. "We service the smaller, surrounding towns. My name's Maureen Doyle. How may I help you today?"

"I'm looking for your selection of poetry, and my fiancée would love to catch up on her cooking and fashion magazines."

Maureen stood and walked around her desk to direct the couple. "Our downstairs level caters entirely to children. They are free to play with puzzles, read books, or play computer games. On our stage, a local puppet company is performing, "How the Elves Saved Christmas," which should be concluding shortly. What you are looking for will be available on our second floor." Pointing in the direction of two flights of stairs divided by a landing, she continued. "Upstairs, just past the coffee shop, you'll find a wide variety of magazines. There are comfy alcoves for your browsing pleasure. Magazines are along the back wall, and poetry, to the left."

As Jasper shifted his weight, Maureen looked down at his cane. "We do have an elevator at the back of the library, towards the restrooms. Follow the yellow brick road through story time village; it'll lead you right to it."

"Ah, yes," said Jasper, "From Dorothy's adventure in *The Wonderful Wizard of Oz*. Thank you, Miss Doyle." Jasper and Olivia carefully maneuvered around three dozen school-age children leaping up and down, *politely* yelling instructions to the puppets performing in a live performance.

At the bank of elevators, Olivia studied a Christmas-themed poster. "Today is 14 December, is it not?"

"I believe you are correct, my dear," Jasper replied.

Olivia cast her eye over the poster. "This afternoon the library will be hosting a Christmas Gala for the children. There will be snacks and games, a book scavenger hunt, sing-a-long fun, ornament making, and a special reading of the book titled, *The Polar Express*. What a delightful afternoon of merriment organized for the children."

"Delightful, indeed."

Maureen joined them at the elevator. "I see you made your way around the wiggly-giggly children at this morning's puppet show."

"Their silliness was quite animated," Jasper said. "I was glad to see the elves found Rudolph in time for Santa's on-time departure. I trust the children learned a valuable message today regarding the importance of helping each other."

"I'm sure they did." The elevator doors opened, and Jasper and Olivia stepped into the vacant cab. Maureen firmly placed her hand against the opened door until she was sure the couple was safely inside. "Current magazines for purchase are adjacent to the coffee house and out-of-date, line the far wall. My mother, Evelyn, will direct you to our poetry corner. Do you have a favorite author?"

"Perhaps you would suggest a preferred American poet."

"I've always enjoyed, Robert Frost and Walt Whitman. Then there's my favorite children's authors: Shel Silverstein's *Up the Down Staircase,* and for humor, Dr. Seuss's *Green Eggs and Ham.*"

"Your recommended authors do sound most agreeable. We shall look for them straight away."

"*Green Eggs and Ham?*" asked Olivia after the doors closed.

Jasper shrugged.

In comparison to the gaily painted walls, fairy-tale tiled flooring, and the spirited behavior in the children's library, the second-floor reflected warmth, elegance, and contentment. Its walls displayed the same highly polished mahogany paneling as the main foyer. The scuffed oak flooring creaked with age from more than seventy-five years of foot traffic. Along one wall, cozy nooks and crannies were carved out. Pairs of high-backed brocade chairs with velvet footstools faced floor-to-ceiling windows. Lit sconces dotted the ends of the short bookshelves separating each reading nook. In the center of the room, library patrons utilized long wooden tables and chairs, marred by age. A 1,000-piece unfinished jigsaw puzzle depicting a colorful image of several dozen teacups with matching saucers occupied one end of the table. Jasper and Olivia couldn't resist sitting down and inserting a piece or two.

"Livy, the audible rumbling sounds emitting from my stomach tells me it is midday, time for lunch. On our way through town, we passed a charming restaurant called Pauly's Soup and Sandwich Shoppe. The establishment advertising their homemade soup of the day is Italian wedding soup. Why they were in need of advertising that, I do not know. Aren't all soups, homemade?"

"In a cooking magazine, they referenced a cooking pot which will cook a fork-tender pot roast in mere minutes instead of hours. Where is the pride in that? Meals take time to prepare. Time to simmer. Not minutes."

"You take pride in cooking our meals. And I… take pride in eating them," Jasper said, patting his rounded midsection.

"I'll wager that a hearty cup of soup and a piping-hot pot of freshly brewed tea is merited. I'll powder my nose, then meet you by the lift."

Jasper and Olivia waited as several library patrons exited the elevator car.

"What a shame," a woman said, to her acquaintance, "the Children's Christmas Gala has been canceled. Why do you suppose that is?"

"Canceled?" Olivia asked the woman. "Why in heaven's name would such a festive occasion for the children be canceled?"

"We don't know the particulars," the woman said. "Maureen just hung a canceled sign over the downstairs poster."

"Thank you for your kindness," Olivia said. "I must return this to her at the front desk. We'll inquire there."

"Miss Doyle," Jasper asked, "Might I inquire as to why the Christmas Gala for the children has been canceled?"

"Mrs. JoÚson is the Gala coordinator. Earlier this morning, she had to take her foster son, Travis, to the hospital."

"How unfortunate for the lad. But surely there is someone else who can fill in for them?"

Maureen shook her head. "With budget cuts, we are already spread too thin. We must rely solely on volunteers for holiday crafts and readings."

Olivia looked at Jasper. "Can anyone volunteer?"

"Yes, but for the safety of the children, we always run a background check on our volunteers. I'm afraid there's no time for that now."

"But it's Christmas. And it's for the children," Olivia said. "We'd love to volunteer. I am Mrs. Olivia Winters and this is my fiancé Dr. Jasper Aldridge. We're here on holiday from Manchester, England. We'll be staying in Kringle through Christmas."

"You're a doctor?" Maureen asked.

"I am a Doctor of Optometry, licensed in England."

"Well, that is very kind of you folks to give up part of your vacation to help the children of Kringle. As you said, it is Christmas and it is for the children. If you'll excuse me for a few minutes, I'll check with my supervisor."

Jasper and Olivia waited nearby. "Why the library would deem it necessary to check our backgrounds is a mystery to me."

"For the safety of the children, she said."

"My supervisor was quite reluctant, but she knows there is no time to notify the families of the cancellation. She agreed because she will be in the adjoining area working with teens on their Christmas poetry."

"Wonderful," Olivia said. "If you show me the crafts and the story to be read, I can familiarize myself with them. Jasper can play the piano during song-time."

"On behalf of all the children, and the entire library staff, I thank you both! Dr. Aldridge, the sheet music is on the piano bench." Maureen removed a manila folder from her desk drawer and handed it to Olivia. "These are the patterns for the children to choose from. All the art supplies will be on the craft cart. The children will cut out the ornaments, add tons of glue and glitter, then hang them on our tree in the lobby. Several of the moms have already signed up to provide snacks and drinks. If we run short, the library always has a stash in the kitchen." Maureen picked up the day's story time book. "Then they'll settle in while you read *The Polar Express*. Can you return around 1:15?"

"Yes. That time frame should work perfectly." Olivia thumbed through the delightfully illustrated picture book.

"It's been a Kringle tradition for over twenty years. Fifty-two children would have been extremely disappointed. And at this late time, we would not be able to notify each parent of the event's cancellation."

"Twenty years?" Jasper asked, reviewing the children's listed names. "Can't break tradition now, can we?"

"Miss Doyle, you say that the Johson child went to the hospital? Nothing too serious, I hope," Olivia asked.

"I'm afraid we don't know yet. Jake Hollister brought his daughter Penny and her friend Travis in earlier today. Travis began complaining of a bad stomachache. Penny's father is a firefighter and an EMT. The boys' cheeks were flushed and he was running a high fever. Mr. Hollister notified Travis's foster parents and recommended he be taken to the hospital right away."

"That certainly does sound serious. Where is the hospital? We'd like to check in on him if it is permissible."

"Travis has been taken to Lexington General Hospital. Make a right at the corner of Maple and Main. Go east on Route 9, then turn south on Lexington Avenue. It's the four-story, red-brick building at the end of the street. You can't miss it."

"I'm sure we'll have no trouble locating the facility. Thank you for the information," Jasper said.

Maureen accepted the magazine from Olivia. "I'm sorry I didn't take the time to return this to its proper location. Was Penny's name on the list of children who signed up for the Gala?"

Maureen checked the event's registration. "Yes, and her friend, Travis, too. Here is the list of the attendees." A tremor of a smile came to Olivia's lips.

Jasper removed his pocket watch. "Suddenly, I'm not quite as hungry as I thought. We have plenty of time to check on the boy's welfare and return in time for today's festivities."

Olivia turned her back and tapped her butterfly pin. "Lady Vanessa, please inform Raphael that we require a healing request. Travis is young and strong, but the healing powers of an archangel is just what the doctor's ordered."

Jasper smiled. "You're such a good woman, Olivia."

Chapter Twelve

COCOA'S PRESENT

COCOA BOUNDED DOWN THE INN'S main staircase, Jake and Penny not far behind. Chelsi was in the living room curled up under a blanket, leaning against the arm of an oversized sofa. She muted the television's local news station, *Kringle Today,* but kept an eye on the weather report ticking along the bottom of the screen.

"That was quite an emotional overload you faced earlier, Chels. How are you feeling?"

Chelsi drained the remainder of her pale pink infusion and placed the teacup on its saucer with a tiny clink. "Better now, thank you. There's nothing like a hot cup of herbal tea to help settle the soul. And… the English shortbread cookie was a nice added touch."

"My dad let me pick out the tea for you, Miss Chelsi. He said it has healthy rose pips in it. I hope you liked it."

Chelsi and Jake smiled at the slipup about the rose pips, but neither had the heart to correct her.

Jake's attention was drawn to the waning fire. He gripped the drawcord, but the fireplace screen resisted his first attempt. After a bit more force and a lot of wiggling, he coaxed it open. He shifted the wood around, then added a fresh log on top.

"Jake, I really need to talk to you about the paperwork I found at my dad's house. Before you and Penny visit Travis in the hospital, can we go somewhere to discuss it? Then, maybe drop me off to pick up some new clothes? I want to investigate further, maybe go into the attic, to see if there are any more clues."

"Sure thing, Stitch," he said with a grin. "Let's go for coffee a bit later. I'll contact the power company so you at least have heat and light before venturing into the attic."

Penny tilted her head, making eye contact with her father. "Daddy, why did you call Miss Chelsi 'Stitch'?"

"I'll let Miss Chelsi tell you that story."

"Oh, boy. I *looove* stories."

Penny climbed onto the couch, pulled the end of Chelsi's blanket over her lap, and snuggled up close to her. Look at how Penny's taken to Chelsi, he thought. She's never trusted anyone like that since—

Cocoa let out a series of barks telling Jake it's time to get going.

"All right, girl. Let's go," he said. "Back in a few," he winked at Chelsi, then closed the front door.

"Are you all set for me to tell you a story about me and your daddy?"

Penny snuggled a bit closer. "You bet!"

"Once upon a time, there were two friends named Jake and Chelsi. They were about your age, and boy, were they inseparable."

Penny looked up out of the corner of her eye. "Like me and Travis?"

"Just like you and Travis." She tapped Penny on the top of her nose. "Your father was very smart; he got A's on all his tests. Me, I liked sports better than studying. I always had a baseball and glove in my hands. One hot summer afternoon, I climbed up the tree in my backyard—"

"The big one where your treehouse is?"

"Yup, that very same one, only we hadn't built the treehouse yet. Anyway, I looked up and saw the tops of the tree branches swaying in the breeze and thought it'd be cooler if I went up higher. So, I climbed up the tree trunk. One hand pulling down on the branches, one foot pushing up 'til I found a sturdy branch, and then I sat there."

"Was my daddy there too?"

"Afraid not. He had to finish his chores first."

"My daddy's like that." Chelsi could feel Penny's head bob up and down under her chin.

"I sat on the tree branch, feeling pretty good about myself. I swung my feet back and forth thinking, okay, now what? So, I took a ball out of my pocket. Well… I started tossing it up and down a few times, then your dad came riding up on his bicycle and distracted me. I missed the ball and fell out of the tree. Your dad jumped off his bicycle and ran inside and got my mom."

"Like I ran and got my dad when Travis was sick?"

"Just like that," Chelsi said, with a snap of her fingers.

"Did you need to have an operation, like Travis?"

"Well, sort of, but it was different. Fortunately, when I hit the ground, I didn't break any bones, but I did get a real bad cut under my chin and had to go to the hospital to get stitches. Your daddy came with me in the car and held an ice pack under my chin. I got five stitches. Right here." She lifted her chin and pointed to the area.

Penny rubbed Chelsi's chin. "Did it hurt?"

"Well, not really. First, the doctor came in and put my chin to sleep. That hurt… just a tad, but my mom was there, holding my hand the whole time."

"I don't have a mom," said Penny. "She went to heaven when I was five."

Chelsi kissed the top of Penny's head. "I know, sweetie. Your daddy told me. You know what? I didn't have a mommy either growing up. She went to heaven when I was ten."

"Ten?"

"Yup. But I had my dad, just like you do. When I came out from the emergency room, your daddy was sitting in the waiting room. My chin was swollen, my favorite shirt all bloody, and I had a big white bandage covering up the stitches. He handed me my ball, and said, 'Here ya go, Stitch.' He's called me that ever since."

"Miss Chelsi, that was a nice story." She sat up quickly and added, "Not the part about you falling out of the tree and getting stitches, but you're a good storyteller."

Playing with Penny's hair, Chelsi smiled, "I knew what you meant."

Jake came in the back door and stomped the snow from his boots. After wiping off Cocoa's paws, the dog came barreling into the living room and dropped something on Chelsi's lap.

"Cocoa, what did you bring me?"

"A pinecone!" yelled Penny.

Chelsi rolled it around in her hand. "Do you know what we can make with a pinecone?"

"A bird feeder!" Penny said, excitedly.

"Exactly. With all the snow, the birds have a hard time finding food. Does your grandpa have peanut butter and maybe some birdseed?"

Penny shrugged. "I know he's got a jar of peanut butter with jelly stripes."

"I don't think jelly is very good for the birds. Later let's bring a paper grocery sack outside and collect as many pinecones as we can and let them dry. When we go shopping for dinner, we'll get a spool of string, a plain jar of peanut butter, and a bag of wild birdseed."

Penny's face lite up. "Oh yeah, I saw that on YouTube. You tie a string around the pinecone, load peanut butter on a butter knife and spread it on the pinecone. Then, you roll the pinecone into the birdseed and hang it on a tree branch."

"You watch YouTube?"

"Yeah, Grampa doesn't like it, but my dad lets me watch craft videos on Saturday mornings. Last week, I made sparkly red slime."

* * *

JAKE STOOD PROPPED AGAINST THE kitchen door jamb, observing his daughter's interaction with Chelsi. *Look at them. Penny nestled up against Chelsi, taking in every word she says. The two of them snuggled under a quilt, chatting away, and Cocoa, curled at their feet. It looks like Penny is enjoying Chelsi's company. I know I am. If only—*

"Daddy, Miss Chelsi told me all about when she fell out of the tree and hadda get five stitches. She was so brave."

"Yes, she was."

"Oh Jake, I didn't see you there."

"That's okay. I didn't want to disturb your craft project story."

"Tomorrow, we're gonna make bird feeders from pinecones. Wanna help?"

"Sounds like fun, Squirt."

Chelsi looked down at Cocoa. "She's quiet now, but how do you manage her when the inn has guests?"

"That's my fault. She's always well-mannered when we're here and usually doesn't bring her 'treasures' inside. Today, I knew she had the pinecone in her mouth. She looked up at me as if to say, 'Please, dad? Can I bring it to her?' So, I told her, 'Go ahead, girl. Bring it to Chelsi.'"

Jake saw a mischievous twinkle in Chelsi's eyes. "So, you were talking to Cocoa about me?"

"You'll have to ask Cocoa," he said, with an innocent look.

"I liked Miss Chelsi's story about when she got her stitches. Before good-night time, can she read me a book?"

His daughter interacting with Chelsi looked so... so natural. Chelsi looked over at Jake. He smiled and nodded. "I would like that very much, Pen."

Chapter Thirteen

TWO IMPERFECT HALVES

"JASPER... SHE KNOWS!"

"Yes, I see. Our Chelsi took the news quite well for someone who had just learned the truth about her biological mother."

"Should we ring the bell to the inn or continue to the hospital?"

"Let's take a quick look first."

"Oh, my! Will you look at that," Olivia whispered, peeking through the Strawberry Inn's living room window. "Chelsi, Jake, and Penny already look like a loving family. I think our work here is almost complete."

"Now, Livy, let's not get ahead of ourselves."

"You are absolutely correct. As Vision Ambassadors, we knew they were fashioned to be together since grade school. Jake is a trusting soul and a loving father, whose heart is incomplete. Chelsi must learn to trust again so she can open her heart to Jake and allow their love to flourish. Two imperfect halves, joined together, becoming whole."

Jasper looked over at Olivia's shoulder. "Lady Vanessa, please stay with Penny this evening. I'm sure she'll have questions and possibly doubts about her new feelings for Chelsi."

* * *

OLIVIA TOOK JASPER'S ARM, WALKING through the entrance of Lexington General Hospital. A hospital attendant, wearing a white lab coat and colored scrubs, hurried to their side with a wheelchair.

Looking from one to the other, she asked, "Good evening, folks. Which one of you requires emergency care?"

"Oh, I'm sorry, Ma'am," Jasper said. "Neither one of us is in need of medical assistance. My name is Dr. Aldridge and this is my fiancée, Mrs. Winters. We are here to see a young boy named Travis Reid. We were informed he was admitted into your infirmary with stomach pains."

The attendant nodded her head gesturing towards the seating area. "Please have a seat in the waiting room. Help yourself to a cup of coffee and homemade Christmas cookies, and someone will be with you shortly."

Olivia looked at the attendant's name tag. "Thank you, Dr. Tanisha. You have been most kind."

"Oh, I'm not a doctor, ma'am. It's just Tanisha," she smiled, as she spoke.

Jasper moved towards a long table covered in a green tablecloth with red poinsettias. Two plates of cookies sat next to a half-empty coffeepot, powdered creamer, sugar, and wooden stirrers. But no cups.

"Why does everyone in this town boast about something being homemade?"

"A sign of progress, I suppose," Olivia said, keeping her voice low.

"Dr. Aldridge?" Tanisha asked, "If you'd both please follow me, Travis's attending physician said you may have a short visit. They are prepping him for surgery."

Olivia's white-gloved hand flew to her mouth. "Surgery?"

"Yes, ma'am. His foster mother, Mrs. JoUson, is with him now. She will explain everything."

Jasper and Olivia were led down one long hallway and entered a hospital room across from the nurse's station. Travis occupied the first of two beds, with his mother sitting in the visitor's chair. Removing her glove, Olivia extended her hand to the woman. "Good evening, Mrs. JoÚson. We heard about your foster son's illness from the librarian. How is he feeling?"

Fern JoÚson set her magazine aside to take the stranger's hand. "I'm sorry, but do I know you?"

"Please forgive our boldness and kindly do not formulate an opinion that we are insensitive to the boy's health condition. My name is Dr. Jasper Aldridge, and this is my fiancée, Mrs. Olivia Winters. We were visiting the library this morning and were informed the Children's Christmas Gala had been canceled due to Travis's illness."

"Yes, unfortunately, you are correct. May I ask why are you here?" asked Mrs. JoÚson.

Olivia looked at the young boy lying in bed, playing with a hand-held object, fluids being administered into him through an IV. "We wished to offer kind words of encouragement to you and the young lad for his prompt recovery."

"Thank you for your concern, Mrs. Winters, is it?"

"Yes."

"Thank you, both of you. I can assure you his condition is not life-threatening. His appendix is inflamed and needs to be removed. He should return—"

"I'm afraid everyone must leave now," Tanisha said. "We're ready to take Travis down to pre-op."

"Your foster son will be in our prayers, Mrs. JoÚson. If it is permissible with you, may we return later for a short visit?"

She looked over at Travis. "It's up to you, Trav."

"I guess it's cool," he said. "Hey, can you bring me a book? They have no books here for kids to read."

"No books? What a travesty," Olivia said. "The library has allowed me the honor of reading, *The Polar Express*, in place of your foster mother this afternoon. I'm sure it would be acceptable with Miss Doyle if I borrowed the book long enough to read it to you."

"*The Polar Express* is one of my favorites. Thanks, lady."

"Folks, I really must insist you all leave, now."

"Yes, yes, of course," Jasper said. "You have a patient to attend to. Livy, after you."

Leaving the hospital, Olivia said, "Jasper, did you hear what Travis said? The hospital doesn't have any books for the children to read. Let's return to the store and gather up all the books and toys we can and donate them to the hospital. For a child, it's a terrible notion to be hospitalized, especially at Christmastime."

"You are an angel, Livy," said Jasper, with a wink.

* * *

OLIVIA PICKED UP THE REMAINING chenille stems and scraped glittery glue from the wooden craft tables. "The last of the children have taken their leave. I believe a most delightful time was had by all. But what I found to be most peculiar was Penny not being in attendance."

"I think you are quite right, Jasper. I'm sure there was a logical explanation for her absence. But I do pray for her good health."

"We'll return to the store, have a much-deserved cup of tea and a quick biscuit, tend to the dogs, then gather up our donated items for the children's ward. I am most anxious to check on the welfare of young Travis," she said.

"Thank you very much for donating the gift of your time to the children of Kringle," said Maureen. "My supervisor said you have quite a knack with the children; she's never seen them so well-behaved. On their way out, the children were all excited to hang their ornament on the lobby

Christmas tree. You see, our tree is unique; every decoration is displayed within the child's reach. When asked about story-time, each child identified for their parents their favorite part of the book. Each was different. Each just as animated. Maybe you can return in the spring for our next holiday event. The Easter Eggstravanganza."

"We would be delighted if we are in town," Jasper said. "But now, we must return home to see to our four-legged companions before we return to visit young Travis Reid at the hospital. On our first visit to the hospital, we noticed the extracurricular activities for the youngsters were quite sparse. We have an abundance of children's items in our secondhand store we wish to donate to the hospital."

"The hospital will certainly appreciate your donations. There's never enough to go around. Your dogs, are they certified therapy dogs?" Maureen asked.

"Therapy dogs?"

"Yes. The hospital encourages pet therapy for their post-op patients. The kind eyes and loving personalities of the dogs have quite a calming effect on patients, and they tend to return home quicker."

"Though our dogs are not certified, they are quite spirited animals, yet exceedingly loving. We shall bring them along as well. Thank you again, Miss Doyle, for allowing us the privilege of today."

* * *

"DADDY! LOOK AT THOSE DOGS," Penny said. "They have such short little legs and like… no tail. Can I go over and pet them?" Jake was at the coffee table on his fourth, or maybe fifth, cup of the day. "Pen, it's 'May I pet them?' It's fine with me, but please introduce yourself and ask their owners for permission."

"Hello. My name is Penny Hollister, and over there is my dad, Jake. We're here waiting to visit my best friend, Travis. I have a dog, too. She's a chocolate lab. Her name is Cocoa. May I pet your dogs?"

Reaching out, Olivia shook Penny's little hand. "Cocoa. Like the delicious, sweet, hot beverage overflowing with marshmallows?"

Penny looked down at their connected hands.

"Ah-huh."

Jake nodded at Olivia. "Penny. Such a lovely name for a pretty young girl. It is my pleasure to make your acquaintance. My name is Mrs. Winters, and this is Dr. Aldridge."

Penny climbed on the chair next to Olivia and made herself at home. "A doctor? Is he going to make my best friend all better?"

"I'm afraid I'm not a medical doctor, young Penny, but we too are here to visit Travis. Hopefully our dogs, Maximillian and Gwendolyn, will help send your best friend home quickly."

Penny touched the brooch Lady Vanessa pinned on the outside of Olivia's coat. "What a pretty butterfly pin. It's so sad... she's a little broken."

"Yes, Penny, it is a shame. Damaged or not, she is very much loved. Love offers second chances." Penny closed her eyes, her fingertips remaining on the pin. "Thank you," she whispered.

"Who are you thanking, Pen?" asked her father.

"I know now that Travis will be okay, and he'll go home tomorrow. I feel it in my heart."

Olivia placed her hand on top of Jasper's and smiled.

Max and Gwen sat patiently waiting for their turn to greet the young girl. Penny sat down on the floor between them, and Olivia gave them the okay sign to greet her. It didn't take them long before they bestowed upon her a plethora of doggy kisses.

"Mr. Hollister?" Tanisha asked. "Travis is out of surgery, and they've transported him from recovery to his assigned room. Mrs. JoÚson said you and Penny may visit him now."

Max and Gwen looked at her and let out a series of short, low woofs. Tanisha smiled and ruffled their ears. "I'll check with the attending physician for any pet allergies the patient may have before approving your therapy dogs. Folks, if you'll please wait here for the Hollister's to vacate the room, then you may visit Travis. He's on the third floor. Room 3212."

* * *

TANISHA WALKED INTO THE WAITING room, her arms laden with several sleeves of hot beverage cups and a fresh tray of cookies. "Here, let me be of some assistance to you." Olivia took the tray of cookies from her hands and placed it in the center of the beverage table. She admired the oval ceramic dish mounded high with festive holiday cookies of various sizes and shapes. Covered in plastic wrap, the platter was thoughtfully finished with green curling ribbon and an artificial silk poinsettia. "My, these cookies certainly do look delicious."

"My mom sends me with several trays of homemade cookies every day. One for the employee lounge and the others for the waiting-room guests to enjoy. 'A little love from home,' she calls it."

"Tanisha, may I ask you a question?" Olivia asked.

She glanced at her watch. "Sure, I have a minute."

"Why is it so important that people know it is homemade? Isn't everything made in your kitchen?"

"These days, a lot of people are spread pretty thin. Between busy schedules like day jobs and night college, folks are forced to buy store-bought stuff from the local grocer for speed and convenience. My mom was a stay-at-home mom, so she had the time to cook a balanced meal every night and always baked us homemade treats."

"She sounds like a love—"

Penny came skipping down the hallway and returned to the waiting room. "Miss Olivia, Travis is awake, but he's talking funny. Mrs. JoÚson said it's the medicine the 'ceeziologist gave him to go to sleep."

Olivia smiled. "My, that is a mighty big word for a little girl. Mark my words, he will be all better in two shakes of a lamb's tail."

"Ah, here are the Hollister's now. Dr. Aldridge, your dogs have been approved to visit Travis and any other patient who would enjoy their company."

Jasper returned the magazine he was reading to the side table. "Splendid. Thank you, Tanisha. We shan't be more than a quarter-hour. The boy needs his rest."

Chapter Fourteen

A ROMANTIC RIDE

HOLIDAY MUSIC PLAYED QUIETLY WHILE the aroma of sizzling burgers and freshly brewed coffee welcomed Jake and Chelsi inside the Kringle Diner. Jake nodded to the waitress, then helped Chelsi off with her jacket.

"Sit anywhere you like, kids," said the tall woman, with sparkling eyes and a broad smile. "I'll be with you before you can name all the reindeer. And no fair looking it up on your cell phones, either!"

Chelsi smiled. "My, she's certainly a lively soul."

"That, she is." Jake put his hand on the small of Chelsi's back and directed her to an open booth. He kept his puffer vest on, but hung Chelsi's jacket on the hook between the booths. Chelsi slid across the red tufted bench seat while Jake sat opposite her. The diner was decked out in full-on Christmas. A five-foot tall silver artificial Christmas tree was decorated with white coffee filters cut into snowflakes, three types of sugar packets, and plastic utensils. The furnishings in the diner had seen better days, and the booth they sat at had B & R carved into a one-inch heart, so this was, apparently, their booth.

Chelsi skimmed her hand down the sleeve of her new green top. "Thanks for taking me shopping before we went for coffee. I mean, wearing your sweats is okay while hanging out at the inn or rummaging through my dad's stuff, but I feel better dressed *correctly* in public."

"You look good in what you're wearing. But I admit, I liked the purple top better."

Chelsi removed a sugar packet from the white caddy, put it on the edge of the table, then with her thumb and middle finger, flicked it across the table at Jake. "Yeah, you would. This top is more seasonal, and the other was cut on, how should I put it? A bit on the slender side."

His eyes held hers. And what was wrong with that? Jake had been admiring Chelsi ever since she returned to Kringle. Though he'd always love Amelia, Chelsi had a side to her he'd forgotten about. Playful, challenging, stubborn, loving. Why he'd never asked her out in high school was the question of the century.

Chelsi tilted her head to the side. "What was that look for, Hollister?"

Jake shied away from her gaze and flicked the sugar packet back to her. "Oh, nothing. I'm glad we were able to get some alone time. Chels. It's been a whirlwind ever since you arrived." He put on his reading glasses and nodded toward her handbag. "Let's see what you've uncovered."

Feeling the raised Wisconsin notary public seal, Jake read the words on the birth certificate, then studied the photo of the two women. "Wow, look at how young your mom was here. There's no denying it, you do resemble your aunt more than your mom. How much older was your mom?"

"Seven years."

Jake turned the picture over again. "The back stamp says it was printed in September of '70. How old would that have made your aunt?"

"*Um,* Mom was born in '44—"

"So, she would've been around nineteen."

"Okay Einstein, how'd you figure that out so quickly?"

The waitress, carrying two coffee carafes in one hand and a small white pitcher of milk in the other, walked quickly to their table. She had silver jingly bells tied into the laces of her shoes and wore red Christmas bulb earrings which blinked off and on with every movement of her head.

"Hey darlin'," she said to Jake, turning over their white coffee mugs. "Today's special is: The Nutcracker. It's a turkey-Swiss wrap with walnut and cranberry chutney, fresh green beans with bacon and crispy onion strings, and to finish, a slice of sweet potato pie."

Jake gave the server a suspicious look. "Sounds a lot like your turkey club meal, but with a fancy name."

She looked at Chelsi and gave her a wide toothy grin. "Who've you brought in with you tonight?"

"Hey, Katrina. This is Chelsi Burnett. Growing up, she lived across the street from us on Cottage Lane. She's in town for the week till Carlos can put her Jeep back together again."

The waitress held up two carafes of brewed coffee.

"Regular, please," said Jake.

"I'd like decaf, please."

Pouring their coffee, she gave Chelsi a side look. "So, you're the one who slammed her Jeep into the tree on Old Post Road."

"Boy, I forgot how fast word travels in Kringle," said Chelsi, reaching for three sugar packets.

"That and Katrina here is my sister-in-law Jessica's step-mom."

"Very nice to meet you. I'm sure our paths will cross again soon."

"You can count on that, honey," she said, setting the carafes down on the table. Katrina pulled one of the two candy cane pens from the elastic band of her curly raven bun and suspended it over an order pad. "Can I bring you today's special?"

"We don't have that much time today. What pie do you recommend?"

She looked over at the counter. "Blueberry. But there's not much left, so order quickly."

"That settles it." Jake pointed to Chelsi. "Just the coffee and we'll split whatever blueberry pie is left."

"Do you want that a la mode?"

"Nope, we're good," he said.

Katrina scribbled down their selection and slid the order pad back into her red Christmas apron pocket. "I'll have that out to you shortly."

Jake lightened his coffee with milk, then added three packets of sugar. "So, by your calculation, Aunt Ann Marie got pregnant her first year of college?"

"It sure looks that way."

"When did your parents get married?"

"May fifteenth, '68, I think." She, too, added three packets of sugar into her mug. Absorbed in thought, Chelsi watched the crystalline sweetener swirl around, infusing into the fragrant aroma from the full-bodied, steaming beverage. "I suppose I should be grateful I'm here. She could've gotten an abortion."

Jake covered her hand with his. "I'm glad she didn't. I kinda liked growing up with you."

Chelsi looked down at her encircled hand and smiled. A smile that tugged at his heartstrings. "I have to continue my search. There's *got* to be more information."

Katrina approached their table and Jake removed his hand from Chelsi's. "Here you go, kids," she said, placing their oversized portion of dessert and two forks in front of them. "Welcome back to Kringle, Chelsi. Pie is on the house."

"Thank you, Katrina. That's very kind of you."

She put her hand on Jake's shoulder. "Looks like you both could use a pick-me-up tonight." Jake was ready to delve into his pie when the waitress continued. "Don't forget, the horse-driven sleigh rides through town began last night. Perhaps you would consider taking Chelsi here for a spin?"

"We did see a family enjoying a ride when I parked the truck. I think a promenade around town is just what the doctor ordered."

"Good boy," she said, topping off their mugs, then jingle-belling away.

* * *

CHELSI WIGGLED HER TOES INSIDE her new warm socks and fluffy, fleece-lined boots as she and Jake waited for the family of four to exit the horse-drawn carriage. The crisp air smelled like a pine tree forest scented from the array of decorated Christmas trees each business displayed outside their storefronts. Each window depicted a different mural skillfully painted with red and green holiday greetings.

Grinning like a Cheshire cat, Jake offered Chelsi his hand. "M'lady?"

"Quite the gentleman, now, aren't you?" She wasn't sure if it was the zing of electricity from him holding her hand, or his little boy grin that released a rainbow of butterflies deep within her belly. She stepped onto the floorboard of the restored antique buggy and slid partway across the smooth, black leather bench seat, leaving Jake *just* enough room. Jake unfolded the blue and white snowflake blanket and covered their laps.

"Warm enough?"

Chelsi rubbed her chilled hands together and scooted as close to Jake as possible without sitting on his lap. "Getting there."

They both laughed.

The costumed coachman tightened the leather reins and clicked his tongue. "Walk-on Lulu Belle," he said to the gentle brown and white mare. Jake found a partially used jar of bubbles in a box on the floor. He dipped the long wand into the jar, then blew out several dozen bubbles in varying sizes. "Since it's not snowing, let's make believe these are round snowflakes flying around us."

That's the sweetest thing ever! Was there no end to the incredibleness of this man?

The carriage driver turned his head and gave Jake a thumbs-up. He turned on a Christmas CD. Bing Crosby's "I'm Dreaming of a White Christmas" emanated from speakers behind their heads.

"*Mmmm*," Chelsi said, resting her head on Jake's shoulder. "I know it might sound cheesy, but I feel like we're in a Hallmark Christmas movie. Snuggling under a cozy blanket with someone you care about on a romantic horse-drawn carriage ride. And Bing Crosby serenading us while the clip-clop of the horses' hooves stride leisurely through Main Street. It doesn't get any better than this."

"I like cheesy." Jake closed the jar of bubbles and returned it to the box on the floor. Sitting back, he snaked his arm under Chelsi's hair skimming the back of her neck and rested it on her shoulder.

"Bubbles," he whispered. "You forgot about the bubbles."

Chelsi smiled, looked up into Jake's eyes, then down to his lips. She moistened her lower lip. "The bubbles—"

"Can I…" he interrupted, "can I kiss you?"

Not waiting for her to answer, Jake leaned down and pressed his lips onto Chelsi's. Soft, yet firm. The gentle touch of his lips wasn't long, but it was a memory that would last forever.

Heat rushed from Chelsi's toes up to her cheeks. *I've been waiting over thirty years for our first kiss.* She adjusted her glasses and smiled. "…were amazing."

The second squadron of butterflies took flight. *Oh, my God!* What a perfect kiss! Short. Tender. Playful. Not *movie*-perfect, so… *Can we please have another take?*

She laid her head on Jake's shoulder and they enjoyed the rest of their ride in silence. Not an awkward silence. A happy silence. Though not quite dark enough to get the full effect of the holiday lights, their twenty-minute ride around Kringle's town square was lovely. The town's barren trees were alive with over a million white twinkly lights and animated cascading icicles. Since it had recently snowed, the town wasn't concerned with covering the ground with artificial-looking snow, which helped when a few teenagers decided to build a family of snow people, including a pretty good resemblance of a snow dog. Or, maybe it was a cat. Anyway, it was endearing.

Chelsi was disappointed when Jake's cell phone rang, interrupting their moment. "It's okay, I know you need to take the call."

"Sorry." He pulled out his phone and checked the screen. "It's my dad." He picked up. "What's up, Pop?—Oops. We'll be home in fifteen."

He disconnected the call. "We gotta get going. I forgot Pop and Gloria were going out tonight."

Chapter Fifteen

GLORIA'S MISHAP

"WHAT A DELIGHTFUL SHOW, JASPER," Olivia said, buttoning her coat. "The music was exceptional and the premise of the angels, most intriguing. I'm glad we were able to have a short conversation with a few cast members after the performance."

"I couldn't have said it better myself." Jasper took a stronger hold on her elbow. "Please mind your step, Livy, the temperature has dropped considerably, and the sidewalk might be rather slippery."

Olivia patted the strong hand of her ever-concerned fiancé. "I'll be careful, my dear."

Jasper craned his neck to see around the departing concert-goers in front of them. "There appears to be an incident near the corner; I do hope no one is seriously injured. Lady Vanessa, please pop over if you will, then shed some light as to what all the commotion is."

"Ah," he said, "the gentleman is Jake's father, Mr. Jim Hollister. His acquaintance, Mrs. Gloria Sanchez, has fallen and is indeed injured," he repeated.

"Quickly, Jasper."

"Will everyone please take a step back and provide this woman with some air." Jasper offered his hand to Jim. "Sir, my name is Dr. Jasper Aldridge, Doctor of Optometry. My fiancée and I are on holiday from Manchester, England. May I be of some assistance here this evening?"

Jim looked up at the man and accepted his extended hand. "Yes, thank you. My name is Jim Hollister. Gloria slipped on the ice and may have a broken wrist. Would you mind staying with her while I bring the car around?"

"Not at all. There is a bench a few meters ahead, she can rest there."

Jim looked down at his empty hand and blinked several times. "Gloria, I'll only be a few minutes."

"I'll be fine." She nodded, and he left for the car. Wiping away some grit from her palm, Gloria said. "You are so kind to stop and help me. I don't know what happened. We were walking along, talking about the performance when my foot went out from underneath me."

"How unfortunate you had to experience this anguish after such a lovely evening as tonight." Sitting next to Gloria, Olivia patted her leg just above her knee and left her hand resting there. "Please try not to move your wrist for fear of further injury. Everything will be just fine."

"*Muchas gracias.*" Gloria looked down at Olivia's gloved hand resting on her leg. "*Señora*, ever since you sat next to me, my worries, they seemed to have… disappeared." Gloria looked from Jasper then to Olivia. "You were at tonight's performance, weren't you? I think you sat in front of us."

"I believe you are correct, *Señora. Ah,* Mr. Hollister has arrived with his vehicle."

Olivia stood and moved next to Jasper. "May we accompany you to the hospital, Mrs. Sanchez?"

"No, thank you. You both have been so kind. What is your name?"

"Forgive me. It is Olivia Winters."

"Thank you, Mrs. Winters. I hope to see you again soon."

"Jasper," said Jim, "if you and the missus aren't busy tomorrow evening, why don't you join us at the Snowberry Inn B&B. It's on the top of the hill on Belmont Avenue, say around four-thirty? My late wife started the tradition when our first guests arrive for Kringlefest, we watch the movie, *It's a Wonderful Life*. The McIntyres, a lovely family of five, will be arriving early afternoon from Arizona. We'll have a variety of hors d'oeuvres and beverages for the adults, and grilled cheese sandwiches for the children. With only the light from the crackling fire, we'll snuggle under warm quilts, eat popcorn, drink hot apple cider, and enjoy the classic movie. The more, the merrier."

Olivia gave Gloria a concerned look. "Will you be up for entertaining so soon after your injury?"

"Don't you worry about my Gloria. I've got that all taken care of. She'll stay with us at the B&B for the night. She'll sit there like a queen, with her hand on a pillow, and order me around."

Jim helped Gloria to stand. "Come along now. Let's get that wrist X-rayed."

"Oh, and please have the hospital staff address her right knee as well," Olivia said.

"Her knee? Why is that?" Jim asked.

Olivia and Jasper glanced at each other. "I observed her limping and when she sat, she winced."

"*¡Oh, Dios mío!* Tomorrow. The bakery!" Gloria cried. "What will I do? I will not be able to lift or carry hot trays one-handed."

"Don't worry, Ria, we'll get you some help. Let's get you to the hospital before your wrist swells any further." Jim shook Jasper's and Olivia's hand. "Lookin' forward to seeing you folks tomorrow."

"Such a lovely woman," Olivia said after they parted ways.

"Mrs. Sanchez owns the bakery in town, does she not?"

"You're so right, Jasper. I'm sure she has enough staff to fill in in her absence."

He winked. "I think we know someone who has the time and will be willing to help out for a few days."

Olivia nodded in agreement. "Perfect."

* * *

"GOD BLESS MOMMY IN HEAVEN. God bless Grandma in heaven. God bless Daddy. God bless Grampa. God bless Cocoa and Whiskers. God bless Miss Gloria, I'm sorry she's gotta have a cast on at Christmas. God bless Travis, I'm really glad he's coming home tomorrow. And, God bless Miss Chelsi. Daddy, I really like having her around. Can she stay?"

"Well, Pumpkin, Miss Chelsi doesn't live here. She lives in Massachusetts."

Penny climbed onto her bed and Jake covered her with her comforter. "She could move... she could move back into her house and get a job here. Then we could all be together. I can tell her that moving wasn't so scary. Daddy, isn't that what you told me before we moved here from Washington?"

I was afraid this would happen. Penny's become too attached to Chelsi. Jake picked up Rosie and tucked her under the comforter. "It's complicated, Sweet P." Jake looked away, deep in thought. Having Chelsi here had been wonderful. She fit right in, not only with him, but with Penny, too. He didn't want her to leave.

Why did I kiss her? But it had felt so right. Still, Penny was his life and he didn't want to see her get hurt when Chelsi went back to Massachusetts.

Penny sat up in bed and picked up Rosie. For emphasis, she criss-crossed her arms holding her favorite doll close to her heart. "Daddy, I like being a kid. When you're a grownup, why does everything have to be so complicated?"

Chelsi stood in the doorway and knocked on the bedroom door. "Who's up for a bedtime story?"

Penny leaped out of bed and ran to Chelsi, giving her a big hug. "Miss Chelsi, Miss Chelsi, I've already said my prayers." She took her hand and led Chelsi to the bookshelf. "Here. Pick one."

"Wow, you sure do have a lot of books." Chelsi scanned the books and chose *Tea for Ruby* by Sarah Ferguson, The Duchess of York. She held it up. "How about this one?"

"Oh, I looove that book!" Penny hopped back into bed and snuggled down further under the covers.

Chelsi looked through the children's book, scanning the comical illustrations of a little girl named Ruby learning proper tea etiquette. "While I'm here, Penny, why don't we have a tea party."

Penny's eyes widened. "Can I invite my best friend, Reese?"

"Of course! As long as it's okay with her parents."

"And you can't skip any pages either. She knows each one of them by heart," Jake said.

"That's good to know. Just give me ten minutes to dry my hair."

Jake looked at her fresh from the shower. Barefoot. Hair wrapped up in a towel. Wearing his sweats. What happened between us today? Why didn't I kiss her thirty years ago? Our kiss was… was electric. *Glad I'm a firefighter, I'm still on fire.*

Chapter Sixteen

COFFEE AND CHAT WITH DANIEL

CHELSI PUSHED THE PARTIALLY OPENED door to Penny's room open and tiptoed in to check on the sleeping child. She couldn't believe the girl had zonked out so quickly. *Look at her, sound asleep. So innocent. So much heartache for one so young.* Her room was decorated with twinkling snowflake lights draped across her ceiling in a scalloped pattern. Above the bed, sheer curtains were gathered in a tight knot and fell open on either side of her headboard, creating a castle-like appearance. Chelsi lifted her arm and tucked it under the comforter, then leaned in and kissed Penny on the top of her head.

"Sleep tight, sweetheart. If only…"

Chelsi's cell phone chirped. Cringing, she backed out of Penny's room, thankful the sound didn't wake her.

Not hearing any signs of activity downstairs, she knocked on Jake's door.

"Jake? Jake… are you in here?" Chelsi whispered. Listening for any signs of movement inside his room, she tilted her head to the side and put her ear on his bedroom door. *Guess he's out walking Cocoa.* Looking both ways down the hallway, she turned the knob. It wasn't locked. With one hand on the doorknob, she pushed with the other. It didn't budge. What if he was in the shower and didn't hear her knocking? She wondered which room was Jim's. *Why do I feel like I'm still in high school?* She took a firmer grip on the doorknob and shoved it open.

Chelsi peeked around the door and looked at his bed. "Jake?" She stepped inside, closed the door behind her, and inhaled the essence of him.

I shouldn't be in here. What if he comes back?

Oh, just one more minute.

Why did I come here in the first place?

Adjusting the glasses higher on her nose, her vision zeroed in on the dresser along the short wall. Was he building a model ship? She took a closer look. The detail, so many tiny pieces...it was incredible. The USS JoÚ C. Stennis. It must've been one of the ships Jake served on.

Chelsi, what are you doing? Get out of this man's room. Now!

Cocoa bounded down the hallway and pushed her way into Jake's room. *Busted!*

"Hey, girl, where's Jake?" she whispered, scratching the dog's head. "Oh, he's on his way up the stairs now, is he?" She put one finger across her lips. "Shhhh. Let's keep this our little secret, 'kay? I owe you a t-r-e-a-t, or two, tomorrow." Chelsi scooted out of Jake's room and headed toward the stairway, Cocoa following close behind.

"Jake!" she said, running into him at the top of the stairs. "I just checked on Penny, and she's down for the count. I was just about to make a cup of tea and do some reading. Care to join me?" *Phew, quick thinking, girl.*

"Tea's not my thing, Chels, but we do have some decaf coffee pods for the Keurig."

"I'll take care of our hot beverages if you put another log on the fire."

"Deal."

As they walked past each other, Jake reached out and grasped Chelsi's hand. They stopped shoulder to shoulder. The reaction of his thumb caressing her knuckles sent her mind into a tizzy. It was the feeling when she had an uncontrollable smile on her face and couldn't string two words together coherently…yeah, *that* feeling.

"Glad you're here."

She smiled. "Me, too."

Cocoa joined them in the living room and stood there facing Chelsi. She whimpered, then licked her lips as if to say, *Um, I'll take that treat now*. Chelsi could've sworn the dog winked at her.

"Come on, girl, you can help me in the kitchen." Compelled to oblige, Cocoa obediently trotted after Chelsi into the kitchen.

"Got any Christmas CDs out there?" she asked.

"Already on that."

Jake's cell phone dinged with a text message. He read the message and went into the kitchen to relay the message, but was distracted by Chelsi singing and dancing to Gwen Stefani's jazzy version of "Santa Baby."

Chelsi didn't know Jake was standing there, but Cocoa, on the other hand, knew the moment he had approached.

The whistling tea kettle alerted Jake that he should return to the living room before he was caught spying on her.

The inn's nine-foot, live balsam fir Christmas tree was the focal point of the gathering room, the nickname Jake's mother, Jane, so lovingly named it. Jake's favorite decoration, the Christmas angel, graced the tree's tallest branch. Many years ago, the angel's original white skirt had been damaged due to mold, and his mom had replaced it with a rich shade of burgundy satin. The trees' trimmings were plain yet elegant. Jane Hollister had bought a similar set of gold garland beads she had seen in a photo of The Plaza's Christmas tree. She draped it from bough to bough and suspended hundreds of gold and white ornaments from hooks adorning the tree's branches. The twinkling white lights darted on and off like bubbles popping in the air.

An old-fashioned black mesh screen sat in front of the dancing fire, which cast an everchanging reflection on the glossy oak flooring. A dozen pea-sized burn spots dotted the wooden floor from years of rogue sparks.

Chelsi carried the cups, trying not to spill their contents. Jake looked so comfortable and confident sitting on the couch that all she wanted to do was curl up next to him and become one. She handed him his coffee. "My, doesn't this look cozy."

"I thought we could use some more alone time after the past few days we've had."

"You've got that right." She stood in front of the fireplace, gazing into its warm, mesmerizing flames, inviting her to unwind. Chelsi enjoyed her time more and more at the Snowberry Inn, and she didn't want it to end. She knew her feelings for Jake were growing, but he lived here, and she didn't. This wasn't reality. Reality was back in Massachusetts.

Paris, on the other hand, was a definite possibility. She'd applied online to *Le Cordon Bleu* the night she'd arrived and could hear of her acceptance any day now.

Chelsi sat close to Jake, cradled the warm mug, and inhaled the calming aroma of chamomile and peppermint leaves. Dried hibiscus flower and rose blossoms offered the blend a perfect shade of light pink.

Jake took a quick swig of his coffee. "Sorry, I have a confession to make," he said with a sheepish grin.

"What's that?"

"You've got some pretty good dance moves."

"What are you talking about?" Then, the light bulb went off in her mind. "Were you spying on me?"

Jake shrugged. "I came to tell you to call my dad but got distracted. I heard you singing and was hypnotized by your boogie-woogie."

She slapped him on his shoulder. "Your dad wanted me to call him—why didn't you tell me? Is everything all right?"

"He said Gloria broke her wrist, and you should call him."

"What?" She picked up her cell phone and looked at him over the rim of her glasses. "Number, please?" He gave it to her, and she dialed.

"Hi, Jim, this is Chelsi. You're on speakerphone. What happened to Gloria? Is she okay?"

"She feels stupid," Jim said. "She slipped and fell on an icy patch on the sidewalk and landed on her hand. Broken in two places. Her knee is pretty banged up, too."

"That's terrible! What does Gloria need me to do?"

"She's called her assistant, Virginia, but she's gonna need more help. Gloria wants to know if you can you be at the bakery tomorrow morning? At four?" Chelsi could hear the sound of Jim cringing when he told her what time to be at the bakery.

"Of course. I'll have Jake drop me off. Please tell Gloria not to worry. I've got her covered."

"Will do," he said.

"Bye, Jim."

Jake forced a guilty smile. "Sorry, Chelsi. What did he say?"

"You heard him. He said you have to get up at 3:30 tomorrow morning and take me to—"

Chelsi's phone rang. She didn't need to check the caller ID to see who was calling. She recognized the ringtone she had set for her ex-fiancé, Daniel.

What does he want? She excused herself and ducked into the kitchen to take the call.

"Hello, Daniel. What do you need?"

"Can't I call to see how my favorite girl is?"

Her shoulders sagged. "*Ugh.* In case you've forgotten, Daniel, I'm not your favorite girl anymore. How's the catering?"

"Couldn't be better. No one could ever replace you, but I hired a male chef to take over the position. His name is Randolph. He has impeccable credentials, from an accredited cooking school in Chicago."

Chelsi rolled her eyes. "Have you cancelled the cookbook yet?"

"I miss you, Chels. Any chance we can meet for coffee and talk about it?"

What are you, nuts? "No! I'm not coming back to Massachusetts now, or any time soon."

"Well, I'm sure there's a diner in your little town of Kringle. You name the time and place."

"How did you know I was in Kringle?"

"I didn't until now," he said.

I can't believe I fell for that. Chelsi gave herself a mental head slap. "Daniel, you're nothing more than an egotistical, self-absorbed individual. You don't care about me, only what you can get *from* me. Have you moved out yet?"

"Babe, you know I love you."

Chelsi rubbed her throbbing temples. "Don't sugarcoat your response. When I asked you about moving out, there's only *one* answer! And, I've been in contact with a lawyer, so don't forget to cc me when the book is cancelled, or you'll be served. Goodbye, Daniel." She disconnected the call.

"Of all the nerve!" she said, sitting back down next to Jake.

"Who? What?" Jake asked.

"My ex! He called to say that he missed me, and then wiggled it out of me where I was staying."

Jake waved her off. "You have nothing to worry about with Daniel. He's licking his wounds."

"What about Gloria's bakery?"

Chelsi took a long sip of her tea. "She asked me to help Virginia for the next few days. I'll bake while she helps out with the front counter."

"I'm happy for you, Chels. What would you say to a game of 500 rummy?"

"I'd love to, Jake, but not tonight. I have a busy day tomorrow, not to mention getting up at zero-dark-thirty. When do you have to be back to work?"

"I have a ton of vacation time, and Randy said he'd be happy to pick up a few extra shifts from me."

"*Um,* before I'm permanently in the doghouse, we're having a welcome get-together tomorrow evening. The inn's first guests will be arriving from Arizona late afternoon. Dad serves hors d'oeuvres, then we all settle in and watch *It's a Wonderful Life*. The McIntyre's have been celebrating Christmas at the inn ever since I can remember."

Chelsi stood and collected Jake's coffee mug. "What a great family tradition."

"Unless you're taking the rest of your tea to your room, I got this, remember?" He removed the cups from her hands and brushed a light, feathery kiss on her cheek.

"But I didn't cook anything."

"You prepared the coffee and brought it to me." He flashed her a big smile. "My house, my rules."

* * *

JAKE COULD NOT FALL ASLEEP. All he could think about was Daniel surprising Chelsi by coming to Kringle and sweet-talking his way back into Chelsi's life. Jake didn't know Daniel, but he'd known the type. He'd be charming, bring her engagement ring with him, and apologize about the cookbook. He would tell her he'd canceled the contract with the publisher and want to take her back with him to Massachusetts.

Jake would do everything in his power to make sure that never happened. The more he thought about it, the more he knew he was falling in love with Chelsi, again. This time, he would not let her go. Jake wanted to go into her room and warn her about Daniel's antics, but it was already two a.m. and her alarm would be going off at three. Since he couldn't sleep, he decided to get up, get dressed, and go for a run.

Chapter Seventeen

JIM'S RETIRING

"FLORENCE, JOSEPH, MERRY CHRISTMAS, AND welcome back to the Snowberry Inn!" Jim Hollister said while piling coats and hats in his arm. "Girls, Penny will be down in a few minutes, something about gettin' her hair just right."

"Thank you, Jim," Florence said, admiring the decorations of the season. "And Merry Christmas to you and your family. The inn's gathering room never fails to delight me. Your late wife paid particular attention to every detail."

"She sure did have the knack."

Penny raced down the stairs screeching, Cocoa padding close behind. "Mary, Katie, Jackie, I can't believe you're finally here." The four girls leaped up and down, giggling, arms linked around each other.

"All right, all right," Jim said, "let them come and warm themselves by the fire. You have all week to catch up." Jim gave the dog a stern look. "Company, Cocoa. Manners." She slinked away and curled up in front of the fireplace.

"Sorry, Grampa," she said. The four of them scurried off to the kitchen in search of a snack.

Jim led the grownups into the gathering room. "Gloria, these are the McIntyres, Florence and Joseph. This is Gloria Alverez, a very good friend of mine. She owns the bakery in town."

"Good gracious, Gloria. Whatever happened to you?" Florence asked.

"I admit, I look worse than I feel." Jim and I were at the theatre last night, and I slipped on some ice. My wrist is broken, and my knee is pretty sore." Casting a look at Jim, she added, "He worries so."

Jim ladled eggnog from a crystal-cut punchbowl into clear-glass footed mugs. He topped each one with fresh whipped cream and sprinkled the tops with a dash of nutmeg and a candy-cane-striped straw. He offered the ladies theirs first, then picked up the bottle of brandy for a splash if they desired.

"Tell me, Joe," Jim said, "how is sunny Arizona treating you these days?"

"Pretty well. During the heat of the summer, we abscond to a small town south of Flagstaff. It's at least fifteen degrees cooler than down in the valley. We rent a small A-frame house. The girls love it, and I can work from anywhere."

Jim winked at Gloria.

"Are you thinking of retiring?" Joe asked.

"We sure are. Gloria and I have been talking about retiring to Florida." He picked up Gloria's hand in his. "Especially now, with Ria's accident and all."

Florence looked around the room, then heard the girls' playing cards in the kitchen. "Go fish!" Penny said.

"But your family is here. What are your plans for the inn?"

Cocoa got up and walked over to Jake standing in the doorway. "What do you mean—what are your plans for the inn?"

"Sorry, son. I didn't want you to find out this way. We are tired of all this frigid Vermont weather, and I'm just gettin' too old to run the inn. It needs new, younger blood. Besides, Gloria and I are in love; time we started thinking about ourselves."

Jake couldn't believe his ears. His father was selling the inn, the pride of his mother. When was he going to tell him? Jake shook his head. That would mean that he and Penny would have to move, just as Penny was beginning to show major improvement ever since they moved back to Kringle.

Jake shoved his hands in the pockets of his jeans, not sure what to say. "I sure didn't see this coming, Pop. Any idea as to the timeframe?"

"Jake, let's discuss this later."

"Gloria, what about the bakery?" asked Florence.

"I've already told my assistant Virginia. She's been with me for years and is thrilled to take on the responsibility as manager. All she'll need now is an assistant."

Jake's cell phone chirped. He took it out of his pocket and read the message from Chelsi: About done for the day. Can you pick me up from the bakery?

"Mr. and Mrs. McIntyre, it's nice to see you again. Back in a few, Pop. Heading to the bakery to pick up Chelsi." Jake walked through the front room to the kitchen. "Pen, I'll be back soon. I'm picking up Miss Chelsi."

"Good, 'cause we're getting really hungry."

He shrugged on his puffer vest. "Then I think it's grilled cheese and tomato soup o'clock for the muncŠins."

"Yeaaah!" they yelled in unison, tossing their playing cards in the air.

* * *

JAKE LEFT HIS TRUCK IDLING at the curb in front of the Kringle Bakery, then jogged to the front door. It was flanked by two four-foot-tall whimsically outfitted wooden Nutcrackers. One soldier held a crystal plate which offered the arriving customers a generous slice of strawberry shortcake. In place of his tall hat was a cupcake frosted with sparkling red icing, complete with a swirled dollop of fluffy whipped cream. Jake could swear there was a smudge of whipped cream on the corners of the Nutcracker's mouth. The other walked a small gingerbread dog carrying a red star with the word 'Believe' painted in white letters. The Nutcracker wore a red sequin-studded jacket, green sparkle pants, and white boots. Atop his red and green candy-stripped top hat was a marshmallow snowman with a carrot nose and a matching silk hat.

Turning the knob, Jake felt a twinge of apprehension. He was still in shock over the news of his father wanting to sell the inn. He wished his father would've told the family in private, instead of blurting it out like *oh, by the way, you and Penny have to move, and I'm selling the inn your mother so loved.* If it hadn't been for Amelia's passing, they'd still be in Washington living a full and happy life, and it wouldn't have bothered him as much. But ever since returning to Kringle and living at the inn, he couldn't imagine living anywhere else.

The bell clanged over the front door, announcing Jake's arrival. The bakery, like the other business owners of the town of Kringle, took pride in the wares they sold. Many shops, like Sal's Shoe Repair Shop and Wong's Chinese Restaurant, had been passed down from parent to child, but Gloria had taken over the bakery after the original owner sold it and moved away.

Jake inhaled deeply. The sweet and savory aroma of the bakery sent his stomach craving, well… everything. He walked around the glass display counters towards the kitchen. A fine haze of white flour hovered above a three-foot tall institutional mixer.

"Knock, knock!" he yelled out.

Chelsi emerged from the backroom. She was wearing her country club uniform, and her hair was up in a ponytail. Removing her flour and icing-covered apron, she said, "Boy, am I glad to see you."

"Tough day?"

"No. Different. I'm used to being behind the scenes, not waiting on customers. I can't believe how many people welcomed me back. And meant it!"

"They did the same for me and Penny when we moved back."

"I didn't have the heart to tell anyone my stay in Kringle is temporary."

Jake felt his jaw tighten. He didn't like the sound of the word 'temporary.' If he had anything to say about it, she'd stay right here in Kringle. After all, what did she have to go back to Massachusetts for? Her apartment? Her ex-fiancé who's trying to wiggle his way back into her life? She's unemployed and could easily find work here in Kringle.

"Bye, Virginia. See ya tomorrow at four. You sure I can wear jeans?"

"I'm sure," they heard over the dough hook clanking on the sides of its institutional-size metal bowl.

When they stepped outside the bakery the wind had subsided, but it was cold. Bone-chilling cold. Jake opened the truck door for Chelsi, then ran around to the driver's side.

"*Hmmm*. Nice and snuggly warm in here," Chelsi said, rubbing her hands together over the heater vents.

"I left the truck running while I went inside. Where are your gloves, young lady?"

She leaned over and kissed his cheek. "I think I left them at work."

"With your boots?"

"Yes, with my boots. Hey, have you heard? Gloria is retiring and moving to Florida."

"Yeah, I heard the same thing a few minutes ago," Jake said, pulling away from the curb. "She's retiring with my dad!"

"And this surprises you?" she asked, buckling her seatbelt.

"I guess I don't see my dad in that way. I mean, dating and all." He shuddered. *It's the "and all" I can't quite fathom.*

Chapter Eighteen

ROSIE'S SAD

"MR. AND MRS. MCINTYRE, THIS is Chelsi Burnett, a friend of mine from our childhood. She's staying with us at the inn while her vehicle is being repaired." Chelsi removed her coat and greeted the newest guests to the Snowberry Inn B&B.

"Very nice to meet you, Chelsi. Where do you call home?" Florence asked.

Chelsi set her handbag on the floor next to the couch and her cell phone on a side table. *That is the question of the day!* "Just a few hours south of here in Massachusetts. I'm a… I was a pastry chef at a golf course country club."

"She was an angel today and helped out in my bakery," Gloria chimed in. "Virginia texted me earlier to say you looked like you'd work there your whole life. What are your thoughts?"

"I thought it went well," she said, with a half-smile. "Didn't take me long to get into the groove. Virginia is a terrific teacher."

"Yes, and she will make a great owner… someday."

And hopefully, I can be her assistant. "Sorry, I'd like to go up and clean up before the welcome party. I have flour *everywhere*. If you'll all please excuse me."

"Of course. I know how temperamental the mixer can be." Gloria fidgeted with the sling which restricted the use of her arm. "I don't know where my head is these days."

Jake looked from Gloria to his dad. He could only imagine where Gloria's mind was. Retiring away from this frigid weather. Playing pickleball, whatever that was, and walking hand in hand with his dad on some sunny beach in Florida.

Jake headed into the kitchen. "Pop, I'll get the kid's supper going. Chelsi will prepare the hors d'oeuvres when she comes down."

Jim tilted his head to the side and squinted his eyes at Jake. "Does she know this?"

"Yes. I told her last night."

Chelsi's cell phone chirped from the side table. Instinctively, he glanced over at her illuminated screen. It said: Happy Birthday Eve, Chelsi! Sorry, but Daniel wiggled it out of me where you're staying. I think he's planning…

"That's private, son. You shouldn't be eavesdropping."

"No, Pop. Glad I saw this one. Only read a portion of it. On our way home, she told me she was expecting a text from the repair shop. I thought this was Carlos. I read that tomorrow's Chelsi's birthday. *Umm…*" He thought for a minute. "She's turning the big 5-0!"

Gloria placed her uninjured hand over her heart. "We must do something special for her."

"You're right," Jim said, walking to the fireplace. As if angry for the interruption, the freshly stoked fire popped and spewed out another spark. Luckily, Jim stomped out the glowing ember before it added another burn mark on the wooden floor. "She's been such a big help to me around here."

"Don't fuss too much, Pop, she's not like that. Why don't we order catering trays from Bernard's Bistro? Beef and pasta dishes appeal to everyone?"

"Yes," they all answered. "Oh, but Mary is vegetarian these days," Florence replied, "or so she says. All the girls in junior high school now are trending in that direction."

"Geesh!" said Jake. "Is this what I have to look forward to with Penny?"

Joseph came over to Florence. "I'm sure she'll be fine."

Chelsi came downstairs. She had changed into jeans and a Christmas sweater, her hair freshly wound up in a messy bun. "Did I miss anything?"

Jim nodded in his son's direction. "Jake's volunteered you to help in the kitchen tonight."

"Yup, it's what I do," she replied. "What are we serving, Jim?"

"Jake's got the kids' grilled cheese and tomato soup under control. I've got a list on the counter that shouldn't take you too long."

"On it," she pivoted on one foot and headed for the kitchen.

The doorbell chimed, directing everyone's attention to the foyer. "Almost time for our final guests, Jasper and Olivia, to arrive. Jake, please get the door."

"From the hospital, Jasper and Olivia?"

"Yes! For heaven's sake, son, don't keep them waiting!"

Jake opened the front door. A cold squall of December wind mixed with a flurry of silvery snow preceded their guests. He took Olivia's hand and helped her inside.

"Jake, so nice to see you again," Olivia said, in her unmistakable British accent. "Has young Travis been discharged from the hospital?"

"Yes, he went home earlier this afternoon."

"Oh, That's jolly good news. Now he'll be sure to have a Happy Christmas."

Olivia moved her black handbag from one hand to the other while Jim helped her remove her coat. "Florence and Joseph McIntyre, Jasper and Olivia are on vacation from England. They were at the same show Gloria and I were at last night and were a tremendous help when my Gloria fell."

Jasper shook Joseph's hand, then Jake's, and finally Jim's. "Thank you for inviting us and including us in your Christmas festivities." Jasper walked over to Gloria. Her newly casted hand resting comfortably in a royal blue sling and her leg propped up. "I see the invalid is following doctor's orders and is staying off her feet."

"I'm making sure of that, Jasper," Jim said. "I put her up in the room next to mine for the night."

Olivia produced a white notecard with a phone number written on it. "Your color has certainly improved since last we met. If there's anything else we can do for you, please don't hesitate to ring us. We hope to stay through Christmas Day."

* * *

"I THOUGHT I HEARD FAMILIAR voices!" Chelsi said, serving her first appetizer. "Jasper, Olivia, it is so nice to see you again. Did you bring Max and Gwen?"

"Max and Gwen?" Jim asked.

"Our two corgis," Olivia said. "They are such endearing rascals."

"Please, bring them along next time you're in the neighborhood. Cocoa doesn't get many four-legged visitors."

"Thank you, you are very kind, Jim. We'll do just that."

Chelsi balanced the serving tray on her hip. She handed off the first dish of plated hors d'oeuvres to Gloria. "Oddly enough, ever since I've been back in Kringle I've begun to see my life in a whole new light. I feel like… like I make a difference. That my talents are appreciated. Something I haven't felt in a very long time."

"Where there's a new vision, there is hope," Jasper said, adjusting his bowtie.

Gloria looked down at her plate. "Now, if you will please explain this lovely dish to us."

"It'll be my pleasure. This first course is a tomato, basil, and mozzarella salad with a balsamic vinaigrette dressing. Next up will be smoked salmon wraps with cucumber, sprouts, and a creamy dill spread. Finally, I'll bring out softened cream cheese topped with a sweet chili glaze, served with crispy noodle strips for scooping."

Jim's bushy eyebrows knit together. "Darlin', those don't resemble any of the food items that were on my list."

"Oh… no?" She winked. "I could've sworn I prepared your suggested menu items… to perfection."

Chelsi delivered the remainder of the first appetizer to the inn's guests. "These are all recipes from my late Aunt Ann Marie's B&B back in Wisconsin. In addition to her decadent breakfasts, at 7 p.m., the Willow Creek Inn served an assorted selection of wine and cheese to complement the evening's light entrées, including a seasonal soup. After my mom passed, I'd spend summers with my aunt until after I graduated high school. My time spent with her was when I fell in love with baking and the whole idea of bed and breakfast hotels."

"It is our home away from home," Florence added.

"Precisely! When I went back for my aunt's funeral, my uncle gave me her treasured recipe binder with all the inn's recipes, then he sold the B&B and took a part-time job at the local hardware store."

"That's quite a tale," Florence said. "So, all of her recipes are your legacy."

"Exactly."

Jake came up behind Chelsi. He put his hand on her shoulder and whispered something into her ear. "Excuse me, I have a phone call," said Chelsi. "Please, everyone, enjoy your first course."

Chelsi slid the green button on her cell phone. "Hello, this is Chelsi," she said, in a high, chipper voice. "Uh-huh. Okay—The steering what?—Sure, I'll wait for your call tomorrow."

Jake folded the kitchen towel, then hung it on the oven door. "Anything wrong, Chels?"

"That was the repair shop." She cleared her throat. "My Jeep should be ready tomorrow late afternoon."

"Nooooo!" Penny yelled from the kitchen. "Miss Chelsi, I don't want you to leave. Ever!" She ran out of the kitchen and continued running up the stairs until everyone heard a door slam.

Jake and Chelsi, along with the three McIntyre girls, joined the other guests in the gathering room.

"What happened to upset the little one so much?" Olivia asked.

Disheartened, Chelsi collected the soiled plates. "My phone call, I'm afraid. It was Carlos, the owner of the repair shop. He said the final repairs on my Jeep should be completed by tomorrow afternoon, then I can be on my way. They are just waiting for the steering mechanism parts to arrive." She gave her best effort at a smile.

"I was afraid this was going to happen." Jake looked down at the floor, then raked his fingers through his hair. "I told Penny not to get too attached to you, that when your Jeep was repaired, you'd be going back to your home. Back to your life in Massachusetts."

Believe me, Jake, I don't want to leave. There's nothing left for me there.

Cocoa got up and stood next to Jake. Her hopeful brown eyes gazing up at him. "I know, girl. I'll go and check on her."

"If you don't mind, may I go to her?"

"Sure, I think she'd like that." Jake ruffled Cocoa's ears. "Go ahead girl, go with Chelsi."

Giving Penny a few minutes alone to vent, Chelsi walked slowly down the upstairs hallway to her room. She stopped at the entrance to her room and admired the artwork Penny had taped to her door. She was glad to see that Jim had given her permission to decorate her space so freely. Cocoa scratched at the door, then looked up at her as if to ask, *Aren't we going inside?* Chelsi listened at the door another minute until she was sure Penny was finished with her one-sided conversation with Rosie.

Chelsi tapped lightly on her bedroom door. "May Cocoa and I come in?"

"Okay," sniveled Penny, "but only the two of you."

Chelsi stood in the doorway and looked at the child. Fresh tears dotted her bright pink pillowcase. Holding Rosie tightly to her chest, she rolled over onto her other side. *Poor thing. Maybe I should start with some light chit-chat.*

"I love how you've decorated your room."

"Rosie's sad, she doesn't want you to leave."

All righty then. So much for small talk.

"Scooch over a bit, Pen." Chelsi took off her shoes and climbed on the bed, leaning back against the headboard. "May Rosie sit on my lap?" she asked, stroking Penny's hair, who nodded and handed her doll off to Chelsi.

Fidgeting with the doll's dress, Chelsi asked, "Rosie, why are you sad?"

No answer.

"Rosie it's okay. It's just us girls in here." Cocoa climbed on the bed and curled up at Penny's feet.

"She's shy," Penny said, wiping her runny nose with the palm of her hand.

"I see that. Well, how 'bout if she whispers her feelings into your ear. Will you speak for her?"

"I guess." Penny rolled over and curled up under Chelsi's arm.

Chelsi positioned the doll's face close to Penny's ear. Penny squinted, attentively listening.

"Rosie said, she doesn't want you to go."

"Rosie, why is that?"

"She said you're very pretty and you make her laugh. But 'specially ever since you've come to stay with us, Penny doesn't miss her mommy as much."

Chelsi pulled her lips into a tight line. *Oh! my goodness, this is killing me. Please Lord, help me say the right words.* "I see. Well, Penny, your daddy is very handsome, *and* he's funny. He makes you laugh, right?"

"I guess."

"And your grandpa, well, he simply adores you." Her heart ached for Penny's loss and her bravery. She knew what it was like to grow up without a mother. The loneliness. The questions about the changes in her body. Someone to fuss over her when she came home crying because the boy she liked sat next to her best friend at lunch. "But you know it's okay to be sad sometimes too, right?"

"I know." Penny's words were just about a whisper.

"And sweetie, your mommy knows how much you love and miss her, but I know she wants you to be happy."

Penny reached over and held Chelsi's hand. "I guess."

"That a girl." Chelsi closed her eyes tightly, fighting back the tears.

"I heard my daddy talking to Uncle Randy on the phone today. He said, he's happier than he's been in a long time, and your laugh is contagious, whatever that means."

So, Jake had been talking to his brother about her? Well, she was happier now than she had been in a long time, too. *And when your dad smiles at me, it sends flip-flops through my whole body.*

Chelsi pointed to the draped fabric over Penny's bed. "You know what this reminds me of, Rosie?"

No answer.

"It reminds me of my treehouse. I loved being up there. I'd climb the stairs, and my worries seemed to fall to the ground, especially when Penny's daddy was with me. He was a good listener. On the weekend, his mom would make us PB and J sandwiches, and we'd spend hours up there just talking and laughing. Besides baking, my treehouse was my happy place."

"Rosie said, it sounds like fun. She wishes she had a treehouse."

Chelsi crossed her fingers. "And Rosie, what would Penny say if I asked her dad if the three of us could go to my treehouse later this week?"

Penny's face lit up brighter than all the twinkle lights in her room. "I would say yes! Can we go tomorrow… and bring Travis too?"

Chelsi tilted her head to the side. "Of course, Travis can come, too. But maybe not tomorrow. He needs more time to rest."

"I suppose."

"Does he have any other foster brothers or sisters?"

"Nope, just Travis. He's my best friend." She looked up at Chelsi, her eyes still moist from tears. "Like my dad was your best friend. I hope we're still friends when we get old like you and my dad."

Chelsi scrunched her face into an over-exaggerated frown. "Hey, I'm not that old." She thought about it for a minute. "Oh, my goodness, I am. I turn *fifty* tomorrow!"

"What?" Penny perked up. "Tomorrow's your birthday? We *have* to have a party for you. Wait till I tell my dad."

Penny scrambled out of her bed as quickly as she could and ran down the stairs, yelling, "Dad, Dad, tomorrow is Miss Chelsi's birthday. We have to buy her a cake, some ice cream, and streamers and party balloons and…" she put her index finger on her chin, deep in thought. "What kinda games do grownup people play at their birthday parties?"

Everyone downstairs began to laugh. "What a darling daughter you have, Jake," Olivia said.

"Yeah," said Jake, his arm around her shoulder. "She's a keeper."

Chapter Nineteen

WE'RE NOT IN HIGH SCHOOL ANYMORE

"MMMM... ARE WE HAVING PANCAKES and *bacon* for breakfast?" Penny scrambled onto her usual seat at the table with Rosie at her side.

Jake kissed the top of his daughter's head, then put a plate of two, six-inch banana pancakes in front of her. "Well, good morning to you too, Penny. Glad to see you finally came down for breakfast."

She took a long drink of her orange juice. "Where is everybody?"

"Right now, it's just us. Grampa took Miss Gloria home to pick up a few more things, Chelsi is at the bakery working, and the McIntyres took the train into the city."

"That sounded like soooo much fun. The girls told me yesterday that their daddy has a meeting in the morning, so their mom made an appointment at the American Girl Doll Store to get their dolls' hair done. While they're waiting, the girls and their mom will get their nails done, too." Penny inspected her unadorned fingernails, then began meticulously spreading peanut butter, in a swirly pattern, on top of her pancakes.

Jake's shoulders sank watching his precious daughter talk about her friends spending time with their mothers, though he had no idea why the dolls needed to get their hair done. He missed his late wife tremendously,

A New Vision: A Recipe for Love

but his heart had completely opened to the idea of Chelsi being part of their lives. After a two-beat pause, he said, "Hey, don't forget we have to decorate for Miss Chelsi's birthday before she gets home from work. I think we still have some decorations in the pantry."

"Oh, that'll be fun, too," she said, scraping the warm peanut buttery pancakes from the roof of her mouth. "How 'bout we hang balloons and streamers in front of her door. But you'll have to help me blow them up. And tie them. And hang them."

Jake smiled. "I can do that," he said, drying the electric griddle. "Say, how would you like to come with me to the fire station today? We're organizing the toy and canned food drive. Uncle Randy said he could use our help sorting."

"Sure! Maybe I can go across the street to the bakery and give Miss Chelsi a birthday hug. Can we bring Travis, too? I miss him so much. Miss Chelsi told me last night she was going to ask you if we could go to her house after work one day and show us the treehouse and—"

"Slow down, little one. I'm sure glad you didn't put any sugary Vermont maple syrup on your pancakes. You're already pretty wired."

She wants to take them to the treehouse? Hmmm... I wonder why she didn't say anything to me about it this morning. I guess she forgot.

"Sure thing, but we'll need to run it by Mrs. JoÜson."

Penny stood on her tippy toes to kiss her dad. "Thanks for breakfast, Daddy. It was delicious. Can I call Travis now?"

"Yes, you may."

* * *

THE OVERHEAD STATION DOORS WERE open, and the townspeople were buzzing about getting a close-up view of the gleaming fire trucks. Each shift had spent extra time waxing them and shining all the nozzles and levers. Randy's wife, Jessica, baked five-dozen sugar cookies and mixed up plenty of red and green colored icing for the kids to decorate them.

"Thanks for your donations, folks," Randy said. "My niece Penny will put the toys in the appropriate bins, and her helper, Travis, the canned foods."

"Yo, bro, a little help here." Jake's concentration was focused more on Chelsi at the bakery across the street than helping his younger brother. She stepped outside carrying a square white box tied with red and white bakery twine, then ran across the street to the fire station. Today was the first time Chelsi had seen Jake in uniform. He wore his usual navy-blue puffer vest over a long-sleeved blue-collared shirt with Kringle Fire Department embroidered around a fire department shield, and navy-blue cargo pants.

Jake saw Chelsi crossing the street and ran over to her. "Chelsi, what are you doing outside without a jacket on?"

She handed Jake the box. Looking back across the street, she said, "It was like a hundred yards, door to door."

"Penny, please take this box and put it over there on the table," Jake said.

"Sure thing, Daddy." Penny and Travis ran up to her, each giving her big birthday hugs. "Mrs. JoÚson said Travis can come with us when we go to your treehouse."

She looked at Jake, then back at Penny. "That's great, guys! I can't wait for you to see it." Off they hurried to put the box away. "Yeah, about that. Sorry, I forgot to mention it to you this morning. I thought Penny seeing where we spent our childhood days would boost her spirits last night. She was so upset."

Chelsi began to shiver. "You're freezing. Come inside and stand by the heater." Jake took her hand and lead her to the table near where the kids were decorating their cookies. He grabbed a wool blanket from one of the supply lockers and wrapped her up like a sweet, creamy, ricotta-filled cannoli. He rubbed her upper arms, trying to get some warmth back into them.

"Chels, you know Gloria won't be back on her feet for a while. Maybe you can stay and help out through the holidays. Pop doesn't typically rent the Rudolph room." *And I wish you'd stay here with us, forever.*

A gust of wind blew through the open doors of the stationhouse. "Well, my apartment and everything I own is back in Massachusetts. And besides, I haven't left for home yet."

Jake's cell phone vibrated. He looked at the screen and declined the call. "What's in the box that you had to run across the street for, in twenty-degree temperature, without your jacket on?"

"Oh, I baked a kringle! I noticed Gloria didn't have the Danish pastry in her files, so I pulled out Aunt Anne Marie's recipe. After all, we are in the town of Kringle, are we not?"

"Well, you've got a good point there." Jake briskly rubbed his hands together and picked up her hands, sandwiching them between his own. "You're still freezing. You'd—"

"Well, there you are, Jake," said, a familiar-looking woman. She reached inside her flashy designer handbag and removed a small white envelope. "Here's a gift card for your little toy drive, though, I don't know why the parents of Kringle can't simply go out and buy their little darlings Christmas presents." She looked over at Chelsi and pasted a saccharine sweet smile on her ruby-red lips, then turned on the charm. "I've been calling you all afternoon, but you've not answered your phone."

Jake scratched at the stubble on his chin. "Chelsi Burnett, you remember Laura Schaefer from high school, don't you? She was on the debate team with me."

Recognition danced across her face. "Yes, of course. How are you?"

Laura shouldered her way between Jake and Chelsi. "Much better now since Jakers here has returned from living out west." Laura wrapped her right arm around Jake's waist, then possessively tapped his chest with her other hand. "I bring him and darling little daughter, Penelope, food all the time. We've been *utterly* inseparable ever since."

"Bremerton."

"What?" Laura asked, looking mildly confused.

"We moved here from Bremerton, Washington," he said, pulling away from her, "after my wife passed away."

Laura gave him an *I-could-not-care-less* look. "Chelsi, unlike you, I returned right after college. Did you know I own the only real estate business in town?" Laura toyed with the two gleaming diamond bracelets on her left wrist. "And doing quite well too, I might add."

"I thought that was your face I saw plastered on all the for-sale signs around town."

She reached into her pocket and pulled out a business card and handed it to Chelsi. "On your way out of town, back to wherever it is you're living these days, stop by my office. I'll give you a fair price to sell your father's old house."

"That's very generous of you, Laura," Chelsi said.

Moving closer again, Laura said, "Oh, and Jakers, I heard your dad's going to retire. I'm meeting with him after New Year's to discuss selling the B&B. I already have a prospective buyer."

"Boy, that was fast. We only found out yesterday. Hopefully, the inn will be sold to good people."

Laura flicked her hand in a dismissive gesture. "They're not keeping the inn, silly, they're investors. They plan to demolish everything. There's enough property there, between the house, the cottages, and the three-car garage to build an eighteen-hole miniature golf course."

"A what?" Jake and Chelsi said in unison.

"Yup, state of the art. The city has already approved the plans."

Yeah, and it helps that your father is the mayor. "We'll see about that!" said Jake.

"Well, I'd love to stay and chat, but I've got to get back to the bakery." Removing the blanket, she looked from Laura to Jake. "Jake, can you pick me up at two?"

"Of course. Happy Birthday!" he said, kissing her cheek. Jake and Laura watched Chelsi cross the street and disappear into the store.

"So, Chelsi's a little bakery girl. I thought after high school she was jetting off to Paris to study at some famous cooking school."

"Gloria broke her hand. Chelsi's been a huge help to her at the bakery." *Not that it's any business of yours. And Jakers? Come on. We're not in high school anymore.*

Chapter Twenty

LITTLE BLACK DRESS

COCOA RAN TO THE FRONT door, barking.

"How does she do that?" Jake excused himself from visiting with the McIntyres to respond to Cocoa's inquisitiveness as to who—or what—was on the other side of the door. "One minute she's sound asleep, chasing squirrels in her dreams, the next…"

Accompanying their newest guests, snow flurries danced their way into the inn's foyer. "Jasper, Olivia, nice to see you again." Cocoa brushed past Jake sprinting out the door, welcoming her two, four-legged visitors on the front porch. "So, this is what had you on high alert, huh girl?" Jake bent down and ruffled Maximillian and Gwendolyn behind their ears. "And, it's *very* nice to see you two loveable pups again. Cocoa will be happy to have playmates for the evening."

"Please, come in. Chelsi's still getting ready and my dad should be back any minute with Gloria. Penny and the girls are at the kitchen table making Christmas cards for the kids in the hospital. Make yourselves comfortable."

"Pen, please take Dr. Aldridge and Mrs. Winters' coats."

"Coming."

Olivia reached down for Penny's hands. "Oh, what an adorable jumper."

She looked at Olivia quizzically. "Jumper?"

Olivia ran her fingers over the sleeve of Penny's sweater. "Oh yes, of course. We Brits call this... a jumper."

"Oh, thank you," she said, pulling at the sweater's hem. She looked down at the moose head design, which was knit into the pattern. "It was a Christmas gift last year from the JoÚsons. I have a hat just like it."

Jasper reached inside his sport coat pocket and removed a maroon pipe tobacco pouch. After scooping a bit of fresh tobacco into the barrel, he pulled the silky cord, closing the well-worn sack. "Peculiar, when we were at the library the other day, Miss Doyle said it was against the law to smoke inside a public building. How can that even be possible?" Clenching the mouthpiece tightly between his teeth, he tapped down the fresh tobacco with his thumb and lit it. A puff of fragrant smoke released from between his lips as he drew on the mouthpiece.

Jake looked around the room. "*Um,* yes, Jasper, I'm afraid it is a nationwide law, but I'm sure it'll be fine with Pop. He used to smoke a pipe years ago, but Mom made him smoke on the porch."

"On the porch? In winter?"

"'Fraid so."

"Penny, where is young Travis?"

"Travis had some chores to finish before Mr. JoÚson would drive him. Daddy, it's getting late. Can we go and pick him up?"

"No, Pumpkin, I'm sure he'll be along any minute. Besides, Miss Chelsi, our guest of honor, has yet to arrive."

"Did I hear someone say my name?"

Jake turned at the sound of Chelsi's voice, and all the breath whooshed from his lungs. Their eyes locked in a steady gaze as he followed the spectacular beauty slowly descending each step. Jake admired how the cut of her little black dress accentuated her curves. And what curves they were.

I haven't admired the look of a woman in a very long time. I like what I see, and how alive it makes me feel.

He kissed her cheek, reached for her hand, then tucked it into the crook of his arm. "Chels, you look… stunning," he said, and escorted her to greet her guests.

The front door opened and a swish of cold air preceded Randy and Jessica. "Hello, everybody!" they said in unison.

"Hi Uncle Randy, Aunt Jess!" Penny said, giving them quick hugs. She looked over and pointed to Chelsi. "Doesn't Miss Chelsi look beautiful?"

Jessica looked at Chelsi and winked. "She absolutely does."

"Daddy, it's getting really late. Can you *pleeease* pick up Travis?"

"Oh, no need. We saw him turning up the drive when we parked."

The men shook hands with introductions to Jasper and Olivia. Jessica hugged Chelsi, whispering, "So, what did Jake say about your LBD?"

With two fingers, Chelsi grasped the fabric at the side seam, then spun around. "He was speechless, then said I looked stunning."

"As I predicted." The two grown women giggled like junior high school-age girls. "It's only once that you turn the big 5-0."

* * *

"TRAVIS, THIS IS MARY, KATIE, and Jackie. They live in Arizona. Their family's been coming to the inn every Christmas since before my dad and I moved here."

"Hi," he said, somewhat short-tempered. "I moved to Kringle a while back from Long Island."

"We were excited to see it had already snowed here, but we still hope it snows on Christmas Day," Mary, the eldest McIntyre sister, said. "Where we live it hardly ever snows. If we want to go see the snow, it's a two-hour drive up north."

"You drive to go see snow?" he asked, his eyebrows knit together.

"Yes, then we come home and barbeque out by the pool and warm up in the hot tub."

"That's cool if you like that sort of thing."

"Travis, I don't think that was very nice of you to say that. When I lived in Washington, it rained a lot. We don't know what it's like to live in Arizona."

"You're right, Penny. I'm sorry. I got some news before I got here. I should be happy about it, but I'm not."

Penny looked around the kitchen at the girls sitting at the table. "What is it, Trav?"

"Not polite to tell secrets in front of anyone, that's what Mrs. JoÚson always says. I'll tell you later."

Cocoa came into the kitchen with her two guests trotting close behind. Giving her dog head scratchies, Penny asked, "Whatcha looking for, girl?" Max and Gwen sat down and licked their mouths. She put her hands on her hips, trying to look stern. "Now Cocoa, did you tell them there were treats in the kitchen?"

Max let out a low woof, followed quickly by Gwen. "Well, at least you both have manners enough to say please."

"Travis, the doggie treats are on the third shelf in the pantry. Can you please get it down for me? I'm going to make sure it's okay that they have one," Penny asked.

He sat unresponsive at the table.

"Earth to Travis."

"What?" he snapped.

"The dog treats are in the pantry. Please get them for me?"

"Okay! Geez, you don't have to be so bossy!"

Penny rolled her eyes and went to the gathering room. "Mrs. Winters, is it okay if Max and Gwen have a doggie treat?"

"But of course, my dear. I'm sure they would love a biscuit."

"*Um…* which one is which?"

Olivia gave her a slight smile followed by a nod. "The white strip on Max's head is wider and goes farther back than Gwen's."

"Got it," she said, and hurried off.

"Mary?" her mother, Florence, asked, "how would you like to play some Christmas carols while we're waiting for Mr. Jim to arrive. I'm sure everyone would love to hear how much you've improved."

"I'll be right there, Mom. Just let me wash my hands, they're kinda sticky."

"We'll meet you there in a minute," Travis said. "Pen, meet me in the pantry, I've got to show you something."

"Can it wait until after Mary's song?"

He handed Penny a piece of paper folded in thirds. "No. Just read it."

Mr. and Mrs. Johnson,

As you know, the adoption case regarding your foster son, Travis Reid, has been opened. For the past year, a couple has shown growing interest in adopting Travis. It is extremely difficult to find a permanent home for a ten-year-old boy; most couples want a child considerably younger. The prospective adoptive couple's visitation will take place at your home on December 26th from 4 until 6 p.m. I will forward you the prospective adopting parents' information. Upon approval, a court date to be set at a later date.

Yours truly, Emory Addams

USA Adoption, St. Albans, VT.

Penny's eyes closed and her chin sank heavily toward her chest. Her limp arms dropped to her sides like a lifeless rag doll. She stood motionless until her fingertips opened, allowing the heartbreaking letter, Travis's fate, to float to the floor. "St. Albans, Vermont? This can't be happening!"

In a one-page letter, Travis's whole world came crashing down upon his young shoulders. "December 26th? That's in *ten days*, Penny! I don't want to go! I can't leave you. I'll say I'm sick again. I'll run away. That's what I'll do. I'll run away."

* * *

CHELSI LOOKED AROUND THE INN. Everything was perfect. Jake and his younger brother Randy were in the kitchen laughing about whatever it was brothers laugh about, Jasper and Olivia were deep in conversation with the McIntyres, and in the distance, she could hear the kids in the kitchen playing with the three dogs.

"You know, Jess, I've only been back in Kringle a short while, and I can't imagine going back to my other life. This feels so right. It feels like home."

"So, don't leave. Move back into your dad's house. See where your relationship with Jake goes."

Chelsi shrugged. "I didn't know by coming back to Kringle I'd feel so at home. But the night I arrived back I applied to *Le Cordon Bleu*, in Paris. The admissions office said there was a cancellation for this semester and they would fast-track my application. I should get confirmation shortly. The only problem is that I'd have to leave on the 24th. Orientation and classes begin on the 26th."

Jessica looked surprised. "You applied to go to school in Paris? Does Jake know this?"

"I haven't told him yet. I've been so busy here it slipped my mind. But I know it'll break Penny's heart if I don't see her perform at Kringlefest. That's all she's been talking about since I arrived. She even drew me a picture of her singing."

"So, what made you want to study in Paris?"

"It's been my dream ever since I can remember."

"What's been your dream?" Jake sidled up next to Chelsi and his sister-in-law carrying three tall glass mugs of hot mulled cider, each dressed with a twist of orange, fresh cranberries, and a cinnamon stick.

"I'll fill you in later, Jake. After the party."

"Well then, a toast to the birthday girl," he said.

"With many more *Kringle* birthdays to come, I hope." Jess pipped up.

"Jake," Jim said, coming in the back door. "The caterers have arrived, and they could use a hand."

Jake leaned over and kissed the birthday girl. "On it, Pop."

"Gloria, come join everyone in the living room." Jim helped her off with her coat and handed it to Penny.

"I'll be there shortly, Jim. I need to fix my wind-blown hair."

"Oh, Ria… you always look perfect, but if you insist."

Chelsi and Jessica were the only ones left in the kitchen. Running her hands down the front of her dress, Chelsi said, "Thanks for lending me this dress, I noticed it's a J. Hollister original," her voice a mere whisper.

Jessica smiled. Growing up, she loved to design clothes. She'd been sketching outfits from fashion magazines since she was a teenager. She'd use the bodice from one, sleeves from another, then altering the skirt flare, a new creation was born. Six months before her junior prom, Jessica had begun designing her one-of-a-kind formal. Living in a small town, she'd wanted her dress to be like no one else's. The final design had been a bit more grownup than her father had agreed upon, but she was delighted with the final results.

The first semester of her senior year in high school, Jessica applied and was accepted into the Fashion Institute of TecÚology in New York City. After receiving her bachelor's degree in fashion design, she returned to Kringle and her old job waitressing at the diner, until she made up her mind which fashion house to apply to. Randy had proposed to her that summer and encouraged her to spread her wings when she was afraid of taking a business risk. Six weeks after their wedding, the doors to Jessica's Bridal had opened.

* * *

THE CATERERS HAD DONE AN exceptional job setting up the buffet. Jake had made sure to tell them it was a birthday celebration, not Christmas, but couldn't remember Chelsi's favorite color, so he told them to provide pale pink linens.

Jake announced the buffet table was ready to receive guests, making sure Chelsi was first in line for her birthday dinner. He stood behind her, savoring the essence of her. *I know she's a baker, but how does she always smell like... like cherry pie?*

After filling their plates, everyone moved into the gathering room and sat across from the fireplace. Before taking a bite, Jake's gaze lingered on Chelsi's hazel green eyes. Tonight, the flickering glow of the freshly stoked fire reflected golden streaks dancing in her eyes. *I want to burn this image into my memory forever.*

"Daddy, we didn't want to bother you, but Jackie's glass broke. We were sweeping it into the pan when she got a little cut on her hand. It's not bad. We washed it off in the bathroom sink, but I can't find a bandage or the peroxide."

"Thank you, Pen. Please go tell Mrs. McIntyre about the cut and tell her I'll be happy to take care of it."

"Okay, Dad."

Jake slid his hand down Chelsi's arm. "I'll be right back."

"You guys look so good together," Jessica said. "I hope you decide to move back. You can't deny the chemistry between you two. He's totally mesmerized by you, and it's not just the dress."

"I admit I'm happier now than I have been in a really long time."

Jessica's concentration was interrupted by casual glances into the kitchen. Chelsi searched her friend's eyes. Something had changed since they were together earlier in the day. She picked up her partner in crime's hand. "Jess, is everything all right? You seem distracted tonight. What's going on?"

"Nothing we can discuss now, but soon, I promise."

Chelsi was pleased with how quickly their relationship had rekindled. Over thirty years ago, Chelsi and Jessica were high school softball teammates. Jessica on Junior Varsity, Chelsi Varsity.

"Hey, remember when varsity won state your senior year?"

"How can I forget! Our final championship game started late. By the time we boarded the bus for home, coupled with the three-hour drive back, we didn't pull into the school's bus lane until 5:30 a.m."

"And you had to be back at the school for graduation at what, eleven-thirty?"

"Yeah, and none of us got any sleep. I was wondering why my dad was so insistent upon washing my uniform stuff right away. Only to find out Coach Mo called the parents of the four graduates saying Principal Lennon agreed to let us wear our green uniform socks and cleats with our cap and gown to the graduation ceremony."

"That was so cool. Didn't Jake begin his valedictorian speech by congratulating the team?"

"He *did*."

"My senior year, we were eliminated in the final round of regionals. We didn't even come close."

* * *

"HEY PENNY, COME JOIN MARY and the girls in singing Christmas carols. This will allow you to practice your songs for the pageant."

"*Um…* be right there, Dad."

Jasper glanced at Olivia. "Did you hear the tension in Penny's voice?"

"Indeed. I'll go check on her," she said, in a low voice. Olivia crossed the room at a slow pace as to not draw attention to herself.

"Penny, dear, might I have a glass of water?"

"Of course, Miss Olivia."

Penny hopped onto the counter and opened the cupboard door. Olivia placed her hand lightly in the center of Penny's back for safety. "I didn't mean to be such a bother, dear."

"Oh, it's no bother, I do this all the time." She glanced over at Travis. He shook his head slightly as if to tell Penny not to say anything, then folded the piece of paper and stuffed it into his jeans pocket.

"Penny, you seem preoccupied this evening. Is everything all right dear?"

"Preeeeoccupied?"

Olivia stroked Penny's head. "Is anything bothering you, child? You appear troubled."

Travis came up next to Penny and helped himself to a glass of water. "We're okay. Travis had a problem at home, is all. He thinks he's got it taken care of."

Olivia turned to face Travis and touched the young boys' shoulder. "Travis, your future may be brighter than what it appears to be. Trust those who love, guide, and protect you."

"Thank you, Mrs. Winters," Travis said, looking down at the floor. "I'll try."

"Penny! We're all waiting, Mary has finished her warmup scales."

"Coming, Dad, I promise."

"You two get a wiggle on," Olivia said. "You don't want to keep everyone waiting."

"Munch, did you feel all warm and fuzzy inside when Mrs. Winters touched your back?" Travis asked Penny.

"Yeah, you too? I thought it was just me. Whenever I'm near her, I feel like… like it's Christmas morning, and my mommy's in the kitchen making Christmas tree pancakes."

"How does she do *that*?" he asked.

"I remembered she'd mix a few drops of green food coloring into the batter before they went on the griddle. After they were cooked, she'd use a big Christmas tree cookie cutter and cut out as many tree pancakes as she could. My favorite part was the red gumdrops we'd put on for ornaments. Before we sat down to eat, my dad would put on Christmas carols, and we'd sing 'O Christmas Tree.'"

"Sounds like you had a great mom."

"I did, and you will too, *someday*."

When the children were out of sight, Olivia touched her butterfly broach. "Lady Vanessa, please convey a message to Michael. I believe we're going to require the assistance of a twelve-year-old Mikey Shields this evening."

* * *

CHELSI LOOKED AROUND THE ROOM at all the friends who'd come out to celebrate her birthday. Jasper and Olivia were considerably quieter than the night before, but their pooches were happy to have another fur friend to play with, and they devoured the extra attention from the children. Jim and Gloria were so cute together. He watched over Gloria the entire evening, not allowing her to lift a finger. He refilled her beverage, fluffed the pillow under her foot, and brought her seconds of the delicious catered food.

After being married for over twenty years, Randy and Jessica still acted like newlyweds. They adored Penny. Chelsi wondered why they never had any children. Jessica had owned a lucrative business all these years, with a dedicated staff. She would've been free to stay home and raise their children.

Her eyes shifted to the McIntyres. Family traditions. Husband and wife devoted to their three charming young girls. That had been her family too until her mom was diagnosed with breast cancer.

Jim passed around glasses of sparkling wine to the grownups and sparkling cider for the children. "Everyone, let's hear from the birthday girl. Chelsi… if you will."

"Thank you all so much for a lovely evening. I can't remember ever having a more enjoyable adult birthday."

"Here, here," the McIntyres said in unison.

"We're pleased to have been included in such a lovely affair," Jasper said.

"*Feliz Cumpleaños,* Chelsi," Gloria added.

"I'm enjoying my stay back in Kringle more and more every day. Everyone has been so kind. Thank you all for taking the time out of your busy holiday schedules to grant me birthday wishes."

"Any news on your Jeep?" Randy asked.

"Well, oddly enough, the repair shop was only waiting on one part, something having to do with the steering. Since my Jeep is pretty old, they can't seem to locate the part anywhere. The next option is for Carlos to scour the local salvage yards for a used part, but that could take a while."

"And what would the problem with that be?" Jessica asked.

Chelsy shifted her eyes to Jim. "I'm not sure how much longer I can depend on the generosity of the three Hollister men. Jim with taking me in, Jake with carting me around, and Randy for taking on extra shifts."

"I told ya before darlin', stay as long as you need," Jim said.

"But then again, in a few days, I just might have the answer."

"Chels?" Jake asked.

"I wanted to tell you in private, but the opportunity hadn't come up."

"This sounds serious."

"Could be. To see if my application had been approved for Paris." She looked at Jake's dismal expression, then quickly added, "The night I arrived, after we baked Penny's cookies, I applied to *Le Cordon Bleu's* Patisserie Diploma program. It's a sixteen to eighteen-month-long curriculum."

"Paris?" Jake's eyebrows knit together. "I thought you'd given up on Paris."

"But certainly, there are other locations in the States which offer the same type of program?" Gloria asked.

"I'm sure there are, but there's nothing like studying under the blue ribbon of excellence in the culinary arts. My dream was to follow in my aunt's footsteps as proprietress of a B&B with the additional concept of afternoon tea. I live for the day I can frame my credentials and prominently display them in the kitchen of my establishment. My ex-fiancé, Daniel, laughed at me asking why would I want to cater to tea totaling women. Jake celebrated my Paris vision with an Eiffel Tower keychain for my high school graduation gift. When he left for the Navy, he thought I'd be off to Paris."

"Why in tarnation does it look so gloomy in here," Jim said, arriving from the kitchen. "This is a birthday celebration, not a funeral!"

"Excuse me," Jake said, marching out of the room. "I'm going outside for some air."

"Jake, wait! Please don't leave."

He ignored her plea and continued out the front door.

"Chelsi, why is he so angry?"

She looked down at the floor, trying hard to control her emotions. "It's a long story, Jim. But I applied to a culinary school in Paris."

Jim released a long, low whistle. "Paris! Well, that'll do it. No wonder he's upset. I thought you were happy here. I thought you two might—"

"I *am* happy here, Jim. Everyone's been great. I won't be gone forever. Sixteen to eighteen months. Two years tops. Besides, I haven't been accepted yet."

Penny and Travis came into the front room and stopped in front of the cookie tray. "Miss Chelsi, are you're leaving?"

Chelsi walked over to Penny and opened her arms, hugging her undersized body. "I'm not sure yet, sweetie."

"But you can't leave me!" First, my mommy left me, then my grandma. I love you, Miss Chelsi. My daddy and Grampa love you." Her pint-sized voice escalated with each sentence.

Reacting to the commotion, Cocoa trotted in. Her short shadows, Max and Gwendolyn, scampering close behind. "Even Cocoa loves you. We don't want you to leave us. Miss Chelsi. Ever!"

She stroked Penny's hair, then kissed the top of her head. "Peanut, I don't know for sure. But please believe me when I tell you I will love you and your daddy for the rest of my life." Chelsi closed her eyes. *Did I just say, out loud, that I loved Jake?*

Chapter Twenty-One

NEWS FROM PARIS

JAKE COULDN'T BELIEVE HIS EARS. After all this time, the love of his life—yes, he finally admitted to himself that he loved Chelsi, always had, always would—could be leaving him for Paris. Not only had he fallen in love with her, again, but now she'd stolen Penny's heart, too.

He looked up at the sound of the front door closing and footsteps walking towards him. "Isn't it a tad bit cold to be sitting on the porch swing without a jacket?"

Jake continued looking down at the chips in the painted porch floorboards. "No, Pop. I'm pretty heated from what I just heard."

Jim Hollister stood in front of his son and lightly grasped his shoulder. "Well, let me ask you this, son. Have you made your intentions known to her?"

"What are you talking about, my intentions?"

"Don't you dare talk to me in that tone," he said, pointing his index finger. "You know full well what I mean. Do you love her?"

Jake looked up at the feel of his father's penetrating stare on him. Deep-set eyes once hardened with grief from losing the love of his life, now strengthened by the joy he shares with Gloria. "I don't know, Pop. But now it's too late."

"Do you need a swift kick in the rump or at least a push in the right direction? It's *never* too late to tell a woman you love her. Especially if it's Chelsi. She's good for you, son." With a curt nod, he concluded, "She'll do right by you… *and* Penny."

A gust of wind rustled through the barren branches of the inn's Japanese maple tree, sending broken twigs clattering to the ground. "I won't ask her to choose between me and Paris. Heck, I don't even know how she feels about me."

"Well Jake, you won't know 'til you ask her. Now come back to the party. We have guests."

* * *

"DADDY, IS IT CAKE TIME?" Penny's head vigorously bobbed up and down before Jake had the chance to answer her question.

Her father scratched the stubble on the side of his cheek. "Well MuncŠin, I know… there's a breakfast time, lunchtime, and suppertime. Then there's bath and good night time, but I didn't know we had a *cake* time."

Jessica moved closer to Penny. "Jake, it's *always* cake time."

"See, Dad," Penny replied. "I guess it's a girl thing, right?" she whispered to her aunt.

"Well, I guess then it's cake time. Aunt Jess, a little help in the kitchen."

"Yay!" all the kids yelled. "It's cake time!"

The front doorbell chimed.

"I'll get it," Chelsi said, rising from the couch. "It must be Rosaria."

Her black strappy shoes clicking across the hardwood flooring drew everyone's attention to her. Before opening the carved mahogany front door, she looked over at Cocoa and her two dog buddies. The three pooches, content in making short work of their new rawhide bones, showed no interest in joining her.

When Chelsi opened the front door, her friend Rosaria stood there and said, "Chelsi? Is that you?" and extended her arm for a hug. Stepping back, Rosaria picked up Chelsi's hand. She twirled her around, admiring her attire. "Look at you, all fancy-schmancy."

"It's great to see you too, Ro," she said hugging her back. "I have Jake's sister-in-law, Jessica, to thank for this *gorgeous* outfit."

"And I simply adore the new look."

"New look?"

"Ya glasses, girlfriend."

"Oh, yes. I love them, too. Jasper—you'll meet him in a minute—is an optometrist. I broke my glasses in the car accident. The frames, he said, chose me and that my vision will guide me. I didn't understand that at first," she paused and looked around the gathering room, "but now I'm beginning to."

Still dressed in her Country Club at Redfield catering whites, Rosaria handed off a bakery box to Chelsi. "These are for you, birthday girl. I baked ya birthday scones."

"Birthday scones?" asked Gloria.

"Yes, ma'am. I tweaked a recipe I found online."

"I can't wait to try them, Ro, and not a minute too soon. Please, come inside and meet the fam. You're just in time for cake."

Rosaria licked her lips, then rubbed her stomach. "*Mmmm*, cake time, my favorite time of day."

Penny stood next to her father with her hands on her hips. "See Daddy, even Miss Chelsi's friend said there's an official cake time."

"I'm Rosaria Pingerelli," she said, to Penny, extending her hand, "Chelsi here's my best friend. We used to bake together. And who is this lovely young lady?"

Penny accepted Rosaria's offered hand and shook it matter-of-factly. "Miss Rosaria, it's very nice to meet you. You talk funny. I'm Penny Hollister. I have a loose tooth. This is my best friend, Travis Reid. He doesn't have any loose teeth. We're official coat-takers."

"Yes, I do talk funny. Ya see, Penny, I grew up in Brooklyn, New York. In Brooklyn, a lot of us talk this way. Don't forget to put your tooth under your pillow, so the tooth fairy can leave you a surprise. And hello, young Travis. It's my pleasure to make your acquaintance, too," she said.

Penny stood there, impatiently wiggling her fingers, waiting for Rosaria to remove her jacket. "Oh, you're waitin' on my jacket. I see you two take your jobs very seriously."

Handing Penny her jacket, Rosaria added, "But will I get my jacket back at the end of the evening?"

Penny crumpled her face into a questioning look. "My grandpa only hired us to *take* everyone's jackets, not to *return* them, too." And off they went, disappearing without another word.

The grownups all laughed.

"Please, darlin', show her in." Jim stood and patted the seat he just vacated. "There's a spot here, right next to my Gloria."

"Sure, Jim. Come on, Ro, I'll introduce you around."

In the foyer, Rosaria slipped off her snow boots, revealing a pair of hot-pink Christmas socks. They were covered with sparkly snowflakes, decorated Christmas trees, and the likeness of Rudolph catching snowflakes on his tongue. Rosaria followed Chelsi through the gathering room, stopping first to warm herself by the fire. Jake stood and offered his hand, but she waved it off and pulled him into an affectionate bear hug. "Nice to finally meetcha, Jake."

He smiled at the sound of her accent. Memories of Marisa Tomei, in the classic movie, *My Cousin Vinny*, instantly came to mind. "Nice to meet you too, Brooklyn."

"Who'd think after fifteen years of livin' in Massachusetts I'd still sound like I did when I was growing up in Brooklyn?"

"Go figure," Jake said, teasingly.

"Rosaria, tell me about your family," Olivia asked.

"Back in the day, my grandparents saved every penny they could and moved from Palermo, Italy to Brooklyn. They opened an Italian deli on Flushing Avenue not far from the Brooklyn Navy Yard. One afternoon, this *really* handsome twenty-four-year-old sailor walked into my grandparents' deli. Papa was busy so he called my mom out from the back to wait on customers. The sailor ordered a sausage and pepper hero with two meatballs on the side. The rest, as they say, is history."

"That's quite a memorable meeting," Jasper said. "I hope, one day, we get to visit this infamous Brooklyn."

Rosaria smiled. "At their twenty-fifth wedding anniversary party, my dad toasted to the love of his life. He confessed when he first met her, he thought she was 'quite a dish.' Mom said she was instantly attracted to his broad smile, brown wavy hair peeking out from his squared-off sailor's cap, and his smoldering, Robert Mitchum eyes."

Jake smiled at the thought of a young sailor meeting his prospective bride in a delicatessen. He remembered being too career-focused until the accident ended his Naval career. *Whoever said the way to a man's heart is through his stomach is one-hundred-percent correct.*

Jake never thought he'd open his heart again to love after the loss of Amelia, but his main focus was protecting Penny. He'd do anything to make sure she didn't get hurt, but he was afraid she'd already become too attached to Chelsi. He saw the void in his daughter's life. She needed a mother, and Chelsi would make a darn good one. As a husband, all he had to offer her is this broken-down man, with a hole in his heart the size of a fist. But he loved her too much to interfere with her dreams of Paris.

* * *

CHELSI HANDED ROSARIA A GLASS of hot mulled cider and a plate of food. "Sorry, Ro, there's not much left. So, how's work going?"

Spirited, she held up her hand in the stop position and shook her head. "Don't *even* get me started! Ever since ya left, Daniel's been a complete…" Stopping before Rosaria finished her sentence, she looked at the children within earshot. "… completely impossible to work with."

She paused long enough to scarf down a bit of her dinner. "This is delicious, Chels. Is it one of your aunt's recipes?"

"No, Jake didn't want me to cook. He had it catered in from a local restaurant. But I have been working these past few days in Gloria's bakery during her absence, perfecting some new recipes."

"The Kringle Bakery? Oh, my, goodness, it's so adorable! I rubbernecked at it the whole way through town."

"I agree. I love the lace window treatments in the bay window, and wait 'til you see the interior. The other day, I made a kringle pastry. After all, it is our town's name."

Our town. Chelsi couldn't believe how easily that rolled off her tongue. "So, who did Daniel replace me with?"

"The afternoon you left, he interviewed, then hired a pastry chef, if you can call him that. Randolph's from another catering hall. This whole week he came in late and left early. All he does is order us around. Daniel doesn't seem to mind 'cause ya know, he's got…" Rosaria cleared her throat, "talent? Well, if you ask me, he has no business being in a kitchen. To pick up his slack, we've been putting in twelve-to-fourteen-hour-days, with no time off! Half the bakers have already quit, with two more threatening."

Gloria looked stunned at Rosaria's description of her workplace. "They can't do that—it's against the law."

"We know that, hon, but the pay is diddly-squat, and we're all desperate for the OT."

Chelsi put her arm around Rosaria's shoulder. "My savings aren't going to last forever, but I haven't missed that place for one second." She planted a kiss on her friend's cheek. "Except for you, of course."

Rosaria looked from the gathering room, through to the kitchen. "Jim, how many rooms do you have?"

"Seven, plus two cottages out back that Jake and I usually occupy," he said. "We have another young couple arriving tomorrow afternoon. Then we'll be full up."

"Jim, I'll be more than happy to return to my house tomorrow, if you need another room. My knee's feeling much better," Gloria said.

"Nonsense, darlin', I've enjoyed your company these past few days. We'll manage just fine."

A train whistle sounded from Chelsi's cell phone, announcing she had a new message.

"Excuse me a minute. I've been waiting for an email."

Chelsi unlocked her phone—and her eyes widened. "It's from *Le Cordon Bleu*!"

Staring at the unopened message, she whispered, "This is it." The room went silent; not even the logs in the fireplace dared to crackle.

"Why is it so quiet in here, Daddy?" Penny asked.

Jake looked up to see all the kids standing in the doorway of the kitchen.

"Miss Chelsi is waiting to see if she was accepted into her special cooking school, Pumpkin."

"The one that's far away? In Paris?"

"'Fraid so."

Penny climbed on her father's lap while the rest of the kids sat on the floor.

Chelsi's hands were shaking. She looked around the room, then clicked on her message. All eyes were locked on her, waiting to hear the outcome. Adjusting her glasses higher on her the bridge of her nose, she read through the documents. Her jaw dropped open, then snapped shut. Stuttering, she said, "I… I got in!"

A rising round of celebration and cheer erupted in the front room.

"Nooooo!" Penny yelled, scrambling to her feet. "I don't want you to go!"

"That's great, Chels," Rosaria said. "So, when do you leave?"

She scanned the itinerary, then closed her eyes. "Ro, my flight leaves from Kennedy on the 24th."

"But you can't leave then! It's Kringlefest. You'll miss my pageant and Christmas!" Penny cried.

Travis took Penny by the hand. "Come on, Munch, let's go inside and work on the puzzle. It's almost done."

"No, I don't want to work on the puzzle. I'm bored with that now. And, don't call me Munch!"

"Trav, it's almost nine, and I promised the JoUsons I'd have you home by nine-thirty," Jake said. "In the meantime, how about you get the playing cards out from the pantry and play a few hands of rummy."

"Sure thing, Mr. H., but you don't have to take me home, I rode my bike."

"Nonsense," Randy said. "You shouldn't be out this late on your bike. Jess and I are ready to go. I'll load your bike in the back of my truck and have you home on time."

"But I want to hear more about Paris," Jessica said.

Randy jerked his head in the direction of the door. "We should head on out now. I have an early shift tomorrow, remember?"

"It's best we get going too, Livy," Jasper said. "You know the dogs rise before the crack of dawn."

"Penny, will you and Travis bring everyone their coats?" Jake asked.

"But—"

"Now please, Penny."

"Okay, Dad," she said with a huff.

Travis followed Penny to the laundry room where all the coats were stored. "Penny," he whispered, "when no one was looking, I put a bag of snacks out on the back porch. I'll be back around eleven and stuff it in my backpack."

"Are you sure you still want to do this, run away and all?" she asked.

"Yes, if I get adopted and move away, we'll never see each other again. You saw what's happening to your dad and Miss Chelsi. I don't want that to happen to us."

"But where will you—"

"Penny! Everyone's waiting for their coats. Please get a move on."

Piling the last of the coats onto Travis's arms, she sang out, "On our way."

"I'm coming with you. I'll show you a shortcut to Miss Chelsi's house."

"Are you sure you want to? I'll understand if you don't."

Jake came into the laundry room. He looked from Penny to Travis, then back to Penny. "What's going on in here?"

She crossed her fingers behind her back, knowing she was telling a lie. "*Um…* walk around with Travis after the tree lighting. *Um…* he wants us to share a bag of kettle corn."

"We'll talk about that tomorrow."

Jake put his hand on Travis's shoulder. "Everyone is waiting for you in the foyer."

"Sorry, Mr. Hollister. Night, Pen."

"Night, Trav."

Jasper helped the ladies with their coats, then donned his own. Shaking hands, he said, "Jim, thank you for such a special evening."

"Yes, thank you all, it was lovely," Olivia added.

Jasper turned to Chelsi. "My dear, do not brood. You are *not* wedged in the ruts of your destiny. You *do* have the power to break free, change your vision and see a whole new life for yourself. Look in front of you for your future, not behind."

Chapter Twenty-Two

A SHADOW IN THE STREETLAMP

"WHAT IS IT, GIRL?" COCOA had woken Jake up from a sound sleep. Bleary-eyed, he looked at the bedside clock. "This better be good. It's not even one a.m."

To hurry Jake along, she let out a low woof. "I'm coming, I'm coming," he said, jumping into his sweatpants. "If you know what's good for you, you'd best not wake up the entire house. We have guests, in case you've forgotten."

Cocoa sprinted down the hallway, her paws muffled by the thick carpeted flooring. She stopped and nuzzled Penny's door open. Jake heard Penny's guinea pig, Whiskers, busily running on the exercise wheel inside her cage. Cocoa pawed at his daughter's bed. "Easy girl. Penny's asleep, you goof ball, but I'll check on her if it'll make you feel better."

During cold nights, Penny would hunker down toward the bottom of the bed and burrow her head under the plush comforter, like a hibernating turtle. Trying not to wake her, Jake carefully moved her covers down to uncover her face. His breath caught in his chest. Instead of uncovering his daughter peacefully snoring away, her unoccupied bed revealed a row of pillows neatly aligned to look as if she were asleep.

"What the hell?" He threw back the covers, wildly picked up each painstakingly positioned pillow, and flung them onto the floor. "Penny, what have you done!"

The hallway light switched on. The sound of quick footsteps padded down the hallway, or was it the sound of his heart pounding? He looked up from the dimly lit room to see Chelsi's silhouette standing in the doorway. "Jake, what is it?"

"Penny's not in her bed. I have to call the police."

"Oh, my goodness! I'll get dressed."

* * *

JESSICA HOLLISTER ENTERED THE FOUR-DIGIT security passcode into her smartphone and scrolled through the long list of contacts. She looked over at Randy driving, his eyes darting from one side of the street to the other. "Do we have an after-hours number for the adoption agency? I think we should notify Emory that Travis is missing."

"I spoke with Erik JoÚson before we left the house about the disappearance of his foster son. He said he'd contact the answering service immediately." Jessica reached down and picked her handbag up off the floor. Placing it on her lap, she unzipped a side section and slipped her cell phone safely away. Randy looked over at his wife's unsettled demeanor, then reached over and squeezed her knee. "It's just a matter of time before we find them."

He made a right turn onto Main Street and drove slowly through the center of town. Except for the diner and the historic Kringle Hotel, all the shops were buttoned up tight. Double parked, they perused the last of the moviegoers heading toward their cars.

"Won't Penny and Travis be surprised to hear they'll soon become cousins?"

No answer.

"Jess?"

Not wanting her husband to see her cry, Jessica turned her head and looked out the passenger side window.

Randy cleared his throat, breaking the deafening silence. "*Ahem*. Receiving a copy of the letter yesterday from the adoption agency was reassuring. These past ten months since we had begun the adoption proceedings for Travis, the time seemed to have dragged on forever. So many interviews. So many forms. But within a few weeks, Travis will officially be our son."

"Too bad we couldn't tell him at the party tonight. Maybe then we wouldn't be searching for them now." Jessica gave in to her runny nose and reached into the glove box for a tissue.

"I don't get it," Randy said. "He's an intelligent boy. What devastated him so much to cause him and Penny to run away?"

He glanced over at the clock… then down, to the outside temperature gauge. Twenty-nine degrees and still falling. Below freezing. He made a right turn off Maple Lane, then south towards Lexington Avenue. Kringle's familiar four-story, redbrick building came into view.

Jessica's eyes widened. "The hospital? Randy, are we checking the hospital?"

* * *

JIM HOLLISTER PACED BACK AND forth between the inn's gathering room and the kitchen for what seemed to be the hundredth time. He removed the mug from the kitchen table and ran his calloused thumb over the personalization, 'Grandpa's Cup.' Hoping for a refill, he poured its dregs into the sink, then removed the glass pot from the coffeemaker's warming plate.

"Damn," he said, forcefully returning the almost empty carafe onto its base. "What's keeping them? Why haven't we heard something yet?"

"Jim, we'll hear something shortly. I'm sure Jake wants to keep the phone lines open," Gloria said, rinsing the coffeepot. "Here, let me make us another pot."

Jim put his arm around Gloria's waist, pulling her closer to him. He leaned in and kissed her forehead. "You're probably right."

"Say, after I put the pot up, let's take Cocoa out for a quick walk. I think the fresh air will do us both good."

At the sound of her name, and the word *out*, the dog stood up, walked to the back door, and let out a low woof.

"Simmer down, now girl. Give Gloria a few minutes here." Cocoa laid back down and let out a long yawn.

Florence McIntyre stood at the entrance of the kitchen dressed in her robe and slippers. "Did I hear you say you were making fresh coffee?"

"You sure did."

"Might it be decaf, by any chance?" she asked.

"Not this pot, Florence, but I'll join you in a cup of decaf." Gloria opened the kitchen cabinet and removed the canister of ground decaf beans, along with the coffee mug that had been Florence's favorite since they'd arrived.

"Jim, please get the four-cup coffee pot from the pantry."

"Thanks, but I think I know where the kitchen appliances are in my own house." Jim opened the door to the walk-in pantry closet and removed the coffee maker from the shelf. Jane Hollister had a thing for kitchen gadgets. If it plugged in to an electrical outlet or made prepping breakfast for the many Snowberry Inn guests easier, his wife had to have it.

"Sorry, ladies, I'm a mite crusty tonight." He placed the coffee maker on the counter and plugged the cord into the outlet. He brought tonight's leftover dessert to the table and gave his best attempt at a smile. "Might as well finish off the remainder of Chelsi's birthday cake. Don't think she'll mind too much."

Cocoa stood at the kitchen's backdoor and whined.

"Okay, okay, hold your horses, girl." Jim removed his jacket from the coat rack in the laundry-room and shrugged it on. Removing the dog's leash from the doorknob, he said, "Ladies, will you please excuse me for a few minutes while I take Cocoa out to do her business? Gloria… rain check?"

"Certainly."

Cocoa sat patiently while Jim attached her leash to the pink collar around her neck, then danced around in circles, waiting for him to unlock the door.

Jim sent a wink to Gloria and closed the back door.

"He sure is sweet on you, Gloria," Florence said, taking her seat at the table.

"I know. Isn't it wonderful? Our love grew over this past year. We don't even know when it started. It just happened."

The familiar aroma of fresh brewing coffee permeated the inn's kitchen. "It was only a few days ago we went on our first *official* date." For emphasis, Gloria performed double air quotation marks. "He casually asked me to accompany him to the hotel's opening night of "Angels on Assignment, A Journey of Love." I accepted and shamelessly suggested we grab a bite to eat beforehand."

"Atta girl," Florence said. "These men of ours are so oblivious at times. Before I turned fifty, my hair had begun to turn grey. As it progressed, my hairdresser suggested highlights to camouflage it. A week went by, and Joe *still* hadn't noticed the new highlights."

Gloria shook her head. Florence poured two steaming mugs of decaf and divvied up the last of the cake. Leaving Jim's on the counter, she carried both mugs in one hand, their dessert-laden plates in the other.

"One evening, Joe and I were in line at our local grocery story. My favorite cashier, C.C., complimented me on the new highlights. Joe got this goofy look on his face, and said, you highlighted your hair?"

Laughing, Gloria raised her mug and they toasted to men's lack of observation.

* * *

"WHAT'S GOING ON WITH YOU, girl? Why are you tugging so dog-gone hard on your leash?" Jim chuckled at his comment to Cocoa about how hard she was pulling him. "Looks like you're hot on the trail of something."

Unyielding, Cocoa forced Jim to cross the street and cut through a neighbor's yard. "*Hmmm…* Interesting." He ducked his head low, shifting his eyes from one side of the yard to the other. "Gotta be important to you if you're making me cut across someone's yard," he whispered. "It's late enough, but I sure hope no one catches us."

Jim and Cocoa emerged, undetected, onto the next street. "We'd better call home Cocoa or the soon-to-be Mrs. will think twice about letting me put a ring on her finger." Jim tapped his front pocket for his cell phone. Then back pockets. Finally, his jacket pockets. No phone. "Great! Must've left my cell phone on the hearth in the gathering room."

Cocoa abruptly jerked the leash from Jim's firm grip. "Hey! Who's walking who?"

Taking full strides, the determined dog ran ahead, dragging the unencumbered leash behind her. She stopped, picked something up, then sat down. Jim raised his voice above what he should have at this time of night. "Now, what was so confounded important that you nearly dislocated my bum shoulder to get to it?"

One porchlight flickered on. Then another. A flashlight beam focused on Jim's face. "Everything okay out here?" the homeowner asked.

Jim raised his hands to eye level, blocking the shaft of light which temporarily blinded him. "Sorry to wake you, sir. I was walking my dog and she pulled away from me is all."

"Okay, well, goodnight."

Jim looked over at Cocoa, then whistled. "Well, come here, girl. Let's see whatcha got."

She trotted back, sat down, and presented him with her prize.

"Good girl," he said, patting the dog's head. Staring in disbelief, he removed the recognizable item out from Cocoa's tender hold.

"Is this Penny's doll, Rosie?"

"*Woof!*" barked the dog.

He wiped some debris from the doll, then turned it over. Jim Hollister clenched the cloth doll tighter and tighter until his hand was balled into a tight fist.

"Blood?"

* * *

JAKE PUT THE VEHICLE INTO park, barely waiting for it to come to a complete stop. He slammed his palm on the steering wheel. "What the hell were they thinking? *Everyone* is out there searching for them!"

"They're on foot, Jake, and couldn't've gotten very far. When I spoke to Fern JoÚson, she said Travis's bike was still in the garage. It's just a matter of time before someone finds them."

He glanced at the digital clock on the truck's dashboard. "We've been combing the streets for over an hour." Restless, he reached inside his vest pocket and pulled out his cell phone. Pushing the home button for what seemed to be the hundredth time, he clicked his tongue. "Still no word." His mind wandered to when Cocoa was a puppy and she dug a hole under the fence, escaping the backyard. He'd driven for an hour searching the neighborhood for their family pet. But this time, the stakes were much higher. This time, his daughter had gone missing.

"It's all my fault! When I asked Penny to get the coats, she and Travis were in the kitchen. They looked like they were plotting something. I asked her if everything was okay. She said it was. I should've known. I should've pushed harder."

"You can't beat yourself up like this, Jake. Someone will find them, or maybe they'll just come home."

Chelsi snapped her fingers, then pointed to Jake. "Home! That's it! Why didn't I think of it sooner?" She settled back into her seat. "Jake… let's go!"

He looked over at her, put the vehicle into drive, and sped off. "Chelsi, what's going through that beautiful mind of yours?"

She chuckled. "Jake, take the next left. My house. I'll bet they went to my house."

He slid his cell phone back into his pocket. "But we've already been through your neighborhood… twice."

"Yeah, but we never went around back." Folding her arms across her chest, she continued. "More specifically… the treehouse. Remember, I promised to take them this week. Take the shortcut, you remember, through Dooley Farm."

"Like we used to when we were kids walking home from school?"

"Uh-huh."

Jake reached over and squeezed her hand. "Chels, I could kiss you right now."

"Okay, lover boy, let's wait for the kissin' to commence until *after* the kids are tucked safely in their beds."

Jake turned right on Marion Avenue, then through the entrance of Dooley Family Farm. Clusters of dried corn stocks flanked the weathered black and white sign. Jake remembered Dean Dooley, the family's youngest son, hand-painting the sign one summer. It was the first day of a week-long summer basketball camp. Dean rebounded, came down awkwardly and broke his ankle, sidelining him from basketball for the entire summer.

Chelsi looked over at Jake. He was strumming his thumbs against the steering wheel, eyes fixed on the vast snow-covered field ahead of him. "What's wrong with the truck?" she asked.

"Huh?" Jake looked down at the truck's instrument panel. The tire icon flashed red. "Damn! I think we've got a flat. We could've run over *anything* on this dormant field."

Jake put the truck in park and left the ignition running. "Stay in the truck where it's warm."

He exited the truck. A minute later, he heard the sound of the ignition being turned off and Chelsi standing right behind him.

Handing him the trucks keys, she pointed to her feet. "Boots."

He opened his cell phone and clicked on the flashlight to better see the rear tire. "Will you look at that." He kicked the tire where a chunk of wire had penetrated the sidewall. "That tire's shot."

"Do you have a spare?"

"Yeah, it shouldn't take me too long to change it." Jake turned to face Chelsi. "Hop back into the truck and *stay there* this time."

She stood there and waited for Jake to open her car door. She'd become accustomed to his thoughtfulness. Randy had displayed the same respect toward Jessica at the party. Their mama had certainly trained her boys right. "Okay, if you insist."

Clutching the inside grab handle, Chelsi pulled herself up. Something caught her attention. "Hang on a sec." She stood on the running board and adjusted her glasses, focusing on an area further down the farm. "Jake, I think I see footprints."

He looked out on the moonlight field. "Where?"

"Over there. At the top of the ridge, to the right of the headlight beams." She jumped down and pointed back and forth. "Ya see? Right there. Two sets. They're heading for that clearing between the trees."

"Huh. Well, I'll be." He licked his lower lip. "Now I really will kiss you." Jake took Chelsi's hand. He spun her around and gripped her tightly in his arms. Cradling the back of her head against the palm of his hand, Jake pulled her toward him, closing the gap between them. He kissed her. A kiss that was firm... and fabulous.

Jake broke away first from the kiss. In a breathless whisper, he said, "Now, let's go find those crazy kids."

Chelsi shook her head and let out a long breath.

Jake jogged around to the other side of the truck, opened the door, and retrieved a high-powered flashlight from the console. Switching it on he held out his hand. "Come on Chels, let's follow the footsteps and pray they lead us to Penny and Travis."

"But what about the truck?"

He kissed the back of her hand. "I'll fix the flat later." Hand in hand, they cut across the field, eyes fixed on the meandering footprints.

* * *

JAKE LOOKED OVER AT CHELSI. Having her by his side felt so natural. So right. Even amidst this crisis, Chelsi remained calm and helped him stay focused. Not even Amelia possessed these qualities. His late wife was a vision of beauty... a compassionate soul. Jake's very own Florence Nightingale. Or so he thought. The day after the surgeon put his leg back together, Jake remembered her accompanying the doctor during morning rounds. A freak accident aboard ship kept him stateside for the remainder of his active tour. Lieutenant Amelia Jenkins, a Navy Physical Therapist, was assigned to Jake for his three-month rehabilitation at Bremerton Naval Hospital in Washington. His first impression of her was beautiful and compassionate. Until... his first rehab session. Then, well, she was still beautiful, but about as compassionate as an escaped birthday balloon coming in contact with the unforgiving, needle-sharp point of a rosebush thorn. Vulnerable meets invincible.

"Have you noticed how similar the friendship between Penny and Travis is to when we were their age growing up?"

Chelsi's words, echoed by visible wisps of cold air in the bright moonlight, brought Jake's thoughts back to the present. "Yeah, at least *we* didn't run away in the middle of the night, *in* the dead of winter. If we did something *that* crazy, my dad would've taken me behind the garage and given me the 'what for', for scaring the heck out of my mom."

"Ouch! And I bet Randy would've loved to have seen the effects that punishment had on his perfect older brother."

Jake rubbed his backside. Oh, believe me, we each had our fair share of, um… discipline."

"Say, did you know Travis has a nickname for Penny?" she asked. "It's super cute."

Jake knit his eyebrows together and turned to Chelsi. "He has a nickname for my daughter?"

"Yeah, Einstein, just like we did."

"Well, don't keep me in suspense."

"Munch."

"Munch, what?"

She rolled her eyes. "Jake, Munch is his nickname for Penny."

"Why Munch?"

Chelsi put her free hand over her heart, then dragged Jake to a stop. "Did you see that?"

Jake looked around. "See, what?"

"A shadow. In the streetlamp. Jake, give me the flashlight."

To steady her shaking hand, Chelsi gripped the flashlight with both hands and shined the beacon of light ahead of them. "There!" she yelled. "That's them! I'm sure of it!"

"Penny?" Jake yelled. "Penny, Travis, are you there?"

Penny stopped and grabbed Travis's jacket sleeve. "Huh?"

"What?"

"Is that my daddy?" she said, above a whisper.

"Travis! Penny!" They both yelled in unison.

Porchlights illuminated. One after the other, after the other.

"Daddy?" Penny screeched, then raced in the direction of her father's voice.

Rapidly closing the gap, Penny jumped into her father's waiting arms. Jake swung her around and around. *Thank you, God! For keeping my baby safe.* He didn't know what he would've done if any harm had come to her.

"Daddy! I was so scared," she said, crying into her father's shoulder.

He kissed the top of his daughter's head. "I'm here baby, I'm here. We were all so worried. Are you okay?"

"I'm okay, but I lost Rosie."

"Travis?" Jake asked.

He lowered his head to his chest. "I'm okay, too, Mr. Hollister."

Chelsi walked over to Travis. She put her arm around the top of his shoulder, rubbing it. More so for her contentment than his.

"I'm sorry, Mr. Hollister. This is all my fault."

"There'll be plenty of time later to discuss who is… or is not, at fault. Right now, we have several calls to make. There's a lot of folks very concerned about your whereabouts."

"Yes, sir."

"Chels, please call Erik JoÚson and tell him that Travis is safe. Also, I'd be happy to drive him home after we fix the flat. Or if they prefer, they can meet us at the truck. I'll call my dad on his cell. I'm surprised we hadn't heard from him all night. He'll notify everyone at the inn that the children have been found."

"And don't forget Randy."

He looked back and forth between Penny and Travis. "No, I haven't forgotten. He'll be the next one I notify."

Jake looked up and sent another message of thanks to the heavens above for the safe return of these two children. He could never imagine his life without his precious daughter. Or Chelsi.

Penny looked up at Jake, her little mouth drawn into a tight, thin line. "*Um…* Daddy? Do you remember, a few days ago you said you'd put a change of clothes for me in your truck before went to Kringlefest. Just in case?"

"Yeah, why?"

"I *sure* could use them now. This time Daddy, I really *did* wet my pants."

Chapter Twenty-Three

THE ATTIC

"GOOD MORNING, SUNSHINE." THE BOX spring on Penny's bed squeaked when Jake sat on the edge of her bed. He loved watching her sleep–so young, so innocent—but he couldn't wait any longer to find out why his daughter felt the need to run away last night.

"*Mmm...* mornin', Daddy." She sat up and flung her arms tightly around her father's neck. "I'm sorry, Daddy. I really didn't mean to run away last night. I was only showing Travis the shortcut to get to Miss Chelsi's house. He was going to hang out in her treehouse until he figured things out."

"So you said last night. What you *did* do was called sneaking out, and you scared us to death. But why?"

"At Miss Chelsi's party, Travis showed me a letter Mr. and Mrs. JoÚson got from an adoption agency. It said there was a couple interested in adopting him, and he was going to meet them on the 26th. They live all the way in St. Albans."

"St. Albans, huh? And Travis took a letter addressed to the JoÚsons to the party? Is that what you were doing when everyone was waiting for their coats?"

Penny crawled out from underneath her covers and sat on her father's lap. "Yes."

"Why did Travis bring the letter?"

"I don't know," she answered, sniveling, "but I was very sad when I found out Miss Chelsi was leaving. Is she really going all the way to Paris?"

"I don't—"

A knock sounded on her bedroom door. "Is Penny feeling up to building a snowman with us?"

"Thanks for checking on her, Jackie. Maybe after she's had breakfast."

"Okay."

"So… Travis was going to hide away in Miss Chelsi's treehouse? What made you two decide to come home?"

"Mikey."

Jake's blinked several times. "Who's Mikey?"

"This kid we met at the treehouse. He said his name was Mikey Shields. He was a little older than us, said he was just passing through. Daddy, his clothes were ratty and he had no socks on under his sneakers!"

"He didn't hurt you, did he?"

"Oh, no! I felt very safe. He said he was hungry, so Travis shared his PB and J with him. He had a really cool bike that he did tricks on. Mikey said he'd been on his own before and had been to juvie. And, if we didn't get home soon, the police would arrest us for breaking curfew *and* Travis would get twice the sentence 'cause he brought me along with him. Do you know they give you an orange jumpsuit, sneakers with no laces, and pink tighty-whities to wear when you go to juvie?"

"*Hmmm…* Juvie, huh?" *I'll have the police run an inquiry on him.*

"I was glad to go home. I was cold and had to pee really bad. That's why when you swung me around, I wet my pants."

"Let's go downstairs and have some breakfast. You know, Penny, you can *always* come and talk to me about anything, got it?"

"Promise," she said, crossing her heart.

At her doorway, Penny stopped. "Daddy, what are 'tighty-whities'?"

"Huh?" Jake shook his head. "Oh, old-style men's cotton underwear." He kissed his little girl on the top of her head. "That's my girl."

* * *

WHEN JAKE PULLED UP IN front of the Kringle Bakery, Chelsi was tucked tightly into the alcove of the bakery waiting for him. The sun was out, but the wind had picked up throughout the day, with gusts so intense that, at times, Jake's truck was knocked about.

Even with her winter jacket pulled tightly under her chin, Chelsi was so chilled she didn't wait for Jake to open her car door. She ran to the truck, closed the door, then leaned over and gave Jake a quick kiss on the side of his cheek. "Thanks for picking me up early today. I want to get back to my house to continue my search."

"No problem. I got a text earlier today from my connection with the power company. He said due to the power outage from the last storm, they're still running behind with reconnects but promise to be out first thing tomorrow. And as far as I know, the water has been turned on today. Make sure you run the sinks a while to flush out the lines and fill up the toilet tanks."

"Will do. How's Penny this morning?"

"She's doing okay. We had a good talk this morning. I know she doesn't understand the severity of her actions now, but will someday. I hope! They forgot to cover this kind of stuff in dad school."

Chelsi looked surprised. "They have such a class?"

He winked at her. "No, not really. It was a joke between me and Amelia. I'd ask her how she knew how to do something, and her response was, 'I learned it at mom school.'"

Jake pulled up in front of Chelsi's house. They both stared at the front of it, then Jake turned his head and looked across the street to his old house. "We had good times growing up here, didn't we?"

"The best! Except for Mom passing away, it was the best childhood I could ever hope for."

Rubbing her shoulder, he asked, "Are you sure you'll be okay on your own this afternoon? I can tell dad I'll be back later."

"Nope, I'll be fine. But I appreciate it, though. See ya later." Walking up the front walk, a gust of wind was so strong, Chelsi had to grab onto the stoop's wrought-iron railing for balance.

She hung her jacket on the coat rack and went into the kitchen to turn on the faucet. The water sputtered and spit, then ran at a steady stream. She took a bowl from the cupboard, then headed to the bathroom to fill the toilet tanks. Because she didn't expect to be there too long, she didn't build a fire.

Chelsi stood in the doorway of her parents' bedroom. "Okay, Dad, let's see what else you and Mom have hidden regarding my biological mother."

She checked under the bed. There was nothing there but a lone discarded sock and some dust bunnies. The nightstands on either side of the bed were also empty. "Where to next? Guess I should check the attic for boxes."

The attic entrance was hidden inside the upstairs closet next to the hall bathroom. Chelsi opened the door. At the back of the closet was a wooden panel held up by two, two-inch hook and eye latches. She flipped the hooks, one at a time, and grabbed hold of the panel on either side, lowering it out of the closet. She hadn't been inside the attic since high school and hoped she would still be able to hoist herself up onto the attic flooring.

After only two attempts, she was finally successful. Chelsi was able to stand up in the attic, but needed to be careful of the low trusses. She flinched at the sight of several petrified squirrels who'd decided their attic would be a great place to keep warm for the winter.

Using her cell phone for light, she flipped the covers open from the top box, revealing only Christmas tree decorations. She put that one off to the side. The same with the next and the next.

She spied an old black steamer trunk. How the heck had her dad gotten that thing up here? Outside, the wind howled through the attic air vents, and tree limbs scratched against the roof as if they were begging to be let in.

Along one wall lay her family's camping gear. Her dad must've carefully walked each item to the side, for there was no plywood flooring underneath. "None of this is any good now. Why didn't Dad get rid of this stuff years ago?"

Something moved and her breath hitched in her throat. Mice? Squirrels? Ghosts from her past? Not thinking, she threw her water bottle in the direction of the noise. Two mice scurried out from between the boxes, and Chelsi let out a little scream.

Not too smart, Burnett.

As carefully as possible, Chelsi went down on all fours and shimmied across two beams to reclaim her bottle, which had landed between the wall and the camping gear. She lifted one sleeping bag and tossed it to the side. Thankfully, no more critters jumped out, but underneath her bottle, something colorful caught her eye.

"What the heck?" Moving another sleeping bag, she was able to scoot closer to the object. *Is that my Hello Kitty lunch box? Why has it been hidden all these years?*

She tucked it under her arm and crawled backward, retracing her steps. Sitting on the plywood walkway, she took a quick swig of her water, then flipped the latch and opened the lid. "Letters?"

A ruthless gust of wind, followed by what Chelsi thought was thunder, slammed unsympathetically against the house.

Boom!

Craaaaccckkkk!

Thud!

Pop! Sizzle!

* * *

BEEP, BEEP, BEEP, BEEP—

The alarm tone Jake had set for emergencies at the fire station went off on his cell phone. He pulled out his phone and quickly read the text: Utility pole down. 28 Cottage Lane. Live wires. Roof compromised. Occupants to be determined.

"*28* Cottage Lane? That's Chelsi's house!" Jake called the dispatch officer at the station.

"Barbara! Hey, Barbara, are you sure it's 28 Cottage Lane?"

"Yup, a neighbor called it in. Mrs. Wagner was in her room reading when she heard a clap of thunder, then a deluge of sleet. When she looked out her window a bolt of lightning had hit the wooden utility pole splintering it. Said it was the Burnett house. Jake. Jake?" But Jake had already disconnected the call.

"Come on, Chelsi, answer. Answer!" But it went straight to voice mail. "Her phone's dead. I'm on it." Jake ran to Penny.

Emotions sliced through Jake's heart like a steak knife through butter. It was the same feeling he had experienced when the paramedics called him that evening informing Jake his wife was involved in an accident.

"Penny, I've got to go. There's been an accident at Chelsi's house. Stay with Grandpa."

Penny looked up at Jake, tears welled in her eyes. "Save her, Daddy."

* * *

THE SIGHTS AND SOUNDS OF emergency vehicles resounded through the small town of Kringle, Vermont. Occupants neighboring 28 Cottage Lane stood at their front windows peering down on their ordinarily, sleepy street. Blaring sirens faded to silence, while red and blue strobe lights reflected off mounds of freshly plowed streets.

"This is Captain Randy Hollister of the Kringle Fire Department," echoed a voice from behind the bull horn. "Folks, for your safety, please remain in your homes. I repeat. Remain in your homes. We have a damaged utility pole with several live, sparking, wires. Vermont Power Company is en route. They will cut the electricity to that transformer. When the repair has been completed, your power will be fully restored."

Chelsi was among the occupants at the living room window watching. Waiting. Each firefighter meticulously executing their rehearsed rescue drill.

As long as I stay put, I'm in no immediate danger. She sighed. *But I wish Jake were here. I need his strength. I need his comfort. I need him.* She looked at Randy. He was focused. Prepared. Like a soldier going off to war. To think, the man in charge is Jake's younger brother. She mouthed the words, "Thank you." He acknowledged back with a comforting smile and a tap to the brim of his helmet.

A second emergency vehicle arrived at 28 Cottage Lane. Lieutenant Josephine Bobinski exited the cab. "Capt'n, when we pulled up the info on this residence, the computer said it was unoccupied."

Randy nodded toward the figure standing at the front window. "Until a few days ago, it was. JoBo, meet Chelsi Burnett."

"So, *that's* who I saw him with yesterday. I was pulling into the diner just as they pulled out. Katrina told me about her car accident. Tough break. But I'll bet he's happy she's here."

"Yup."

She adjusted the shoulder harness of her air pack, then joined the rest of the team.

Jake's truck jumped the curb, then came to a skidding halt in the middle of Chelsi's snow-covered front lawn. Jumping out from the truck, Jake said, "Randy, I heard the scanner alert from my phone. Is she safe?"

"Yup. See for yourself," he said, gesturing toward the window. "Lightning took down the utility pole. Transformer's still connected, but live wires, from the neighboring houses, sparking on the roof. I was going to text you, but I knew you'd get the phone alert."

Chelsi stood in the front window, one hand grasping two quilts wrapped around her, the other, the lunch box. There's Jake. *Finally.*

Unaware that two electric company vehicles had arrived, Jake's focus was solely and completely on Chelsi. "Come on, man, why can't we get her out?"

Randy heard the trepidation in his older brother's voice. "Your girlfriend's safe inside. VPC's pulling up now. Let us do our jobs."

"Girlfriend?"

Randy patted his brother's shoulder and walked toward the arriving crew. He turned around and nodded. "Tell her about fifteen minutes."

* * *

JAKE SHOVED HIS HANDS DEEP inside the pockets of his jeans. Not for warmth, but for not knowing what else to do with them. Helpless, he paced back and forth in front of the house, waiting for the all-clear signal. *Save her, Daddy,* repeated over and over in his mind. To hear the pleading in his daughter's voice, and see the tears welling up waiting to be shed, he was determined to do just that. After Amelia's car accident, there was nothing he could do to save his wife.

"All clear," the power company's crew leader said to Randy.

"It's about time!" With too many years of deep-seated passion locked away, Jake took off in a slow sprint through the trampled-down, snow-covered front lawn. He wasn't used to being told to adhere to the fifty-foot perimeter rule; he was usually the one enforcing it. The past several days with Chelsi flashed before his eyes. He flew up the porch steps and flung open the front door.

Chelsi darted through the living room, abandoning a mountain of comforters in her wake. In one fell swoop, Jake whisked Chelsi off her feet and cradled her in the safety of his arms. Their eyes locked. Jake was lost in a sea of hazel green eyes. He pulled her closer. His mouth claimed hers. Unyielding. Savoring her, he deepened the kiss. He tasted love. He tasted future. He tasted completeness. Jake felt the rise and fall of her body embraced in their passion. Her breath irregular against his stubbled face.

Randy walked into the foyer and cleared his throat. "Sorry to interrupt folks, but we need to secure the residence before the power company can vacate the premises."

In between kisses, Jake said, "Captain… I think you know… how to—"

"Access the attic," Randy Hollister said. "Yes, we know the way. Carry on."

Chelsi laughed and buried her head into Jake's chest. "*Um*, I think you can put me down now."

"So much for timing," he said, steadying her on her feet.

She looked up and smiled. Though it was not their first kiss, Chelsi had finally kissed Jake where mistletoe once hung.

Chapter Twenty-Four

TWO CHOCOLATE EGG CREAM SODAS

JAKE PUT THE TRUCK INTO gear and headed in the direction of the Snowberry Inn. "I'll bet that was quite a scare for you, Chels. Glad it didn't take too long to clear the house."

"Yeah. I was afraid the roof was going to catch fire, but seeing you there reassured me, and I knew everything was going to be okay."

Jake placed his hand on Chelsi's knee. "Trust me, Chels. I'll always be here for you."

"I know you will be," she said, covering his hand with hers.

Jake knew he was falling in love with Chelsi, again, but didn't realize just how much, until now. Sure, he'd dated other girls in high school, but nothing too serious. With his father away at sea for months, even a year at a time, never knowing if he'd make it home for holidays or birthdays, Jake had struggled with his feelings for Chelsi. He'd decided it was better to stay friends than break up when he left for the academy. He'd do everything in his power, now, to protect her.

He glanced over to her lap. "Hey, what's with the lunch box? That thing's seen better days."

Chelsi ran her hand over the colorful cover and removed the remaining attic dust. "I know. I found it in the attic after I tossed my water bottle at the wall."

"You threw your water bottle?"

"Mice."

Chelsi shook the lunch box. "Guess what's inside?"

"I sure hope not a thirty-year-old PB and J!"

"No, silly." Chelsi lifted the latch, then flipped open the lid. "Letters!"

At the stop sign, Jake leaned forward to get a closer look. "Letters? From who?"

"Aunt Ann Marie to my mom after my aunt left for college. I had just found it when the transformer blew."

"Anything about your birth father?"

"Not yet. I only glanced at the first one. Nothing interesting there. Just about her course load and getting a job in the student union. When we get back, do you want to join me at the table and see what kind of juicy college life my birth mom had back then?"

Jake rubbed the back of his neck. "Do you really want to know?"

"I'd like to know my father's name," she nodded. "Maybe he's still alive." Chelsi turned her head and looked out the passenger window. Barely above a whisper, she said, "I wonder if he even knew I existed."

"I've called Pop to tell him you're safe, and the house is still in one piece." He drummed his thumbs on the steering wheel, then checked the time. "Better idea. There are too many eyes and ears at the inn. Before the dinner rush, let's go to the diner where we can have some privacy."

"Good thinking, Einstein."

Jake winked. "I thought you'd see it my way, Stitch."

* * *

"HI, KATRINA," JAKE SAID.

"Afternoon, kids. Sit anywhere you like. Today's special is Hog Yule Log. It comes on a six-inch sub with beans, coleslaw, a side of fried pickles, and a slice of apple pie." Lifting a pot, she asked, "Coffee?"

"*Hmmm…* sounds familiar. I had the exact same thing a few weeks ago, but the menu said it was your pulled pork sandwich combo. We'll pass on the Hog Yule Log and the coffee," he said, "I have a different beverage for us in mind." Jake chose a quiet booth at the far end of the diner.

The waitress placed a few menus on the table, then scurried off. She must've lost one of the bells from her sneakers. Only one foot rang out with every other step.

Chelsi slid the white scalloped paper placemat off to the side and placed her once-treasured lunch box in front of her. Nervous, she cleared her throat and repositioned her eyeglasses a bit higher onto the bridge of her nose. She looked across the booth. "Let's see if we can discover who my birth father is."

"Even though she's been gone for forty years, don't you feel like you're prying into her personal life?"

"Kinda, but wouldn't you want to know if the situation were reversed? Besides, why would Mom keep the letters all these years unless she hoped, one day, I'd find them? And why did dad put my original birth certificate in a place where I could easily locate it?"

"I guess. How many letters are there?"

"Seven." Chelsi put the envelopes in postmark order and passed the first one across the table. "Look, back in 1969, a postage stamp was only six cents. Now, with buying forever stamps, I don't even know what the going rate is."

"Sixty-three cents," Jake said, reaching inside his vest pocket for his reading glasses. "The rates are constantly rising. I think the United States

Postal Service is losing money with everybody paying their bills online and sending ecards."

He watched Chelsi scan the single-page letter. "Not much here. She wants to bring her roommate, Sue, home for the Thanksgiving holiday. Her parents will be on a cruise to the Bahamas—"

"Have you two decided?" the waitress asked, ready to take their order.

Jake cocked his head and gave Katrina an inquisitive look. "Do you have any lactose-free milk?"

"Sure do, Sugar."

"Great. We'll have two large chocolate egg cream sodas, with lactose-free milk, and an extra pump of chocolate syrup, please."

"Whipped cream and chocolate sprinkles?"

"Ooooh…sprinkles would be great," said Chelsi.

Katrina pulled out one of two ballpoint pens from her ponytail. They each had a red poinsettia attached to body of the pen. She scribbled down their order, then said, "Coming right up."

"A chocolate egg cream? I haven't had one of those in *forever*!"

"Me neither. I figured after your ordeal today, we'd enjoy a drink from our youth while we get to the meat of these letters. Hopefully, the lactose-free milk won't cause you any stomach problems."

"If it does, I'll be back at the inn and can take something for it. Anyway, let's see what's in this next letter."

"Nothing much here, except her roommate, Sue, sounds like a real hell-raiser."

"Same here. They sure do go to a lot of parties. Sounds like my mom was majoring in guys, instead of—"

"Two, large, chocolate egg cream sodas, lactose-free milk, extra chocolate with sprinkles."

"Looks great! Thanks, Katrina." Jake removed the paper wrapper from Chelsi's plastic straw and slid it into her foamy, chocolatey, indescribably delicious-looking beverage.

"Enjoy!" and the waitress rushed off, her one sneaker jingling away.

Chelsi took a long sip from her frothy drink, then rolled her eyes. "Oh, my. I think I've died and gone to heaven."

"Okay, Burnett, less dying and more reading. We've gotta get back to the inn sometime soon."

"Geesh! Tough crowd here. Let's see, this one's postmarked February fifteenth. Yadda, yadda, yadda. Wait! This one mentions her meeting a guy named Nick last night at a Valentine's Day frat party. Says here he's on the lacrosse team. That's a start. We could go online, get a copy of the yearbook, and look him up."

Chelsi removed a picture of her aunt and her roommate wearing short, low-cut, red dresses. Written on the back, she read, "Off to party," then handed it to Jake.

"Wow, look at them! They could have their pick of guys dressed like that."

Chelsi stared at him over the rim of her glasses. "Don't forget, Hollister, that's a picture of my birth mother! And besides, we don't even know if this Nick guy is my dad. Read on."

"Uh-oh. Aunt Ann Marie doesn't sound too happy here. She had to cover a second shift at work and arrived late to the Spring Fling frat party. By the time she had arrived, Nick was already canoodling with some blonde. And she wrote her grades were slipping."

Jake took a long swig of the remaining beverage. Slurping up the last bit of chocolate through his straw, he reached into the lunch box. "Only three letters left."

"I'll summarize this one," he said. "There was a snowstorm that dropped eighteen inches of snow overnight, and administration canceled classes. She spent the day with Nick and they "frolicked" in the snow for an hour building a snowman, then had a snowball fight with the other students. She actually used the word *frolicked*."

He leaned forward, elbows on the table. "We'll find him, Chels."

"This one's from March twenty-second." Chelsi slowly unfolded the letter. She didn't say anything but simply handed it to Jake.

I'm late! I'll call you after I see the doctor.

"Well… we knew that was coming," he said. "So, it looks like someone named Nick is probably your father."

"Here, I can't read the last one. You do it."

Jake took the last letter and stared into Chelsi's eyes while removing it from the envelope. "This one's postmarked April twenty-seventh."

Dear Marion,

I don't know how else to say this, but I'm pregnant, and Nick is the father. I told him yesterday after I got home from my doctor's appointment, and now I can't locate him anywhere! I went to the frat house, and they told me he'd moved out. My last hope was the admissions office. The only thing they were permitted to tell me was that he withdrew from the university two days ago. What am I going to do? Dad is going to kill me. I have money in savings, but I don't want to have an abortion. When I can get some privacy on the hall phone, I'll call you.

Love, Ann Marie

A single tear rolled down Chelsi's cheek. He folded the letter, added it with the rest in the lunchbox, and closed the latch. "We could do an internet search for him after we find out his last name."

"No, Jake. He knew about the pregnancy and split, leaving my mom to raise her baby, *their* baby, alone. I *don't* want to know his last name, and I *never* want to meet him. I had a happy childhood with wonderful parents. Aunt Ann Marie, my birth mom, made a huge mistake, and after I was born, her loving sister and brother-in-law adopted me. At least they kept me in the family."

Without finishing her beverage, she picked up the lunch box. "Thanks for today, but I'd like to leave now."

Helping her on with her jacket he placed his hands on her upper arms and held her gaze. "Sure thing, Chels. Anything else I can do for you?"

"I think I need some alone time to process the events of today."

"Take all the time you need." He kissed her forehead. "Don't forget, you don't have to do everything alone. We're both in this, together." *Forever, I hope.*

* * *

PENNY HEARD THE TRUCK PULL around the back of the inn and ran outside without her jacket on to greet them. Through chattering teeth, she wrapped her arms around Chelsi. "Miss Chelsi, I'm so glad my daddy saved you."

Chelsi's heart was breaking. She took off her jacket and wrapped it around the shivering child. "Yes, Penny, your daddy was very brave. Uncle Randy and his team were, too."

Taking Chelsi's hand, then Jake's, she looked up at her father and whispered, "Thank you, Daddy."

Jake kissed his daughter's head. "You're welcome, Pumpkin. Now, let's get you girls into the house. Miss Chelsi needs to go upstairs and rest for a while."

"Sure thing, Daddy. Maybe we all should go upstairs and take a nap. I know, I sure could use one now."

* * *

CHELSI BARELY HAD TIME TO change into her comfy clothes when she thought she heard a faint tap on the other side of her door. She closed the lid to her lunchbox, crossed the room, and opened the door only to find the hallway empty. *Humph. Must've been my imagination.* Resuming her position, stretched across her reindeer comforter, she removed the first letter.

A million questions ran through her head, starting with, *Didn't Grandma Singleton talk to you about waiting until marriage? Or…*

"There, now I know I heard someone at my door." Penny stood outside her door with a bright smile on her face. "Penny? Cocoa? How nice of you two to join me." Cocoa offered Rosie to Chelsi, then curled up at the foot of her bed. "Well, thank you, Cocoa," she said, accepting the doll from the dog's mouth.

Penny walked into Chelsi's room like she owned the place, her unicorn slippers blinking on and off with each step. She unloaded her favorite quilt, a few books, and her sound machine onto Chelsi's bed.

"My hands were full, so I asked Cocoa for help." She spread her quilt across the bed; neatening it just so, and put the books into one pile. Penny looked over at Chelsi. "I promise I'll be careful," she said, plugging in the sound machine. "Which sound do you want to listen to while you rest?"

Chelsi smiled. "Which one do you recommend?"

Penny crooked her head to the side, looked up at the ceiling, deep in thought. "Well, my favorite sound is the ocean waves. But then there's crickets chirping, popcorn popping, and a lightning and thunderstorm."

Both Chelsi and Penny's eyes grew wide, while they shook their heads in unison at her last suggestion. "No thunder and lightning, thank you very much. I don't think I'd like the thought of crickets in my room, and popcorn popping would make me hungry, so I agree with you, Pen, the sound of the ocean waves will be perfect." *How darling,* she thought, *Penny coming in here bringing all her favorite things to help me rest.*

Penny turned down the quilt, climbed up onto Chelsi's bed, and made herself comfy. "This is a really nice room, Miss Chelsi," she said, looking around. "I looooove all the Rudolph stuff Grandma put in here."

"I like it, too. Your grandma had the knack for decorating."

"And baking!" pipped up Penny.

"Yes, and baking."

Penny patted the empty spot next to her, then fanned out the books like a deck of cards. "Pick one."

"Let's see, how… 'bout… "The Elves and the Shoemaker"?"

"That's a good story. My dad said the story teaches us good things come from working hard, and the shoemaker and his wife were rewarded by the elves coming to help in their shop."

"Your daddy is such a smart man."

"I know. Now, lay back, Miss Chelsi, and I'll tuck you in." Penny slipped her doll under the quilt sandwiched between the two of them. "Rosie likes to be held while she listens to the story. This way when she falls asleep, she won't get cold."

Chelsi rolled onto her side and held Rosie close to her. "Once upon a time, there was a shoemaker—"

Penny stopped reading at the sound of someone knocking on Chelsi's door. "Who is it?" she asked.

Jake opened the door and smiled at the vision before him. "It's Daddy," he said. "What are you doing in here, Squirt? Miss Chelsi is supposed to be resting."

"She *is* resting, Daddy. I just tucked her in. Now, I'm reading her a story so she can fall asleep."

"I see that."

Chelsi mouthed the words, "It's okay. She's fine."

"Well, don't be too long."

"I won't be, I promise."

Jake winked at Chelsi and closed the door.

"Now, where was I? Oh, yes. Once upon a time…"

Chelsi smiled, then closed her eyes, listening to the most adorable child reading her a bedtime story.

Chapter Twenty-Five

AMTRAK

THE NEXT SEVERAL DAYS FLEW by in an instant, yet seemed to drag on forever. The steering mechanism Carlos ordered finally arrived, and Chelsi's Jeep ran better than she had in years. Jake and Chelsi had spent an entire day clearing out and reorganizing her garage, so, while she was in Paris, her vehicle would be protected from Vermont's bitterly cold winter nights and hot and humid summer days. Each knew the other was thinking about Paris, yet she and Jake had avoided the subject, and were simply enjoying their time together.

Chelsi had removed her bed linens and placed them on the floor near her partially opened door. Folding Jake's NAVY tee-shirt, she brought it up to her nose, closed her eyes, and inhaled. Filling her lungs, she hoped for a hint of his essence. Exhaling, she sniffed again. Disappointed, she debated slipping this little piece of Jake into her suitcase, but thought better of it and placed his shirt on top of the laundry pile instead. Nightly, she surrounded herself in the warmth of his shirt despite the drafty windows of the nearly fifty-year-old inn. Chelsi had seen Jake in his long-sleeved Kringle Fire Department uniform shirt, which stretched tightly across his well-defined chest accentuating every muscle. Why are firefighters so darn hot? During the interview process, did someone rate their level of hotness on their application, and if so, how could she get a dream job like that?

Glancing at the clock on her bedside table, Chelsi realized she didn't have time to fully launder her linens, but at least she could put one load into the washing machine before leaving for the train station.

Her eyes caught her reflection in the cut crystal mirror above the antique dresser. She ran her fingers along the etched scrollwork on the outer frame, then over raised crystal roses which cleverly hid four screws. Mrs. Hollister had quite the eye for decorating. Was this mirror an antique, intricately fashioned by hand, or a mass-produced piece that followed a computer pattern to create the illusion of antiquity? She presumed she'd never know.

She double-checked each drawer for any articles of clothing left behind. The lowest drawer stuck and needed to be jiggled closed. Cringing at the sound, Chelsi looked over at her friend still asleep on the roll-away bed in her room.

"Good morning, Ro. Sorry to wake you."

"Wake me?" her friend moaned, rolling over onto her side. "I never fell asleep." Taking the white eyelet comforter with her, she sat up. "Girlfriend, you were grindin' your teeth all night. It's a miracle you have any teeth left to chew a steak."

"Well, for your information, Miss Smarty Pants, I *know* I grind my teeth. I have an appliance I wear to bed so I don't grind them down to smithereens, but it's back in my apartment in Redfield. You forget, unlike yourself, I arrived in Kringle with only the clothes on my back."

"*And* your jar of jellybeans."

"You're right, and my jar of jellybeans, along with—"

A gentle knock on the door was followed by Penny's head peeking inside. "Miss Chelsi, Miss Rosaria, is it okay if I come in?"

"Of course, you may." Rosaria opened her quilt, and the heavy-eyed child clambered onto her lap. Encompassing the child with the oversized comforter, Penny's petite body looked as if she was on an expedition traveling to the North Pole.

"Good morning, Penny. Where's Rosie?"

"She's dirty. Grandpa had to put her in the wash on account of I was holding her when I lost my tooth. I got some blood on her dress."

"She'll be as good as new, you'll see."

"I didn't expect to see you up and about this early today," Chelsi said.

"At two, we have dress rehearsal for today's Christmas…" A frown grew quickly on her face when Penny saw Chelsi's unmade bed and an overnight bag at the foot of her bed.

"Are you really leaving, Miss Chelsi?"

Her lips pressed into a tight thin line. Chelsi glanced to Rosaria, then motioned with her head in the direction of the doorway. She scooted Penny off her lap, then got up. "Excuse me, girls, nature calls."

Chelsi sat next to Penny and put her arm around her. "'Fraid so, MuncŠin."

"But you'll miss the pageant!" she cried. "You promised." As if to emphasize her disappointment, she repeated: "You promised."

"I—"

Penny scrambled to her feet and hopped off the rollaway bed, sending the fluffy comforter tumbling to the floor. At the door, she stopped and turned. Through tearful eyes, she said, "Don't call me MuncŠin. You don't have the right to give me a nickname. My name… is Penny." She ran down the hallway to her room, passing Gloria along the way.

Chelsi lowered her head and buried her face into her palms.

"That didn't go very well, now did it?"

The sound of Gloria's voice startled her.

"I'm sorry, Gloria. It seems by my decision to go to Paris, I'm letting a lot of people down."

"Oh, she'll be all right. Don't forget, Christmas is right around the corner. Once she sees her new bicycle under the tree, she'll forget everything."

"Jake got her a new bike?" she whispered.

"He did. He bought it on his way home from work the morning of your accident. It's being stored in my garage, away from prying eyes."

"Smart," she said, nodding.

"And don't you worry about letting *anyone* down. We all knew your stay in Kringle was temporary. Chelsi, you're an extraordinary pastry chef despite your vision of needing tangible validation. Baking comes from the heart, not from schooling, and I'm grateful for the time you gave me in my bakery. I've promoted Virginia to manager and asked Rosaria to take your place in the bakery full time. She can't wait to start, but has to go home to give her job and roommate two weeks-notice before she can move here."

Chelsi pulled Gloria into a warm hug. "That's great about Rosaria. She'll be a great fit here, both in your bakery and as a new Kringle resident."

"And why is Paris so important to you?"

"Shortly before Mom died, she and I baked Dad's favorite cookie. They were nothing special, peanut blossoms, you know, a peanut butter cookie, rolled in sugar, with a Hersey's kiss pressed into the center? Anyway, my dad complimented me so much on it, Mom said, yes, I was an extraordinary baker, and someday I'd have my name on a certificate from the best culinary school in the world."

"So, who is this really for? You? Your mom? Your dad?"

"For me, in my parent's memory, I suppose."

"What time is your flight?"

Chelsi unlocked the screen of her cell phone, then checked her flight schedule. "Rosaria's going to take me to the Amtrak Station in town. The train leaves Kringle around 1 p.m. and arrives in Penn Station, New York

City, at 6:30. From there, mass transportation will deposit me directly into terminal one at JFK airport. Then, it's on to Paris at 9:30 p.m."

"Yup, that's right," Rosaria said, returning to their room. Side-hugging her friend, she continued. "My girl here's finally gonna fulfill her dream and become a bona fide pastry chef and study at the legendary *Le Cordon Bleu* in Paris. I already bought ya a picture frame for the certificate. This way, Chef Chelsi here can hang it in her office, above the desk in her very… own… kitchen."

"This way, I will finally be taken seriously as a baker," Chelsi added.

"Not everyone is like your former boss," Gloria said. "Trust me. You are incredibly talented and don't ever forget that. I wouldn't let just anyone work in my kitchen."

"Thank you, Gloria. You do have an incredible bakery."

"Coffee. I need coffee. And lots of it."

"Me, too."

"Me, three!" Gloria chimed in.

Scanning the room, she reflected on the past few weeks. She really loved it here. Everyone had welcomed her, unconditionally, into their lives. *Am I doing the right thing by leaving Kringle and everyone behind?* She'd totally fallen for Jake, again. He was so loving and trusting. But did he have the same feelings for her?

Chelsi moved her overnight bag to the doorway, then picked up the pile of sheets. There were several reputable catering halls in the vicinity, she told herself. After she graduated from *Le Cordon Bleu*, she could come back to Kringle, move into her dad's house, and find a highly regarded position. But would Jake still be here? And available?

"Need any help with your bag, Chels?" Rosaria asked.

"Nah, I'll get it later," she said, juggling the bulky load.

"He does love ya, you know, right?"

"Well, if he does, he has a funny way of showing it." Chelsi slammed her suitcase closed. "And I've fallen head over heels in love with him too, but now, I have to concentrate on my career."

Glancing at the nightstand clock, Chelsi said, "Ro, I'd like to leave by eleven. I've allotted enough time to stop by A New Vision, to have Dr. Aldridge adjust my glasses. They've been slipping."

"Sure thing, kiddo. Looking forward to seeing the doc and Olivia again."

Leaving Chelsi's room, the three of them ran into a scurrying Penny heading back to her room.

"Do you think she was sitting outside my door eavesdropping?"

"No, I don't think so," Gloria said. "I think she wants to spend as much time with you as she possibly can but was embarrassed about her actions before."

* * *

JIM REACHED INSIDE THE KITCHEN cupboard for three coffee mugs. "Ladies, regular or decaf?"

Rosaria rolled her eyes. "Oh, puleeease Jim, what's the point of drinking coffee if you don't get your daily dose of caffeine?"

Everyone laughed.

Jim handed Gloria her cup of coffee and gave her a good morning kiss on her forehead. "Where did the McIntyres go?" she asked. "Their suite was empty when I got up this morning."

"They left early this morning for some last-minute Christmas shopping, then on to Manchester Park."

"What's in Manchester Park?" Rosaria asked. "Sounds like something right up the doc and Olivia's alley."

"The Manchester Theatre is hosting a traveling ballet troupe, which is performing The Nutcracker, but their performances were already sold out.

The McIntyres were fortunate there was a cancellation at the Manchester Park Inn for afternoon tea. So, after shopping, they will be seated at three p.m."

"Why so far for afternoon tea? Isn't Manchester Park like two and half hours northwest of Kringle? Surely there's someplace closer."

"Chelsi, according to the Vermont Travel Bureau, it's *the* place to go for tea," Jim said.

"*Hmmm… pity.*"

Chelsi adjusted her glasses higher on her nose. "Why, Gloria?"

"It would be perfect for you. You said you grew up at your aunt's B&B. Didn't she serve afternoon tea?"

"Yes, and I'd love to consider that too, someday. Today, I'm on my way to Paris. It's always been my dream."

"Dreams can change," Jake said, his shoulder propped against the doorjamb.

Chelsi's heart flip-flopped at the sound of his voice. "Jake, we went through this last night."

"Just sayin' is all."

He removed the dog's leash from the hook. "Come on, Cocoa. Let's go for a run. A long run."

Cocoa raced through the kitchen doing her wiggly dance, waiting for Jake to hook up her leash."

"We'll be back soon. Pop, don't hold breakfast for me."

"Okay, son."

Chelsi stood there looking at the closed back door, hoping Jake would return to kiss her goodbye. "I thought Jake was covering a shift today?"

"Me, too," his father replied.

She opened both doors of the institutional side by side refrigerator/freezer and stood there assessing its contents. "Gloria, did Virginia bring croissants today?"

"Yes. I believe she delivered a dozen this morning, why?"

"Perfect. Breakfast is on me today."

"You don't need to fuss non, darlin'. I'm sure you have a lot to do before you leave."

"It's my pleasure, Jim. This is the least I can do to repay you for your hospitality and putting up with me."

"If you insist. No complaints from me."

"I do. Let's see… there's not a whole lot of time, but how does blueberry-stuffed croissant French toast… with bacon sound?"

"Where ya gonna find blueberries this time of year?"

"In the freezer. This week I was experimenting with different kringle recipes and only used half the bag. The other half is still in the freezer."

Jim rubbed his hands together, "Well, whatcha waitin' on, darlin'?"

"Ro, grab an apron from the pantry. While breakfast is cooking, I'll fill ya in on the two batches of dough I have chilling in the fridge. One's the kringle entry for the pageant, the other is Penny's angel cookies."

"Sure. Just like old times, huh, Chels?"

"Old times, Ro? I've been gone less than two weeks."

"Well, for me, it seems like…" with a colorful hand motion, she ended the sentence with, "forever!"

"Morning, Grampa. Morning, Miss Gloria."

"Good morning, Penny," they said, in unison. Jim added, "But there are others here in the kitchen, too."

"No worries, Jim. Penny visited with us earlier this morning."

"Still, it ain't right."

Penny got her usual bowl from the cupboard. "I hope it's okay, Grampa, but my belly's only hungry for cereal this morning."

"Well, if you're sure that's all you want, then okay. But you'll be missing out on Miss Chelsi's French toast made with Miss Gloria's delicious, buttery croissants."

"With blueberries," Gloria added.

"And bacon," pipped up Rosaria. "Who doesn't love bacon?"

"*Hmmm,* I do love bacon. But I'm sure. And Grampa, would it be okay if I take it up to my room?" She drew an 'X' over her heart. "I *promise* to be careful."

"What's so important in your room that you won't join the rest of us at the table. Miss Chelsi is leaving in a few hours."

"I know, but I'm working on a special project, and it's almost done."

"Okay, but get a larger bowl so the milk doesn't slosh out over the sides."

After Penny filled the bowl with her favorite cereal, she took a banana from the red ceramic fruit bowl on the table and tucked it under her arm. "Thanks, Grampa."

* * *

"ARE YOU SURE YOU WOULDN'T rather Jake take you to the train station?"

"No, I'm sure, Ro. We talked last night. I told him you'd take me on your way back to Massachusetts."

"Never you worry. Always glad to help ya."

"Thanks. And I'll give you the key to my apartment when we get to the station. If you would please box up my clothes and bathroom stuff and bring it to my house when you come for Kringlefest, that would be great. I know Daniel hasn't moved out yet, so I texted him and told him I'm on my way to Paris and he can sublet until my lease runs out in March."

"Sure. Hey Chels, can we swing by your house so I can see the place. I can't wait to see where you and Jake grew up."

"Of course. It is a nice house. Needs some work, but she's got good bones."

"You're lucky to have grown up here. Kringle is a great town."

"Funny, growing up I couldn't wait to spread my wings and leave Kringle. Now I don't want to leave. It's home."

"Hey, Ro, I have a great idea. Since you'll need a place to live when you move here, why don't you stay at the house?"

"At your house?" Chelsi saw her friend's face light up.

"I would be honored. Ya know, growing up in Brooklyn, we lived in an apartment house. I've never lived in a house before." Rosaria scanned the inn's front room. "But I can't believe you're leavin' all this behind. I think you're crazy to go to Paris now. It sounded like a terrific opportunity, until I came here and met these wonderful people, in this wonderful town, and your wonderful Jake."

Reaching for the last of her newly purchased luggage, she said, "I know. I'll miss the inn, Kringle, and everyone in it." *Especially Jake.*

Chapter Twenty-Six

SAGE ADVICE

"SON, WHERE ARE YOU GOING all full of salt and vinegar?"

"Don't worry, Pop," Jake said, thrusting his arm into his puffer vest, "I'll be back in time to take Penny to dress rehearsal."

Jim gave his son a sharp look. "Now simmer down, Jake Hollister, and hear me out. After that, I promise not to say another word."

Jake stood and hooked his thumb into the pocket of his jeans. "Yes, sir."

"We both had our first loves taken away from us too soon. Not a day goes by that I don't miss your mother. With Gloria, I *have* my second chance at love, and by God, I'm taking it. It's okay to miss Amelia. She was a good wife and a loving mother to Penny."

"What's your point."

"Let me finish, son… and listen with your heart, not with your ears."

Jake shifted his weight to the other foot.

"This metaphorical merry-go-round we call life is waiting for you to step up onto the platform and embark on your journey. First, you must have the wisdom to buy your ticket. If you don't buy that ticket, and Chelsi boards the plane, she just might get on that carousel in Paris and choose to never get off. Purchase your ticket, son. Grab that brass ring and live your life to the fullest… with Chelsi."

"She's made it perfectly clear about her feelings for me and Kringle by leaving us all behind for Paris."

"Did you asked her to stay?"

"Well… no," he answered, in a flat tone.

"Why the blazes not? I know I've asked you this before. Do you love her?"

I've always loved her. He walked to the kitchen counter, pulled out a barstool, and sat. "I've always had feelings for Chelsi, but I tried not to open my heart, knowing she was leaving town." Jake raked his fingers through his hair. "But I think I do love her."

"Make up your mind, son. Either you do, or you don't. There's no guessing when it comes to love."

"Do you remember how letters from home got us through lonely tours at sea until the next letter arrived?"

"Yeah, and the care packages too! At our last Navy reunion, the guys were still talking about Mom's jam thumbprint cookies. She even made a separate batch for the guys who had nut allergies."

"Your mother *was* quite the baker. But that was not the point I was getting at."

"So, what is the point?"

"The letters."

"Letters?"

"Yup. It's one of the oldest forms of communication."

"Pop, what does a letter have to do with Chelsi leaving for Paris?"

"People come into our lives for a reason. Some good comes out of it, some not. Like the Earth's magnetic field causes a compass needle to point

North, Chelsi was pulled by the same magnetic force to Kringle." With a wink and a nod, Jim continued. "I saw the way you looked at her when you thought no one was watching. But you still haven't answered my question. Do you love her?"

A smile tugged on Jake's lips as long-forgotten memories combined with newly formed remembrances bubbled up like an ice-cold IBC root beer float at a Memorial Day picnic. He thought he'd made a terrible mistake by letting her go, but he hadn't wanted to stand in the way of her lifelong dream. *She's barely been gone an hour, and I already feel so empty inside.* Jake couldn't deny it any longer; he was head over heels in love with her.

"Yes, sir. I do love her. Chelsi is my true North." A long whoosh escaped from Jake's mouth. He felt so liberated to finally say the words out loud.

"If you love her; fight for her, Jake. *Tell* her your feelings. And none of this cold, unfeeling texting. Go upstairs and write her a letter and tell her how you feel. On your way, you might want to pick up some flowers, and maybe a box of chocolates. There, I've said my peace. You're a grown man, Jake Hollister, take it or leave it."

Jake checked the time on his cell phone. "Her train leaves at 1:06."

"Then I suggest you hurry."

* * *

"SLOW DOWN, MARIO ANDRETTI, OR you'll drive right past Jasper and Olivia's place." Chelsi pointed in the direction of the house converted to a store. "There's A New Vision. I've built enough time in for us to have tea with Olivia. Her scones, with a dollop of thick clotted cream, smothered with homemade jam, taste like a little piece of heaven."

"*Hmmm*, temptin'. I would love to see Olivia and Dr. Jasper again, and I certainly love a heavenly scone, but I have to pass. My gas tank is pretty empty from the trip up. How 'bout I drop you off and be back here in say thirty minutes?"

"Did I tell you A New Vision has an antique store inside called A Second Chance? I know how much you love to shop for antiques."

"Not fair! Okay, fifteen."

* * *

"MAX, GWEN WHAT ARE YOU two doing outside?" Chelsi said, accepting a face full of doggie kisses from them.

Jasper walked toward her from the side yard. "Hello, my dear. I do let the dogs romp about the woods this time every day. A family of squirrels live in a hollowed-out tree. Every morning, they forage for food and nibble on snow for hydration. It's the dogs' daily dose of entertainment."

"So, what do we owe the pleasure?"

"I'm leaving for Paris today. My train leaves a little after one for JFK."

"JFK?"

"Sorry. It's an international airport in New York."

"I see. Please, please come inside. Olivia just put the kettle on."

"Allow me." Jasper said, opening the door.

Chelsi smiled. "I'll miss you, Jasper."

"Yes, yes. After you, my dear," he said holding open the door, "we mustn't let our tea get cold."

"I can't believe it's been a little more than a week since I first met you and Olivia. Where has the time gone?"

"Chelsi, dear," smiled Olivia, "we're so glad you could take the time to see us before you embark on your new journey. You will stay for tea, won't you?"

"Yes, thank you, I'd love to."

"The scones are cooling, and the tea needs another minute to steep."

"Olivia, how did you know I would be arriving at this exact time?"

She looked heavenward. "Sometimes I have that uncanny ability, and this was one of them."

"Is there anything I can help you with?" she asked, removing her coat.

"No, but thank you for offering. Jasper has our tea tray assembled. Please sit and tell me all about Paris."

To make room for the arriving tea tray, Olivia fastened the slender embroidery needle, threaded with two strands of lavender-colored floss, off to the side of the embroidery piece she had been working on since their arrival in Kringle.

Chelsi extended her hand. "May I?"

Passing her fingers over the intricate embroidery stitches, sewn with love, Chelsi read the inscription. "'Love: Bears all things. Believes all things. Hopes all things. Endures all things. Love never ends.' This is a beautiful scripture, Olivia. Jasper is a lucky man to have a woman in his life who loves him as much as you do. Looks like you might have this piece completed in time for your wedding."

"Have what completed?"

"Nothing," they said, echoing each other.

The sound of porcelain teacups jingling atop their saucers brought a smile to Chelsi's face.

"Would you mind sharing your thoughts?" Olivia asked. "Your expression was a lovely recollection of the past."

"Or a premonition of occurrences yet forthcoming."

"Wait. What, Jasper?" Chelsi asked, pushing her glasses higher on her nose.

"Oh, don't mind him, dear, please continue."

"I remember Aunt Ann Marie saying, 'Enjoy the little things in life because one day you will look back and realize they weren't so little.'"

"She was a wise woman, Chelsi." Olivia lifted the basket and uncovered her fresh-out-of-the-oven scones. Chelsi could not help herself. She brought the basket to within six inches of her nose and inhaled deeply. The sight of the freshly baked confection was a treat in itself with its shaggy golden crust, baked to perfection, but when it was combined with a hint of sweetness in the moist, flaky, inner crumb, then slathered with fresh-fruit jam topped with the almost nutty flavor of clotted cream, it made her mouth do a happy dance.

Mmmm... Chelsi placed a dollop of rich clotted cream, followed by a healthy serving of jam on the edge of her dessert plate. "I remember, Olivia," she said, breaking the tender scone horizontally in half, "jam first, then the cream; just like the queen."

"Indeed, Her Majesty takes this issue quite seriously."

Chelsi watched Jasper deliver their pot of fresh-brewed black tea, noticing for the first time a slight limp. "I'm going to miss you both."

At her feet, Max and Gwen each let out a low woof.

"Oh, I'll miss you too," she said, bending down to give them head scratchies.

Olivia poured their tea. Returning the teapot, accented with butterflies, ladybugs, and a honeybee to the tea tray, she said. "Jasper, you seem to have forgotten the sugar. Would you be a dear?"

"Yes, yes, of course, Livy."

Jasper returned momentarily, sugar bowl in one hand, fancy silver sugar tongs in the other. "One lump or two?"

Chelsi adjusted her glasses. "Two, please."

"My dear, I see your glasses appear to be in need of adjusting. It should take me but a minute to complete the simple task."

"Thank you, Jasper. If you don't mind, we'll wait 'til after we've finished our tea. I don't want to miss a single crumb of Olivia's delicious scones."

"That is a capital idea, my dear. Capital indeed."

Chelsi dipped the tip of her spoon into the jam before spreading it on top of her split scone. "Olivia, what flavor is this jam?" She tasted the last bit of the delectable, cooked fruit still clinging to her spoon. "I can taste sweet strawberries and tart cranberries, but there's a hint of something my taste buds can't decipher. It tastes… florally."

"You are quite right, Chelsi. This is my special blend for Kringle. I've added just a hint of organic elderberry flowers from The Country Store in town. I call this recipe Three-Berry Kringle Christmas Jam."

"The taste is remarkable. Penny would love this jam on top of her pancakes."

Penny. Chelsi felt horrible letting her down. Would she ever forgive her? Chelsi had promised she would be at the festival, and now she would miss her performance.

"Olivia, next year, you should set up a table at Kringlefest, make a big batch of this incredible jam, and sell it. Lots of vendors sell homemade goods. I bet you could sell out the first day."

Olivia locked her gaze onto Jasper's. "I will certainly keep that in mind."

Popping the last bite of scone into her mouth, Chelsi stood and walked across the room to the window. "I hope Rosaria didn't get lost. I'm a nervous traveler and can't relax until I've arrived at the gate, waiting for the plane, or in today's case, the train to arrive. What is keeping her? She should've been here by now."

Jasper clicked open his pocket watch. "In due time, my dear. In due time." He guided Chelsi toward the opened door of his examination room. "Why don't you step into my office while I adjust your glasses; then when your friend arrives, you'll be ready."

Olivia removed the basket of remaining scones, but left the teapot on the tray. "Chelsi, may I offer you some of the remaining scones for your trip?"

A New Vision: A Recipe for Love

"Yes, please. The Amtrak leg is a long one."

"Now make haste," she said, with a grin. "Jasper is waiting. Though I'd love for us to continue our visit, your vision is far more important."

* * *

"NOW, LET ME SEE WHAT adjustments I can make to your glasses, my dear." Jasper stood behind the examination chair until Chelsi was comfortably seated.

"Sorry, they're kinda smudged," she said, after he removed them from her face.

Jasper held her glasses up to the light, closed one eye, and peered through them. "And a fine dusting of flour too, I see. Not to worry. I will take care of that directly." Jasper walked across the examination room to the sink. He turned the faucet on and held the frames under running water, drenching both sides. Reaching for a dry cloth, he said, "If you wouldn't mind, please read the eye chart on the far wall. But this time, there is no need to cover either eye."

"But, Jasper, you've already given me a thorough examination. I read the eye chart last week. Surely my vision hasn't changed in a few short days."

"This is a new eye chart, my dear. You'd be surprised how altered your vision can become after only one day." Motioning to the chart, he continued. "Please, if you will."

She forced a quick smile. "'Your vision will become clear only when you can look into your own heart. Who looks outside, dreams; who looks inside, awakes.'—Jasper, why do you have these bizarre eye charts? How does this even challenge my vision?"

"The words written on this chart are quoted from the prolific Swiss writer and philosopher, Carl Jung. You see, Chelsi, when we look inside our heart, we discover who we are and where we're meant to be."

Chelsi stood and looked back to the eye chart. "But Jasper, I know who I am, and I'm on my way to Paris. My flight leaves in a few hours."

Jasper made the final adjustments on her glasses. "Chelsi, what does your heart say? Will studying in Paris make you happy?"

"*Um…* I think so."

"Ah, Livy, right on time. If you would, please hand Ms. Burnett the mirror?"

Chelsi shook her head. "That won't be necessary, Jasper. I've already seen what my glasses look like on me."

"Oh, but I do insist, my dear," he said, centering the glasses on her face. "There, now how do they feel?"

"Much better, thank you." Jiggling the arm of her glasses, she said, "I don't think they'll be sliding down anytime soon."

"Chelsi, do you remember the first time you were here, you looked into the mirror and saw Jake's reflection? Let's see what your heart sees now."

Her eyebrows knit together. "So, you're saying when I saw Jake's reflection in the mirror instead of mine, it was because he was in my heart?" She looked again at the antique, jeweled, handheld mirror, then turned it over, examining the other side. "When I came into the store that day, the furthest thing from my mind was a new relationship."

Jasper put his arm around Olivia's shoulder and nodded to Chelsi. She lifted the mirror. Her eyes widened and locked onto the image. "Jasper?"

"What do you see, child?"

Straightening her back, Chelsi leaned forward. She directed her answer to the mirror instead of Jasper. "It looks like… like Kringlefest." She shook her head. "But that's… impossible. Kringlefest doesn't start for several more hours!" She searched Jasper's eyes for answers. "I don't understand. Again, it should be *my reflection* I see in the mirror."

"True. But those who look *in the mirror* look at their reflection; those who look *into the mirror* look into their hearts."

She stood up and lowered the mirror. "This can't be happening!"

"Chelsi, what is the last line of the quote?"

"...who looks inside, awakes," she repeated.

"Precisely. Many people think that happiness is in the objects they desire, *and* in the job of their dreams. Getting in touch with one's inner peace is the cornerstone for achieving that much-needed balance."

"Please be seated again, my dear."

Chelsi sat down. Once again, she brought the mirror in front of her face and looked. Really looked.

"My dear. Tell us what you see."

"I see the townspeople of Kringle browsing festival booths, eating cotton candy, and drinking hot and cold beverages."

"Very good. Anything else?"

Chelsi repositioned her grip on the mirror's handle. "The children's bell choir is performing in front of the Christmas tree. They're wearing white gloves and red Santa hats. Oh, that's a shame, a little boy tripped and lost his balloon."

"What color was his balloon?"

"*Um*, red."

"*Mmm-hmmm.*"

"Penny, dear. Do you see Penny?" Olivia asked.

Her voice quivered, "No, not yet." *I hope she's there. Please, tell me she's there.* Chelsi moved her head around the vision of Kringlefest as if she was trying to look around the townsfolk. "Wait, there she is. She's with Randy and Jessica." She pointed to the mirror. "Oh, and Travis, too. Penny and Travis are walking Cocoa on her leash. What on Earth is the dog wearing?"

"Oh, how adorable. I forgot the pet parade. Penny must've dressed Cocoa up to look like Rudolph."

"Is that all?"

Chelsi's eyebrows knit together as she moved closer to the mirror. "I see a gold ring. A very *unusual* gold ring which has the likeness of Rudolph." She drew her hand up and placed it against her chest. "*Oooh!* And here's a beautifully decorated gazebo. Looks like it's set up for Valentine's Day, an intimate wedding perhaps."

Chelsi stood so fast it made her head spin. "This is crazy, Olivia," she said, her voice elevated. "You can't see the future in the reflection of a mirror."

She held the mirror at arm's length, offering it first to Olivia, then Jasper. "Olivia, Jasper, you look into the mirror. What do you see?"

"Oh, that won't be necessary, child. You see, our fate has already been chosen."

She gave them an inquisitive glance. "Jasper? What do you mean… your fate has already been chosen?"

Maximillian and Gwendolyn laid down in front of Jasper and Olivia, then Lady Vanessa flitted in, resting on Olivia's shoulder.

Jasper looked into Olivia's eyes, then back to Chelsi. "You see, we are all angels."

Chapter Twenty-Seven

LETTER, FLOWERS, AND CHOCOLATE

"DADDY, WILL YOU PLAY WITH me?" Penny asked, sitting alone at the kitchen table.

Jake opened and closed several kitchen drawers. "Not right now, Squirt. Looks like you're already in the middle of a Monopoly game."

She stared at him for a few moments before replying. "I'm playing two players."

"Well, it looks like you're winning."

"You know I always win when I'm the Scottie Dog."

"*Mmm-hmmm.*"

Sidling up next to her father, she asked, "Whatcha looking for?"

"Notepaper and a pen for a letter. Do you know where some might be?" he asked, closing the pantry door.

"Sure, Daddy. I'll go get them," and off she ran.

Jake turned toward the sound of his daughter's thundering feet, running across the inn's classic oak flooring. "Walk, please."

"Sorry," she said, running up the stairs.

He shook his head, then took his place at the kitchen table. *Letter. Flowers. Chocolate.* Now, what should he say to Chelsi? Jake drummed his fingers against the top of the table. *Wait, I've got it!*

Jake couldn't remember being this nervous. Well, except for the time he asked Lisa Newberry to go with him to their senior prom. She'd been the most popular girl in school, and he'd been certain she was going with the school's star baseball pitcher. His mouth went dry. *I hope I'm not too late. How could I be so stupid to let her go?*

Penny marched back into the kitchen as confident as a qualified applicant would enter into a job interview. She unloaded her overflowing arms in front of her dad. The black composition notebook was first, followed by a box of fifty assorted colored pencils, silver glitter, and a squeeze container of white craft glue. "Here ya go, Daddy. I couldn't find a pen, so I brought you my box of colored pencils."

"I see that." Jake picked up the book. "But this is your story journal, Pen. I know how special this is to you."

"It's okay," she said, her mouth curving into a sweet smile. "You can tear a page out from the middle. I did it this morning with my special project for Miss Chelsi, and nothing fell out from the front."

Sitting a brown stuffed bear on top of the table, Penny reclaimed her chair. "Here you go, Mr. Bear. You can be the race car."

Jake gave the bear a sidewise glance. "Did you get that bear from Miss Chelsi? He looks like an antique."

"*Um…*what's an antique?"

"That means it's really old."

"Oh, like Grampa?" she asked, her head bobbing.

Jake lowered his head and tried not to let Penny see him laugh. "Yeah, something like that."

"Yes, Miss Chelsi gave him to me this morning before she left. She said that Miss Olivia wanted him to have a good home, and she couldn't think of a better home than ours."

"That was really nice of Miss Chelsi." *Maybe there's hope yet.* He opened the notebook to the center stitching and carefully tore one sheet out. "I only need one, Penny. I'll leave this extra one here for the next time you need one."

Jake opened the familiar box of colored pencils, blankly staring at his options from one end of the box to the other.

The cuckoo clock, counting down the hour, directed Jake's attention to the time. He sucked in a breath. "Noon. Gotta get a move on… her train leaves in an hour. So much for a letter."

"Daddy, is the letter you have to write for Miss Chelsi?"

"Yes, Squirt, it is."

"How will you give it to her?"

Jake folded the paper and tucked it into his pocket. Grabbing his keys from the hook near the back door, he said, "Hopefully I can catch her at the train station before she boards for New York City."

Penny crossed her arms. "You know, I wrote Miss Chelsi a letter this morning, too. When she wasn't looking, I hid it in the front zippy part of her little suitcase."

"Why didn't you give it to her?"

"She was busy, and I wanted to surprise her with it. I was sad when she told me she was leaving for Paris and would be gone for a long time. So, I wrote her a letter and drew a picture on the other side. I told her I loved her and don't forget to come back to us."

"That was very thoughtful of you, Penny. My letter pretty much says the same thing. Listen, Sweetheart, thanks for your help, but I gotta go. Grandpa is out in the garage. I'll tell him I'm leaving. If I'm not back in time, Grandpa will drive you to the pageant."

"I'll be fine, Daddy."

"My cell phone number is on the fridge if you need to reach me."

Penny gave her father a thumbs-up. "Dad, I know. Please don't be late."

* * *

JIM LOOKED AWAY FROM HIS workbench toward the sound of the side garage door squeaking open. Pop's garage was as organized as a hardware store. Along one wall, next to his workbench, were two brown, four-foot by eight-feet wooden pegboards with every hand tool imaginable hanging on long pegs. Jake could tell immediately which tool his father was utilizing from the tool outline on the panel, sans the tool.

"What's the project for today?" Jake asked.

"Just puttering around."

"Okay, Pop. Well, I'm leaving."

"Got everything you need, son?"

"Yep, I'm good. Penny's in the kitchen, playing a game."

Jim picked up a blue shop towel and wiped some dark grease from his hands. "Gloria will be over soon. We'll take Penny out for lunch before the pageant begins."

"She'll love that, thanks."

"Good luck."

Jake rubbed the back of his neck. "You got that right! I need all the luck I can get. I'll text Randy and let him know I'm taking the truck."

Before starting the engine, Jake pulled out his cell phone and sent a text to his brother that said:

Hey bro. Taking the truck to catch Chelsi at train station. Back soon.

10-4 Jake.

"Twelve-fifteen, not much time," he said, tucking his cell phone into his vest pocket.

Pulling out onto Belmont Avenue, Jake rehearsed what he wanted to say to Chelsi, but nothing sounded quite right. Too rehearsed. What had Pop said? *Speak from the heart.*

Kringle's highway department was in full force, setting up road blockades for Kringlefest, and the townsfolk had begun arranging food tables and holiday booths. *Crap, now I'll have to backtrack around the hospital to get to the train station. I* can't *afford any more delays.*

Jake's cell phone chimed. Removing it, he glanced over at the screen. "No, not now, Randy." Jake pulled the truck over to the side of the road to read the incoming text:

Flat tire. Corner of Woodland and Arthur. Maria. 2012 White Honda CRV. Reply.

"You've gotta be kidding me!" Jake yelled, at the cell phone screen.

Tell motorist thirty minutes. He texted back.

No, now Jake! Motorist is safe, but two kids in car.

Seriously?

Yes! Now. Everything else can wait 'til motorist is on her way.

Through gritted teeth, Jake ended with:

On my way.

Frustrated, Jake slammed the palm of his hand against the steering wheel, then pulled back into traffic. "This will have to be the fastest tire change in history." He vaguely remembered traveling the four blocks to the intersection where the stranded motorist waited.

"Thank you for arriving so quickly," the young woman said, following Jake to the rear of her vehicle. "My kids are late for hockey practice."

"*Mmm-hmmm,*" he replied, opening the rear hatch.

Jake eyed two, three-foot black long duffle bags among various other sports paraphernalia. "Oh, sorry," she said, "hockey equipment bags. I suppose I should've emptied the back while I was waiting."

Yup. That would've helped me out! "Let me guess, Chandler and Mason?"

Maria looked at the embroidered personalization. "Good guess." She reached into the back. "Here, I'll help you with these."

"It's okay, ma'am, I've got them," he said, grabbing both handles with one hand. "I'll have you back on the road in no time."

She leaned against the side of the SUV. "Thank you."

He simply nodded.

Jake removed the spare tire from its carrier, bounced it off the pavement, then rolled it around the side of the car. After adding a few pounds of pressure from the portable air compressor, he made short work of removing the flat tire.

"Everything okay?" she asked.

"Almost done, ma'am."

Jake secured the damaged tire and replaced the carpeted trunk lining. With a loud clunk, he returned the two duffle bags to their original location and closed the rear hatch. He jogged to the driver's side window. "You're all set, ma'am," and turned away.

"Wait," she called out, rummaging through her handbag. "How much do I owe you?"

"Merry Christmas," he yelled, jumping into the driver's side of the tow truck.

He glanced at the digital clock on the dashboard. *Crap*—12:55. He'd never make it in time. Chelsi was probably already on board.

Committing several posted speed limit infractions, Jake finally arrived at the Kringle train station. He slammed the gear shift into park, grabbed a few things from the seat next to him, then leaped out. Leaving the truck's door open, he ran toward the loading platform. Jake stood helpless watching the last car of the 1:06 p.m. Amtrak train, bound for New York City, pull away from the station.

His shoulders slumped as he watched the receding train until it was completely out of sight. Disbelief drained every ounce of hope he had at asking her to stay in Kringle with him and Penny.

Glancing towards the truck, he said, *Shake it off, Jake.*

He was *not* giving up this easily. He would drive to New York if he had to. Hell, he'd even fly to *Paris* if it meant bringing Chelsi back. He thought for a minute. This was Amtrak. The ticket counter inside had to have the schedule of stops. With renewed enthusiasm, he jogged toward the station house. He'd get the day's schedule, drive to the next stop, and meet her train.

Jake pushed open the swinging door, nearly running into a janitor mopping the contents of a spilled coffee cup.

"Slow down, son, where's the fire?" the elderly gentleman asked. Jake looked around at the empty lobby.

"I'm terribly sorry, sir. The Amtrak train that just pulled out, where can I get the schedule for the upcoming stops?"

"The 1:06 bound for New York City?"

"Yes," he replied, a little too snappy. Was there any other Amtrak train that just left the station?

Moving the *Wet Floor* sign, the janitor motioned with his head in the direction of the empty Amtrak ticket counter. "'Fraid you'll have to wait 'til tomorrow, he just left."

"He left?"

"Yup, only one Amtrak train a day."

"Could you go back there and look at the schedule?"

The janitor continued mopping up the remaining liquid. "Nope. 'Gainst policy. Don't work for Amtrak."

"Against policy?" Jake said, raising his voice. "You mean you can't go behind the counter and—"

"Jake?"

He turned his head in the direction of the familiar voice. Chelsi stood in front of the Women's restroom door, drying a wet spot down the front of her jacket with a few brown paper towels.

"Chelsi? What are you still doing here?"

Her face lit up. Jake had never seen anything more beautiful. A smile that made the little hairs on the back of his neck stand on end. "Me? What are *you* doing here?"

Jake's heart thumped wildly. It pounded so loud he was sure the arriving travelers for the next train could hear it. But his vision was focused on only one person, the most incredible woman in the world standing a few feet away from him. Jake took Chelsi's hands in his. Neither one moved. He stared silently into her eyes. Reluctant to blink. Hesitant to breathe. The last time he'd held a woman's hands in his like that, he and Amelia were professing their love for each other on their wedding day. He loved Chelsi. He needed Chelsi's love, not only for himself, but also for Penny. She would make his heart complete again. But now was Jake's turn to acknowledge his love for Chelsi. Right here. Right now. His strong fingers wrapped around Chelsi's delicate hands.

"Looking for you."

She took in a ragged breath and released it slowly.

"Chelsi, since the day you came back into my life, not a moment has gone by that I haven't thought about the curly-haired, hazel-eyed tomboy who'd stolen my heart all those years ago. From the way the smell of cherry pie seems to encircle you, to the way the little hairs on the back of my neck stand up whenever you smile. We have something good here, Chels. Something real. I think we both know it."

Tears pooled in her eyes. "I waited. I hoped. But you never came. I was certain my feelings for you were different from yours." She let out a short laugh and could not hold back the tears any longer. "Jake, what took you so long?"

Chelsi took a half step closer. But when she did, the sound of a sticky substance stuck to the bottom of her shoe made them look down. They both laughed.

"I can't believe I almost lost you… again." Jake reached up. With the pads of his thumbs, he wiped away a duo of escaped tears. "I didn't want to stand in the way of your dream. I know how much Paris meant to you."

"Dreams can change, Jake. Isn't that what you said this morning?"

"Paris was right there in front of you for the taking, why didn't you get on the train? What changed your mind?"

She reached into her jacket pocket and removed a folded piece of lined paper. Holding it up, she said, "This. I sat here and watched the joyous faces of children, dressed in their Sunday best, eagerly waiting to visit their loved ones for Christmas. I secretly yearned to be one of those families."

Jake looked at the folded paper she held between her fingers.

"It's a long story, but the short of is, after I left the inn, I went to say good-bye to Jasper and Olivia. Jasper noticed my eyeglasses were slipping, so he offered to adjust them. On the back wall of his examination room hung a quote by Carl Jung. It said that a new vision begins within your heart, but you have to look *inside* your heart to see it. Penny drew me this picture. I sat here and truly looked inside my heart, asking myself if Paris is what I really want?"

He recognized the lined paper as a sheet coming from Penny's writing journal. Unfolding it, he smiled. "So, this is the secret project Penny was working on this morning."

Jake looked down at the front of her jacket. "An exuberant child bumped my hand, and I spilled my entire cup of coffee. I reached into the zippered part of my bag for some tissues and that's when I found it. She must've snuck it into my carry-on bag when I wasn't looking."

He cupped her face, searching her eyes. "Chelsi, there's something I have to give you." He handed her a folded piece of paper, an unopened bag of semi-sweet chocolate chips, and a broken stem from a dormant snowberry bush.

"What on Earth?"

"This too is a long story. It was sage advice from my dad. He told me to own up to my feelings in a letter and bring you chocolate and flowers." He lowered his gaze to his feet. "This was the closest thing I could come up with on short notice."

Chelsi tucked the bag of chocolate chips and the twig into the crook of her arm, then unfolded the paper. She looked up at Jake and turned it over. "But there's nothing written here."

"I know, I wanted to tell you in person." Jake inched forward. He put his finger under her chin and raised it. "On January 1st, my dad and Gloria are renting an RV and traveling to Arizona. He wants me to manage the inn and hopes you'll join me to preside over the kitchen."

Her eyes sparkled brighter than the luster of the Christmas Star. "Me? He trusts me, in your mom's kitchen, to cook for his guests at the Snowberry Inn?"

"No, Chelsi. In *your* kitchen. For *our* guests. You once told me you hoped you could follow in Aunt Ann Marie's footsteps and run a kitchen in a B&B."

"I remember," she whispered.

Jake inched forward and sucked in a huge breath. "This is me, fighting for you. Chelsi Ann Burnett, I love you. Stay. Stay in Kringle with me and Penny."

Chelsi's arms became as limp as a rag doll. The point of the twig stuck to her jacket, the bag of chocolate chips fell to the tile floor with a splat, while Penny's picture fluttered downward. "Well, it took you long enough, Jake James Hollister."

Hungry for the taste of her lips, he reached out and ran his fingers down the side of her cheek and tilted her face up to his. With the tip of her tongue, Chelsi moistened her lower lip, then fluttered her eyes closed. Jake brushed his lips against hers, soft at first, just long enough that he could feel the warmth of her breath as his mouth joined her tender lips. She tasted sweet. Like birthday cake, cotton candy, and warm cinnamon rolls on Christmas morning all rolled up into one.

Chelsi broke away and stared into his eyes. "Jake, I love you, too."

Drawing him closer, Chelsi snaked her arms up and encircled Jake's neck. He stared into her eyes, greedily drinking in the essence of her. The electricity that surged between their eyes ignited a lightning bolt sending white-hot blood coursing through Jake's veins. Feelings awakened deep inside his soul that he thought were lost forever.

"And Paris?" he asked.

"Paris isn't what I want, Jake… *Kringle* is. Kringle. The Snowberry Inn. Penny. And you."

Chapter Twenty-Eight

KRINGLEFEST

IT WAS A CHILLY CHRISTMAS Eve, and the temperature was dropping. The midafternoon sun had played hide-and-seek behind low-lying clouds, teasing festival goers with her warmth. *Kringle Today* had forecast four to six inches of new snow beginning before nightfall. It looked like the children of Kringle, Vermont, will enjoy the merriment of a white Christmas.

Kringlefest was in full swing. It had been over thirty years since Chelsi participated in the town's extravaganza. She had been a senior at Kringle High School and attended with the sisterhood of her softball team. Today, a gaggle of giggling girls ogled over the varsity football players who volunteered at the kids' game booths. They looked especially daunting wearing home jerseys, shoulder pads, and sporting elf hats instead of football helmets.

Holiday music drifted throughout the grounds, and enthusiasm grew as Chelsi and Jake mingled with animated festival-goers of all ages. Neighbors, friends, and family members greeted each other with warm wishes and holiday hugs at Kringlefest's Golden Jubilee. More than sixty decorated booths lined the town's cobblestone streets, leaving the sidewalks vacant for pedestrians to pop in and out of businesses with extended holiday hours. Like children gravitating to Santa Claus in a shopping mall, the enticing aroma of freshly roasted cinnamon-sugar pecans, from More Than Nuts, attracted patrons to the vendor's rolling wagon.

Jake and Chelsi walked hand in hand browsing through endless craft tables, decked out in holiday lights, brimming with hand-made treasures. Excited children waited in line to give Santa Claus their last-minute wishes, while others chased each other around resulting from too many cookies, candied apples, and their all-time favorite, cotton candy.

Jake stopped at the Fifty Shades of Fudge booth. A petite, rather curvy woman stood behind the table. The short side of her edgy, asymmetrical hairstyle was accented with bright fuchsia highlights. She wore stylish black ripped jeans, exposing rhinestone fisÚet stockings underneath. Her paisley print top in bold shades of purple, fuchsia, and lime green was not very Christmassy but complemented her flamboyant style. She donned a red Santa hat which displayed her name, "Pinkie," in hot pink sparkle paint along the brim.

"Hi, Pinkie!" Jake said, scanning the plethora of mouth-watering fudge samples. "Chelsi, come meet Pinkie. She and her wife, Zenora, own the newest business to open in town. They sell incredible homemade fudge, gourmet popcorn, and hand-twisted soft pretzels. You should've seen the line on down Main Street on National Fudge Day."

Chelsi extended her hand and greeted the woman. "It's very nice to meet you, Pinkie, I'm Chelsi Burnett. I saw your shop the other day but didn't have the time to stop in. Is there actually a national fudge day?"

"Oh, yes," she replied. "It's June 16th. We have contests and a countdown to all our national food holidays. Popcorn Day is January 19th, and Soft Pretzel Day, April 26th."

"Chelsi, how does Baileys, white chocolate chunk, and marshmallow cream fudge sound?" Jake asked.

"What's not to love?" Chelsi watched Jake interact with the shop owner. Jake is so caring. Not at all like Daniel who only thought of himself.

She thought back to the day of her mother's funeral when Jake had brought a plate of food to her on her front stoop. Why didn't I see that sooner? To think…

Chelsi had to shake the memory of her mother's passing out of her mind and concentrate on the affectionate man in front of her. "Wait! Pinkie, do you have any lactose-free fudge?"

"Say no more. Chelsi, here are the lactose-free options, made with sweetened vanilla almond milk."

Chelsi browsed through the nine or ten lip-smacking options. "I'd love to try the amaretto chocolate chunk, please."

"Excellent choice."

"And I'll take the snickerdoodle, please."

Pinkie shook her head. "Jake, you always get snickerdoodle. One of these days maybe you'd want to liven things up with, say, red velvet or white Russian fudge?"

"Nope. I'm good."

Pinkie cut a lion's share of each sample and offered them to Jake and Chelsi on small imprinted paper napkins.

"Did I hear someone say amaretto chocolate chunk?" asked a beautiful woman, approaching the table. She was about five inches taller than Pinkie and dressed quite differently, outfitted in an off-white turtleneck sweater under a fitted green leather jacket, similar style faded jeans, and zippered ankle booties. Zenora looked like she was going for a magazine photoshoot, instead of manning a festival table.

"Z. You *finally* made it back!"

Wheeling a utility cart loaded with supplies, she said, "I should've walked here from the shop, it would've been quicker." She stored her handbag under the table, then continued. "Hi, Jake. Nice to see you again."

"Hi, Z. Yeah, I think we got the last spot next to the church dumpsters."

Pinkie began arranging the freshly delivered reinforcements. "Where *are* my manners?" Pinkie asked. "Chelsi, this is my wife, Z. We moved here from Surprise, Arizona, last year. We'd had it with the heat."

"And the scorpions!" Z added, with a shudder. "Even though we had an exterminator spray inside and out regularly, those scary little suckers *still* managed to get into our house. When a friend from church told us his sister was stung by a scorpion, *in bed*, on the *second* floor, we decided it was time to move."

"On behalf of the whole town, we're glad you're here," Chelsi said.

"Thanks for the samples. But if you see my dad, please *don't* mention the scorpions. He and Gloria are traveling to Arizona after the first of the year."

"Scorpions? What scorpions?" Z answered, with a wink.

Energized children of all sizes, along with their pets, rushed past them. "I must say, the kids went all out for the pet parade this year. I can't wait to see Cocoa dressed up as Rudolph."

Jake spied a smudge of fudge on the corner of Chelsi's lower lip. With the pad of his thumb, he ran his finger over her lip and removed the confectionary mixture of powdered sugar, cocoa, and butter. Licking the remnants from his finger, he asked, "Rudolph? How did you know Cocoa would be dressed as Rudolph? As of this morning, Penny hadn't decided."

Chelsi led Jake away from the fudge table, and they took a seat on a nearby bench. She looked into Jake's eyes. Her reply was barely above a whisper. "My vision."

* * *

"YOUR WHAT?" HE ASKED, DRAWING out his words. Jake was as intrigued by her statement as he was by the seriousness of Chelsi's expression. He knew the importance of communication and hated it when husbands dismissed what their wives said even before they had the chance to explain themselves.

"I had a vision of Kringlefest today."

Jake searched the candor in her sparkling hazel eyes and remained silent. A Vision? How could Chelsi have a vision of Kringlefest when we've only just arrived? His cell phone chirped inside his vest pocket, but he refrained from accepting the unwanted interruption.

"After Jasper adjusted my glasses today, I looked into the mirror and had a vision of Kringlefest. In the image before me, members of the children's handbell choir wore white gloves and Santa hats. They had just begun to play "Angels We Have Heard on High" when a toddler ran past the performers. He tripped and his red balloon escaped."

"Well, *there* you two are," Jim said, in his booming voice. "Chelsi, what's that age-old expression?" Jim looked up to the sky as if the answer were written in the clouds. "Ah, yes, coming home brings you back to where you belong. I'm very happy to see you've decided to stay with us in Kringle."

Chelsi gazed into Jake's eyes. "So am I, Jim." She reached over and took Jake's hand in hers. "It took me longer to realize that Paris was *not* what I was looking for in my life. Kringle was. Kringle is home. Now… I'm home."

Thank you, God, Jake thought, gently kissing the back of her hand.

Gloria reached in for a hug. "I couldn't be happier for you. Have you told Penny yet?"

"Not yet." Jake's cell phone vibrated again. "Jake, please go and check your message. I don't mind," Chelsi said.

"It's probably from your brother."

He pulled his phone from his vest pocket. "Yep. It's Randy. He said to meet him and Jessica at the skating rink. They have something important to tell us."

"We were on our way to the rink when we ran into you two. Let's see what has your brother all fired up." Jim said, patting Jake on his shoulder.

The lively sound of children's laughter could be heard above the din of enthusiastic festival-goers. The town of Kringle had ordered two truckloads of snow. A snow-removal team, along with two empty dump trucks, were sent to the higher elevations in Vermont. They scooped untouched snow from empty fields and trucked it home. It had always been a festival favorite, and not only by children. Adults enjoyed some friendly-fire snowballs thrown and deflected in the grown-up-only area.

An old basset hound named Sadie, wearing a red and green argyle dog sweater, waddled alongside her person. Vocalizing her excitement, the croon of her deep gruff bark reverberated through the vast sea of strolling legs. After that, twin boys took turns pulling a red wagon decorated like Santa's sleigh. Belle and Pantera, two short-haired Chihuahua's, dressed as Santa and Mrs. Claus, occupied the driver's seat.

Gloria had removed the red itinerary flier stashed inside her sling, then checked her watch. "The pet parade will begin in thirty minutes. All entrants, along with their person, will meet in front of the skate rental kiosk for a group photo. They will line up single file and promenade around the outside of the rink. Bowls of water and a tasty treat will be waiting for the participants at the end. A winner will be chosen for the best costume, and every participant will receive a ribbon."

"Gloria, what does the schedule say about the kringle pastry competition?"

"We've already seen Rosaria at the judging arena, Chelsi. She said there weren't many entrants willing to tackle the kringle pastry, but the Cream Puff Bakery, from Massapequa Park, New York, took home the blue ribbon. Rosaria was awarded second-place."

"Well, that's wonderful," Chelsi said, her face beaming with pride, "she's never made a kringle before. There'll be lots of time for her to practice making one for next year."

"Miss Chelsi!" Penny yelled, as she and Travis, along with an excited Cocoa, meandered their way through the crowd of people and pets.

Jake stared at Cocoa in disbelief. Cocoa was dressed as Rudolph. Just like Chelsi had said in her vision.

Wound-up from the activity of the festival, Cocoa pulled a bit harder on her leash than usual. Handing the leash over to Travis, Penny ran into Chelsi's embrace. "Did you miss your train?"

Crouching down, Chelsi said, "No, sweetie. I didn't get on the train. The most clever child in the whole wide world wrote me a very touching letter and colored an amazing picture. When I was at the train station, I needed a tissue, so I looked inside my carry-on and found this hidden treasure." Chelsi removed the folded-up paper from her handbag. She held up the hand-colored picture of a man, woman, child, and a dog sitting in front of a Christmas tree with "Miss Chelsi's Official Baking Certificate" on the other side. "This made me realize that Kringle is home, not Paris. Too bad it wasn't signed. I'd have loved to thank the artist."

Penny jumped up and down, clapping her hands. "That was me, that was me! I didn't want you to leave us and go to Paris, so I drew you the picture. I'm so glad you're staying here with us. Now you have your baking certificate to frame and hang above your desk."

Even Cocoa joined in in the excitement, showering Chelsi with doggie kisses and wiggly tail wags.

"Sweetheart, when did you decide to dress Cocoa up as Rudolph?" asked Jake.

Penny adjusted the dog's costume. "Doesn't she look adorable? Miss Gloria bought her a Rudolph costume from the pet store this morning. It came with a red nose, too. But she kept taking it off, so we left it home."

"Randy," Jake called out, "just got your text, bro. Hey, sorry I forgot to text you when I completed the job. I took care of the lady with the flat but didn't stay long enough to collect the fee, so I owe you for the call."

"Forget it. I hated to send you out. I knew you were on a mission and your time was short."

"So, son, what's the news?" Jim asked.

Jessica took her husband's hand, and Randy put his arm around Travis's shoulder. "We have exciting news. We didn't want to get anybody's hopes up, so we kept this a secret. We got notification earlier—after months of waiting, we've been accepted to adopt a child. A ten-year-old boy. We're adopting Travis!"

A hush hovered over the Hollister family. Travis stood there, not knowing what to say. His gaze bounced from Randy to Jessica to Penny and back again. "Adopted? Mr. Randy? You and Miss Jessica are adopting me?"

Randy kissed the top of Travis's head. "Yes, son, we are."

Speechless, Travis looked at Penny.

"Fern and Erik JoÚson received a letter from the adoption agency. Ms. Addams told them there was an interested, approved couple who were very excited to adopt you. That couple was us."

"You're the family that wanted to adopt me? I thought I'd be taken away from Kringle and Penny and have to move to St. Albans."

"St. Albans?" Randy asked. "That's the town where the adoption agency is located. Travis, did you see the letter that was written to Mr. and Mrs. JoÚson?"

Travis lowered his head. "Yes, sir."

"Is that why you ran away? Because you didn't want to leave Kringle?"

Penny sidled up close to Travis. "Yes, sir."

"Well, now that is all settled, come here Travis, and give me a big ol' hug," Jim said. "After all, I *am* your grandpa now."

Everyone applauded and hugs went around the circle.

"Dad," Penny whispered, "so is Travis now like… my brother?"

"No, Sweet P, he's your cousin."

Penny thought for a minute, then tugged on Jake's vest. "*Um*… Dad. What's a cousin?"

Jake smiled. "A cousin is a family member. Uncle Randy is my brother. Any children he and Aunt Jess have are… your… cousins."

"Cool," she said.

With the adoption news, Chelsi was beaming. She went over to Jessica and pulled her into a sisterly hug. "Congratulations, Jess. I couldn't be happier for you and Randy."

Jessica hugged her back. "You, too! I can't imagine Kringle without you." In a hushed voice, she continued, "Jake is a terrific guy and a wonderful dad. He's been smitten with you ever since you've returned to Kringle."

"May I have your attention please," said a women's voice over the loudspeaker. "Will the participants in this year's pet parade kindly make your way to the start/finish line. The parade will begin in twenty minutes. Twenty minutes."

"That's you, Penny," said Jake. "We'll meet you back here when you're finished."

"Can my cousin come with me?" she giggled.

"If he wants to."

Not allowing Travis to respond, Penny grabbed Travis by the sleeve of his jacket. "Come on, cousin, we have a pet parade to get to." The three of them bounded off, with Cocoa in the lead.

The sweet and silvery notes of the children's handbell choir warming up gave Jake pause. He turned and viewed a dozen children going through this afternoon's pre-concert routine. With each strike of their bells, the resonance captivated festival-goers of all ages.

He faced Chelsi. "In your vision, a child will trip and his balloon will slip through his fingers?"

"Yes. A red balloon."

The backdrop for the handbell choir was a forty-foot decorated Christmas tree the town purchased every year. To support local businesses, they continually purchased their holiday trees from Vermont-owned Christmas tree farms.

"Thank you all for attending Kringle's Golden Jubilee," the director said. "The children's handbell choir worked tirelessly this month to present you with not only a feast for your ears but your eyes, too. We will be performing three numbers. Please stick around after our final performance for the mayor's lighting of the Christmas tree, followed by the children's choir and the Live Nativity. For our first number, we will perform "Angels We Have Heard on High.""

Jake's curiosity had his eyes glued not on the performers but on the crowd assembling in front of them. Then he spotted it. A single red helium balloon tethered a few feet above the festival attendees. Several measures into the number, the balloon began to dance. A scampering toddler broke away from the confines of his mother, letting out a playful screech when she caught up to him. He tripped. Landing on all fours, the red balloon released from his tiny grasp. In an instant, his laughter turned to tears as he watched his red balloon sail up to the heavens.

Jake turned and stared into Chelsi's eyes, neither one uttered a word. I can't believe it. She's two for two on her visions. Not that I ever doubted her, but still…

Jake approached the mother, asking if the little boy was okay. "Thank you, he'll be fine," she said, wiping away small pebbles from the scraped pad of his hand. "He's more upset from losing his balloon than anything. He wriggled free from my grasp when I attempted to tie it onto his wrist."

Satisfied the child was not seriously injured, Jake took Chelsi's hand. Weaving their way toward the skating rink, he asked, "Do you have any other hidden talents I should know about?"

Chelsi gave him a sidewise glance. With a twinkle in her eyes, she said, "The day isn't over yet. But we do need to hurry. The parade's about to begin."

Jake and Chelsi joined Jim, Gloria, Randy, and Jessica already in position near the center of the parade route. Children waved at the cluster of onlookers standing nearby while their parents snapped hundreds of pictures with cameras or cell phones. A dog pulling a fire hydrant. A cat in an elf costume. Even a hamster spinning in his decorated cage filed past several judges holding clipboards, each one vying for the best costume rosette.

"There's Penny and Travis," piped up Chelsi, grabbing hold of Jake's elbow. "And look, doesn't Cocoa look adorable?"

"Gloria, thanks again for getting Cocoa the costume," Jake said. "Time ran away from me."

Glancing Chelsi's way, she smiled. "I knew you had a lot going on."

Penny, Travis, and Cocoa wove their way around the crowd to catch up with their family. "Daddy, did you see us? Did you see us get our picture taken?" asked an excited Penny. "The lady from the newspaper tried to get a picture with all the pets, but some were more interested in the treats left for them at the finish line. The photographer took our picture and the boy with the hamster. She said Cocoa looked like a winner, but the judges gave the best costume to the dog from the firehouse. His person was dressed like a firefighter, and the dog was pulling a fire hydrant."

Cocoa sat looking proud of the participant ribbon pinned to her costume. Jake took her leash and ruffled Cocoa's ears. "You did great, Cocoa. We'll get 'em next year, girl."

Cocoa let out a woof in agreement with Jake's comment.

"Time for you and Travis to head over to the church to line up," Gloria said. "Travis, what part are you playing in the Live Nativity?"

"This year they cast me to play the first wise man. We each have a line." Travis got all serious and struck a pose. "Where is He that is born King of the Jews?'"

Randy put his arm around Travis's shoulder and gave it a little jiggle. "My son the actor."

"Come on, Pokey," Penny yelled. "We gotta get a move on. Bye, Dad."

"We'll see you aft—" but, the remainder of his words were heard only by the remaining adults standing near him.

"I see Mayor Shaefer now," Gloria said, pulling out the festival schedule. "The children's choir and Live Nativity participants will process from the church shortly. The tree lighting ceremony will begin shortly after."

* * *

FOR THEIR FINAL NUMBER, EVERYONE joined the children's choir by singing "Joy to the World." The children stepped off stage, then scrambled to the assigned booth to return their costumes and pick up the baked cookies they brought from home. Since the kringle baking contest had long been completed, Rosaria was more than happy to volunteer in distributing the baked goods to the correct child.

Penny and her friend Reese paired up. Rosaria had baked almost five-dozen angel cookies decorated in flowing white icing robes. She surprised Penny by placing a yellow-colored M&M for their halos. The children were excited to offer festival-goers their homemade cookies, and the recipients were *more* than happy to accept them.

Holding her serving tray, Penny asked, "Daddy, did you watch me sing?"

"We sure did, Pumpkin. You all did a wonderful job."

Reese elbowed Penny. "Oh, yeah, thank you for coming to the Kringlefest Pageant. Would you like a cookie?"

"I'd love one," Jake said, helping himself to one of Penny's.

Reese held her tray out, offering cookies as well. Chelsi glanced at Penny's cookies and those of her friend, too. "Miss Rosaria did a beautiful job in decorating the angel cookies, didn't she, Penny?"

"She sure did." Holding the cookie tray closer to Chelsi, Penny asked, "Would you like one?"

Accepting an angel cookie, Chelsi replied. "Yes, I'd love one."

Reese offered hers as well. "My mommy baked her special lemon cookies."

"And they do look quite tasty." Jake took one, but Chelsi did not. "I do so love a good lemon cookie."

Penny had moved onto the next family group, but Reese stayed put. Still holding her tray out, she said, "There's plenty, Miss Chelsi. I have a second tray back at the table."

Chelsi hesitantly chose one of her cookies. "Thank you, Reese. I'd love one. Please tell your mommy thank you."

Reese took off to catch up with Penny.

"What's up, Chels? Why the hesitation?"

Chelsi looked at the delicate pale-yellow scalloped cookie sitting on her napkin, then back to Jake. "Jake, these are lemon *poppy seed* cookies. Poppy seeds are black."

He sucked in a breath. "You don't have to eat it, Chels, if you don't want to."

"No. It's about time I put my big girl pants on and face my fear of not eating black foods."

Chelsi looked down at her cookie and took a deep breath. "But you know what? I can't change what happened in the past, but I'm ready to change my future."

"Atta girl."

She broke off a piece of the lemon poppy seed cookie and popped it into her mouth. She closed her eyes. "*Mmmm*, the bright hint of citrus from the grated lemon zest is lovely."

"And the poppy seeds?"

She took another bite. "Nutty. Crunchy. A great complement to the lemon zest."

"How do you feel about it?"

Finishing the cookie, she smiled, "I feel good. I wish I had another one."

Jake smiled. "That's my girl."

* * *

"WELL, THERE YOU TWO LOVE birds are," Randy said. "As soon as Penny finishes handing out her cookies, the kids want to go on the carousel. You game?"

Chelsi's face lit up. "Oh, Jake, that sounds like so much fun. I haven't been on a carousel in… forever."

"*Um,* not sure about that, bro. But, Chelsi, you can go on with the kids. Don't let me hold you back."

"Why not?" Randy asked. "I haven't been on one since mom took us to Coney Island when we were kids."

"Me either, but don't you remember?"

Randy rolled his eyes. "Don't tell me you won't get on because you fell off grabbing for the brass ring?"

"I thought I broke my arm."

"But you didn't," his younger brother said. "*And* the area was padded, 'cause you weren't the first kid to fall off his carousel horse."

Jake looked at Chelsi. "We'll see."

Patting his older son on the shoulder, Jim said, "We need to get going. Joe McIntyre just texted me, and they will be returning to the inn in about forty-five minutes."

"Do you need me to go with you to prepare a light dinner?"

"That won't be necessary, Chelsi. Rosaria put a Mississippi Pot roast and veggies in the crockpot before she left this morning. You kids enjoy the rest of Kringlefest." He stared into his son's eyes. "I understand a ride on the carousel might be in order for you. A lot of people have been successful in grabbing for the coveted brass ring. All you have to do is take that next step, son. Believe in the process. Grab hold of that ring. Happiness is a right we all have in life, and it's completely in your hands. If you don't do it, nobody else will do it for you."

Not responding to the subject of the carousel *or* the brass ring, Jake asked, "You taking Cocoa?"

"Yup. Dog's gotta eat," Jim said.

"We'll see you at home, Pop."

Chelsi smiled. "Bye, Jim. We have a lot to talk about over the next few days."

"Don't you worry non, darlin'. The Snowberry Inn practically runs herself."

"But it's the times when she doesn't that we need to discuss."

Reaching for Jake's hand, Penny said, "Come on, Daddy, the line is super short for the carousel ride. It looks like so much fun."

"Why don't you and Travis go first; this way I can take your picture."

"But you said—" she protested.

"Penny, I know what I said. Tell you what, you pick out your reindeer and I'll get you buckled in safely."

"Hurry, Daddy! I really want to sit on Rudolph."

"Okay, I'll see what I can do." Despite the weather cooling down, Jake felt moisture beading up on his forehead at the thought of riding a carousel after all these years. Though he was just a child when he fell off, he remembered it as if it was yesterday. This should be a snap. It's a kid's ride for goodness sake, and Penny has her heart set on riding Rudolph.

Penny stepped up onto the wooden platform and walked quickly around the empty reindeer figures, but stopped short. "Ohhh no, Daddy look! Rudolph has already been taken. Can we wait and take the next ride?"

"It's getting late, Pen. We need to eat, take a bath, read *'Twas the Night Before Christmas*, and get you to bed so Santa can come tonight."

"Munch, they're all the same," Travis said. "We can be next to each other if we sit here. Do you want to try for the brass ring?"

Penny vigorously shook her head. "No way! Too scary."

Travis looked at the names of the carousel reindeer. "Okay. Then you ride Cupid, and I'll ride Comet."

"Well, I guess."

Jake lifted his daughter onto Cupid's back and securely buckled her in. She picked up the leather reins and tried them out.

"Giddy up, Cupid. Let's get this ride going."

Chelsi stood nearby, ready to photograph Penny and Travis as they passed by her.

"Mommy, I'm scared," said a young child, sitting upon Rudolph's back.

"There's nothing to be afraid of, sweetheart. But, if it will make you feel safer, I'll stand right here with you," said her mother.

"Sorry, ma'am," said the carousel operator, "no one is permitted to stand while the ride is in motion."

The toddler picked up the buckle and shook it. "Down, down. I want to get down!" she cried.

Stepping onto the platform, Jake asked, "May I help you with the child?"

The little girl's wails grew louder as she pawed at the safety buckle.

"Yes, that would be wonderful. Thank you."

Jake helped the child off the ride and looked back at Penny. She hadn't noticed that Rudolph had unexpectedly become available.

He looked over at Chelsi. She smiled and signaled to him to get on.

If Chelsi could overcome her fear of eating black foods, then I can certainly spend three minutes on a child's amusement ride.

The warning bell rang. "On or off?" the ride operator asked.

Jake took a deep breath. "On." He mounted Rudolph, and before he knew it, the ride began. The reindeer ascended and descended to the song, "Rudolph the Red-Nosed Reindeer."

The sweat-fest Jake had going on began to run down his temple. The on-lookers, surrounding the carousel, were all waving and happily taking photos. He looked down at his hands, not realizing he had white-knuckled the galloping pole in front of him. Loosening his grasp, he took a deep sigh of relief. *So far, so good.*

Looking over his shoulder he thought he caught a glimpse of Jasper and Olivia with their dogs, but when he looked again, they were gone.

Carnival-goers were applauding loudly. Jake noticed several of the outer reindeer riders had captured a ring from the brass ring dispenser. Okay, Hollister. You can do this. Grab that brass ring.

He spotted a young boy standing next to the ring dispenser, then shook off the notion that a butterfly had flitted several feet above his head.

Chelsi smiled, waved, and snapped a few pics when he passed her. *A ring for Chelsi.* He watched as the brass ring dispenser approached. He leaned closer towards it. The rider in front of him reached out and grabbed a ring, but when Jake approached the dispenser, there was no ring in the shoot. *Crap! I hope I'll get another chance before the ride concludes.*

Just as Jake feared, the carousel lights blinked off then on. *Now or never!* He held tightly to the pole with his left hand and leaned in as close as he could. There it is. I can see the ring. He set his sights on the target, cocked his index finger like he was shooting a gun, and locked his finger around the ring, drawing it in. Closing his eyes, he thought. *I did it!* I got the brass ring and didn't fall off. It only took me forty years to overcome that fear, and now I'm awarded a ring for my efforts.

The ride came to an end. He tucked the ring safely into the front pocket of his jeans and walked across the platform to get Penny.

"Daddy, did you see me? I couldn't find you in the crowd."

"Yes, Squirt, I saw you. I hope you had a fun time."

"I did! And Travis got a brass ring. Isn't it wonderful?"

Travis opened the palm of his hand to reveal a brass ring. "Look at that, kiddo. Merry Christmas. It's not every day you find out you've been adopted and got a brass ring all in the same day.

"That was soooooo much fun, Daddy. You really missed out."

Jake gave Chelsi the universal *shhhh* sign, indicating to her not to let on he had been on the ride. Though Penny had a fun time, she would've been disappointed that she didn't get to ride Rudolph.

"Hey, Travis, did you see Mikey?" Penny asked.

"Yeah, I saw him standing by the brass ring machine, but then he was gone. I wonder where he went?"

"Well," Jake said, putting his arms around Chelsi and Penny. "It's time to get my girls home. Let's stop and pick up the cookie tray and talk to Rosaria."

"Oh, I saw her a little while ago. She went home with your dad and Gloria. Said she had to wrap a few gifts and wanted to get back to the inn in time to serve tonight's supper."

Oh, no! I didn't buy a Christmas present for Chelsi. Why didn't I think of that sooner today? Jake put his hand into the front pocket of his jeans and rolled the brass ring around in his fingertips. *I know exactly wha—"*

"Jasper, Olivia, I thought I saw you earlier," Chelsi said, shaking Jasper's hand.

"Lovely to see you this evening, Chelsi," he replied. "I see you have decided against Paris."

"I did indeed," she said. "I recently read a poem by an amazing Swiss philosopher who advised me to look inside my heart. I did. And here I am!"

Olivia gazed at Jasper. "We're delighted about your decision."

Bending down to greet Max and Gwen, she asked, "Did you two enjoy Kringlefest? I bet you met lots of fur friends today, huh?"

"They certainly did," Olivia pipped up.

"Chelsi, would you be so kind as to help me find the loo?"

"Of course, Olivia. It's inside the lobby at Saint Michael's. I don't blame you for not wanting to use the porta-potty. They can be quite ripe at this time of day. Penny, why don't you come with us, too. Jake, we'll meet you at the truck."

"Sounds good," he said, kissing her cheek.

A young boy approached Jake, then removed his hat. "Excuse me, mister. I saw you won a brass ring, but you disappeared before I had a chance to talk to you."

"I thought I saw you near the dispenser. What can I do for you, son?"

"You waited a long time to get your brass ring today. I have a box for you to safely store your prize in."

"No, that's okay, the ring is safe in my pocket," he said, tapping his jeans.

The boy looked down at the ground and began to walk away. Jake studied him for a minute. His hair looked rather unruly, in need of a good cut. His too-long jeans were frayed at the ends, and there was a hole in his glove.

Jake glanced at Jasper, then back to the boy. "On second thought, yes, of course, I'd love a box." The boy reached down into a well-worn paper bag and removed a three-inch square white cardboard box. It too was a bit tattered. A few dollar bills fell out of the bag, floating to the ground. Jake helped gather the youngster's earnings.

"Thanks, mister."

"What is your name, son?"

"Mikey."

Jake noticed that this youngster fit the description Penny had given him of the boy, Mikey, who they met when they ran away. "Are you the same boy who helped Penny and Travis the other night?"

"I didn't do nothin' wrong, mister, honest. We just talked."

Jake took out his wallet and gave the youngster a five-dollar bill.

"Thank you, mister!" he said, stuffing it into the bag.

"You know, Mikey, there are agencies that can help. You don't have to be alone. Come by the firehouse anytime, we'll be happy to assist in any way we can."

Jasper nodded to the boy. "I gotta go, mister. Thanks for buying my last box."

Jake looked away for a moment to place the ring in the white box. When he went to answer the boy, he was gone. "Boy, Jasper, he was quick."

"On the merry-go-round you sat upon Rudolph, did you not?" Jasper asked.

"Yeah, my daughter wanted to sit on Rudolph, but it was taken, and then it wasn't." Jake reached into his pocket and removed the brass ring. "This is kinda special to me. Silly I know, but when I was a child, I fell off the carousel reaching for a brass ring."

"May I see the ring."

Jasper put the ring in the palm of his hand, and covered it with his other hand. Returned the ring to the box and handed it back to Jake. "Not silly at all. I'm sure you'll put it to good use."

The church bells tolled seven times. Jasper clicked open his pocket watch. "We must mind the hour. It's well past suppertime. Jake, what time are the Christmas services at Saint Michael's?"

"Nine and eleven o'clock on Christmas Day, and there is a Christmas Eve service tonight which begins at eleven-forty-five. It's a lovely service, with lots of singing, and the adult bellringer choir performs."

"I fear I'd fall asleep during the pastor's Homily," Jasper said, in a whispered voice. "And I snore as loud as a fully loaded, fast-moving freight train."

Poor Olivia! "Well, we're all going to the eleven o'clock service tomorrow morning. Why don't you and Olivia come to the inn around eight? Chelsi told me she and Rosaria have an incredible breakfast planned. After breakfast, we'll all go together."

"What a splendid idea. I think we shall do just that." Jasper put his hand on Jake's shoulder. A spark of excitement ignited deep within his soul. It was like the first time his dad took him out for a driving lesson, seeing his daughter take her first step, and kissing Chelsi, all rolled into one. When Jasper removed his hand, the feeling faded away.

"Oh, there's Olivia," Jasper said, seeing the girls across the parking lot. "I must dash."

Jake stopped and stared at the shoulder Jasper had touched. He shook his head when he couldn't figure out what had just happened, then continued to meet up with Chelsi and Penny.

Chapter Twenty-Nine

CHELSI'S RECIPE FOR LOVE

AHHHH... IS THERE ANYTHING BETTER than that first bite of your fresh-baked, cranberry-orange cinnamon roll dripping with warm cream cheese frosting on Christmas morning? Absolutely! It's the animated sounds coming from four excited little girls after they've snuck down to scope out the presents under the Christmas tree. But to their dismay, the children's packages were cleverly tagged with Dasher, Dancer, Prancer, and Vixen, so no one knew whose gift belonged to whom.

A few short hours ago, the Snowberry Inn bustled with the sights, sounds, and smells of Christmas morning: the captivated expressions as the children tore open their festively wrapped presents, three worn-out family pets warming their backs in front of the crackling fire after a brisk romp in the snow, and familiar Christmas carols being played on the Hollister family record player.

Florence McIntyre had joined Olivia on the winged chairs for tea. Twisting her wrist back and forth, she ran her fingers over her new Christmas present... a diamond tennis bracelet. With each movement of her hand, the twinkling lights from the Christmas tree played tag with the diamond's faceted edges.

Olivia leaned closer to Florence. "I've never seen such a beautiful bracelet. You must have been quite surprised by it."

Straightening the clasp, Florence replied. "Yes, I was. Joe didn't want me to see him shopping in a jewelry store, so he bought it in Arizona before we left for Kringle."

"That's a mighty fine driver the Mrs. bought you for Christmas, Joe. I bet you can't wait to take it out on the links."

Joseph McIntyre removed the six-inch red bow and unwound the ribbon from the golf club his wife had bought him. "You got that right. I was able to test drive this one in the store's golf simulator. But hopefully, I can carry the fairway bunker on Arrowhead's first hole, then hit it over the trees on the second."

"Jasper, do you play?"

"Can't say I ever fancied the game. Now, Olivia and I *do* enjoy a riveting match of croquet."

The console record player, which played the sounds of the holiday season, turned off with a final click. Jim looked through the large selection of LPs housed behind the cabinet doors. "Any requests?" he asked.

"You've got quite a selection of records, Jim," Olivia said. "Your choice of music today has been most enjoyable."

"Ah, the classics… can't beat 'em," Jim said, shaking his head. "My late wife, Jane, had quite an extensive collection. She'd ask me to stop at antique stores and yard sales so she could browse their selection of Christmas LPs or Broadway show tunes. I've got about three-dozen packed away in the garage. Too many scratches. But I can't bring myself to get rid of them. Of all the holidays, Christmas was her favorite. Thanksgiving morning she'd start playing her favorite album as soon as Santa Claus had made his appearance at the end of the Macy's Thanksgiving Day parade. Then she'd say, 'the Christmas season has begun.'" Removing the vinyl record from its cover, he looked in the direction of the kitchen. "I can still see her now.

She'd be in her favorite apron, kneading bread or baking cookies, singing to them all day long. This next one was her favorite."

The unmistakable voice of Judy Garland singing, "Have Yourself a Merry Little Christmas" emanated from the speakers in the mid-century stereo console.

"Florence, how very thoughtful of you to buy me this lovely gift," Olivia said. "You shouldn't have."

"Nonsense, you and Jasper are part of the Hollister family now. We all are."

Olivia opened her new book on the celebrations of afternoon tea. "Tea is a huge part of our British upbringing." Bringing the book closer to her nose, she said, "I do love the sound and smell of being the first person to open a brand-new book."

"Wait till you smell… and *taste* Christmas dinner. Chelsi followed Jane's recipe for Bacon-Roasted Turkey. My wife smeared the bird with seasoned butter, then crisscrossed strips of bacon over the entire turkey. After a few hours, she basted it with maple syrup tapped from the inn's maple trees."

"It does sound most delightful, Jim," Olivia said. "But—"

"Last batch of cinnamon rolls fresh from the oven. Any takers?" Rosaria passed a second tray of cinnamon rolls. The sweet fragrance of freshly grated orange zest combined with the tart chew of the dried cranberries set everyone's taste buds watering, again. Four girls trotted down from Penny's room to the gathering room, their new Barbie dolls in tow. "Oh, me. Yes, please!" they yelled, in unison.

"I thought as much. I've already set your pastries and glasses of milk out on the kitchen table for you."

The back door closed, alerting the dogs to greet whoever had arrived. "Rosaria, have you seen Chelsi?" Jake asked.

"Yeah, I just left her. She's in your dad's office going over stuff with him and Gloria." Rosaria gave Jake a sly look. "I know I just met ya, Jake Hollister, but whatcha got goin' on?"

He gave her half a grin. "You'll see."

"Oh-a. My. Gawd!"

"*Shhhh*," Jake said.

"You okay in there, darlin'?"

"You betcha, Jim. No worries. Just me and Jake in here conversing about nothin' at all."

His father's office door was open, but Jake lightly knocked on the door frame. "When you get a few minutes, Chels, I'd like to talk to you."

"Sure." Chelsi pointed to the vacant chair next to Gloria. "Have a seat, we're almost done here."

"*Umm*." He shook his head, then held out her jacket. "Alone, if you don't mind."

"That's my cue," Gloria said, standing up. "I think it's time I get ready for church."

Gloria smiled when she walked past Jake, but his eyes were focused only on Chelsi. "I've got something to show you, Chels, but you'll need your jacket on."

She rose from behind the desk and allowed Jake to help her with her jacket. "I see you're ready for church. It shouldn't take me long to change."

He kissed her forehead. "You look beautiful in what you're wearing right now."

"Pop, Chelsi and I will be right back."

"We have to leave in an hour, so don't be too long."

His words were left unheard by his son, for the back door had already closed. "I must say, that boy's been more nervous this morning than a long-tailed cat in a roomful of rocking chairs."

Randy chuckled. "You got that right. Jess, I think we need to collect our son and head home to change. Pop, we'll see you at church."

Jessica kissed her husband. "Our son. I never thought I'd ever hear those words."

Olivia, we're excited you and Jasper are joining us this morning. It's such a beautiful service. Last year, Pastor Ross carried the baby Jesus, wrapped in a white blanket, and placed him in the empty manger between Mary and Joseph. It was quite moving."

Jasper looked at Olivia and gave her a brief wink. She smiled, rested her porcelain teacup back onto its saucer, and placed them onto the side table.

"Yes, thank you, Jessica. It would be an honor to join your family," Jasper said. "You see, Olivia and I are leaving Kringle today."

"Oh, no! We'll miss you. Does Chelsi know?"

"Not yet. We spoke to your vicar yesterday at the festival and scheduled an appointment to see him right after today's last service."

"Thank you again for helping my Gloria when she fell, Jasper. Please come back and visit us next time you're in town."

Jasper walked across the room and stood behind Olivia's chair "We absolutely will." He looked down into her eyes and gave her shoulder a little squeeze. "If our work brings us back here."

Their attention was drawn to the methodical popping sound coming from the record player needle.

"Darn it!" Jim lifted the curved tonearm and repositioned the needle to play the next song. "I forgot about that scratch."

"Grandpa, I can't find Daddy, and Cocoa needs to go out. I can put the leash on her and walk her out to the clearing near the gazebo. Is that okay?"

"Yes, but next time, please come and ask me instead of yelling halfway across the house."

"Sorry."

* * *

THE SUN'S RAYS WERE BRIGHT, but not warm enough to take the chill out of the midmorning air. It *was* December in Vermont, after all. During the night, the Kringle countryside accumulated three additional inches of wet, heavy snow, the kind that was perfect for building a snowman.

Jake and Chelsi walked hand in hand in silence through the pristine snow. Their attention was drawn to a rustling sound high in the branches of the century-old trees. "See, even the squirrels are smart enough to stay out of the snow."

"That's probably because he's forgotten where he buried his Christmas dinner and is going elsewhere for supper." They both laughed. Chelsi was beaming with happiness. It felt nice to be in the thick of things. To be part of a community again. To trust a man enough to open her heart to love, *and* to return the love. Many of the townsfolk had remembered her from her childhood. It was humbling. Heartwarming. Coming back to Kringle had transformed Chelsi's life. Day by day, she was building a new life her for herself. For Jake. For Penny.

She caught Jake stealing glances at her from the corner of her eye and wondered what was on that incredibly handsome mind of his. "Where are you taking me, Jake Hollister?" she asked, pulling on his hand to stop him. "Can't you see I'm not exactly *dressed* for a romp in the snow?"

Narrowing his eyes, he gave her a slow, lopsided grin. "I can take care of that in a New York minute, Chelsi Burnet." Jake bent his knees, put one arm around her back and the other behind her knees. In one fell swoop, he scooped her up and cradled her in his arms.

Chelsi let out a little squeal, then laughed. "That works, too." She stared into Jake's eyes. She knew he was mere seconds away from kissing her, and she couldn't wait. They were good together. She deserved Jake. She was perfect for Penny, and they adored each other.

"Are we there yet?" she asked, like a child on a family road trip. "Almost. But now, you've gotta trust me."

"I trust you, Jake."

"Good. Close your eyes."

Nuzzling the side of her face into the warmth of Jake's embrace, she took in the intoxicating scent of his confidence. His mystery. Blend them together with his love languages of quality family time, encouraging words, and commitment to community was his recipe for love. Jake was the complete package. *Hmmm… I could get used to this.*

The subtle sound of snow crunching under Jake's footsteps subsided. Repositioning his hold around Chelsi's body, he stomped off the excess snow, tousling her a bit.

"Not that I mind you carrying me around, and I'm tremendously grateful you didn't throw me over your shoulder in a fireman's carry, but can I open my eyes yet?"

"Fireman's carry? Now, where's the romance in that? I'll put you down now but keep 'em closed."

"*Hmm-hmmm.*" Not promising she wouldn't peek, Chelsi separated one of the fingers she had covering her eyes, but all she could see was white. *What is he up to?*

"Take my hands," Jake's words were low and soft. Chelsi took in a long cleansing breath, then released it slowly.

Pondering his next move, she extended her hands in search of his. The intimate touch of his hand taking hers sent her emotions in a whirlwind. His essence melted into hers. Everything stilled. It was just the two of them. He raised her left hand to his lips, turned it over, then kissed her palm. The sensation zinged straight down to her toes.

Chelsi's breath caught in her throat. "Jake," she whispered.

He reached down and stroked the line of her jaw with his fingers. She opened her eyes. Those same eyes were looking at him now with a mixture of anticipation and wonder. "Chelsi, I know this might seem fast, but we've known each other for a lifetime. We were best friends when we were ten years old and we still are."

He sucked in a huge breath. "Chelsi, I love you."

Jake locked his gaze onto Chelsi's eyes and lowered himself to one knee.

Ohmygod... Ohmygod... Ohmygod...

Covering her mouth, a tiny squeal released from deep within her throat. Time stood still. Not wanting to break eye contact, Jake reached into his vest pocket and pulled out the little white box. He smiled and removed the lid. "Chelsi, will you marry me?"

Chelsi helped Jake to his feet. He reached down and tilted her chin up so he could look directly into her eyes. Eyes that had released her warm, salty tears of joy.

Chelsi smiled. "Rudolph?"

"Rudolph? What are you talking about?"

Jake looked inside the box. "This was supposed to be the brass ring I won on the carousel. I was going to take you to the jewelry store tomorrow to pick out your engagement ring."

"But, you see, this was another part of my vision. A ring with the likeness of Rudolph."

"Jasper," Jake whispered. "He had the brass ring in his hand."

"*Umm...* Chels. Now, will you please give me your answer?"

"My answer? Oh, Jake, yes! Yes. I'll marry you!"

A tornado-like wind swirled around them. It created an unbroken ring of snow which began at their feet, swirled past their heads, then dissipated returning to heaven.

He removed the ring from its box and slipped it onto the third finger of her left hand. Chelsi grabbed his face with both hands and pulled his mouth to hers. Hard. Lips locked, Jake picked her up and swung her around in circles.

Cocoa's bark echoed through the snow-covered yard. Jake and Chelsi looked over in time to see Cocoa barreling down at them at full speed, her leash dragging behind in the snow, Penny in a slow run trying to catch up to her escaped dog.

Cocoa was first to reach the couple, sending them both tumbling onto the fluffy snow. "Wait for me!" Penny yelled. She jumped on the growing pile and rolled around in the snow.

"Daddy, what are you two doing out here?"

"Penny, I just asked Miss Chelsi to marry me. You're the first to know."

She gave Jake and Chelsi a group hug, with Cocoa joining in on the excitement. "I'm so happy for you—did you say yes, Miss Chelsi?"

Chelsi reached over and tucked an errant clump of hair behind Penny's ear. "Yes, I did, precious. Look at the magnificent ring your daddy gave me."

Penny's eyes widened. "Oh, it's Rudolph! I love it." Penny rolled over and gave Chelsi a big hug, then a kiss on her cheek. "Oh, Miss Chelsi, I love you! I'm so happy you're going to be my new mom. You know my mommy is in heaven. Is it okay if I call you Mom?"

Chelsi looked over to Jake. "Did you know about this?" Without a response, he motioned for her to answer Penny's question.

"Penny, I love you, too. I'd be honored to have you call me Mom. You know I never had children of my own, so may I call you my daughter?"

"Sure!" she said, throwing her arms around Chelsi. "Boy, this was the best Christmas ever! I get a sparkly red bike, my very first cousin, and a new mom in two days!"

"Does anyone else know?"

Jake helped his bride-to-be off the ground and wiped some of the snow out of her hair. "They suspect. So, let's go inside and make it official."

"Daddy, will you give me a piggy-bank ride back into the house?"

"Sure thing, kiddo." Jake reached for Penny's hand, helped her walk up his body, then climb onto his shoulders. He held onto her ankles and gingerly galloped away.

"Hey, Jake! Don't worry about me... and Cocoa... I've got this," she yelled after them.

Jake waved his hand in the air and continued the celebration with his daughter.

Cocoa was lying in the snow, licking the snow out from between the pads of her paws. "I see you forgot your boots too, huh?" The dog sat up and looked at Chelsi. "Looks like it's just me and you, girl."

* * *

"GRANDPA, GRANDPA, GRANDPA! DADDY ASKED Miss Chelsi to marry him, and she said yes!" Penny yelled, running from outside into the kitchen.

"I had no doubt," Jim replied.

"And Grandpa, wait 'til you see her pretty ring. It's a Rudolph ring!"

"Well, I'll be. Ain't that different."

"Penny, dear, why all the commotion?" Gloria asked, coming down the stairs.

Penny led Jake and Chelsi by the hands into the gathering room. "Everybody, my daddy asked Miss Chelsi to marry him, and she said yes! I saw them in the field when I took Cocoa out. He kissed her hand, then put his knee into the snow."

¡Dios mío! ¡Felicidades, Chelsi!

"Yes! Congratulations!" The McIntyres said with their girls giving Penny hugs.

Olivia looked over at Jasper and whispered, "Did you hear that, Jasper? Jake asked Chelsi to marry him."

Jasper reached for Olivia's hand. "Yes, indeed. *Now* our work here is complete," he replied, quietly.

"Thank you, everyone," said Chelsi, looking down at her rather unconventional engagement ring. "I'm still in shock!"

"All right missy, time to get ready for church. I purposely took Miss Chelsi out in the backyard so we could have a few minutes to ourselves."

Jasper reached his hand out to Jake. "Well, congratulations, my good man. Chelsi is a remarkable woman."

"Yes, sir, she absolutely is. We'll all celebrate tonight with Christmas turkey and sparkling wine." Jake looked at Jasper and continued. "I'm sure your meeting with the pastor won't last too long, and I hope you and Olivia will join us all for Christmas dinner."

"We'd love to, but you see, we're leaving directly after our meeting."

"We're getting married!" Olivia blurted out.

"What? Married?" Jake asked.

Jasper tapped the breast pocket of his sportscoat. "I've been carrying around her ring for as long as I can remember."

"Everyone, did you hear that? Jasper and Olivia are getting married after church today."

Applause could be heard throughout the inn. Even Cocoa, Max, and Gwen were running in circles.

Penny came up to Olivia and whispered into her ear. "I didn't know angels could get married."

"My dear, what makes you think we are angels?" Olivia asked, in an equally low voice.

"Well, it happened the night of Miss Chelsi's party. I was talking to my mommy and fell asleep. You know she had a bad car accident and she's in heaven."

"Yes, precious girl, I know."

Penny nodded. "Anyway, Mommy told me she was happy in heaven, but she missed me and my daddy... *a lot*. She said she wants my daddy to be happy and hopes he gets married again. Then I saw you and Dr. Jasper in my dream, too. You were there with my mommy."

"Did that frighten you?" Olivia asked.

"Oh, no. I'm happy Mommy has friends in heaven. Did you have a car accident—"

"Penny, *please* go upstairs and get ready for church. We have to leave in fifteen minutes."

"Okay. Sorry, Daddy."

"Go on, dear. Listen to your father," Olivia said, "we can talk more later if you wish."

Penny leaned over and kissed Olivia on her cheek. "Thank you, Miss Olivia, for being my mommy's friend."

* * *

THE RED BRICK STRUCTURE OF Saint Michael's Church was built across from the town square, at the end of Main Street. Its gleaming spires, rising toward the heavens, were visible for blocks. Century-old maple trees stood dormant in the bitterly cold winter of Kringle, Vermont, eagerly waiting for spring's rebirth. But that day was Christmas, the day Christians celebrate the birth of Christ. The congregation, eager to take their seats, climbed the church stairs, then filed through the redwood double doors, to the sound of the church bells tolling.

"We're late, Chels. I'll drop you and Penny off, then park the truck."

"I'll text you with our location. Hopefully Randy and Jessica arrived early to save us enough seats."

Chelsi held Penny's hand, guiding her up the stairs. "Penny!" Travis said, as if he hadn't seen her in years. He was waiting in the vestibule to usher them to their seats. "We saved pews C14 and 15, and now everyone is here."

"Except for my daddy. He's parking the truck."

"You kids go ahead, I'll let your dad know where we are."

Chelsi hadn't finished her sentence before the two of them had strode away, hand in hand.

Jake didn't attempt either of the church's two parking lots, but headed right for the overflow lot, parked, then jogged across the street.

Taking the stairs two at a time, he found Chelsi waiting for him just inside the door. The choir had already begun singing their entrance hymn, "O Come, All Ye Faithful," and, as in previous years, Pastor Ross ceremoniously walked down the aisle cradling the baby Jesus wrapped in a white blanket. Jake and Chelsi stood next to the empty Wish Tree, which at one time held wishes for families in need. Jake, and the rest of the Kringle FD had hand-delivered hundreds of wrapped gifts, all donated by the children and families of Kringle. They spotted Maximillian and Gwendolyn along the back wall of the church, just behind the last pew. Jasper did say they were leaving Kringle right after their wedding.

The Christmas service was as beautiful as everyone said it would be. Though the choir was still performing their recessional hymn, "Joy to the World," the congregation had begun filing out.

"Jasper, you got a few minutes?" Jake asked. "It looks like the pastor will still be a few minutes wishing everyone a Merry Christmas."

Jasper patted his shoulder. "Sure, sure, son. What's on your mind?"

Jake shuddered from a tingle rising up his spine. "Chelsi told me about the visions she saw when she got her glasses. Can you shed a little light on that subject?"

"I'm not sure what you are asking of me."

"When you first made her glasses, she told me she looked into a mirror and saw my reflection instead of her own. Then yesterday, when you adjusted her frames, she looked into the same mirror. It revealed several visions she had of Kringlefest even before it started."

"Ah... you're a smart man, Jake Hollister. Close your eyes."

"Close my eyes?"

"Yes, I want you to see something, a vision, if you will."

Sunday, 22 December 1940

Saint Ann's Street

Manchester, England

6:38 p.m.

Shrouded in darkness, the horrific wail of air raid sirens raged; while silent screams flooded the city streets. German bombers had been identified. Manchester, England, was under attack.

Jasper wished they had declined tea with Reverend Nigel and began their wedding rehearsal earlier. Saint Ann's Church was a short block-and-a-half from their journey's end, but he feared the outcome could end in tragedy for the betrothed couple.

He reached for his fiancée's hand. "Quickly! Olivia!" he yelled. "To the bomb shelter!"

Like a hungry predator, drawing closer to its defenseless prey, the drone of a half-dozen low-flying enemy planes began their massed assault.

The ground shuddered as the first wave of bombs exploded, sending Jasper and Olivia plummeting to the pavement.

Helping her to regain balance, Jasper shouted, "Olivia! Are you all right?"

"I-I believe—" her voice stopped, mid-sentence.

Jasper glanced over his shoulder. Ravenous fires devoured their way through exploded buildings, while columns of thick black smoke ascended skyward, marking the recent destruction.

"We must make haste!"

Olivia's eyes darted from the direction of the closest bomb shelter to Cross Street where their place of business was, and back to Jasper.

"Maximillian and Gwendolyn," she pleaded. "The store… is closer. You know how the dog's howl; the sirens frighten them so."

"You are quite right. We'll all take shelter there."

The couple moved rapidly across the cobblestone street, their clacking footsteps in sync with other civilians fleeing for safety. The once-darkened evening sky now ablaze, illuminated from exploding bombs. A firestorm of orange flames, reaching for the heavens, spewed haphazardly through the cold night air, leaving disaster and death in its wake.

* * *

6:49 P.M. BETWEEN TWO WORLDS

Olivia stood at the entrance of her fiancé's examination room. The green suit she so loved, tattered, covered with dust and debris. A trickle of innocent blood soiled her torn hose. Her once perfectly coiffed hair, now disheveled.

"Jasper, may I come in?"

"Yes. Yes, of course, my dear," he said, tucking his pipe and favorite tobacco pouch into the front pocket of his tweed sport coat.

"I've popped the kettle on. Tea should be ready in a jiffy." She glanced about. "Glad to see your office is still somewhat in order." With a nod over her shoulder, she continued. "I'm afraid the condition of the store is in a bit of a shambles."

"It's not for us to worry about now, Livy. Are the dogs with you?"

"They should be along directly. Gwendolyn is sleeping near the entrance of the store, with Maximillian sitting at her side."

Jasper removed the timepiece tucked away in his vest pocket, then clicked it open to check the time. "6:49, Excellent. Soon we shall all be together on our first assignment."

"Assignment, Jasper? But..."

He looked heavenward. "I've been informed we are all to leave England straightaway."

"Straightaway? But, but...our wedding? It's in three days!" She pleaded with him with her eyes, hoping she could find a way to change his mind.

"Livy. This isn't about us; our lives are no longer our own."

Maximillan and Gwendolyn soon joined them in his office. Jasper held out his hand to Olivia. Enveloping her petite frame in the safety of his arms, he kissed her forehead. "We are now Vision Ambassadors."

"Vision Ambassadors?" she asked, breaking away from his embrace. "What do you mean?"

"I am not quite certain. We shall be completely informed of our duties upon our arrival."

"Arrival? Well, as long as we're all together," Olivia said.

"It's a miracle of Christmas when—" Jasper stopped in midsentence. He removed a broken wing caught in the fabric of her suit jacket. It was a portion of the cloisonne butterfly brooch Olivia had lovingly named Lady Vanessa. "I believe this belongs to you."

He placed the remnant in the palm of her hand.

Olivia looked from her hand to her lapel. "Jasper, look. Lady Vanessa is…is broken."

"Yes, Olivia, she is. If you will, please come with me." Jasper led his fiancée through the examination room into her resale store, with the dogs trotting close behind. He swung his arm open wide, sweeping it across the store.

"Look around, my dear," he whispered. "We all are broken."

Jasper removed his hand from Jake's shoulder. He opened his eyes and stood there unable to speak, trying to process the vision he just saw.

"We were to be wed on Christmas Day, 1940, but the Germans decided otherwise."

Jake looked at Jasper in astonishment. "So, you're, you're—"

"Dead?" Jasper said. "Yes, we are."

"So, how is it that I can talk to you. See you?"

"We're Vision Ambassadors, angels, if you will, on assignment. You and Chelsi were always destined to be together, but you didn't know it. Our task was to show two loving people that they were perfectly suited for each other through 'visions.' We planted the seed and let you do the rest."

The young boy Jake had bought the white box from at Kringlefest joined Jasper, as did Olivia and their two dogs. A butterfly flitted above Olivia's head, then landed on her shoulder.

"Jake, this is who we call Mikey Shields."

"You're the boy that helped Penny and Travis the night they ran away."

"Yes, sir," he replied. "They were never in any danger. Just needed a little guidance."

"Penny told me about you, but you were gone before I could thank you."

Jake looked from Jasper to Olivia and back to Mikey. "Are you an angel too?"

Mikey turned around and looked at the statue of Saint Michael the Archangel. "You could say that."

Chelsi and Penny came up and stood next to Jake. "Sorry we took so long. The line for the Ladies room took forever." She studied Jake's expression. "Jake, is everything okay? Everybody looks so…serious."

He pulled her into a side hug. "Nothing to worry about now, Chels. I'll fill you in later."

Jasper looked at Olivia. "I'm afraid that's not entirely true. As soon as everyone steps outside of the church, all memories of us will be forgotten."

"Mikey!" Penny screeched when she saw him with her dad and the others. "Merry Christmas! This was the most special Christmas since my mommy went to heaven. My best present wasn't under the tree. My daddy asked Miss Chelsi to marry him, and she's going to be my new mom—isn't that great? Oh, and Uncle Randy and Aunt Jess are adopting Travis. He's gonna be my cousin."

"Woah, woah, Pen, take a breath."

"But Daddy, I'm so happy."

Jake reached for Chelsi's hand. "Me too, Pumpkin. Me, too."

Jessica came bustling into the vestibule carrying a white cloth bag. "Sorry I'm late, I had to run a quick errand before the wedding." She faced Olivia. "Olivia, marrying Jasper today will be the most important day of your life. We wished we could've had a proper bridal shower for you, but due to the time constraints, that was impossible. As Jasper's bride, I have a few things for you."

"For me?" Olivia asked.

Jessica nodded. She reached into the bag and removed a clear plastic corsage box, beautifully wrapped in a light blue bow. She untied the bow and removed a single white flower corsage. "A gardenia worn on your wedding day signifies purity, love, and protection. I wish it was a fresh gardenia, but this silk one will last forever."

Olivia looked down at Jessica's kindheartedness and smiled. "How did you know gardenias were my favorite flower? And *where* did you ever find a store open on Christmas?"

"It just looked like you, Olivia." Jessica held up the cloth tote bag with Jessica's Bridal logo printed in blue script letters. "I own a bridal store, remember? It's within walking distance."

Jim Hollister turned to Jasper Aldridge. "Looks like you're all set, old chap. Do you have the ring?"

Jasper tapped the breast pocket of his tweed sportscoat. "Indeed. Right here, close to my heart."

The pastor approached the group. "Dr. Aldridge, Mrs. Winters, if you're ready, we can all assemble now."

"Yes, yes, I'm sure you are anxious to return home and enjoy your Christmas supper."

"Bride's family on the left, groom's on the right. Mrs. Winters, will anyone be giving you away?"

Jake stepped forward and extended his elbow. "Mrs. Winters, it would be my honor to escort you down the aisle."

Penny jumped up and down. "Can I be the flower girl? My best friend Reese was her aunt's flower girl. She said she had the most important job to do. She dropped flower petals from a white basket in front of the bride. Can I, Daddy? Can I be Miss Olivia's flower girl?"

"But—"

Jessica tore open a bag of white silk rose petals and emptied them into the tote bag. "Penny, it's not a pretty basket, but will this do?"

Penny took the cloth bag from her aunt and hugged it to her chest. "Oh, yes!"

"That settles it then," Pastor Ross said. "Everyone, please take your seats."

"We are gathered here today in front of God and these witnesses to celebrate the union of Catherine Olivia Winters to Jasper Gregory Aldridge…"

The information in Jake's mind was spinning. It all happened so fast. One minute Jasper told him they were angels, the next he was walking Olivia down the aisle. How would Jake not remember Jasper, Olivia, and their dogs? The dogs, he assumed they were angels too, as well as the butterfly pin Olivia called Lady Vanessa, even though the pin *tecÛically* was never alive.

He leaned over to Chelsi. "Do you have a pen and paper?"

"Now?" she whispered.

"Yes, I have something very important to tell you and I want to write it down so I don't forget." Jake wrote quickly and told Chelsi about the vision of the day Jasper and Olivia died.

Chelsi had a horrified look as she quickly scanned the note. "This can't be," she whispered, "they look so… *alive.*"

"It's all true," he whispered. "You know what a history buff I am. The Brits called the bombing the Christmas Blitz. The Germans took out half of the Royal Exchange and their store was a direct hit. He handed her his phone. I googled it. Look at the headline on these pictures. '6.50 PM: The top of the Royal Exchange is now ablaze. High explosives have destroyed nearly half of the exchange's floor. The shopping arcade beneath the exchange is also alight.'"

Clicking his phone off, Jake asked. "Didn't Olivia say their store was on Cross Street next to the Royal Exchange?"

"I think so. That explains their '40s attire. The antique store—those were everyday thrift items her store sold. They're stuck in a time warp."

"On our way home, let's swing by the store where you first met them. I've been meaning to do it all week."

"I'd like that very much."

"…you may now kiss the bride," said the pastor.

Jasper put his arms around Olivia and gave her a very discrete kiss. They turned to face the congregation.

"It gives me great pleasure to introduce everyone to Dr. and Mrs. Jasper Aldridge."

Everyone stood and applauded as the happy couple walked down the aisle, husband, and wife.

Handshakes and hugs greeted them, as well as Maximillian and Gwendolyn prancing around, doing their happy dance.

"Well, Mrs. Aldridge, it's time we said our goodbyes to these wonderful folks and thank them for their unending generosity and friendship."

Jim kissed Olivia on her cheek and shook Jasper's hand. "Congratulations, you two. Hope you've got time to come back to the inn for a matrimonial celebration."

Jasper removed his pocket watch and checked the time. "We'd love to, but we need to be going."

"You have such an unusual pocket watch, Jasper. Is that your family crest?"

He unhooked the silver clasp from the buttonhole in his vest and handed it to Jake. "No, it was presented to all the doctors when we graduated from the University of Hertfordshire's College of Optometry. It's the schools' crest."

With Chelsi looking over his shoulder, Jake pushed the button to click it open. *Sunday the twenty-second. Six forty-nine.* Closing the cover, Jake handed the watch back to Jasper. "Thank you, sir. It's quite a treasure."

Jasper put his arm around Olivia's shoulder. "No, son. Now the Mrs. here is quite a treasure."

"Good answer."

"Now, come along, my dear. We have a long journey ahead of us."

"Pop, we'll meet everyone back at the inn. Chelsi and I would like a few minutes before Jasper and Olivia leave."

"Okay, son, but don't be too long. Christmas dinner will be ready shortly."

Jake and Chelsi watched everyone exit the church; Maximillian and Gwendolyn trotting close behind the bride and groom. "Jasper," said Chelsi. "Jake shared the information with me on the last day before—"

"The bombing?"

"Yes. What's next? Where will you go?"

"They're angels," Penny said, "they can go wherever they want."

"How do you know they're angels, Pumpkin?"

Penny covered her heart with her hand. "I just know, Daddy."

"It's time." Jasper helped Olivia on with her coat and pinned her wedding corsage onto the coat lapel.

"Jasper, Olivia, I'll never forget what you did for me." Chelsi looked at Jake and Penny. "For us."

"My dear, it wasn't us. It was destiny for you and Jake to be together from the start. We just gave you the knowledge to look into your heart," Jasper said.

"And I was too thick-headed to see what was right in front of me in high school, or I would never have let you go after graduation."

Chelsi reached out and held Jake's and Penny's hands. "We're together now, the three of us, and that's all that matters."

"Chelsi, I have something for you." Olivia handed her the completed embroidery piece she had been working on.

"I can't accept this, Olivia. You were making it for Jasper. It was his wedding present."

Jasper took Olivia's hand. "I already have my present, dear child."

"Yes, please accept this as an early wedding present. Remember your final vision?"

Chelsi thought back to her visions of Kringlefest. "*Um,* a gazebo set up for an intimate Valentine's Day celebration?"

"Precisely. The gazebo behind the inn. Wouldn't it be wonderfully romantic to marry on Valentine's Day?"

Chelsi looked at Jake, and they both nodded in unison.

"Then it's my honor to pass this on to you." She motioned for Chelsi to put it into the white merchandise bag from Jessica's Bridals.

"Now, Penny dear, open your hand."

The child opened her hand and watched Olivia place something on her little palm, then closed her fingers tightly around it.

She looked down at her closed hand, then up to Olivia. "May I look at it?"

Olivia nodded.

Penny's face lit up when she saw a colorful, shimmering butterfly pin.

"It looks just like yours, 'cept she's not broken."

Penny moved her hand back and forth, admiring it. The butterfly pin sparkled under the vestibule's overhead lighting.

"Would you please pin it on my jacket, Miss… I mean, Mrs. Olivia?"

Olivia bent down and pinned the butterfly brooch on Penny's red jacket. "Thank you." She hugged Olivia. "I'll never forget you. I can't believe an angel gave me a present."

Olivia kissed Penny on the top of her head. "Goodbye, sweet child. Your mother told me she is very proud of you. If I had a daughter, I'd want her to be just like you."

Jake opened the doors and waited until everyone exited Saint Michael's Church. He met up with Chelsi and Penny at the bottom of the church steps.

Chelsi was carrying the bag from Jessica's Bridal. She peeked inside. "What on earth? Jessica must have forgotten to take this beautiful wedding embroidery with her. We'll give it back to her at the inn."

Jake held out his hand. He was holding a piece of paper. Turning it over, he said, "Why am I carrying a blank piece of paper?"

Chelsi shrugged. "What a wonderful Christmas service, Jake. It looks like we were the last people to leave."

"Yeah, I wonder why that is. And where is everyone else?"

"We'll meet them back at the inn. Rosaria said our turkey dinner will be ready at four o'clock, and she prepared a light snack for us when we return from church."

"I can't wait for Mom's maple-bacon turkey. It was her specialty," Jake said.

About twenty yards ahead of them, a man held open the door of a black, antique British car parked parallel to the street. A 'Just Married' wedding banner, written in black scrolling letters, was draped from one end of the sloping rear panel to the other. The convertible top was down, and a young boy and two corgi dogs climbed into the rather narrow, tapered backseat. Before entering the vehicle, a woman turned around and waved goodbye. Penny smiled and waved back. A butterfly, flitting several feet above the receding car, released a stream of silver sparkles. The vehicle, along with its occupants, soon faded away into nothingness. All that remained were the sparkles trailing behind them.

"Good-bye," Penny whispered. "Give Mommy a hug from me."

"*Hmmm...* I've never seen them in town before. They must be visiting family for Christmas," Jake said.

"Silly, Daddy. That's Dr. Jasper and Mrs. Olivia. Mikey is with them, too. They're all angels!"

"Angels? And their dogs?"

"Maximillian and Gwendolyn. They're angels, too. Don't you remember?"

Jake looked at Chelsi. They both shook their heads. "Can't say that I do, Penny."

He touched the butterfly brooch pinned to her jacket. "Squirt, where did that pin come from?"

Penny rolled her eyes. "Dad, Mrs. Olivia just gave it to me before we left the church. I named her Lady Vanessa after the one Mrs. Olivia has."

"Lady Vanessa. That's a pretty name."

"Daddy, after we get home, can I ride my new bike over to Travis's? I promise I'll be careful."

Jake put his arms around Chelsi and Penny's shoulders. "I think that would be an excellent idea. Chels, we have extras in the garage. How 'bout we all take a nice bike ride before dinner, as a family."

Chelsi smiled. She held out her left hand and watched Rudolph's red nose sparkle in the Christmas morning light. "As a family. I love the sound of that."

* * *

JASPER AND OLIVIA LOOKED AROUND. They were surrounded by robin egg blue skies and delicate, billowing clouds. Lady Vanessa fluttered a few feet above Maximillian and Gwendolyn, but only the tips of the dogs' ears were visible.

"I think our first assignment, as Vision Ambassadors, went quite well don't you agree, Jasper?"

"Yes indeed, my dear. Yes indeed. Jake is a loving and trusting soul. And with Chelsi by his side, as Jake's wife and Penny's mother, the Hollister family is whole and complete."

"And Chelsi has her priceless certificate to frame, and will preside over the B&B's kitchen. So, both of their prayers have been answered."

"But Jasper, I do have one question. Before we left England, you began a sentence and we were interrupted. Would you mind terribly finishing it?"

"What was it that I started to say?"

"Something about a miracle of Christmas."

Deep in thought, Jasper cocked his head and scanned the enormous expanse. "Ah yes, now I remember. "It's a miracle of Christmas when… angels come to town."

THE END

Chelsi's Favorite Recipe From

A NEW VISION: A RECIPE FOR LOVE

Aunt Ann Marie's Roasted Garlic Rosemary Bread

- 1 ½ tsp. active dry yeast
- 1 cup warm water, 110-115 F.
- 2 tsp. sugar
- 1 ½ tsp. table salt
- 3 Tbsp. extra virgin olive oil
- 3 ½ cups bread flour
- 1 Tbsp. fresh rosemary, chopped
- 1/8 tsp. cracked black pepper
- 3-4 large garlic cloves, unpeeled, roasted with 1-2 Tbsp. olive oil
- Extra olive oil for brushing on top
- Coarse sea salt and cracked pepper for sprinkling

Roast unpeeled garlic cloves in an aluminum foil wrap with 1-2 Tbsp. olive oil, 400 degrees F., 25-30 minutes. Set aside to cool.

In the bowl of a stand mixer, add 1 cup warm water and sprinkle yeast on top. Mix in sugar and salt. Let sit for 10 minutes. Mix in olive oil. Add flour to yeast mixture and knead by hand or mixer/hook for 10 minutes. Add rosemary and black pepper. Knead another 5 minutes. Smash roasted garlic and add to dough. Mix for 1 minute. Dough will still be a bit sticky. Place dough ball in well-oiled bowl, turning dough so the surface is completely coated. Cover bowl with plastic wrap, then a kitchen towel. Place in a warm, draft-free area, for 1 hour. (Inside a turned off oven with the light on works great.)

Gently punch down. Turn out dough onto counter and shape into one large round loaf or cut in half for two. Place rounded loaf onto parchment-lined baking sheet. Using a sharp knife, make a crisscross design on top. Cover with large mixing bowl inverted over it. Make sure bowl is large enough that it gives your loaf room to rise. Let rise until doubled again, approx. 1 hr.

Place a metal baking pan on lower shelf and preheat oven to 400 degrees F. Gently brush loaf with olive oil, sprinkle with sea salt, pepper, and a bit more rosemary, being careful not to deflate. Heat 1 cup water and carefully pour onto heated pan, (this provides steam as the bread bakes). Bake 25 minutes. Raise oven temperature to 425 degrees F. and bake 5 additional minutes, watching carefully not to allow bread to get overly brown. Listen closely to the song of your bread, as it comes out of the oven. If you can, let bread rest 5 minutes before cutting into it. Enjoy with butter or a blend of olive oil, cracked black pepper, and balsamic vinegar.

Yields: 1 large round or 2 smaller round loaves.

Note: This recipe has been adapted, and printed with permission, from Amy Dong at Chew Out Loud

Author Bio

After living in Balboa Canal Zone, Panama; Long Island, New York; and Glendale, Arizona; Janet Jensen has finally found her home in Fort Worth, Texas. Ms. Jensen has had a lifelong love affair with cooking, baking, floral design, and all things related to tea. After recently downsizing, she has now reduced her tea sets to five so her tearoom is always ready for guests. When not writing, she can be found in her kitchen perfecting bread, scone and soup recipes. Please feel free to email her at janet.jensenwrites@aol.com.